D1558155

promise
full
of
thorns

JEAN HARKIN

Dear Carolyn –
Here's to writing and
publishing without
thorns! Love –
Jean Harkin
2/20/23

BROWN POSEY PRESS

an imprint of Sunbury Press, Inc.
Mechanicsburg, PA USA

an imprint of Sunbury Press, Inc.
Mechanicsburg, PA USA

For information about special discounts for bulk purchases, please contact Sunbury Press Orders Dept. at (855) 338-8359 or orders@sunburypress.com.

To request one of our authors for speaking engagements or book signings, please contact Sunbury Press Publicity Dept. at publicity@sunburypress.com.

FIRST BROWN POSEY PRESS EDITION: January 2023

Set in Adobe Garamond Pro | Interior design by Crystal Devine | Cover by Lawrence Knorr | Edited by Abigail Henson.

Publisher's Cataloging-in-Publication Data
Names: Harkin, Jean, author.
Title: Promise full of thorns / Jean Harkin.
Description: First trade paperback edition. | Mechanicsburg, PA : Brown Posey Press, 2023.
Summary: Alice doesn't feel she is a strong woman or up to the challenges of her life until she discovers her husband Charlie's decades-old betrayal. Her attempt at revenge goes beyond her control.
Identifiers: ISBN : 978-1-62006-957-8 (softcover) | ISBN : 979-8-88819-037-1 (ePub).
Subjects: FAMILY & RELATIONSHIPS / Love & Romance | FAMILY & RELATIONSHIPS / Marriage & Long-Term Relationships.

Product of the United States of America
0 1 1 2 3 5 8 13 21 34 55

Continue the Enlightenment!

Dedicated in memory to my parents and grandparents.

And to John, my lovest.

Foreword

Inspiration for this novel came from a romantic anecdote from my parents' courtship days. But this story is not about them. The characters in this book inhabit a parallel universe of the imagination. Their personalities, struggles, and destinies do not reflect the lives of actual persons. This is a work of fiction. Similarities to persons living or dead are fleeting and coincidental.

I offer a heartfelt thank you to my editors, Abigail Henson and Teri Brown, and my readers—especially Nancy, Charlie, John, Marty, and Sheila—who have offered excellent comments and suggestions, resulting in the finished work. Please see further acknowledgments at the conclusion of the story.

He never knew her, always tried
To see the way her mind worked
See the thoughts she held inside
He never knew her anyway.

He never knew her, took her hand
And bore her to his brand of dream
He promised more, to understand
But never knew her anyway.

He never knew her, stole her heart
And parted her from innocence
The scents of dreams grew sour and tart
He never knew her anyway.

—*From "Building an Island"*

1

Alice rummaged for the scissors. Her warped fingers reached into the kitchen drawer through a tangle of string, like a fishnet trapping old tape dispensers, empty glue sticks, and broken-off pencils. She remembered something she'd once hidden in this drawer—and a summer day long ago when daughter Judy, then ten years old, discovered her secret—the stash of *Lucky Strikes* hidden in the farthest reach. Alice's main worry for weeks, maybe months back then, was that Judy would tell her dad about the cigarettes. But Judy had kept quiet. Alice now realized that secrets hurt in unexpected ways. She thumped her chest with a tight fist as a cough rattled in her throat.

Sighing, she located the rusty scissors that had cut up yards of string, bunches of herbs, and stalks of rhubarb through the years. Her fingers brushed against a hinged two-sided object she hadn't touched for ages—that metal bread holder she'd used during the war for slicing a piece of bread vertically, stretching a loaf twice as far. Alice smiled at the memory of that paper-thin bread you could barely taste.

The clock on the high-gloss gray kitchen wall made its scraping sound as the minute hand lurched toward the half-hour. Alice adjusted the apron over her cotton print housedress and prepared to cut up chives for a salad. Before rinsing the savory strands in the porcelain sink, she reached over to the kitchen table to click on the radio. The Philco—the same little radio on which they'd listened to President Roosevelt's Fireside Chats, received the shocking news of

Pearl Harbor, and heard the miraculous announcement of Dr. Jonas Salk's cure for polio. And the music—Louis Armstrong, Benny Goodman, Frank Sinatra, their old favorites. Now Phil Collins was starting to sing *Another Day in Paradise*. "Uh huh," and Alice clicked off the radio.

The *Scramble* puzzle page from the newspaper lay next to the radio. A frisson of temptation almost persuaded Alice to abandon the chives. The puzzle was her daily pride and joy, keeping her mind active. It was authored and syndicated by her son Ben Lukas—Benny, who had been labeled *unteachable* and probably unfit for the functioning world. She felt pride, like a blessing of sunshine touching her heart.

Lunchtime drew near, so Alice whispered "later" to the newspaper page and picked up the scissors. She busied herself cutting the fresh chives, releasing their oniony essence into the stale-coffee air of the kitchen. She looked at her hands, rough like sandpaper, crooked, and wrinkled. Her wedding diamonds winked darkly. When had her hands ever looked young? Before the war, before cooking and cleaning, before babies. Her veins ran like ridges across a parched landscape of skin. Snake hands, Judy's daughter Amy had called them.

The floor shook as Charlie stomped up the steps from the backyard and entered the screened porch. Alice paused, waiting for him to take off his muddy gardening shoes, but he marched into the kitchen without stopping. Alice sighed, turning to look at her husband in his tattered tan shirt covered with sweat and grime, his baggy pants caked with mud. Sudsy gray foam, spattered across the lenses of his glasses, concealed his eyes. She held her scissors in one hand, a bunch of chives in the other. Mirroring her pose, Charlie held out a large, luminous pink rose. "Ta-da! It's Charlotte Armstrong—a rose in her prime."

"Lovely," said Alice, her tone edged with sarcasm. "But can't you ever remember to take off your shoes when you come in the house?"

Charlie laid the rose on the nearest surface—the stove. "Aw, Alice," he said, frown lines pinching his forehead. "You know I'm going right back out. It's wasted effort taking off my shoes."

Alice shrugged. "Oh, you always have an answer for everything." She turned back to the kitchen counter and cut into a tomato. She wrinkled her nose at the odors of sulfur and earth emanating from Charlie's clothes. Sniffing, she turned to face him. "And another thing—why don't you wear your garden hat? Your hair smells like spray."

"At least it's the right color to match my hair," Charlie said.

Alice rolled her eyes and returned to the lunch preparation. A sidelong glance at Charlie revealed him breathing in a long draft of the rose's perfume as he tenderly moved it from the stove to the faded kitchen table. As Alice focused on the salad, she heard the door shut and the floor rumble as Charlie retreated to his backyard haven.

It isn't just the mud, thought Alice. Yesterday he had taken a bucketful of roses to Theresa Hawkes, along with an assortment of tulip bulbs for her St. Francis garden. He had even stayed to plant them for her. Squinting her eyes in Charlie's direction, she knew with bitter certainty that her husband hadn't tracked mud into Theresa and Ted's kitchen when he stayed to enjoy lemonade, cookies, and conversation. "He hardly talks to me," mumbled Alice, a knot of sadness in her chest—or was it anger? "Maybe it's time to teach Charlie a lesson."

Her mind brightened with creative possibilities. What if she hid the radio and painted the table geranium-red? She couldn't stifle a little laugh from bubbling over. A red table would match a red-faced Charlie; she could repaint the table later. Or might it be time to replace the timeworn table that was scratched, dented, stained, and repainted over fifty-four years of marriage? She would, of course, manage to *find* the discarded radio in the trash. She would miss its conviviality, but maybe it was time for a new radio.

Smiling about the possibility of new shiny things, she plopped the bowl of salad onto the table. Chimes from the seminary chapel across the street announced the noon hour. Alice watched from the back door as Charlie worked beneath the gnarly peach tree. "Well, come on in when you're ready for lunch," Alice said under her breath. Although hobbled by the canister of Black Leaf 40 on his back, he valiantly aimed the sprayer wand at suspected aphids on the tree's aging limbs. He reminded her of Don Quixote jousting with windmills. "This fair lady might get tired of waiting," she mumbled.

Turning toward the fragile, perfect rose on the table, she said, "Let's get you in water then, Charlotte." She went to the tall cupboards hanging over the counter on either side of the window and sink. Reaching for a leaded glass vase, Alice remembered how roses had once held such significance for her and Charlie and how she fell in love with him over fifty-four years ago when they were young, beautiful, and long in the stem.

Her lips clamped tight, she watched Charlie lay down the heavy sprayer and advance toward the house. What has happened to us over the years, she mused, and when did the bloom start to fade?

2

ALICE LEA LIVED with her parents, John and Flora, who had owned their three-story Victorian brick house on Brook Street since they married at the turn of the century. Signs of neglect had crept into the once-fashionable neighborhood during the Depression years. In good weather, Alice walked to her job at the Bureau of Internal Revenue in a tall building downtown. Pigeons often roosted on the sooty ledges outside the office windows—a citified version of the natural world.

Inside the offices, the clackety-clack of typewriters, adding machines, and the clicking of secretarial high heels on granite floors tapped the workday rhythms. Alice saw more of the director, Mr. McNulty, than the other secretaries did, as she was his personal, confidential aide. The old man of the department, in his fifties, occupied the most spacious and venerable office, furnished in comfortable old leather and black walnut. Alice's plain oak desk sat nearby in a cubicle with frosted panels for privacy.

The outer offices of the Bureau of Internal Revenue hummed with the energies and hormones of younger people, among them handsome, eligible bachelors who worked as accountants and attorneys. Alice's brother Allen teased her about nabbing one of these young men. "After all, you'll be twenty-nine in July—almost an old maid. McNulty's trying to do you gals a favor."

"Why don't you and Catherine fix me up with someone?" Alice suggested. And they did—with Catherine's brother Charlie, a dark-haired man with screen-actor good looks who dressed like a model for men's wear.

Alice didn't talk about Charlie to the other BIR secretaries over lunch. Maybe she would mention him someday to Carol, her best friend at work, if a relationship blossomed. Alice thought it might bring bad luck to talk about Charlie too soon. Besides, he was the best-kept secret from young single women plotting to catch handsome men.

At lunch in the building's spartan but clean cafeteria, the secretarial pool buzzed about dapper ex-king Edward VIII of England and his outrageous American bride-to-be. The lead secretary, her dark hair in elegant waves on one side, clipped with a rhinestone butterfly on the other, said, "Imagine Wallace Warfield—a divorcee, no less—winning that scrumptious royal man!"

Carol, whom Alice knew had long held a crush on Edward VIII, said, "And he chose her instead of the throne of England!" Carol's dark red fingernails curled a loop of her long pearl necklace. "And she'll be a duchess sleeping with her duke."

Alice replied, "Would you like to meet my dad sometime? He looks a lot like King Edward." Carol dropped her pearls and turned to Alice, her mouth open but unable to reply. The other secretaries laughed.

Despite the secretarial fixation on Edward, Alice was fascinated by the former king's unflappable fiancée, who had been named *Time* Magazine's "Woman of the Year" in 1936. The future Duchess of Windsor had the qualities Alice felt she lacked: independence, a strong will, and outspokenness—even to the point of insulting her future husband's exalted position and England itself. Mrs. Warfield shook her fist at power! Alice would have traded her cashmere sweaters, sparkly jewelry, her suede high-heels, and perhaps her feminine charms for the future duchess's self-assurance. On the other hand, she might need most of her assets to capture Charlie Lukas's heart.

At home in her bedroom haven, Alice sat on her window seat—a balcony overlooking the theater of Brook Street. On a late Saturday afternoon, she watched the neighborhood activity. Was it her imagination, or were people walking faster, looking happier, now that the Depression days were approaching a foreseeable close? She smiled, spotting a woman she thought had lost her home. Edging closer to view the neighbor she hadn't seen for a while, Alice put a hand to her heart and whispered, "Thank you, President Roosevelt, for giving us back lost hope."

Her attention was diverted by Allen's car pulling up to the curb as he returned from a short afternoon at Pauling's laundry and dry-cleaning establishment downtown. She watched her brother wave to the woman across the street, then hasten up the sidewalk to the front door. His huskiness and tight curly hair amused Alice when she compared him to the rest of the family: her father, fair-skinned and tall with gangly baseball-pitcher arms; her mother standing chest-high to John, even in the tiny heels she wore on her plump feet; and Alice herself—petite with stick-straight reddish-blond hair and perfect creamy complexion.

Downstairs, Alice heard the front door slam behind Allen's entry. Then he was in the kitchen inaudibly conversing with Flora, sometimes referred to as "Queen Victoria." Their mother was a force to be reckoned with.

Alice expected her brother to charge up the stairs to change his clothes in the bedroom next to hers down the hall, with windows looking out to the brick house next door. She would see Allen at dinner. For now, she tiptoed to her door and closed it. Time to sit on her window seat and write in her diary:

Saturday, March 6, 1937
    I am so happy to see Mrs. Ritchie back home today. Depression days nearly over. Thank goodness Mother didn't have to implement her plan to sell her prized beaten biscuits on the street! Daddy still has his job as assistant postmaster, Allen is still managing Pauling's laundry, and I'm still working.

Pen to her front teeth, Alice gazed out the window as Roosevelt's voice came into her head, "The only thing we have to fear is fear itself." He was proved right, thought Alice, returning to her page:

    But the future is still unclear. Allen is already engaged to Catherine Lukas, though no one speaks of a wedding. Jobs are too shaky—Catherine right now between jobs. Allen's job has been a bit uncertain since the flood nearly destroyed the laundry. I have the creepy feeling we're not out of the woods yet. Someday I hope to find a man as wonderful and charming as Daddy. Ha. Ha. Am I jealous of my own mother? Unless God broke the mold after creating Daddy, I'll eventually find a man as good as he is—maybe even more so, that is, in a financial way. I'd like to have lots of lovely children, a big house, and someone to help me cook, clean, iron, and all those household kinds of things. Also places to go, nice clothes, and so on. Do I need a rich man? I promised Mother I'd never marry for money! Well, not ONLY for money anyhow. I'm thinking about Charlie Lukas. He's handsome, a true gentleman, has a bright future with a federal job at the land bank. AND best of all, I feel safe and happy in his arms.

Her stomach fluttered as she thought of herself and Charlie smooching in the back seat of Allen's Chevy, his hands searching until she had to resist. Driving around the countryside on Sunday afternoons, no one's watching the scenery. She smiled until a tiny cloud of doubt passed across her mind. But does he love me, she wondered.

Disturbed, Alice rose from the window seat to return her diary to its dresser drawer. The mirror above the marble-topped dresser reflected her antique bed behind her, with its carved mahogany headboard reaching toward the ceiling. She searched her face, touching her fingers to a flushed cheek. Daddy sometimes calls me Peaches, she mused, then wondered how Charlie sees her. She stared into her blue eyes framed by long lashes, studied her profile-perfect nose slightly turned up, then made a kissing motion with her rosebud mouth. Yes, all right. According to the secretaries, men favor blondes. But is it only looks that matter? Biting her lip, Alice wished for the vitality of a certain American duchess.

"Dinner Alice!" Her father called from downstairs, interrupting her concerns.

⌒⌒⌒

Alice was growing tired of the grayness of pigeons and smoke-stained concrete. She began dreaming of a garden in the front yard of her family's home. The backyard would be out of the question. Behind the row of three-story brick houses ran an alley bordered by stockade fences. Each family's cobblestone backyard was a space to park the family car and for the coal truck to back up to the cellar door, unloading the winter's fuel supply. In the front yard, a spot of nature would delight people passing along the sidewalk and driving by on Brook Street.

She noted how the front yard consisted of sparse grass—like Daddy's thinning hair—trying its best to grow out of hard-packed clay soil. A two-foot-high concrete retaining wall separated the area from the public sidewalk. Soot-darkened cement steps entered the yard off-center, leading up to a mossy brick sidewalk and more steps to the front door of the house. Alice considered it might be possible to grow desert plants amid some pretty rocks where the yard bordered the concrete wall.

Her mother had always expressed a skeptical "we'll see" about planting flowers and herbs where grass struggled to survive, but Alice focused on hopeful results. From her second-floor bedroom, Alice would be able to sit on the bay window's seat and look through smoke-spotted glass down onto her miniature landscape. Such a bright prospect! She resolved to get started as soon as possible.

A month later, Alice returned to her diary and wrote:

The week after Easter I finally started my rock garden. The oddest thing happened. I needed some tools from the cellar. I walked into the backyard, stepped onto the stones, and realized I never go into the backyard except to get into Daddy's or Allen's car. Turning toward the cellar, shivers like little ants began to crawl up my spine, and my stomach cramped. Reaching for the handle of the cellar door, I almost panicked. I wanted to run away instead of entering that black hole. Uncle Stuart's scary bogeyman stories flashed through my mind. What made me think of those childhood fears? Maybe the dank smell of the cellar unnerved me. It took all my courage to lift the door and go down that dark stairway. The odors of earth and something rotten stunned me. The sight of the coal bin on the left brought tears to my eyes. Shaking and sweating, I groped for the shovel and trowel on a shelf by the stairs, where I knew Daddy put them. As I snatched the tools and ran back upstairs into daylight, I resolved to find another place to store my garden supplies. I refuse to go back into that cellar again.

Alice lifted her head and chewed on the end of her pencil. Her stomach clenched in remembrance. Why had she been so frightened?

On a bright Saturday morning in May, Alice sat on the low concrete wall of her front yard, leaning over to dig in the patch of clay where she'd plotted the rock garden. Sunshine released the organic smell of the earth, and Alice's face grew warm as she stabbed at the hard ground with the point of her trowel. At her feet lay the corpses of succulents—her last plantings hadn't survived the week. She would next try to grow six saxifrage plants between a scattering of rocks—lumps of rose quartz, an amethyst geode, and varicolored calcite rocks. Her centerpiece was a forty-pound block of obsidian that Uncle Stuart, their next-door neighbor, had brought from Wyoming. She couldn't carry it herself, so Allen had to carry it to the front yard for her. The rocks shone, glittering in the sunshine. She kept digging in hopes of making a big enough dent to plant the saxifrages, their tongue-shaped leaves wilting by her side. "This dirt is so hard," muttered Alice, a bead of sweat rolling down her upper lip. Nodding to the plants, she urged, "Don't give up!"

When a car pulled up to the curb, she lifted her eyes to see a 1937 pea-green Plymouth coupe. Alice rose, pitching her trowel. "Charlie!" She held back from running to greet him, embarrassed to be caught in her cotton pleated skirt and Saturday work shirt, perspiring.

Sun-tanned in his perfect white shirt and necktie, Charlie bounded to the sidewalk, tucking gold wire-rimmed spectacles into his shirt pocket. "Hey there, Alice!" He held out both arms to embrace her, but she held him off, arms bent at the elbows, hands careful not to touch his pristine attire.

"Your clean shirt! My dirty hands!" she warned.

"What have we here?" said Charlie, grabbing her wrists and noting her clay-streaked hands. "Don't your parents have a proper gardener?"

Alice smiled, "Just me in my poor rock garden."

Charlie surveyed the scene, from the dead succulents to the live saxifrage, the sparkling rocks, the trowel, and the shallow planting hole.

Alice said, "I'd like to get some moss started too. Why does it grow so well where you don't want it?" She pointed to the cracks between the bricks of the sidewalk leading to the house.

"Earth is building up in the cracks where water collects," explained Charlie. "Ideal for moss."

"Could I try transplanting some in my rock garden?" asked Alice.

"Well, you can try, Alice, but you'll have to water the heck out of this clay. And this slope won't hold much water." Charlie crouched down, picked up the trowel, and began to dig forcefully into the bleak soil. In a few moments he had made a hole big enough to gently place one of the delicate plants. "Luckily, these have plenty of soil around their roots," he commented. "That will help." He went to work digging another hole. When he'd planted the rest of the saxifrages, Charlie stood up. "You'll really need to water these."

"But it might work?" Alice looked up hopefully.

"Yep, it might." He smiled. A curl of black hair had fallen across his broad forehead, and tiny beads of sweat sparkled above his upper lip.

"At least the rocks will survive," said Alice, trying to focus on her garden, not Charlie's gorgeous masculinity.

"Yes, they're looking top-notch." He grinned.

Suddenly Charlie looked serious. He wiped a dirt-soiled hand on his trousers and reached for Alice's left hand. "Alice," he said, "you deserve better than rocks. If you marry me, I'll plant roses and bring you a fresh bloom every day of summer."

Alice's eyes opened wide, and her slim body sat down on the concrete wall with a thud. Was he actually proposing? Was this real or make-believe, where the handsome hero carries off the beautiful maiden? She imagined the trumpet flourishes heightening the drama. Alice blushed, her heart pounded, and her hands felt like clammy dishrags. Charlie stood above her, beaming. Clay stains smudged his shirt and marked his nose where he'd swatted a mosquito. He took hold of her hands and sat beside Alice on the low wall. The warmth of his caress rivaled the morning sunshine. She could hardly breathe.

"What do you say, Alice?" He smiled, watchful but patient.

She searched his face for assurance his proposal was real. His hazel eyes held firm, gazing into hers.

"Roses?" she whispered.

3

CHARLIE'S HANDS GRIPPED the steering wheel as he left Alice's home and drove down Brook Street toward the Fourth Street apartment he shared with his sister. Had he actually just proposed to Alice? Maybe the sun had got to him. "What was I thinking!" he said aloud. He'd been carried away by how cutely mussed she looked, exertion coloring her cheeks. His heart thumped as his future swam before his eyes, imagining himself as a married man—Alice's husband. And Alice, dependent on him—for how much? Children even! A homeowner, maybe someday, with upkeep and taxes. He squirmed in the seat. But she didn't say yes, Charlie reminded himself. He relaxed his sweaty hands on the steering wheel as he stopped for a red light at the corner of Brook and First streets.

Only a week ago he had enjoyed another evening with Bonnie. She was a different type of blonde than Alice. A smoky blonde. He liked it when Bonnie gave him that sideways look, almost daring him to pursue her. She welcomed Charlie's advances while teasing him, pushing him away.

"Well, maybe next time," Bonnie would say. Then she'd let Charlie nuzzle the back of her neck and put his arms around her, with always the promise of desires being fulfilled in the future. But how soon?

The rest of the way home and into early evening, as he helped Catherine prepare for supper, Charlie mused on the fact that he'd proposed to Alice while not really wanting to give up Bonnie. Alice is like a pretty tabby kitten in her rock garden; Bonnie is a slinky city cat, Charlie thought.

He snickered while setting the table in the apartment's miniature dining room and glanced sideways at his sister. If Catherine observed his odd mood, she hadn't commented. He had always been the perfect role model, rarely questioned by his siblings.

After they served their plates and began to eat, Catherine began, "If I may ask—what were you up to today?"

Charlie nearly choked on his sister's thick gravy. "Had the car checked at the garage."

Her brows arched upwards. "Is that all?"

"Stopped by to see Alice a few minutes," he mumbled, wiping his mouth.

"Doing anything tonight? Allen and I are off to the symphony. How about you and Alice?"

Charlie's ears heated, and he hoped his sister didn't notice. He cleared his throat. "I'll see her tomorrow. Tonight's poker night." A panicky thought: Would he have to give up poker night when married?

Catherine nodded. "Oh, that's right. I thought by now Alice might be making you think twice about poker. The way you two are so lovey-dovey in the back seat."

Charlie forced a grin. "Yeah. Maybe soon."

He didn't go out with his poker buddies after all. Suddenly tired, he stretched out on his favorite overstuffed chair in the living room, his feet on the brown leather ottoman, to read the newspaper awhile. Soon he tossed it aside and went to bed.

As Charlie lay in bed, he examined his motives for proposing to Alice. Maybe it had something to do with being one of the last remaining bachelors in the office. Mike Sanders, the latest to take the plunge, had his head in the clouds lately. Charlie was amazed at Mike's willingness to miss Saturday night poker games and the occasional bar night. Charlie wondered if marriage could be the next best thing in his own life. Nearly thirty is a good age to become married, he supposed. Nevertheless, proposing marriage is a big step; he surprised himself by doing it so easily.

He kept thinking about Alice and Bonnie, comparing and contrasting them. Almost like a game. With a jolt, he sat up. What's wrong with me? He had always been Charlie, the straight arrow, the good brother, the hard worker. He'd never considered himself a double-dealer where women were concerned—or with any other concern, for that matter. He scoured his hand across his face and lay back down. Tossing and reconfiguring his pillow, he tried to turn off relentless images of sweet Alice, sultry Bonnie, and himself as a dishonest womanizer. Charlie wished women problems could be worked out as quickly as a column of budget figures and hoped a solution might appear to him in a dream before he saw Alice again. Tomorrow would be Sunday—their day for driving in the country with Allen and Catherine. Charlie shut his eyes tight and gently bit his lip, doubting his dream solution would arrive before tomorrow.

4

DAWN WAS LIFTING the darkness from the apartment on Fourth Street when Charlie awakened. The party-line signal—two short rings—had been part of his dream in which Alice telephoned him. The conversation morphed into one with Bonnie. He was planning a Sunday drive with one of them. The dream vaporized as Catherine's voice reached him from the hallway; she spoke softly into the phone. "When will we know? . . . What can we do?"

He lay in bed, focused on the ceiling, dread curling in his stomach. Phone calls this early couldn't be good. He reached for his glasses, then threw on his brown-and-white striped summer robe, and trudged to the hallway to find out who was speaking with Catherine. What was the bad news?

She leaned against the floral wallpaper, holding the black telephone receiver to her ear. Her other hand clutched the waistline of her cotton wrap-around. Charlie moved closer.

Catherine said, "All right, Allen. So when can I see *you?* . . . Please let us know when you know anything. . . . Please let us do something. . . . All right. This is rough. I'll miss you too. . . . Goodbye." She replaced the phone in its cradle on the table and looked at Charlie, her face pale, eyes close to tears.

"What's wrong? What did Allen want?" said Charlie.

"Horrible news." Her voice choked, and she took a deep breath. "It's Alice. She's very sick. They think she might have polio. That Dr. Richards—you know, Alice's cousin—came to their house about four o'clock this morning."

Catherine reached for Charlie and buried her head on his chest. He embraced his sister as his mind raced.

"It'll be okay," Charlie whispered. "They probably don't know much yet." He remembered Alice's bright eyes and happy smile of yesterday; he couldn't imagine her ill. He thought of her possible future—braces, operations, therapy, an afflicted walk—all the trials his sister Lillian had experienced when they were children living on the farm near Morgantown.

Catherine pulled away. "You're right. We must try to think straight. Allen said they are going to do tests and will know in a few days—"

"Meanwhile?" Charlie interrupted.

"I guess we all wait."

"Can we see Alice?"

"Charlie, she's very sick—with a high fever, sore throat, and stiff neck. The whole family is quarantined for fifteen days." Catherine waved her hand, then crossed her arms across her chest and concentrated her gaze on the ceiling.

As a ray of sunlight found its way into the hall, the gloom of Alice's situation settled on Charlie. His mind leaped to possibilities of the iron lung, paralysis, bone grafts—a life needing constant care.

Catherine pressed her fingers to her cheekbones as if holding back tears. "I'm thinking of Lillian," she said.

"I know," he replied. "But on a brighter note, look at Lillian today—she's got more get-up-and-go than the rest of us."

"Yes," said Catherine, sniffling, "but the way she walks—bent sideways with that limp. And she'll probably never marry and have children—"

"She gets where she wants to go, and she's a career girl. She's happy. That's the important thing. Polio doesn't need to be the end of the world." As further assurance, he continued: "There's FDR—he survived it and became president!"

Catherine nodded, blotting her nose with a handkerchief. As she turned away to go back to her room, Charlie asked, "Did Allen say if there's anything we can do?

Catherine turned around. "He couldn't say right now. The family's so confused and scared to death."

Charlie wondered how Allen would maintain his job, whether Alice's father would go to his work at the main post office. "I'd worry more about all of them if I didn't know Alice's mother," he mused.

Catherine smiled for the first time since Allen's phone call. "I know what you mean. She's a tough little mother hen."

Charlie chuckled, appreciating the farm reference. "Yes, Flora will protect her brood and keep the nest in order. Thank heaven for mothers."

He reflected on how his mother must have suffered when Lillian contracted polio. "Mama was brave. She brought all of us through that hard time."

"Yes, the worst time—until Mama died," said Catherine. She had been thirteen, Charlie fifteen, when their mother died in childbirth with her eleventh child. Catherine waved her handkerchief in front of her face as if to ward off more sad thoughts and dashed out of the hallway.

"We'll get through this," Charlie muttered, wondering how the next weeks would unfold—and beyond.

5

Shortly after noon, Charlie banged a kneecap as he bent to sit at Catherine's dainty phone table. Grimacing and rubbing his knee, he called the Leas' home to check Alice's condition. Allen answered the phone and told him, "She's about the same. Mother is putting cold compresses on her head and thinks the fever is down some."

"Is Alice awake?" asked Charlie.

"Not very, I'm afraid," said Allen, "she's real drowsy."

"I guess I can't talk with her?"

Allen managed a wry chuckle. "No, not possible, old chum. Not at this point. I know how you feel. We'd all like to talk with Alice. Right now it doesn't seem like she can even think straight." Then Allen recanted, "I'm sorry, Charlie—didn't mean to worry you more. It's the fever, you know."

"But it's going down?" asked Charlie. He rubbed his socked foot on the claw of the table leg.

"Yes, down, then up. Doc Richards said it would be this way."

"When will the doctor know more?"

"He'll be back tomorrow to check on Sis. The tests will take a few days," replied Allen.

"Are you and your father working tomorrow?"

"No—forced vacation, wouldn't you know. We're in quarantine for fifteen days! Hope the cleaning biz runs without me—and the post office without Dad. Folks are hankerin' for our jobs these days."

Charlie agreed; they were lucky to have kept their jobs through the Depression years. Catherine hadn't been as fortunate, losing her job as a teller when her bank collapsed. Even with some banks still in trouble, Charlie felt pleased he had taken the road of the future—away from life on the farm. After all, it seemed that farmers and farm workers needed more help than anyone. "Well then, let us know if we can help out." He nervously flipped the pages of the phone-finder on the table.

"Thanks, Charlie. 'Preciate it. Our groceries are being delivered from 'round the corner, so we're okay on that score. We'll keep you posted."

"Take care of yourselves—especially Alice." Charlie suddenly remembered: "Keep her rock garden watered. It needs all the watering you can give it."

Allen chuckled, "Will do. Plenty of time on my hands while I'm off the job."

Charlie visualized his potential brother-in-law, his cheerful nature, husky frame, and that tight curly hair Allen kept cut as short as possible. "Allen," said Charlie, pausing to gain control, "when Alice wakes up, tell her I—tell her 'hi' from me."

"Also something I can do," said Allen.

As Charlie hung up the phone, a frightening thought occurred: Ought he worry about catching polio too? He had been with Alice the day before she became ill. Very likely he'd been exposed to the disease. Then a rational thought: Of all the children in their family, only Lillian had fallen ill with polio. Charlie guessed polio was particular when it came to selecting its victims. He shrugged his shoulders, rose wearily from the chair, and went to locate Catherine.

Later in the afternoon, Charlie took his sister for a drive in the Plymouth. The coupe's interior, smaller than Allen's four-door, emphasized the absence of their Sunday companions. They hardly spoke as Charlie drove through the downtown area, onto the four-lane bridge, across the brooding Ohio River to Indiana. His thoughts wove back and forth from Alice to Lillian, to their mother, to their childhoods on the farm, to his present career in the big city, and back to his deep concern for Alice. Would she live? Be permanently paralyzed? Startled, Charlie realized he hadn't given a thought to Bonnie.

Charlie observed his sister, unusually quiet, her dark hair hanging limp in the summer humidity. Worry tightened her mouth. She was worried about Alice, of course, and was probably worried whether Allen would get sick and if his job would wait for him during the quarantine. Perhaps she worried about getting the job she'd applied for as cashier for the Seelbach Hotel dining room. Charlie reached for Catherine's pale hand, "A penny for your thoughts."

"I sure miss them today." She sighed.

Charlie drove beyond the farm towns, past acres of young corn, not yet *knee-high by the fourth of July*. A gentle breeze stirred the leaves as Charlie's car hummed along the two-lane road. June bugs leaped into the tangled grass in the ditches as the coupe swooshed by, windows rolled down to let in the country air. In the meadows, brown and white cows chewing contentedly, looked up to watch the car pass. Catherine looked out the window. A penny for her thoughts, indeed, thought Charlie, knowing she probably craved a cigarette. Of course, he disallowed it—not in their apartment, certainly not in his prized little Plymouth where the stink of cigarette ash would cling to the gray mohair upholstery, and a spark could scorch the seats and padded doors. He knew she smoked away from home, as he could smell it sometimes on her clothes and breath. He had seen her stuffing a pack of cigarettes into her purse. Perhaps he should stop the car somewhere to let Catherine take a puff or two if she wants to.

With his left arm resting on the window ledge, Charlie proceeded to where they saw the bluish Indiana Knobs—like forested muffins—appearing on the horizon. He slowed, steering the car off the road to park next to a freshly mown clover field. He and Catherine got out of the car, stretched, and inhaled the cooling air mixed with scents of earth and grasses. A rooster crowed in a distant barnyard. "We're a long way from the city," commented Charlie, snapping off a blade of tall grass.

"It's beautiful out here," said Catherine. "I wish Allen and Alice could see this too." She stretched out her arms, twirling around to possess the perfect sky and peaceful countryside around them.

Charlie kept searching the quiet green of early evening, breathing the scents of corn and clover, hearing the gentle sounds from meadows and barnyards. "Crickets sound like a whole choir out here, don't they!" said Charlie.

Another sound moved toward them from the distance as a car approached. As a dark blue roadster passed them, it riffled Catherine's floral-print skirt. Charlie and Catherine returned the driver's friendly wave. After a while, and Catherine having made no sign of needing to smoke, they turned back toward the waiting coupe. Side by side in the front seat, they watched the sun sink over the knobby hills as old as the last glacier.

Catherine finally said, "Allen's mother always says 'God will provide.' We just need to have faith."

Charlie's hands gripped the steering wheel; the light in the sky glistened in his eyes. Before him, the stoic Knobs inspired courage to face the next day and the week ahead, whatever troubles lay in wait. It had not been the usual Sunday drive, but he was glad for the escape from the city and its woes. The setting sun painted cottony clouds with shades of gold, orange, and pink until indigo prevailed in the sky. Charlie felt at peace as the hills darkened. He pressed the starter, shifted into gear, stepped on the gas pedal, and turned the car around.

"Let's go home," he said.

6

ALICE'S EYELIDS TWITCHED as she struggled to focus on her surroundings. She lay in bed beneath the massive headboard and felt unable to move any part of her body. Were the covers so heavy? She heard low voices outside her bedroom door. Forcing her eyes to clear, Alice saw vases and sprays of flowers lined up on her dresser across the dimly lit room. The mirror behind them doubled the effect. Silvery light peeked around the edges and through tiny holes in the shades covering the bay windows—like starlight. She heard an angel singing. It reminded her of a funeral.

The thought scared Alice as her brain struggled to comprehend what had happened to her. How long had she lain here? Days? Weeks? A month? She vaguely remembered strong arms (Allen's?) lifting her out of bed. She recalled her mother's soft, encouraging voice as other legs and arms walked her down the long railroad-car hallway to the bathroom. She remembered, in her confusion, being dragged along past the grandfather clock as it intoned the Big Ben chimes of its famous London counterpart. The head-splitting bong shocked her into wakefulness for a few moments. The last thing she remembered was the suffocating bathroom with its toothpaste scent and the cream-colored wainscoting. She relapsed into dreaming.

Alice gradually became aware of a light tickling sensation on her arm and a voice singing: "Sleep my child and peace attend thee, all through the night. Guardian angels God will send thee, all through. . . ." Alice noticed the freshness of her mother's talcum powder and something cool placed on her forehead. She turned her head to look straight into solicitous brown eyes and tried to move her thick tongue and dry lips to speak. Flora gave her a sip of water through a bent straw.

Flora patted her daughter's hand. "You're all right. You're better now." Alice tried to push herself to a sitting position. Her mother cautioned, "Don't, Dear. You need to lie still and rest."

Alice relaxed a moment, then tried to speak again. She uttered a hoarse whisper, "What happened?"

Flora told her straight out that Doc Richards had just visited her bedside. "You have polio, Alice, but—"

Alice gasped, trying to get up. "Oh no, how bad?" Her legs tingled as she tried to move them. "My legs!" she whined, "God help me!" As she jerked her head, the washcloth compress fell from her forehead to her cheek like a lump of lukewarm clay.

Flora removed the damp cloth. "Mercy, Alice. You're just feeling weak. You've been in bed two weeks. And your fever isn't entirely gone. Please, please—"

Alice sank back on the pillow, stunned. She tried to speak but gagged on her words. Flora caressed her daughter's stricken face. "Hush dear, be quiet. I'll show you the beautiful flowers and cards that arrived for you. Please lie still."

Alice surrendered to her weakness and lay obediently, watching her mother cross the room to gather a basket of cards and a vase of yellow gladiolus.

───

In the hallway, Flora's nephew, Doc Richards, held a muffled conversation with Alice's father regarding the tests and plans for Alice's recuperation. John wrung his big hands as the doctor told him, "Tests show type two polio. Not likely to endure lasting paralysis if she receives proper care."

John's shoulders relaxed as his eyes questioned the doctor. Adjusting the belt around his waistline paunch, Doc continued, "It would be wise for Alice to take the rest of the summer off work, leave the city. Lord knows the soot and haze are no good for anyone's lungs, but for a polio patient—fresh air and rest are absolutely essential. Besides, this is Alice we're talking about. We both know she can be a touch emotional. Leisurely days in the country could do wonders for body and mind."

John scratched the top of his balding head. "Well, it can probably be arranged. Flora and the children used to spend summers at our friends'—you know—the Simpsons' farm in Middlesboro. We can check—"

"If you need me to help you find a place in the country for her, please let me know. I'd do anything to see Alice healthy again. I have some contacts."

John, speechless, reached his long, gangly arms around Doc Richards' girth, hugging him. The doctor stepped back and grasped the older man's shoulder. The two men padded, single file, down the long flight of stairs to the first floor of the house. As John opened the door, the sunshine nearly blinded them.

"No haze today, at least," said Doc Richards, "and things will look brighter for Alice soon. Just get her out there in the country!" John nodded. After the two shook hands, the doctor hustled off to another bedside on his round of house calls.

Inside Alice's bedroom, Flora read get-well messages to her daughter. "These gorgeous glads are from Mr. McNulty. Here's what the card says: Dear Alice, the office misses you. I especially miss my right-hand gal. Get well soon, and hurry back."

Alice offered a tiny smile before drifting into a reverie: She could see her boss opening the frosted-glass door of his office and bursting into the hallway where the secretaries' cubicles were arranged. He labored with an armload of large chunks of shiny black coal straight from a furnace room, as he called out, "Is anyone here? Alice, can you come quickly?" She wondered why Mr. McNulty was carrying coal, as she shook off the dream.

Flora patted Alice's arm, "Alice, are you awake? Of course, he misses you. But right now your job is to get well." Alice opened her blue eyes to stare at her mother. Her body felt heavy with the weight of other people's needs and her own helplessness.

"And you *will* get well," Flora emphasized. "Here's another card. Maybe you can guess who this is from—" Alice did her best to join in a few rounds of guessing. She appreciated the good wishes from friends and family but grew tired of hearing her mother read the notes and trying to concentrate.

Alice looked over at the dresser where the flowers beckoned. "Mother, show me the flowers!"

"Of course," said Flora, her hands shaking as she set aside the basket of cards. She picked up the vase of glads, replaced them on the dresser, and returned with a bouquet of a dozen red roses. Their perfume preceded Flora as she approached Alice's bedside. "Can you guess who sent these amazing roses?"

A memory flickered in Alice's brain. A sense of panic arose—a stabbing pain of loss. Charlie's promise came back to her. "No, Mother. Who?" She almost feared to know the answer.

"Why, they're from Charlie!" Flora beamed. Alice turned her face to the pillow, sobbing. "Alice, what is it?" She set down the roses and hugged her daughter gently. "Alice, dear . . ."

When Alice regained control of her voice, she told her mother that Charlie had proposed to her recently—she was foggy as to the exact day. She tried to shift her legs in bed but felt like a stranded seal unable to roll off a rock.

Flora reached over to rearrange the bedclothes. "Charlie stopped by to see you the day before you got sick," said Flora, "and helped plant your garden."

"That's right," sniffled Alice.

"He asked you to marry him then?" Flora bit her lip. "You didn't tell me."

"I know. I could hardly believe it. I guess I wanted to wait for Charlie to ask Daddy for my hand."

"Well, yes—that *would* make it official." A slow smile replaced the frown on Flora's face. "You didn't really have much chance to tell me before you took sick. Did you?" She wiped her daughter's face with a fresh, cold cloth and looked into her fever-clouded eyes. "Charlie's phoned to ask about you every day. He can't wait until the quarantine is over."

Tears brimmed over again. "But Mother—now I have polio. My legs—they don't seem to work. What if I can't walk again—have to live my life in a wheelchair? Maybe I couldn't have children. Charlie won't want to marry me. Why should he?"

Flora spoke firmly. "You mustn't do this to yourself—letting your fears get the better of you. The worst rarely happens, and whatever does happen, God will give you strength to bear it. You're alive and breathing. Doc Richards says you will get well and must certainly not give in to fear. And I say you will walk again."

"And be normal in every way?" Alice searched her mother's eyes for hope.

At that moment, Alice's father walked into the room. He held out both arms to embrace his daughter. "Peaches—welcome back!"

Alice felt John's soft whiskers bristling against her cheek. She clasped her arms around him and held on tight.

7

THE SIMPSONS' SUMMER home near Middlesboro was the perfect setting for Alice's recovery—and her imagination. The mansion, at the end of a colonnaded drive of elm trees, was one of the grandest in the state. It was modeled after an eighteenth century Palladian-style South Carolina home of brick and sandstone with a slate roof. Classic Ionic columns, in stark white, defined the front of the house. Alice had finished reading last year's romance sensation, *Gone With the Wind,* and the Simpson estate reminded her of Tara, the plantation home of strong-willed heroine Scarlett O'Hara.

As Alice and her parents arrived at the farm, Mattie, the housekeeper, bustled out to greet Alice, Flora, and John and help carry the women's luggage. "Sure is good to see folks for a change—bin plenty quiet 'round here," Mattie said breathlessly. "Here, let me help you, Miss Alice." Mattie's large frame supported Alice as she shifted from her mother's arm. Alice smiled despite the wearying trip from the city and brief walk into the house. She felt her spirits lifting as she breathed the fresh country air and anticipated having 'the run of the place' without the presence of the host family. (Mrs. Simpson was in Europe for the summer; Mr. Simpson would only be at the farm to oversee the tobacco harvest.)

The housekeeper took a hatbox from Flora. "Thank you, Mattie. How nice to see you again!" Flora smiled. "It's been a few years since we've been out here."

"Yes ma'am, Miss Flora. Way too long. I'll get you and Miss Alice settled and help Mr. John with your things." Mattie looked out to the driveway where John struggled with two large suitcases wedged into the trunk of the car.

"Thank you," said Flora. "Allen was on his way to help with the luggage. But he had a delay—at the laundry. These days, they are swamped with the free dry cleaning they're offering unemployed folks."

"That's okay, Miss Flora. I'll have you all settled by the time Mr. Allen gets here." She laughed a deep, wheezy laugh. "Right this way, Miss Alice. We have a comfy bedroom and sitting room set up for you on the first floor. The bath is 'tween your room and Miss Flora's. Meals will be in the dining room. It's all fixed, so you don't have no stairs."

As Alice settled into her summer bedroom and a peaceful reverie, her window view of the fields, barns, and outbuildings melded into a vision of her personal Tara. Looking into the hazy distance, she imagined the future with her own handsome hero—Charlie Lukas. In a rush to confide in her diary, she retrieved it from her handbag and sat down at a secretary desk by the window to write:

Of course, Charlie—not Rhett Butler—is the true gentleman. I imagine Rhett with the same dashing good looks as Charlie, with dark hair and hazel eyes. But as to character, Charlie is kind and loyal, while Rhett is a ruthless devil with a handsome grin. I could never face up to a man like that, but Scarlett took him on. My goodness, they were a pair! I wish I had Scarlett's gumption without her greedy, thoughtless manner. I hope Charlie and I can survive in comfort and style—but without all that drama!

The first two weeks at the Simpson farm passed routinely, with Flora and Mattie urging Alice to walk a bit each day to strengthen her legs. Alice barely needed their encouragement. After a few days she began exploring the house, discovering its paneled woodwork, pedimented fireplaces, ornate plaster ceilings, and the double staircase that provided climbing practice as she gripped the curved mahogany banisters.

Alice's rising spirits energized her weakened legs, as Doc Richards had predicted. At the Simpsons' estate, Alice could move around almost effortlessly, even though the mansion exceeded four times the size of the house on Brook Street. She imagined herself a southern belle like Scarlett O'Hara in her exquisite gowns, ruffles, and hoop skirts, gliding through the mansion.

Walking at short intervals every day, Alice explored the outdoors too. She had made friends with two horses in the west field. Stroking their noses and whispering to the spotted gray mare and chestnut brown gelding sparked a frisson of joy in Alice's heart and made the world seem right. She couldn't wait to share the horses with Charlie.

One morning, Alice dressed quickly, already at the white-washed chicken coop, when Mattie arrived to feed the flock and collect the eggs. "Good mornin' Miss Alice. You're up early!"

"Good morning to you, Mattie. It's the best time of day—nice and cool, so fresh!" Alice spread out her arms to embrace the air. A couple of white hens fluttered up to see if she had food in her hands. The women laughed. "Looks like they're ready for breakfast," said Alice.

"Here—take some, Miss Alice." Mattie's brown weathered hands held out a feedbag full of cracked corn. Alice reached in. A copper-colored rooster and several lively hens flapped around the women. The liveliness of their wings beat the air and flickered across Alice's legs. Charlie would understand her love for the farm.

"Let's go get the eggs now," Mattie said, as she emptied the bag onto the ground.

Mattie helped Alice into the stuffy, low-ceilinged hen house, where the scent of hay and chicken manure assaulted her. Alice followed the older woman's lead among the rows of laying boxes, reaching under the plump, feathered bodies to find the hens' prized eggs. Some squawking ensued as Alice and Mattie claimed the eggs from the nests. Mattie laughed her deep, easy laugh as she brushed away the mad hens. Alice thought what a hard life it must be for these mothers to lay egg after egg only to have their offspring stolen away by grasping hands. Alice preferred to pass over nests in sympathy for the hens, but she knew Mattie would find all the eggs. Charlie would probably smile at her naiveté. The realities of farm life formed his viewpoint, while she was more attuned to storybook chickens with sunny personalities.

Alice took Mattie's arm as they left the hen house, with Mattie carrying the egg basket in her other hand. They stepped carefully among the strutting, agitated chickens. Alice looked around, wary of what she might notice. "Seen any rats lately, Mattie?"

Mattie laughed. "Lands-a-Goshen, Miss Alice—you still remember that? The time you saw me kill a rat with my bare hands?" She shook her head.

Alice shuddered at the memory: A large rodent had slunk through the chicken yard as they emerged from the hen house into the sunlight. Alice gasped, seeing the rat's eyes watching them, lying in wait. She tried to bury herself in Mattie's ample body, upsetting the gathering basket. With her free hand, Mattie picked up a convenient wood plank and smashed the rat. The animal dragged itself away, with Mattie chasing. Her second blow smashed its head.

"Sure was somethin' all right," said Mattie. "But nothin' like that's happened for a long time."

"What a relief!" Alice sighed.

"We have some good workin' cats 'round here now. They do the rat work," said Mattie. The women approached the stairs of the back porch.

"I haven't seen any cats yet."

"Oh, you will. They're not much on folks. They stays around barns mostly. They know me because I feed 'em."

"Maybe I can feed them sometime," offered Alice.

"Sure, but you mustn't do everything at once. Get your strength back first, girl."

"I know." Alice's blue eyes held Mattie's face as the older woman opened the back door to the house.

"Now I'll get some of these eggs cooked for you and Miss Flora."

Alice entered the dining room and sat at the great oak table to await her mother's arrival for breakfast. Alice couldn't get over the immensity of this table compared with theirs at home. At mealtimes, she and her mother occupied a single corner of this table, surely huge enough to seat Mr. McNulty's entire office staff.

Flora entered the dining room, pink-faced, damp curls around her forehead, waving an accordion-fold fan at her face. "Good morning, Mother!" Alice beamed; it amused her to realize Flora would feel cooler if she didn't expend such energy working her fans. "What a pretty dress you're wearing. It looks cool."

"Thank you, Alice. You were up early this morning!" Flora sat down at the head of the table, smoothing the folds of her light gray summer frock.

"Yes—with the chickens!" responded Alice.

"In the chicken yard?"

"Yes, feeding them and gathering fresh eggs with Mattie for our breakfast."

"In your lovely new outfit?"

"Well—" Alice looked down at her lime green skirt and blouse with a ruffled neckline. "I'm not dirty." She wiped at a smudge on the front of her skirt. "Not much anyway!" Alice laughed as Flora cocked an eyebrow. "Oh, Mother," she said, reaching over to pat her parent's splayed fingers. "Don't be cross."

"And another thing, Alice: you mustn't tire yourself out today. You will have a big enough day with Charlie coming to visit."

"I know," said Alice, feeling a blush on her cheeks. "I can't wait. Is Daddy coming too?"

Flora fluttered her silk fan, then snapped it shut on the table. "Yes. He'll be here for late lunch."

The door from the kitchen swung open as Mattie marched in with grapefruit halves in china bowls and a silver carafe of coffee on a tray. "Breakfast is served!" Behind her came the aroma of bacon frying and the sound of fried eggs popping on the skillet. Alice unfolded her linen napkin on her lap.

Flora said to Mattie, "Please bring me some ice cubes. I prefer ice coffee this morning."

"Yes, ma'am, Miss Flora." Mattie bustled back to the kitchen, her forehead glistening.

After breakfast Alice rested on a glider on the porch, reading where she bookmarked her new novel, *Theatre*, by W. Somerset Maugham. The characters already captivated her, especially the pert actress everyone adored. Flora, in a wicker chair, turned from the morning newspaper. "More than a month—still no sign of Amelia Earhart's airplane!"

Alice looked up, shaking her head in sympathetic response. Mother admires such strong women, she thought, and wishes I were more like them. Though I doubt she'd want me off flying myself around the world. She shrugged, resuming her reading. The sun moved higher in the sky while Flora announced tidbits of news, and Alice tried to re-focus on her book after each interruption. When Flora mentioned the lost aviatrix again, Alice slammed her book onto the metal table beside her. Wincing, Alice used the arm of the glider to raise herself. "I'm going for a walk." She felt her mother's eyes pierce her back as she carefully descended the porch steps.

"Take it slow, dear," cautioned Flora.

Not seeing the horses at the fence, Alice headed toward the tobacco barn, where a stir of activity indicated summer harvesting had begun. Along the path leading to the weathered barn, she spotted an orange and white tabby cat and knelt, putting her hand out. "Pretty kitty, good ratter," cooed Alice. When she reached to pet it, the animal hurried off.

As Alice meandered toward the old barn, the image of Mattie and the grisly rat ripped through her mind. The incident loomed as vivid as yesterday. A lot of old memories have been dredged up lately, she reflected. Maybe the fever caused it or returning to this childhood environment. Dreams from childhood tales about Uncle Stuart's bogeymen haunted her sleep recently. In one dream, her uncle had turned away as someone's bony hand grabbed her. What does this mean, and why do I wake up in fear, my heart racing? Alice wondered.

She headed toward the tobacco barn where sunnier memories originated. Mule-drawn farm wagons arrived in a cloud of road dust, loaded with freshly harvested tobacco stalks skewered on long wooden stakes. Alice could almost smell the sweet stemmy aroma from where she stood. Workers came out of the barn, hollering to each other, ready to unload the two wagons. Their shouts and currents of conversation and laughter burst through the peaceful morning air. One of the men looked down the road, saw Alice, and raised his arm. "Mr. Simpson!" She smiled and waved in return. She didn't want to get too close to the barn while the men worked, so she strayed over to rest against the fence and observe from a distance. Alice smiled, remembering when she and Allen used to try to throw a ball over the barn's peaked roof.

The long finger of the depression had even reached out and changed the farm of her childhood. The Negro tenant farmers had been sent away; Mr. Simpson now managed the farm himself with hired help. Neighboring farmers who swapped work helped with the tobacco harvest. Mattie, dear soul, is the last one of her race living here, Alice reflected. She wondered why she had stayed.

A dinner bell sounded from the house—Mattie's signal to the workers for early lunch. The men seemed ready for the break as they jumped off the wagons and vacated the barn. On their way to the house, a couple of young men in wide-brimmed straw hats noticed Alice and waved. Another man nodded as he walked past, buttoning his denim shirt. Alice blushed, turning away to focus on the rows of corn beyond the fence. Mr. Simpson wiped his brow with a white handkerchief before coming over to greet her.

She thanked her host, assuring him, "Your farm is bringing me back to life."

With the men away at the house for lunch, Alice felt safe entering the tobacco barn. The dark interior ascended like a rough cathedral, with its tiers of beams climbing to the tin roof. The men had begun to hang the sticks of pale yellow burley tobacco at the highest levels of the barn. Alice remembered from childhood how the cut stalks progressed from leafy tepees on sticks in the field to a honey-colored tapestry suspended from the barn rafters, ready for market. She also recalled the whisper of the long leaves as they touched together, like wings of great golden bats, when a breeze rippled through the open barn door. And later, the sweet aroma of fine cured tobacco.

The artistry and skillful performance of the tobacco harvest was one thing; smoking cigarettes was quite another. Even though both Allen and Catherine enjoyed smoking, Charlie strongly opposed it. She had tried smoking but choked on it every time—such an easy habit to avoid. Even so, she wanted Charlie to see the tobacco harvest in progress. She knew he would appreciate the hard labor and teamwork from a farmer's perspective. She looked forward to showing him the 'circus act' with workers balanced on the high rafters, housing tobacco sticks at the top of the barn.

Alice emerged from the smothering heat of the great dark barn into the midday sunshine. In the distance, she heard the murmur of a car's motor. It had turned off the highway, the sound increasing. "Charlie!" She primped her hair, licked her lips, and smoothed her long skirt. In a moment, Charlie's little green car came into view, his tan forearm beckoning to her from the driver's window. Alice's pulse thumped against her breastbone, leaving her breathless with excitement; she waved both hands as he drew closer. She wanted to hurry down the lane to him. If only her legs could run!

8

EARLIER THE SAME morning, Charlie relaxed in his chair after breakfast, as Catherine cleared the table in their miniature dining room. The telephone rang. Charlie looked up at the fleur de lis wallpaper. When he heard two short rings—their party line code—he rose from the chair and walked into the hall to answer the phone.

"Well, hello there stranger!" said a voice on the other end.

Charlie took a moment to inhale. "Bonnie!"

"Well, you still know my voice. Good for you!"

Charlie swallowed hard, then rallied to sound in control and ready to banter with vivacious Bonnie. "Of course. How are you?"

"If you cared, you could have phoned me in the last month."

"I'm sorry, Bonnie. A lot has happened lately. I've been busy." Charlie looked toward the dining room to see Catherine watching him from the doorway, her look questioning.

"Busy? Doing God-knows-what?" said Bonnie.

He faked a smile at Catherine, then turned his back to deflect her nosiness. "Well, I've had a lot on my mind. And I've been driving into the country on weekends."

"The country! Whatever for? I don't see you as a country bumpkin."

Charlie lowered his voice in case Catherine was still eavesdropping. "Well, I am you know. Well, maybe not a bumpkin—I hope—but a country boy anyway, grew up on a farm."

"Oooh, so right! Well, that makes you special now, doesn't it."

Charlie smiled. "How's that?"

"Oh, I suspect you know a lot more than I do about earthy things—like birds and bees and pigs and cows," she teased.

"Well, yes. I did plenty of farm chores in my day." He turned to see Catherine standing in the doorway, hands on hips, squinting at him. He frowned and waved her off.

Catherine shrugged, waved back at her brother, and returned to the kitchen.

"No," said Bonnie. "I'm not talking about milking the cows and feeding the chickens—"

"Don't forget slopping the hogs, mucking the barn," said Charlie, suppressing a laugh.

"My goodness, no," sighed Bonnie. "I'm not talking about chores. I'm talking about the basics of life. Animal love in the barnyard. I expect you know more than most city boys—"

"Well, Bonnie. I've seen a thing or two. So, tell me, what's on your mind?" He covered a grin with his right hand.

"Guess I need a hug or two. Can we get together this weekend?"

Charlie experienced a familiar weak-kneed sensation as he remembered her passionate embraces. He sank to the chair next to the phone table, almost toppling it on its spindly legs, and took a deep breath. Alice's condition had him so preoccupied that he had suppressed his feelings for Bonnie. Now the emotions came back in a rush as he tried to maintain his cool demeanor. "I'm sorry. I was just getting ready to drive out toward Middlesboro for the day. I'll probably go again with my sister and her fiancé tomorrow too."

"In heaven's name, what's so interesting out there anyway? You are a country boy, for sure. Are the hens laying?"

Charlie laughed aloud. "No, I'll be visiting a friend, someone sick."

"Oh now I've heard it all. The sick friend, no less. What's going on?"

"Really, Bonnie. Truly—a sick friend, Alice Lea. Allen's sister."

"I don't know who you're talking about. But if you don't want to see me, just don't. You don't have to make excuses." She paused. "I haven't been smoking—much."

"Good. You're better off, you know."

Her tone sharpened. "And maybe better off without you too, Charlie. I have other boyfriends." Was she drawing a line in the sand?

"I don't doubt it. But Bonnie, don't be mad. Can't we still be friends and get together sometime?"

"Maybe. Call me if you want to." Click. Bonnie ended their conversation.

Charlie stared hard at the phone receiver. "Was that nice?" He shrugged, trying to toss off that cloud of being a double-dealing two-timer. As he woefully replaced the phone in its cradle, he vowed to put Bonnie out of his thoughts for now.

Charlie hurried into his bedroom and grabbed car keys and a pocket comb from the dresser. "I'll be back tonight!" he called to Catherine as he left the apartment, heading for his coupe parked out front on Fourth Street.

The light traffic as he headed east to Middlesboro enabled Charlie's attention to wander to his predicament. If he were ready to marry, shouldn't he consider Bonnie as well as Alice? What would his mama think upon meeting Alice? They would like each other immediately. Mama would see Alice's sweetness, her smartness, her enthusiasm for life, though she'd be compelled to remind him that she wasn't Catholic.

But Bonnie? No, she wouldn't like Bonnie.

"Where did you meet her?" Mama would ask, trying to keep the judgment from her voice.

He would be unable to lie to Mama and would have to admit Bonnie had been a pickup. He thought back to events of that day in March when he met Bonnie:

As Charlie left the 620 Building and headed out on his lunch hour, his spirits puffed up like a sail with a full bore of wind. Oblivious to the midday sunshine, the hubbub of traffic, and the bustle of working people out for their noontime break, he daydreamed of career advancement and kudos for his ingenious business proposal. In their private meeting after the other accountants had left, Mr. Benson had even asked for a synopsis of his plan. Charlie was ready to take on the world!

He quickly ordered some lunch at the Brown Derby and found a single unoccupied table. He scanned the crowded café, noticing the other young, attractive working people gathered there. A woman caught his eye; he had spotted her before. Bright and blond, she would soon reveal her name—Bonnie Fines. A man with whom she'd been having lunch got up to leave while Bonnie stayed. She took a cigarette out of her pouch-like purse and lit up. Her motions were graceful and easy, with the air of having lit cigarettes hundreds of times, considering it normal or even boring. Coolly she took her first drag, blowing out the smoke slowly, eyes focused on the ceiling.

Charlie was invincible after his interview with Mr. Benson, so indomitable that he couldn't resist picking up his lunch tray and going over to join this beautiful woman who clouded herself in smoke rings. She pulled back at Charlie's audacity when he sat down across from her at the vinyl-surfaced table. He smiled and introduced himself. Bonnie raised an eyebrow, drawing on her cigarette again. Charlie couldn't help it—he grabbed the cigarette from her slender hand. "You know, you shouldn't do this." He ground the offending object into the ashtray. The dead smell of old ashes burned his nose. He sniffed.

Bonnie, looking shocked, said nothing as Charlie continued with a warning. "Smoking cigarettes is bad for you."

She narrowed her green eyes at him. "You owe me a cigarette, Mister!"

Charlie smiled to disarm Bonnie.

She looked around at several other people smoking in the Brown Derby. "Everybody smokes! What do you know that they don't?"

Charlie didn't have time during lunch hour to explain his understanding of why cigarette smoking is harmful. Instead, he made Bonnie an offer to take her out for dinner some night at the fashionable Leo's Hideaway if she could keep from smoking the entire evening from the time he arrived at her door.

Bonnie agreed to the deal, saying, "You're strange and you've got some nerve, but you look like Cary Grant. I'll take a chance."

❦❦❦

Charlie kept his eyes on the road—Highway 60 to Middlesboro. How could he explain his feelings about Bonnie to his mother? Such romantic matters are not easily explained to one's mother. Of course, Mama would want to know about Bonnie's religion and her faith. "Faith in herself," muttered Charlie.

As for Bonnie's religion, he had no idea. They had never discussed it, nor had Charlie dared to ask. He could imagine Bonnie saying, "For God's sake, I'm an atheist." Charlie chuckled. He enjoyed Bonnie's cocky attitude, exactly opposite of Alice's sweet open nature. Would such an edgy personality be endurable through the years of a long marriage? What if Bonnie decided on a whim she didn't want to cook his meals or darn his socks? What if she took up smoking again, saying, "It's my house too!" Charlie could imagine her doing or saying all of these things. He couldn't picture Alice turning his life upside down like Bonnie probably would in a few years. He pressed the gas pedal.

By the time Charlie reached the long driveway to the Simpson estate, he ardently desired to see Alice and embrace her sweet warmth. As he rounded the wide curve leading to the back of the house, he saw her walking down the long lane from the tobacco barn, waving with both hands. She looked lovely, so desirable in her trim skirt and puffy-sleeved blouse—like a cool green stem with the blossom of her strawberry hair shining in the sunlight. She heard my car, thought Charlie. His heart beat wildly as he double-beeped the Plymouth's horn. He could hardly wait to take her in his arms.

9

T HE GREEN COUPE drove closer, sunlight glinting off the grille's chrome, as Alice's eyes focused on the driver. The car stopped with a sigh of the motor. Charlie, necktie loose at the collar, opened the door, leaped out, and shut the door in one rhythmic sweep. He rushed to embrace Alice, "Hiya kid!" He picked her up, swinging her around off the ground.

Alice giggled and grabbed Charlie's necktie. "Whoa, horsie!" They laughed. "You've worn my favorite necktie with the green and blue stripes. Look how well it goes with my skirt!"

"And your eyes! Are you feeling as good as you look today?" Charlie asked. He set her down gently.

Alice batted her eyelashes. "Much better now that you're here!"

"What are you doing out here by the barn in this hot weather? Shouldn't you be waiting on the porch, fanning yourself or something?"

"Like Mother?" said Alice. They laughed; Flora's fan collection amused them both.

"But seriously, why are you out here?" repeated Charlie.

"I was waiting to take you on a tour of the tobacco barn—smokeless too!"

Charlie hesitated. "Swell, Alice. Maybe later. Sure wouldn't want to miss Mattie's dinner bell."

"Now I know you just came for Mattie's cooking." Alice pretended to pout.

"Funny girl. You are the food of my soul. Let me drive you to the house."

"Oh that's silly," Alice replied, but she allowed Charlie to lead her to the car. Her legs were tired after all, and she gratefully slipped into the coupe.

They coasted less than thirty yards to the rear walkway of the house. Charlie took the car out of gear, preparing to stop. Alice looked across to the west field, spotting the horses at the fence. She pointed, "Oh Charlie! Drive over there. Let's visit the horses."

Charlie shifted into first; the car rolled forward, tires crunching on the driveway gravel. He pulled off onto shady grass under a spreading walnut tree. He helped Alice out of the car; they approached the horses.

"Lady Bug, Honey Boy," cooed Alice, patting first one nose, then the other. The brown gelding whinnied softly and nodded his head enthusiastically. Charlie reached over to pat the horse's long muzzle. The gray mare nudged in to rub against his arm. Alice laughed, "They're happy to meet you!"

"Looks like it," said Charlie, smiling. "They're beautiful. Does anyone ride them?"

"I don't know. Maybe the Simpsons—or their friends. I haven't seen anyone riding them."

"Have you ever ridden a horse, Alice?" Charlie stroked Lady Bug's muzzle as Alice petted Honey Boy.

Her hand stopped, and she squinted her eyes before answering. "A long time ago—when I was just a young girl with no sense. Sometimes I rode a horse here at the Simpsons' farm. Without a saddle!"

"Do you plan to ride one of these horses?"

"Not now. And—I'm afraid to. I can't do it now. My legs—"

"I'll bet you could," replied Charlie. "I can help you do it. Where is the tack room anyway?"

"I guess at the barn," said Alice, pointing in the distance to where the horse barn broke the fence line. "I think there's a separate road to it from the highway."

"Someday we'll do that," stated Charlie. "We'll ride together."

Alice frowned. "Oh no, I'm not ready—"

Charlie interrupted, "A person might be ready to do something, and they don't even know it. All they need is a little push." His raised eyebrows and questioning gaze pierced Alice's composure.

She looked away and shook her head, dismissing the uncomfortable subject of horseback riding. Honey Boy huffed and turned away from the fence with Lady Bug to look for tastier bunches of grass along the fence line. "Let's sit here a few minutes," said Alice as she slid to the ground and patted a spot next to her on the lush grass. Charlie sat down, stretching his legs to the pointy tips of his white shoes.

"Good-looking farm, nice smells," said Charlie, looking around. "Reminds me of when I was a boy." He pulled up a long blade of grass to show Alice how to make it into a whistle by stretching it taut along his thumb. "The first reed instrument."

Alice laughed. "You should've been a musician, Charlie."

"One of my many talents. But a person can only have so many careers—farmer, accountant, banker—"

"Banker?" queried Alice.

"Well, maybe someday." Charlie grinned.

"My Granddaddy Lea was a bank president," Alice informed him.

"And he did all right, did he?"

"Yes indeed! He's the one who purchased my parents' house, also Stuart and Henny's next door—as wedding presents."

Alice contemplated how comfortable a banker's life must be. Charlie fell silent for a moment, chewing on the musical grass blade.

She spotted the tobacco harvesters leaving the house and remembered her earlier intention. "Charlie, have you ever been inside a tobacco barn?"

"Oh, I reckon so. Never thought much about it. Why?"

"I want to show you the Simpsons' barn and the way they harvest tobacco. It's fascinating. The teamwork's amazing; even the mules—"

"Tobacco's a big crop in this state," Charlie interrupted, frowning. "But I'm glad Papa never gave our lands over to it."

Alice examined Charlie's profile for a moment, then leaned forward, hugging her knees. "Why are you so against smoking?" she asked. "A lot of people do it. Even Daddy does occasionally. They always smoke cigarettes in pictures." She thought of her favorite leading men—Clark Gable, Laurence Olivier. . . .

Charlie's jaw tightened. "It's a dirty habit, Alice," He paused, seeming to think back in time. "Papa smoked at our house. Every spring Catherine and my other sisters did a thorough housecleaning. The curtains washed brown with all that tobacco smoke. The house smelled fresh for a day or two, yet after a couple of days of Papa smoking—"

Alice listened intently as Charlie ranted about the nastiness of smoking and chewing. She shuddered, thinking of the fancy ceramic spittoons in the hallways of the Internal Revenue building; she often wondered who cleaned them.

"Even worse," Charlie went on, "Once you're a smoker you can't stop. I've seen it. I'm not about to let a stinking habit get hold of me and drain money out of my pockets. I work too hard for that money." He smiled broadly, clasping her hand, "Well, you asked—"

Alice loved Charlie for being such a hard worker and handling his money responsibly. A banker, yet a farm boy too—so appealing! And how handsomely the curve of his back strained against his starched shirt. She yearned to put her arms around him in a warm embrace. Instead, she lightly touched his arm and said demurely, "Thank you for sharing your thoughts with me."

They had explored a few deep discussions by telephone, but Alice knew more were needed if marriage was in the stars for them. Some issues were not negotiable: she would not work after marriage. Charlie's job choices and most financial matters would be up to him. She knew some things couldn't be planned so far ahead, only dreamed about—a home of their own—and children. "God will provide," her mother often said. However, God figured into a prickly issue facing them—the difference in their religious faiths. They had passed over this subject briefly in their phone conversations, but neither had seemed ready to pursue it. Could this be a sticking point? Was religion an issue for Allen and Catherine? Might it be the reason they hadn't married yet?

John Lea's bluish-green Chevy drove up and parked in the driveway behind the house. Alice waved. "Daddy!" Eager to see her father and learn the status of her rock garden in the summer heat, she tried to get up quickly, but her legs wobbled.

"My little filly!" laughed Charlie, rising to give her a hand. Arm in arm, they walked toward the coupe as Alice's father stood watching them, waiting. Alice noticed a slight frown move across Charlie's forehead like a summer rain cloud. Was there something about Daddy that disturbed him? A pulse of worry crossed her mind. As Charlie helped Alice into the car, he pressed her close. "You know, I really do love you." Her heart lifted, and all was bright in the sunshine of Charlie's glorious words. She vowed to hold onto this moment in her treasure chest of memories, where it would be safely kept to relive in case she ever had cause to doubt his affections.

∽≈∾

While the Leas and Charlie enjoyed Mattie's fried chicken in the formal dining room, the sky darkened, and the midday humidity rolled up into a rain shower. It allowed Charlie to show off the fancy dual windshield wipers on his clever car. After lunch, he took Alice for a spin around Middlesboro in the rain. She expressed delight with the new windshield feature. "Daddy and Allen will be terribly jealous!"

Charlie grinned, pressed the foot feed, and steered around a curve. They toured the countryside, peering through foggy windows and swishing wipers at the ripe tobacco fields and tasseled corn, pointing out sights, laughing, and chatting. On their return to the Simpsons' farm, Charlie pulled the coupe into the sweeping driveway behind the house and turned off the engine. Suddenly he became serious and turned to face Alice, ready to tackle a question that needed answering. "Would you consider becoming a Catholic before we get married?" As Alice appeared stunned, he looked away, watching raindrops dot the windshield. He had dropped a bomb on Alice. Was he being a jerk again? So easy to do lately; handling women was difficult. He turned to Alice again. Her blue eyes looked troubled, as cloudy as the day. And now he'd ruined it!

Alice answered softly, "No, Charlie. I don't want to turn Catholic—at least not right away."

He tried to strike a gentler tone. "Why not?" Then he smiled, hoping not to appear pushy.

"Well, it's the way I've been brought up. My parents, our church, our minister, our friends. They're a part of my life."

Charlie nodded. "I guess I can understand that." He felt the same way about his religion. He remembered the entire family, cleaned and pressed, riding to church in horse-drawn buggies, tramping dust into St. Ann's for Mass on Sunday mornings; Mama's insistence on the children's bedtime prayers on their knees every night; Confession every month, whether or not they had committed *mortal sins*. Charlie realized it would be hard to give up Mama's standards, the precepts he had fostered in his younger siblings after Mama died. His older brother Harold was now pastor at St. Ann's in Morgantown, further tying Charlie to the Catholic tradition.

When a sudden downburst of rain pelted the car's roof, Alice jumped in surprise. Charlie raised an eyebrow, looking at the sky through the windshield. "Shall we make a run for it—I can carry you!"

"Can we wait for just a bit?" She looked so sweetly hopeful—and tempting.

"I think we can," he replied, inching closer, a grin spreading across his face. He reached to embrace Alice as she melted into his arms. Religious differences be damned, thought Charlie, as their lips touched and began to search deeper.

10

THE BLUE MOON BREWERY in Middlesboro planned a grand opening for their outdoor beer garden the night of the full moon on Saturday, August twenty-first. "Speck Green and his Little Big Band are playing," Charlie had told Alice on the telephone, "but you don't have to dance."

"I'll probably want to," she replied, "if my legs are up to it. Anyway, it will be fun just to be there and see it all."

When Flora heard of the young couple's plans over breakfast the next morning, she said, "Of course, we must insist Charlie spend the night here."

"Mother!" Alice set her china cup down with a jolt, spilling coffee into the saucer.

Flora continued in a practical tone: "We have more than enough room here for Charlie to stay the night—we can put him in the opposite wing."

The thought of Charlie sleeping through the night, even in another wing of the house, gave Alice a momentary thrill. She shrugged it off, giggling, "It's not like you suggesting such a thing. If it was my idea—"

"I'd have given it some thought," said Flora, sitting tall. "Of course we don't want Charlie driving down Highway 60 so late at night, especially after drinking beer."

Alice took a bite of toast with orange marmalade. "Charlie doesn't drink all that much." She stopped, not wanting to change Flora's mind. With Charlie spending the night, Alice knew the evening would last longer than usual, with delicious goodnight kisses in the moonlight. "Do you think it will be okay with Daddy?" questioned Alice.

"Of course," replied Flora, picking up a fan lying beside her silverware. "Daddy always accepts my good judgment. Why don't you call Charlie right after breakfast?" Flora dusted the air with her fan.

"I will call him tonight," said Alice.

That evening, Charlie answered the phone in the apartment hallway. "What's up kid?" he said. "You're not canceling on me for Saturday night, I hope."

"No, of course not—I can't wait! I have an invitation for you from my mother."

Charlie laughed when he heard that Flora wanted him to stay overnight. "Better if the suggestion came from you!"

"Well, after all—"

Charlie reflected for a second how this conversation would have played out with Bonnie. She might have already made the bed—only one. "Tell your mother I accept," said Charlie. "And there will be no hanky panky!" he teased.

Catherine, listening in as usual to her brother's end of the phone conversation, caught his attention. He turned from the phone to warn her off with his fiercest look. Back to Alice, he said, "The next day is Sunday, and I need to attend Mass. I wonder if you'd go with me to the Catholic church in Middlesboro on Sunday."

Alice had rolled her hair on soft rags and slept on a satin pillow the night before her date with Charlie to give her bobbed hair the right bounce. In the Simpsons' parlor, awaiting Charlie's arrival, Flora patted and shaped her daughter's hair-do, straightened the hem of her clingy satin dress, then declared, "Now you're perfect!"

"Better than perfect!" echoed John, coming from the hallway. "Wait 'til Charlie sees you. His eyes will pop out."

"Oh, Daddy," said Alice. "It's only me, after all. Charlie is the peacock!"

"Peaches, you always did have a hard time seeing yourself in the right light—"

Flora interrupted, "Better that way than to be vain. Vanity does not become a woman." Flora smiled at her daughter, whose eyes focused on the floor. "Even a pretty one."

Alice looked up at her mother, surprised by the unexpected compliment.

They heard tires disturbing the driveway. "Your carriage arrives." John bowed low to his daughter. Alice's heart skipped a beat as Charlie approached the door. He looked neat, handsome as always, wearing a white shirt with a dark maroon necktie held in place by a gold tiepin. She wondered how long he'd tolerate his suit jacket on such a warm evening.

Charlie greeted the Leas as he eyed Alice from head to toe. He gave a low whistle of admiration. "Are you stepping out with me, Miss?"

"No one else." Alice hooked her hand around his bent arm, hugging it. They headed to the car.

"Have a good time," said Flora.

"And dance one for us," added John, slipping his arm around his wife. Alice looked back and smiled at her parents' closeness. Would she and Charlie grow old together so lovingly?

∽⁀∾⁀∽

Charlie and Alice arrived at the Blue Moon beer garden at dusk, the full yellow moon rising low in the cobalt sky. Alice saw the moon framed perfectly in the gateway entrance—like decorative lighting for the garden. "How magic, how beautiful!" whispered Alice.

"Yes, you are," said Charlie as he pulled a full money clip out of his pants pocket. "Two please," he said to the gatekeeper. They heard the pure notes of Speck Green's trumpet playing *Stardust*. The fumes of fermented hops and the buttery aroma of fresh popcorn invited them into the beer garden.

Charlie took Alice's hand as they entered the flagstone terrace. Round tables, set close together, were occupied by young people in a party mood. Alice imagined the stars had landed in the beer garden when she saw the dazzle of rhinestones bouncing off the women's beads, pins, and hair ornaments. Young men in dress shirts or summer jackets grounded their sparkling female companions. Alice touched the sequins at her neckline and hoped she was dazzling enough for Charlie.

Flowering trees and shrubs bordered the area, except for the arc reserved for the bandstand and a portable dance floor. Alice heard glasses clinking and a hubbub of voices, as Charlie looked around for a table. Suddenly a large hand shot up from the crowd, motioning to them. "It's Mike Sanders!" said Charlie, his brow relaxing as he smiled. "Let's go." He pulled Alice toward his friend's table beside a climbing white rosebush and informed Alice, "Mike and Virginia are the newlyweds."

Mike and another office buddy jumped up to greet Charlie and Alice. Gregarious, red-haired Mike smiled appreciatively at Alice. He introduced his wife Virginia and the other couple, Stan and Jenny. "Crowd in here, you two," he motioned. Stan had procured a couple more chairs, seemingly out of thin air.

Alice glanced around at Charlie's friends. How young the women look, thought Alice, barely old enough to drink beer yet so sophisticated and perfectly in style. Virginia's professionally coiffed brown hair was stunning; Alice hoped her natural bob didn't appear frumpy. She dared a little smile at Virginia. Charlie, already in a joking mood, was laughing with his office mates. Jenny, a vivacious woman with a glowing tan and high cheekbones, stood up as soon as the band began a jumpy swing number. She beckoned to Stan, "Come on!"

On the bandstand, Speck Green tapped his foot and swayed with his trumpet, the bass player and drummer thumping the beat. Alice looked over and tried another smile on Virginia, who reminded her of an aloof kitten with her freckles and pert nose. Virginia seemed uninterested. She thinks I'm too old, thought Alice. The kittenish woman leaned away, whispering to her new husband. Mike nodded attentively, then resumed his conversation with Charlie. Alice had hoped for romance, music, and special moments with Charlie alone, yet here he was, absorbed in a discussion with Mike. Should she tap Charlie's arm to remind him of her presence? Why wasn't he talking to her? Am I less interesting than Mike? she worried. With no one to talk with, she felt like a big, unwanted lump. All around her, chatter buzzed, and laughter resounded to the sky, along with the music.

When Mike and Virginia left for the dance floor, Charlie turned to Alice and muttered, "Virginia's a different sort. Her family's in racehorses. Well-bred, you know." He laughed at his own pun. Alice wished Charlie's friends would disappear. "Why so glum, Alice?" Charlie asked.

She realized her face must show her feelings. Her voice squeaked, "I'm okay. Not glum, just quiet." She smiled, feeling her lips tight against her teeth.

"Maybe you're just dry. Where in heck is a waiter around here?" He stood up to survey for service.

Alice crossed her arms, waiting for him to sit down. She hoped he would appear happy to be with her. Instead, he shot her a puzzled look as he sat down. Embarrassed and awkward, she managed to say, "I'm so glad you brought me here; it's a beautiful night."

Charlie opened his mouth to reply, then suddenly stood up, smiling broadly. Mike, Stan, and their wives had reappeared. "We've got to leave," said Mike. "Need to make the scene at a few more spots before the night ends." He shook Charlie's hand. "Delightful meeting you, Alice." He nodded to her.

Stan slapped Charlie on the back. "Have a heck of a night, old boy." He nodded to Alice, and the women bid each other good night. Alice breathed a sigh as Charlie sat down again. Alone at last, their enchanted evening could restart.

Charlie glanced around at the garden's layout, the beautiful patrons at the tables, and Speck Green's band hammering out Duke Ellington's *Back Room Romp*. At last, a waiter stopped by to take their order. "An ale for me," said Charlie. "Lager for you?" he asked Alice.

"Swell," she replied.

⤫⤫⤫

Charlie removed his jacket and continued looking around. Bonnie would like this place, he thought, realizing she'd be more outgoing with his friends, an equal with Virginia. He stopped. Why am I thinking of Bonnie? I've got my prize right here beside me. His brow wrinkled under the conflict with his conscience. Bonnie's a friend, that's all, Charlie told himself. Don't friends think of friends from time to time? Satisfied, he reached for Alice's hand, his heart warming as she smiled.

⤫⤫⤫

Alice hoped the moonlight made her eyes sparkle as she gazed into Charlie's handsome face. She didn't know what passed through his mind, making him frown for a moment; whatever the reason, the grip of his hand felt reassuring. She briefly closed her eyes, then looked up at the moon. When the waiter arrived with their frosted mugs of beer on a tray, Charlie reached into his pocket for money. The bubbles of beer releasing yeasty flavors tickled Alice's nose. "This is good," she giggled. As Charlie slurped his amber ale, a thin line of foam appeared on his lips. Instead of wiping it off with a cocktail napkin, Charlie planted it on Alice's mouth. "Ooh!" she said in surprise, then licked her lips. She grinned as the evening regained a promising luster.

Speck Green and his Little Big Band gained momentum. The versatile bandleader sang, played his trumpet and harmonica, and rippled out Hoagy Carmichael tunes on the piano while standing. In between musical numbers, Speck bantered with his band members and the beer garden guests. At intervals, Speck raised a mug to "these marvelous post-Prohibition brews produced at Blue Moon." The crowd cheered.

"It's too bad Mike and Stan left early," Charlie said. Alice ignored his comment and turned to watch the band as they started to play. Was she not conversational enough for him? She recalled Charlie's engaging conversations with Mike and Stan, his approving looks at Virginia and Jenny. Am I boring? thought Alice.

When Speck's deep voice beckoned with a song, Charlie touched Alice's chin and turned her head toward him. "Shall we dance?"

Alice smiled. "Yes, if my legs will cooperate."

"Just lean against me."

". . . Will our love come to be? In our hearts we will see," sang the bandleader.

Alice let Charlie's body carry her along. How wonderful to sway in his arms, clinging close to his beating heart, while the band played a song about falling in love. As the moon continued its ascent toward the top of the sky, Speck announced a tune to celebrate "that big man in the sky." The band sped up the tempo, introducing Hoagy Carmichael's *Old Man Moon*.

"I guess we should sit this one out," said Alice.

"No—take off your shoes and hop on my feet," said Charlie. "I'll dance you around."

Alice felt less inhibited than she had for a long time. Maybe it was the moon or the two rounds of lager, but a desire to be daring rose inside her. "Okay!" She kicked away her leather pumps and let Charlie move her around the dance floor on his white shoes. Alice's spirits flew high as Charlie spun and dipped her. They laughed as Speck improvised the song in his own words: "Hey, hey—open your eyes. Shine Moon, turn on for my sweetie tonight."

When Charlie led Alice to her chair, her head was spinning. Exhausted and effervescent, she longed for the comfort and passion of his arms around her. Alice wiggled in her chair, as close to Charlie as she could touch. The sky blackened while the shimmering moonlight intensified the whiteness of the roses climbing on the wall behind them. The midnight fragrance of the flowers competed with aromas of malt and hops under their noses. Alice could hardly wait for moonlight kisses. Charlie pulled Alice's chair closer. The warmth of her *Blue Hour* perfume enveloped them. He reached around to enclose her in a tight embrace and gently kissed her lips. Alice thought of the white rose petals exploding into the night air.

As the band played and the babble of ebullient voices ascended, a shadow fell across their table. Charlie let go of his embrace. Alice looked up to see Allen and Catherine standing there. Alice's heart dropped; Charlie stood up to welcome them. "Glad you could make it!" he said.

"Wouldn't miss it," said Allen. "Good thing you mentioned this to Catherine."

Alice stared at the couple, then hoisted her eyebrows at Charlie.

"Good thing we found you kids," said Catherine.

"Yes, nifty," responded Alice under her breath.

"Sorry we couldn't get here sooner," said Allen, as he held out a chair for Catherine, then lowered his large frame into the chair next to Alice.

"The band's warming up, and the beer's getting colder," Charlie assured them.

The beer isn't the only thing cooling off, thought Alice. She shivered in the night air, and the scent of beer turned stale. Her high spirits deflated even more when she learned that Catherine and Allen planned to spend the night with them at the Simpson house and would join them for breakfast and church in the morning. Had Charlie known about their plans and avoided telling her?

11

Delirious with beer, music, and moonlight, the two couples returned to the Simpson home at about midnight. None thought to double-check Sunday's Mass schedule before retiring to their separate bedrooms.

Charlie awoke to a bright Sunday morning in the second-floor guest wing. Mixed aromas of coffee and bacon rose from the kitchen below. "Uh-oh!" Charlie grabbed his robe and went to knock on Catherine's door. In her wrapper, she opened the door, untangling her hair with one hand. Charlie pointed to his watch. "It's late—and there's breakfast!"

Yawning, Catherine replied, "I hope we can still make it to Mass."

Back home on a Sunday morning, brother and sister would have awakened early to leave their apartment before eight o'clock, skipping breakfast, in order to receive communion at Mass in the cathedral downtown. Here in the country, the Lea family welcomed Sunday morning differently.

"Oh, well," said Charlie. "Let's do it their way."

"Okay," agreed Catherine, her face blotchy from sleeping in an overheated room. "When in Rome. . . ."

"That would have them being Catholic," said Charlie in a wry tone.

Catherine shrugged, half smiling. "Puny pun."

They dressed and joined the Leas for breakfast in the high-ceilinged dining hall. After *good mornings* and *how did you sleep?* Charlie squeezed Alice's hand and whispered a question. Her blue eyes opened wide. "Of course, I know what

time the Mass is! I had it all planned for eleven o'clock. Allen is coming too."
She smiled at Catherine across the table.

After breakfast with the Leas, the young couples prepared to leave for church
in Allen's Chevy. The women's summer dresses billowed gently in the morning's
gentle breeze. Charlie and Allen wore cool seersucker suits and straw Panama
hats. How swanky Charlie looks, thought Alice. His maroon necktie with thin
silvery stripes was an eye-catching note to his summery attire. Alice's short hair
had gone limp. She checked to be sure both sides were tucked securely behind
her ears with enameled barrettes. Ready to start the day with Charlie—and
Allen and Catherine, of course!

St. Joseph's in Middlesboro was a modest white-frame church at the end of a
country lane. As Alice entered, she noticed the dark stillness and the candles in
red glass votives shimmering like stars. The powdery smoke of incense in the air
made her sneeze—as quietly as possible. Her eyes were drawn to the ornate altar
and the wall behind, painted in shades of gold and pink. Three stained glass
windows on each side wall displayed scenes from the life of St. Joseph and the
Holy Family. Alice looked forward to spending an hour in this magical realm.

The men removed their hats upon entering the church. Allen loosened his
shirt collar. Catherine led the way to a pew midway down the aisle, kneeling
quickly on one knee before entering the polished bench. Allen nearly tripped
over her; Alice stifled a giggle. Charlie looked straight ahead at the altar, ignoring them, then bent on one knee like a loyal subject before his master.

To Alice, the Mass was a pageant with the priest in wizard-like robes and re-
galia entering stage left and immediately turning his back on the congregation,
starting to pray. Not understanding a word, Alice was intrigued by the use of
Latin. Charlie hadn't mentioned the language or the pageantry. He must have
wanted to surprise me, Alice concluded.

She noticed her brother frowning throughout the Mass, as though trying
hard to concentrate or keep from showing surprise or amusement during the
ritual. Catherine poked him a time or two.

Alice reveled in the heavenly enchantment of the church as sunbeams
danced with color through the stained glass windows and little bells tinkled
at the altar boys' touch. When the congregation was invited to sing along with
the choir, Alice couldn't wait to hear Charlie's attempt. She smiled as he adeptly
paged through the hymnal. She wondered how his singing voice would sound.
As the music began, Alice could hardly believe the pure tenor notes pouring

from Charlie's throat. Tears welled in her eyes as he sang the Ave Maria. His clear, on-pitch notes were all she heard. Had everyone else stopped singing to listen to Charlie? A piece of Charlie's soul was revealed to Alice, and she loved him even more.

After Mass, the couples took a circuitous return route to the Simpsons' estate through the Middlesboro landscape of the Leas' childhood summers. Allen's Chevy meandered past tobacco fields at stages of harvest; endless rows of ripe corn; meadows with haystacks; and the thistles of late summer, tall and feral along the roadsides. "I'm telling you—we weren't lost," said Allen when they finally returned to the Simpson place. "I took the scenic tour." Alice smirked, knowing her brother never admitted mistakes.

They had time for a short walk around the farm before Mattie served a light lunch. Seated at the great dining table once again, Charlie boldly inquired, "Mattie, do you ever get out of the kitchen?"

Alice noticed her mother's stiffened attention to this informality toward a servant. Charlie is like a breath of fresh air, she mused, as Mattie replied cheerfully, "Yessir, I get out to feed the chickens and do the laundry."

"We couldn't be here without Mattie to take care of everything," assured John Lea, smiling generously at the estate's housekeeper.

Flora fanned herself. "That is indeed true," she said.

Alice beamed at Charlie for taking notice of the help. How kind and respectful he is, she noted.

Mattie bustled around, serving trays of tender roast beef slices and salty country ham. Next came plates stacked with smooth hard biscuits "derived from the hardtack the soldiers carried in the Civil War," Allen informed them.

Alice remembered her mother's fallback plan to make and sell these beaten biscuits during the Depression if the menfolk lost their jobs. She passed a bowl of garden-fresh tomato salad to Charlie and inhaled the summery vapor of cucumber.

The conversation turned to talk of jobs and careers. John told some post-office anecdotes. Catherine gave a progress report on her new job at the Seelbach Hotel restaurant. "I meet lots of fascinating people," she said. "All hungry!"

Flora remarked, "It's a sign of God's providence that you all have jobs these days."

Charlie told them of the business proposal he had made to Mr. Benson. "Heard anything yet, old chap?" asked Allen.

Charlie frowned. "No." Then he added, "Change takes time."

Alice patted his arm. "Even with the best ideas."

"And Sis—" began Allen. "When are you going back to work?"

Alice had trouble swallowing and set down her biscuit. Last week a letter had arrived from her boss, but she hadn't told anyone. Instead, she had tucked the note in her dresser drawer, unanswered.

Flora spoke up. "I noticed a letter came from Mr. McNulty. I was waiting for you to mention it. . . ."

Alice blushed and replied into her plate of food, "Yes—he wonders when I'm coming back to work." Secretarial work had lost its appeal; she wanted this romantic summer to continue forever. Turning to her father with a pleading look, she said. "I think maybe I should talk to Doc Richards first."

"That's a very sound idea, Peaches," John affirmed.

"When do you want to see the doctor?" Flora inquired.

Never, thought Alice. Suddenly sick, she placed her napkin on the table and clumsily stood up. "Excuse me," said Alice. "I have to go."

As she staggered from the room, she sensed a stony silence behind her at the dining table. She regretted leaving them so befuddled but couldn't contain her emotions.

Flora missed dessert to join Alice in her sitting room. "I'm sorry I mentioned the letter, dear. Obviously, you weren't pleased to receive it."

"It's okay, Mother," said Alice, looking up from her bent-over position on the settee. "We can talk later." Flora quirked an eyebrow as if she doubted her daughter's sincerity. "Truly," said Alice.

Flora reached down to Alice and fingered a strand of her blond hair. She informed her daughter that a friend from Middlesboro would soon arrive to pick her up for the afternoon; Mattie would stand by if Alice needed something. "Maybe she can bring you some ice tea," Flora suggested.

"No thanks. Has Charlie gone?" Alice asked.

"No. He's waiting for you."

"Tell him I'll be out to see him soon. Please tell him not to leave."

"I will," Flora promised. "I hope you feel better soon. We can talk later about—" With a glance at her downcast daughter, she left the room.

Alice slumped on the settee. She intended to go to Charlie, but the dilemma about returning to work left her feeling listless. She arose and went to her dresser, opening a heavy drawer with lion's-head drawer pulls. Mr. McNulty's letter lay beside her diary. She stared at the envelope, feeling her stomach churn. She pushed the drawer closed. If she went back to work, would her world return to the way it was before she became ill—before Charlie proposed? Since he hadn't again mentioned marriage directly, did he have second thoughts? When he had asked her about becoming Catholic, was that a turning point? A U-turn, perhaps?

When a gentle tap sounded on the door, Alice half expected to see Mattie with iced tea. Instead, it was Charlie smiling tentatively, in his white shirt open at the collar and no necktie. "May I come in?"

Alice answered with an embrace of both arms, her eyes brimming.

"Tears?" asked Charlie, wiping one away with his index finger.

"I'm so glad you didn't leave," said Alice. She opened the door wider.

He entered her powder-fragrant sitting room where her pink silk robe hung gracefully on the door to her bedroom. His face shown as if seeing a beatific vision.

"We need to talk," said Charlie. "Can we sit down?"

Alice took his hand, escorting him to her parlor settee.

"Something about going back to work upsets you," began Charlie. Alice nodded. "What do you really want to do, Alice?"

She hesitated a moment, then throwing caution aside, she blurted out, "Oh Charlie—I just want to marry you!"

Charlie smiled his broad grin. "I take it that's a 'yes'—after all this time. I was beginning to wonder," he said. "And I really will bring you a rose every day."

Alice exhaled with long-anticipated relief. "Oh, Charlie—I'm so happy! I was worried you had changed your mind about proposing." He enfolded Alice passionately, removing all doubts that he truly wanted her.

They sat together, arms wrapped around one another, relishing their intimacy, tasting each other's lips. Charlie unwound himself from Alice for a moment and walked over to her radio. He clicked it to life. A light shone through the mesh openings of the wood-trimmed façade. Indistinct musical notes floated into the room. As the sound increased and took form, Charlie said, "Listen—from last night!"

Alice heard a jazz orchestra playing *Let's Fall in Love* and remembered some of the lyrics. The magic from the previous evening filled the room, and she relived being in Charlie's arms, pressed close to his body. It seemed so natural when he repeated last night's invitation, "Shall we dance?"

The window blinds were lowered, shading the sitting room from the sun's intensity and casting a sensuous ambiance. When Charlie pulled Alice close to him, she imagined the cool evening breezes and the breath of the white roses. She closed her eyes as he steered her around in a tight circle between the dresser and floral-printed settee. As the song ended, Charlie held her tighter and whispered, "Hold on!" He dipped her backward in a romantic finale as

Alice's standing leg buckled, tumbling them toward the settee. Charlie reached out an arm as they fell awkwardly, laughing. The top button popped off her scoop-necked dress. As he lay across her, Charlie's fingers touched a reddened area below Alice's throat. "That's a bad burn, honey," he said.

"It was at one time," she replied. "From a sunburn I got on vacation a long time ago." She swallowed. "Your hand feels cool there."

From beneath the neckline of her dress, Charlie's fingers traveled further to the edge of her silky slip, seeking the underside of her brassiere. He stopped. Alice, at first startled by his unexpected advance, met his gaze. His fingers continued on their path along Alice's breast to her nipple. She moaned and turned her head. She saw the radio; it reminded her of a little wooden chapel, shining from inside with holy light. Duke Ellington's erotic music pulsed into the room. With the wail of a saxophone, Alice felt a gnawing pang below her stomach; her thighs turned to water, and her heart thumped.

Charlie got up to check the sitting room door and quietly turned the lock. Then he returned to Alice and leaned over her flushed face. "I only thought we'd talk," he whispered. "But here we are. And you did say 'yes' at last."

Alice looked deep into his eyes—brownish with flecks of green. Beautiful! Then she kissed him, and he kissed her harder. On the radio, woodwinds and horns started a conversation. On the flower-crazed cushions, two bodies began to communicate.

Alice responded to Charlie as the music soared. She loved him so much; she couldn't say no. Alice hadn't thought she was ready to *go all the way* with Charlie. Was this what he meant out there with the horses—about not realizing when you're ready? Now the time had surely arrived. The oozing trombones and jazzy rhythms carried them up and over the bumps of making love for the first time in a cramped space on a sultry August afternoon.

༄༅

Mattie, finished with her Sunday kitchen chores, prepared to go outside to take some food remainders to the horses. She noticed Charlie's car still parked outside. She hadn't seen him and Alice for a while and thought she should check on them. The house was quiet as Mattie walked into the hallway from the dining room. As she tiptoed past Alice's sitting room, she noticed the door closed and the radio playing *Ain't Misbehavin*. Mattie chuckled to herself. "No sirree—you sure ain't!" She returned to her chores at the back of the house.

༄༅

As late afternoon light twinkled around the edges of the drawn window shade, Alice and Charlie, warm bodies entwined, emerged from a trance. Flora would soon return from Middlesboro. Charlie jumped up and retrieved his wrinkled, clammy clothes from a pile on the floor. Carrying his shirt and pants, he moved toward Alice's bedroom door. He took her satin robe from the hook and tossed it to her.

Clutching her robe around herself, she said, "Oh Charlie! We must never do this again until we're married."

"Absolutely," Charlie agreed, inwardly smiling yet noticing how vulnerable she looked curled up on the settee. He felt a twinge of guilt mixed with his top-of-the-world excitement. Charlie backed into the bedroom to dress. When he returned, Alice wore her pink robe; her hair hung damp, and her eyes shone misty blue. "I hate to leave you, Alice. But I need to get out of here," said Charlie. "Are you okay?"

Alice nodded, a shy smile curving her lips.

"Your mother will be home soon," he warned. Charlie traced his fingers along Alice's jawline and tucked a damp lock of hair behind one ear. Despite her entreating look, leaving was an urgent matter. He kissed her lips tenderly as if to say, "Sorry."

Charlie hurried out to his car, concerned any second that Flora would return, necessitating an exchange of words. Another pang of guilt—he hadn't thanked Mattie for dinner—but he couldn't afford to waste time looking for her. On the way down the driveway, he passed the car bringing Flora home. "Just in time!" Charlie muttered. He hesitated to wave at Flora but realized it would look suspicious if he didn't return her greeting. As Charlie drove back to the city, he grinned, remembering moments of lovemaking with Alice. How willingly she succumbed as their passion progressed. Then remembering her admonition afterward, guilt piqued his conscience. He realized he needed to go to Confession as soon as possible. Next, he would have to ask John Lea formally for Alice's hand in marriage. The thought of this encounter had already seemed daunting; now, after making love to Alice, the prospect loomed like a thunderhead. Would John Lea find out about their transgression?

༽ⲋ⚬ⲋ⚬

In the early hours of Monday morning, Alice wrote in her diary: *I stayed awake until I knew Mother was asleep. I arose quietly and retrieved some cleaner I'd borrowed from Mattie's kitchen. Despite the printed fabric, the bloodstain on the settee was quite noticeable. I worked and worked on that "damned spot," all the while thinking, "I am Lady Macbeth." I have the guilt to go with it. I never imagined how easy it would be to give myself to Charlie like that. The music coming from that little church of a radio seemed to make it right. And Charlie is so good, how could it be wrong to love him! Now, I realize we did wrong, and I can't let anyone know. Never before have I possessed such an awful—yet wonderful—secret.*

After dozing awhile, Alice awoke to someone knocking on the door of her suite. Alice thought the rapping sounded sharp, insistent. The imagining of her guilty conscience? The tapping grew louder. Mattie wouldn't knock like that, she knew. It must be her mother. As Alice hurried through her sitting room to answer the door, she checked to ensure her robe covered the spot on the settee.

She opened the door to see Flora holding up Charlie's maroon necktie. Her lips formed a straight line.

"Charlie's tie!" Alice laughed as innocently as she could. "Where was it?"

"In the dining room. I thought you might explain why a man would rush off and forget an expensive necktie."

Heat rose in Alice's cheeks as she attempted a casual response. "You know how hot it got yesterday. He took off the tie and then forgot, I guess."

Flora had more. "Not only that—Mattie found his overnight bag and all his things still up in the guest wing. Seems he left in a terrible hurry. Do you know why?"

Alice panicked, then lied to her mother. "All right. We had a brief spat after you left."

The lie had the desired effect on her mother. "Oh no. I'm so sorry, Alice." Flora threw her arms around her daughter. "No wonder you seemed nervous when I came home."

"Don't worry, Mother. We'll make up. I'm sure of it," said Alice. Guilt compounding guilt.

12

CHARLIE AND ALICE sat together, knees touching, on the overstuffed leather sofa in the dim parlor of St. George's parish house. The walls lacked color, except for pastel blues and lackluster reds in the religious paintings: Jesus in the Garden with light rays slanting from the sky, a bearded Jesus holding a tiny planet Earth, and a Botticelli Virgin with Child. The couple faced Father David Devitt, who sat a level above them on a swivel chair next to a highboy desk. Charlie hoped this meeting might pass quickly and that Father Devitt would prove more empathetic than he looked. The priest peered at them, lips pursed, tips of his fingers touching across the mid-section of his heavy black shirt.

Charlie thought back to a few weeks ago when he had faced John Lea to ask for Alice's hand in marriage. Charlie had dreaded that meeting too, but the timing had been fortunate. He congratulated himself for arranging his talk with John soon after the August afternoon he and Alice had made love—before *complications* could have become known. The meeting, on the breezy back porch of the Simpson house, had been casual, between the adoring father of a perfect daughter and the prospective son-in-law. John had barely let Charlie announce his intentions before sharing his own memories of asking for Flora's hand.

The older man had told Charlie, "I remember being a young suitor, sweating at the thought of facing Flora's father. I was trembling—like you!" John had laughed heartily, then continued. "I will never forget that man's blessing, saying that all Flora needed in this world was to be loved. Now I'd like to pass along my father-in-law's kindness and wisdom by saying the same goes for you and Alice."

Charlie recalled John's watery blue eyes as he kept shaking his hand, looking like he wanted a hug. It had been so easy after all; Charlie hoped this meeting with the pastor of St. George's parish might go even half as well.

Father Devitt cleared his throat, interrupting Charlie's thoughts. "Are you aware of the necessary waiting period—three Sundays to announce the banns of matrimony? That places the earliest possible Saturday wedding date at November sixth." Alice squeezed Charlie's hand and looked at him with a pleading expression.

Charlie flashed a smile at Father Devitt, hoping to disarm him. "Well, I hadn't thought about the banns. We just want our wedding the end of this month."

The priest went on. "Highly irregular. Of course, we can request a dispensation from the bishop, but Holy Mother Church has her rules—and good reasons for them."

Alice spoke up, her voice unnaturally high. "What are the banns for?"

Father Devitt smiled condescendingly at Alice. "My dear, we must allow ample notice for the parishioners or others to step forward with reasons why the marriage may not take place. For example, we can't tolerate forced marriages, bigamous ones, or—in cases of divorce, which the Church forbids."

Alice looked down. "Oh, I see."

Charlie spoke up. "You mentioned a dispensation—"

The priest waved away the question. "Only for serious reasons." He hesitated. "Do you have a serious reason?" He narrowed his eyes at Alice. "You're not already in a family way, are you, my dear?"

Alice squirmed on the leather cushion. Charlie squeezed her hand firmly as he replied, "Yes. We are expecting a baby, the end of May."

In the silent gloom, the priest frowned, tapping his fingers together. "I see." Charlie looked at Alice, her mouth drawn with worry. Father Devitt reached behind the desk and picked up a square calendar on a metal stand. "You want to be married the last Saturday in October—the thirtieth? That gives us two weeks of banns starting this Sunday. I will call the archbishop for permission."

"Thank you!" murmured Alice.

"Thank you, Father," said Charlie. "Now, about the wedding arrangements—"

"Well," said Father Devitt, "you don't have much time, do you, so it looks like a church wedding is out of the question."

Next to him, Alice whimpered, and Charlie wondered if the priest had noticed. "We thought we'd like our wedding before the altar, with our friends and family," he said.

The priest glanced at a schedule spread across the desk and shook his head. "If that's the date you want, I'm sorry, but there are already two church weddings that day. My one suggestion is to have a quiet ceremony right here."

"Here?" croaked Alice. "In your house—this room?"

Charlie saw the rectory as a depressing site for their wedding, certainly not the wedding of Alice's dreams. "What about the following Saturday?"

The priest shook his head again. "All the Saturdays are taken up until the beginning of Advent with Nuptial Masses. And, frankly speaking, we do not have Nuptial Masses for marriages with Protestants at any time. Yours would be a short, simple ceremony."

Alice asked, "Could we have flowers and bridesmaids? May I wear a white dress and veil?"

Father Devitt leered at Alice. "If you think it appropriate, my dear, under the circumstances."

Alice glanced at the Virgin and Child on the wall and bit her lip. An inspiration struck Charlie: "Alice loves flowers, Father. Might it be possible at all to have the ceremony in the front yard at Alice's home? She has a rock garden there—over on Brook Street—within the parish boundaries."

"Highly irregular," said the priest, twisting his neck inside his stiff white collar. "I have never done a home wedding. And I don't think the bishop would like to open the floodgates by starting such a practice."

Charlie was tired of backing down. He met the priest's stare. "My brother is the priest at St. Ann's in Morgantown. How difficult would it be for him to marry us?"

Father Devitt raised an eyebrow and leaned forward. "Harold Lukas? In Morgantown? It might be difficult, although not impossible. At least Morgantown is still inside the diocesan boundaries. The bishop must give permission, of course."

Alice broke in, "I love Charlie's idea of having the wedding at my home. I don't want to get married in Morgantown!"

Father Devitt smiled in a friendly way at Alice for the first time. "If the archbishop allows Father Lukas to perform your wedding in this parish, you may have the ceremony anyplace you wish—with my blessings."

Some blessings, thought Charlie, despite his respect for Holy Mother Church. "Thank you, Father," he said.

"Let me know about your arrangements. If necessary, my parlor is available for a brief ceremony at almost any time. However, weekends are tight, as you see."

Charlie winked at Alice. He felt proud of himself for thinking of his brother Harold and wished he had thought of him sooner, possibly avoiding Father Devitt altogether. Charlie knew Harold to be a diplomatic sort who knew his way around the archbishop. With his help, they could arrange a wedding to please Alice. Things were looking up!

Father Devitt continued, "We'll start the paperwork now, and the banns can begin Sunday."

Before leaving the parish house, Charlie and Alice signed a marriage consent form. Father Devitt produced another form for Alice's signature—a promise to raise progeny in the Catholic faith. After Charlie smiled and nodded his approval, she scribbled her name on the signature line. As the meeting concluded, Charlie shook hands with Father Devitt. Alice kept hers clenched tight on her red pocketbook. She nodded goodbye to the priest as Charlie guided her toward the door.

On the porch of the two-story stone house, Charlie muttered, "I'm sorry you're not getting a church wedding."

Alice replied, "It's okay, Charlie. It's only one day in a long, happy marriage. Thank you for the idea to have our wedding beside the rock garden."

Charlie hugged Alice tight and kissed her firmly, hoping Father Devitt saw their silhouettes from behind the curtained front door, perhaps shocking him. Charlie was glad for love and sunshine. He looked at his watch. "Just in time to get back to work! I'll drop you at home first, of course."

"Oh Charlie, do you have to go back to work?" She snatched a handkerchief from her pocketbook as a tear started down her cheek. "Please stay with me this afternoon. We have so many plans to make—so quickly. Can't you?"

Charlie felt himself succumbing to Alice's plea; he realized the morning's appointment had been a trial for her. With a lopsided grin, he said, "I'll see what I can do."

He phoned the office from Alice's home and asked the secretary to tell Mr. Benson "something has come up with the marriage planning." Miss Wilson sounded sympathetic and agreed to smooth things over with Charlie's boss.

"I know what we can do!" Alice piped, suddenly cheerful. "Let's go down to our spot by the river and gather more rocks for my garden. We need wedding decorations!"

Charlie tried to apply the brakes. "Whoa—I haven't even talked with Harold yet about the home wedding!"

"I know in my heart it will work out. Anyway, the garden can always use more rocks."

Charlie didn't argue.

As Charlie drove the green coupe through the downtown area, he kept a lookout for anyone he knew who might see him on a pleasure trip in the middle of a workday. Past the commercial buildings and markets, toward the undeveloped riverine area, they soon reached the little hideaway they'd chanced to find on a picnic one summer day. Their quiet riverside haven was a patch of sand and ground cover, secreted by a curtain of silver maple and black willow. When Charlie and Alice last lingered there by moonlight, she had pointed out a lode of smooth, rounded stones the river deposited during last winter's flood. By daylight the rocks looked even prettier.

"Look at the colors!" exclaimed Alice. "They look like eyes watching the sky." She and Charlie began gathering the most attractive stones: tan with black bands, pure white with ochre patches, green with splotches of black, mauve, and slate gray with mica sparkles. As they piled Alice's treasures into the trunk of Charlie's Plymouth, he frowned and sucked on his lip.

"What's wrong?" Alice asked.

"I'm starting to wonder about the weight on the springs and tires," Charlie said.

"Should we stop then?"

"Maybe." He also noticed the sandy mess in his trunk requiring a major cleaning effort but said nothing, as dirt was the lesser problem. Charlie walked around his car and stooped down to check how the rear axle was holding up. The back end hung lower than usual. "It won't scrape the road yet—a couple more armloads. Choose your favorites—then I think we're done!"

᠄᠊᠋᠎᠐

At bedtime, Alice wrote in her diary:

> *What a day! Charlie's little car got its first flat tire. And all my fault! What a mess—with my load of rocks in the trunk, Charlie couldn't even find his jack and lug wrench. It happened on Market Street, barely into town. Charlie had to borrow a drugstore phone to call Allen. Luckily, Allen was just leaving the laundry on his way home. My brother, the rescuer! He and Charlie transferred rocks to Allen's trunk until they uncovered the tools. Then they took out more rocks to jack up the car easier. What a gritty, gravelly mess in two cars now—so much trouble for my rock garden! Allen made us laugh by offering to dry clean Charlie's trunk.*

The tire disaster nearly made me forget the wedding plans, the awful visit with Father Devitt, and the fact I am having a baby. I can't believe it! Yet today, I had to sign his or her life away—sort of like the miller's daughter who promised her firstborn to Rumpelstiltskin in exchange for spinning straw into gold for the king. I promised to raise our children Catholic. I don't know what's involved. But Charlie turned out well, being raised Catholic. I could do worse than have a dozen like him! At least I didn't promise to turn Catholic myself. And a baby won't care—won't know the difference if he's Catholic or otherwise. I trust Charlie.

13

THE CLOCK THEY called Big Ben struck the half-hour at the house on Brook Street. Alice gazed at herself in the mahogany-framed mirror above the marble-topped washstand, her rumpled bed beneath the antique carved headboard, and the bookshelf wall of favorite books reflected in the background. She brushed her hair (100 faithful strokes) with the silver monogrammed hairbrush and considered her firm breasts swelling beyond the bounds of her white lace camisole. A small smile curved her mouth as she remembered how Charlie had said her increased bosom size was a pleasing feature of her pregnancy. In a few hours, she and Charlie would be married, and it would be all right for him to say such things.

She thought about the baby she carried, wondering when she'd feel it move. Maybe on the honeymoon, thought Alice, when we are lying close together, the baby will kick us both as a reminder of what we've already begun.

From downstairs, Alice heard the ringing clatter of glassware and good china her mother was setting out for the wedding reception dinner. She assumed her father had probably moved out of the way, reading the newspaper, but on call for any tasks Flora assigned.

Her parents had been reasonable about the baby news—considering, Alice reflected. She had told them about her pregnancy two weeks ago Friday, after finishing supper. Allen had already left the table and hurried off for a poker evening with friends. Alice sat alone with her parents; the mood was peaceful after a satisfying meal. When she broke the news, John looked stunned; his Adam's apple jumped in his thin neck.

Flora slapped her hand flat on the table. "Well, I'm surprised you and Charlie couldn't wait. But what's done is done."

John said, "And we know Charlie's intentions were honorable. He had already asked to marry you."

Alice wondered if her father would realize she and Charlie had already made love before he asked. But then she knew Daddy didn't have a suspicious nature.

Flora spoke again. "It would be so much nicer if you and Charlie had time for adjusting to married life first."

"We will have until May before the baby comes," Alice reminded her.

John's sense of humor returned. "Oftentimes the first baby doesn't take nine months. The next ones always do."

Alice smiled. Flora frowned at her husband. "Let's not make light of this." She stared at her daughter. "The thing that hurts is how you broke my trust in you."

It felt like her mother threw scalding water in her face. "What do you mean, Mother?"

"You lied to me, didn't you! The time this pregnancy happened, you told me you and Charlie had a fight. Exactly the opposite occurred, didn't it!"

"But Mother, I knew you'd be upset with me. We only did it the one time—how could I tell you? And I just found out I'm—"

"She's telling us now, Flora," John said. "Please, don't. . . ."

Flora lowered her eyes. "Still. . . ."

"I'm sorry for whatever pain this causes you," whispered Alice.

Alice put down her hairbrush and faced herself in the mirror. All told, her parents had behaved well. She knew they would love their first-born grandchild and hoped they didn't think ill of Charlie. If they did, they hadn't acted unkindly toward him. He would soon prove his worth as an outstanding son-in-law and father.

Alice finished dressing. She didn't feel hungry for breakfast, but the aroma of Flora's fresh-perked coffee beckoned her. At the top of the stairs, she paused to look at Big Ben's face with the phases of the moon above the timepiece. Barely over six hours until the four o'clock wedding! Alice made her way downstairs, holding the banister. She found Flora in the kitchen polishing silver, the scent of tarnish remover making Alice queasy. Allen sipped his coffee, the cup looking dangerously fragile in his big hands. He sat sideways on the ladder-backed chair, glancing at the newspaper, poised to take off at a moment's notice. Alice thought her brother seemed habitually in a hurry—but not for marriage. He looked up. "Good morning, Sis! Big day ahead!"

Her brother seemed genuinely happy for her. Earlier, she had worried about Allen and Catherine's reaction to her sudden marriage—with a baby on the way. If they felt pre-empted by not being the first married, they didn't let on. Allen and Catherine had been enthusiastic about helping with wedding plans. Perhaps, thought Alice, they were relieved not to be in her predicament. Had Allen and Catherine made love, she wondered. If so, perhaps they'd been more careful, more aware that pregnancy could result. Alice hadn't even considered the likelihood of a baby in those spontaneous moments with Charlie on the settee. Even young married women she knew weren't having babies. It couldn't be so easy!

When Alice entered the kitchen, Flora laid down her polishing cloth to serve her daughter coffee. She kissed Alice gently on the forehead. "Yes, today's your big day. I'm already wishing for more hours in it. Charlie and his brother will be here shortly to plan the ceremony."

Suddenly Alice felt butterflies in her stomach. Maybe she was hungry after all—or could it be the baby? Or the smell of that darn silver polish?

"How would you like your egg, dear?" asked Flora.

"Just fine," said Alice absently.

Allen and Flora laughed. "Hello, Alice—are you there?" teased Allen.

"Oh—scrambled is fine, I guess," said Alice.

She managed to stomach her breakfast and felt steadier when the doorbell sounded. Flora bustled to the door. Alice heard Charlie's familiar voice and another she didn't recognize. The two men were ushered into the kitchen. Allen stood to greet them. Alice hopped up to hug Charlie and welcome his sandy-haired brother Harold, the priest. He resembled Charlie, except for blue eyes behind his wire-rimmed glasses and a tucked black shirt with a clerical collar instead of an impeccable white shirt like Charlie's.

"I can offer you coffee," said Flora. "Here or in the dining room."

"Here is perfect, Mrs. Lea," said Harold. "I always feel at home in a kitchen." They settled at the table with Alice and Allen as Flora served steaming coffee.

"Here's my honorary best man," Charlie told Harold, nodding at Allen.

Alice was pleased that Allen was not miffed about not being Charlie's best man and took his replacement with good humor. She and Charlie had wanted him to witness their marriage, along with Catherine as maid of honor, but

Father Devitt decreed both witnesses must be Catholic. So, Charlie's best man would be his sister Lillian, who had arrived by plane the previous evening from Washington D.C. Alice looked forward to meeting Lillian, a fellow polio victim, so brave in overcoming her disabilities and pursuing a career in the capital.

Allen laughed, "Yes, I'm your would-be best man, except—oops—wrong religion! You might say Lillian bested the best man."

"Allen can be best man in spirit," Harold said in his soft voice.

Allen nodded. "Definitely in spirit—and only a few feet away if you decide to use me after all." He looked up at the kitchen clock. "Gotta rush! Catherine and I have a surprise coming." Alice looked up as her brother headed off. "I'm taking Dad with me," he called over his shoulder.

Flora continued polishing the silver. Harold looked around toward the percolator; Alice rose to serve him more coffee. Soon she, with Charlie and Harold, huddled together at the table, planning the wedding ceremony, with Flora listening in.

With plans nearly final, Charlie suggested they go into the front yard and walk through the ceremony. "Before we do that," said Harold, "I brought a surprise for Alice. Charlie, it might be a surprise for you too." He reached into his jacket on the back of the kitchen chair and presented a rectangular box to his future sister-in-law. Inside, on a bed of satin, rested a pearl-cluster brooch on a silver chain, tiny pearls in the cluster swirling toward the larger central pearl.

Alice touched it. "Oh Harold—how beautiful!"

"It belonged to our mama, Josephine. She wore it on her wedding day," said Harold.

Charlie gazed at the pendant. "Really? Mama's on her wedding day? This is really something," a note of astonishment in his tone.

Flora dropped her polishing cloth and went over to the table. "See, Mother?" said Alice, holding up the pendant. "It will look lovely with my dress. Thank you so much, Harold. This is very special." She looked at Charlie, considering how deeply emotional he must feel that his bride would wear a treasure from his mother's wedding day. Charlie sipped his coffee.

Big Ben sounded one bong as Allen and John, with Catherine, returned to the house, followed by a florist's delivery van. Allen dashed into the house, calling, "Sis, come see our surprise!" Alice walked out the front door onto the stoop and saw Catherine and John helping the florist lift large baskets of chrysanthemums from the van. The colors of fall: bronze, deep red, yellow, and lavender. "Catherine and I wanted your garden in bloom for the wedding."

A smile spread on Alice's face as she watched the baskets of flowers emerge from the back of the truck. "What a perfect idea!" In the rock garden, the mosses, sedum, and foliage luxuriated. Cyclamen flowers, poking straight out of the earth like butterflies balancing on slender stems, replaced summer blossoms. Heather snuggled beside the glassy obsidian boulder. Catherine placed the mums at the edges of the *riverbed* of new rocks extending from the front yard wall, along the brick walk, to the house.

John looked up toward Alice and said, "Come on down, tell us where you think these ought to go. You're the gardener, after all!" Allen took his sister's arm and helped her down the concrete steps. Flora, Charlie, and Harold watched from the doorway as the rock garden was transformed for the wedding.

Big Ben had struck the two o'clock hour. Soon after, a cook arrived at the house to prepare and serve the wedding dinner. Elizabeth, a large woman in a crisp gray uniform with a starched white apron, set to work in Flora's kitchen, peeling and chopping vegetables and breading chicken for the frying pan. Rich odors of onion, butter, and rolls baking began floating around the kitchen, invading the house and escaping outdoors.

Alice knew to stay out of the kitchen. She chatted with her father as they rearranged some of the flowers in the rock garden. "So wonderful of Allen and Catherine to do this," commented Alice. "They must have spent a fortune— which they don't have."

John replied, "What is money if you can't spend it on people you love?"

Big Ben struck three, as Alice pulled her wedding dress out of the closet. The dress was dark blue satin with a blousy bodice to gracefully accommodate the slight bump she perceived below her waistline. The soft skirt brushed against her legs as she admired the dress on its hanger. She would wear a matching satin hat with a pearl clip at the crown. Perfect with Charlie's mother's pendant, thought Alice.

Flora had convinced her daughter that a white dress and veil were not appropriate for a bride already in a family way. Her mother and Father Devitt concurred, reflected Alice, a combined force not to be reckoned with. Flora further pointed out that a long white gown and veil would look ridiculous in their small front yard. Alice turned toward a knock at the door and welcomed her mother to help her dress for the wedding.

The doorbell buzzed. In a moment, John knocked on the bedroom door. "Telegrams arriving!" he announced. He handed two to Alice, who had just wiggled into her dress. One message came from her former boss, Mr. McNulty, and the other from next-door neighbors Uncle Stuart and Aunt Henny, who had already left for their winter vacation in Florida.

"How thoughtful of them," said Alice, as she read the yellow forms with typed messages in bold capital letters.

Flora went to change into her wedding finery, and Alice heard Allen clomping up the stairs. As Big Ben chimed three-thirty, Alice, still in her childhood bedroom, heard voices downstairs. Charlie had arrived with his brother and sisters. Although she longed to meet Lillian, Alice decided to delay the moment when her soon-to-be-husband would see her as a bride. When she could wait no longer, Alice checked her reflection in the mirror, and then descended the stairs.

In the parlor, freshly dusted and arranged like a stage set, Charlie stood at attention, looking handsome in his new gray-and-blue tweed suit. His white shirt and tie fit perfectly in place as usual, yet Alice had never seen him so dressed up. It must be the buttoned-up vest, she thought, with a pocket watch chain catching glints of light.

When Charlie saw Alice, his face broke into a wide smile. Warmth like a little candle glowed in Alice's heart as she glided across the room toward Charlie. He picked up a paper-wrapped bundle beside the Tiffany lamp and offered Alice the bouquet of white roses. "For my beautiful bride," he whispered.

The wedding started on time. Only Elizabeth, the cook, remained in the house as Big Ben tolled the hour of four o'clock. In the front yard, decorated with fall blossoms and glittering rocks, Alice stood with Charlie in the pale afternoon sunlight, ready for the ceremony to begin. She inwardly giggled as she saw Elizabeth peeking through the curtains of the parlor window. Harold faced the bride and groom, a black prayer book clasped to his heart. Next to Charlie stood Lillian, the *best man*, a petite young woman with a delicate pointed nose, her dark reddish hair pulled back, revealing tiny silver earrings. She was pretty like Catherine but more petite. What a shame, thought Alice, that polio in Lillian's childhood caused her to stoop sideways, leaning on her pearl-handled cane, her left foot jutting out in a built-up shoe. Alice reflected how lucky she was to be standing on her own two legs next to her husband-to-be-in-a-few-moments.

Catherine beamed, standing tall beside Alice, ready to hold her roses during the ring ceremony. When Charlie placed a diamond wedding band on his bride's finger, Catherine looked over the roses and smiled at Allen. Despite eyes brimming with happy tears, Alice noticed the look pass between them and wondered *how soon for them?*

Then Alice dissolved into her fugue of bliss as Harold pronounced her and Charlie "man and wife." A long kiss followed, as Allen dug deep into a pocket for a handful of rice grains and showered it on the newlyweds. Everyone laughed.

After the ceremony, Alice looked around at the happy faces surrounding her and Charlie. She noticed that her cousin Doc Richards had slipped into the yard. She was glad to see him—the doctor who cared for her during her illness and confirmed her pregnancy by saying only, "Congratulations."

A Western Union courier entered the festive front yard with a bundle of telegrams bearing neatly typed messages of congratulations, best wishes, and love. They came from Charlie's absent siblings, the Simpsons, workplace friends, and church members. Charlie and Alice huddled together to read them. "Oh, I wish they were all here today," said Alice. Catherine, Allen, and Lillian mischievously threw more beads of rice on the newlyweds.

John stepped forward to give his daughter an envelope addressed to *Mr. and Mrs. Charles Lukas*. "One more surprise," he said. Alice didn't know if she could contain further joy as she clasped the envelope to her heart.

Charlie grinned, urging, "Let's see what's inside." He pried the envelope away from Alice's shaking fingers and helped her open the envelope. Inside was a white card with her father's handwriting in black ink, announcing a gala wedding reception for them in two weeks at the Simpsons' home in Middlesboro. Alice looked at her father in wonderment. "It's all arranged, Peaches. Everyone will be there!" Alice didn't know whom to hug first—her father or her new husband—so she hugged them both together, encircling the baby inside.

14

ON A SATURDAY morning between Thanksgiving and Christmas, the first snow of the season fell on Alice's rock garden. Charlie, shivering in shirt-sleeves, watched the snowflakes pile up on the rocks and plants from his vantage point on the front stoop next door. He and Alice were occupying Uncle Stuart and Aunt Henny's house while they wintered in Florida. Charlie felt that the furnished home, available on such short notice, was the best of all wedding gifts. Even so, he was glad the arrangement was temporary; he looked forward to some elbow room apart from Alice's relatives.

Alice, wearing a pink apron Mattie had sent her, opened the front door and joined her husband. Putting her arms around him, she laid her head against his chest and looked over at the Leas' yard. "Oh Charlie—the snow is burying my rock garden!" She hesitated. "But it does look pretty in its new winter blanket. Don't you think so?" She looked up at his chin.

Charlie smiled, assuring her it did. Then he grasped her arms and said, "You'd better get inside, you know. In your condition, you don't need to catch cold."

Age and maturity had suddenly sneaked up on Charlie with the burden of responsibility for Alice and the baby she carried. Life had become more serious. He worried that Alice had only recently recovered from polio and would soon be going through the rigors of childbirth. Alice was concerned she'd felt no movement from the baby yet. Her anxiety, to the point of obsession, had

clouded their honeymoon. He caught her worry and was now awaiting movement as eagerly as she was. They had planned to stay at the Mammoth Cave
Hotel for a week, but Charlie canceled the last three days, suggesting Alice
return to the city and consult Doc Richards about her pregnancy.

As Alice walked back into the house, Charlie glanced toward Brook Street
as snowflakes dusted his coupe parked at the curb. His darling Plymouth would
have to go the way of Saturday night poker and his other bachelor pursuits. He
took a deep breath. Would Bonnie be amused by his new family-man status or
sympathetic? Maybe she missed him. Stop—thought Charlie, as he turned to
follow his wife.

The weekend progressed under bursts of snow with occasional sunshine breaking through the clouds. Slushy sidewalks were treacherous. Charlie's car sat idle,
covered with snow. Charlie and Alice didn't go anywhere. Instead, Alice made
numerous visits to her family next door and fretted about pregnancy concerns.
Doc Richards had assured her that all was normal as soon as she returned from
their abandoned honeymoon trip. Such reassurance had enabled Alice to breeze
through their belated wedding reception at the Simpson estate.

However, at Alice's latest checkup, the doctor still hadn't found a fetal heartbeat. "It's not unusual at this stage," he repeated to his cousin. Yet another week
had passed without Alice feeling the slightest squirm or kick she so yearned for.
Charlie knew she urgently needed confirmation that the baby was okay, so he
tried to be patient with her nervous bouts of crying and his own trepidation.

Sunday afternoon, he sat in the darkened parlor beside Uncle Stuart's Mo-
torola coffee table radio and tuned in to a Wildcats basketball game while Alice
visited next door. Charlie, in a rumpled white shirt, stretched his slippered feet
onto the footstool. He grinned and reached for a frosty bottle of beer to add his
hurrah to the static of radio cheers as the score piled up for Kentucky.

At halftime, Charlie heard a knock at the front door. Good timing—not
interrupting the game, he mused, padding to the door. Seeing his brother-in-
law, he chuckled and slapped Allen on the back, realizing they'd both been
following the game.

"Wildcats on top!" said Allen. "Mind if I join you?"

Charlie appreciated the company and welcomed him into the foyer.

"Had to get out," said Allen. "And Sis seemed like she'd rather I didn't hear
her female troubles."

Charlie nodded. "It's okay. Alice needs her mother right now. Guess it's
hard for us men to understand what it's like having a baby. Care for a beer?"

"Sure thing," replied Allen. "Say, here's something I thought you should see." He pulled a newspaper clipping from his shirt pocket. "In case you haven't already. It seems your business idea has hit pay dirt!"

Charlie seized the article from Allen's hand and read the sketchy report about an undesignated branch of the Federal Land Bank offering to sell bonds to the public. "It could be my idea," murmured Charlie. "Funny, but Mr. Benson hasn't said anything."

Allen went for the beer; he knew the route to the refrigerator, as the layout of his uncle's house was identical to his parents'. Charlie remained staring at the newspaper article until Allen nudged his arm with a cold beer bottle and led him back to the parlor. As the basketball play resumed, Allen hunched over, intent on the announcer's words, and chugged his beer in gulps. Charlie lounged in an overstuffed chair, a beer bottle dangling from his right hand. Thoughts concerning his business proposal distracted him from the game. Did the article he'd just read mean good news or bad news for his future career? And why hadn't he heard about it from his boss?

That evening, as Charlie and Alice finished supper in the kitchen, he discovered that Alice's thoughts had switched from pregnancy concerns to gardening. "I was telling Daddy my latest inspiration this afternoon," she began, "to make a rock garden in this front yard to surprise Uncle Stuart and Aunt Henny when they come home."

"Won't they be back in April?" asked Charlie.

"No, not until May."

"Well, I hate to say it, but you'll be big as a house by then, Alice."

"Of course, but I'll have the garden done before May."

"So that gives you April plus maybe a few warm days in March to plant a garden and put in rocks. The ground will be pretty hard. And you'll still be big as a house!"

Alice laughed.

"I don't want you carrying rocks at that late date," Charlie cautioned. "But I expect you'll have Allen and me doing the lifting."

Alice took a sip of hot tea and looked up at Charlie. "Well, is that too much to ask?"

Charlie wiped his mouth and laid his napkin on the table. "No, of course not. But be practical—we might be more concerned with moving out of here by then. Into our own house somewhere—maybe in the east end."

Alice looked down at her wedding china and gleaming silverware.

He continued, "We're starting our own life, honey. We won't be staying here permanently. And what if Stuart and Henny don't want to take care of a garden. . . ."

Alice answered quietly, with a shrug. "I suppose you know best." She sighed. Charlie reached for her hand, which she quickly removed and began picking up dishes from the table.

Expectant mothers have their moods, thought Charlie. He got up from the table to assist Alice. "Where do these go?" Charlie held a plate with leftover sandwiches Flora had made.

"Here," said Alice, taking the plate. No further words were exchanged.

Alice looked so down in the mouth, Charlie couldn't think of a way to turn her expression into a smile. Her moods so tenuous lately, in exasperation, he thought what the hell and retreated to his chair in the parlor.

The following day, Charlie brushed snow off his car and drove downtown to the 620 Building. He marched into the land bank's suite of offices, tipped his hat to Miss Wilson, and waved to Mike Sanders as he passed his door. In his spartan office, Charlie placed his fedora at the top of the coat stand and was taking off his overcoat when Mike rushed in behind him. He handed Charlie a copy of the office newsletter *Bank Notes*, freshly distributed that morning. "Look at this, Charlie! You could be famous!"

The front page of the slick black and white newsletter featured a headline: *Regional Branch to Issue Bonds Worldwide* and a photograph of Charlie's boss Ed Benson, shaking hands with regional officers of the land bank. Charlie held the newsletter in both hands, shaking, as he tried to grasp the essence of the article. Yes, it appeared that his local branch, along with others in their region, planned to open up consolidated system-wide bonds to the public—internationally—to increase dwindling funds loaned to strapped farmers across the nation. "Just like I proposed!" gasped Charlie, looking over at his friend. Charlie sat down at his desk and pulled his glasses from his shirt pocket. "I suppose I should be pleased." He pasted on a smile.

"And congratulated," added Mike. "I congratulate you, Charlie. It's a hell of a great idea."

"Why wasn't I told? Anyone who saw the newsletter before me knew about this before I did."

Mike looked confused. "I guess I figured you and Benson—"

"He never spoke to me about it after our first meeting." Charlie rubbed his chin. "In fact, now that I think about it, Mr. Benson has kind of avoided me since then."

Charlie clutched the newsletter, rereading the maze of words. He barely noticed Mike's farewell, "See you at lunch—maybe?" Charlie's glasses slipped down his nose as he re-examined the news article. A niggling worry in the pit of his stomach overshadowed pride that top brass was pursuing his business plan. Why had Mr. Benson not congratulated him, even offered him a raise or promotion? It stung that he learned the news from a *Courier-Times* article and the newsletter story handed to him by Mike. It seemed unceremonious and humbling, to say the least. Charlie sneered and thought, this isn't kindergarten, and Benson's not throwing me a surprise party. More likely, the next surprise would be an unpleasant one from the boss.

"Damn blast it!" Charlie muttered to the walls and coat stand.

He rose from his chair, newsletter in hand, and walked to Mr. Benson's larger, wood-paneled, comfortably appointed office. Charlie cleared his throat as he knocked on the door, seeing shadows through the frosted-glass window-pane. He put on his most diplomatic demeanor to approach his boss.

"Come in!" Ed Benson's voice rang out. "Charlie!" he seemed surprised. "I see you have read about the exciting news." He nodded toward the newsletter in Charlie's hand.

Charlie forced a smile. "Yes, it's wonderful news." He expected his boss to come forward with a handshake or a hearty *congratulations, my boy*. Instead, Benson stood still, looking like he expected something from Charlie.

Charlie almost lost his composure as he stammered, "It was my idea—"

His boss didn't offer him a seat. They remained standing, confrontational, as Benson replied, "All ideas coming from the branch are cooperative. We're somewhat like the Communists in that regard. All for one, one for all." He flashed a wide grin.

Tongues of flame shot through Charlie's body. He clenched and unclenched his fists as the impulse rose to punch that grin into the back of Benson's skull. In a carefully controlled voice, Charlie said, "It was your photo in the newsletter, and you weren't sharing any credit in the story. Couldn't I have been included since my folder of ideas started things rolling?"

"Not so fast, Charlie. You seem to think expanding the farm credit debt securities is an original idea. Well, if you'd done your homework, you would have known some East Coast regions are already doing this."

"I thought I had done my so-called homework. I don't believe any other regions have attempted issuing bonds internationally."

"Simply a matter of degree, shades of difference. That's all. Certainly not an original idea."

Charlie swallowed. He had recognized some of Mr. Benson's quotes in the newsletter story as phrases lifted from his business proposal. He squinted his eyes, removed his glasses, and rubbed one lens with his thumb. He realized he was deep into a face-off with his boss but didn't have the fire to continue the third-degree questioning. Charlie felt exhausted, defeated, on the ropes in a losing match as he repositioned his glasses. Hands limp, drained, and sweating under his arms, he could barely breathe. "What happened to the folder I left with you? Why didn't you return it earlier and tell me the idea wasn't new?"

"Your papers weren't returned?" Benson raised his eyebrows.

"No." Charlie's mouth was dry, his chest tightened. Remain steady, he told himself, wondering if his only evidence had been destroyed.

"Hmm . . . ," Benson fingered his puffy lips. "I'll look into it, Charlie. Only misplaced, I'm sure."

Sure, I'll bet, Charlie thought. Did he dare hope his boss would produce that folder? Shoulders hunched, eyes downcast, Charlie let himself out of Benson's office.

The next day at work, Charlie's folder containing his business proposal appeared on the ink blotter in the middle of his desk. On top lay an envelope with Charlie's name underlined. Recognizing Miss Wilson's backward-curling handwriting, he opened the envelope and read:

> *Dear Charlie, I am so sorry about all this. Please be careful! I think Mr. Benson is looking for any slight reason to get rid of you. I heard him say you have a bad attitude. I know that's not true at all. Just be careful, and please don't show anyone this note.*

Charlie's eyes burned as fear gnawed at him. What timing—with responsibilities for a wife, buying a home, and a baby on the way! He sat at his desk, stunned. After a few moments, he began fingering the papers in his folder, then focused on the words. Several paragraphs throughout his original proposal had been marked and initialed by someone—who? Miss Wilson would know. Shuffling through the folder, he found a letter from the regional manager in Chicago, heralding Charlie's bond-issuance proposal. Charlie saw immediately that the initials scribbled on his proposal belonged to this man.

Elbows on the desk, he ran his fingers through his black hair, thinking hard. For sure, he would keep this letter to his boss from the Chicago regional manager, praising Charlie's plan. He might even frame it. Alice will be so proud! He also knew she would be upset that his successful idea was not furthering his career—perhaps exactly the opposite. Charlie dreaded the next chapter of this grim story.

It came quickly. On Friday morning, Benson called Charlie into his office. "Charlie, my boy!"

Charlie accepted his outstretched hand and shook it. Was this cordiality a good sign? "Have a seat," said the boss.

Charlie sat down on the chair opposite Benson's finely crafted walnut desk. Benson began by telling Charlie that his efforts in the office were appreciated and well-regarded. "And good news—you are being offered a transfer to the Evansville office on February first. If you want it."

15

F RIDAY EVENING, CHARLIE arrived home from work in a black mood. Alice had sensed him distracted, in low spirits all week. She hoped the matter didn't pertain to her—and the baby. She had been preoccupied, too, so she hadn't bothered asking about his problems. She watched her husband place his hat on the shelf in the entryway. He hadn't removed his coat before he said tersely, "Looks like we might be moving to Evansville. Mr. Benson is transferring me."

Alice stared. "Why Evansville?" She backed up against the steep stairway and sank to the second step.

Charlie took his arms out of his coat sleeves, turning to the coat stand. When he faced Alice again, he said, "It's a long story. It's been a long week." He went over to the stairs to help her up. "Let's go into the parlor, and I'll tell you the whole thing. Then I'll take you out for dinner."

He began by telling her about the success of his business proposal for the land bank. A frisson of excitement made Alice's heart flutter, but only for a second. What was that about Evansville? As Charlie described Mr. Benson's arrogant ownership of the plan and their confrontation in his office, anger began to throb in her chest. Charlie's conclusion about the possibility of a job and move to Evansville compelled her to hold down a mass of dread rising in her throat. No desire for a nice restaurant dinner now, Alice hurried into the downstairs bathroom and vomited.

Charlie followed her, calling from the hallway, "Alice, are you all right?"

Alice, gagging and sobbing, managed a muffled, "No."

"What can I do?" Charlie asked.

She sat on the bathroom floor, anger, worry, and fear swirling in her stomach. No wonder she was sick. "You can say 'no' to Evansville," she yelled through the door, tears running down her face. Slowly she stood up and looked at herself in the mirror of the medicine cabinet. Her face was ash white, her eyes an ugly contrast with red rims. She pulled a washcloth off a nearby shelf and rinsed her face with cold water, patting her swollen eyes. Then she swished out her mouth with minty mouthwash from the cabinet. Finally brave enough to rejoin Charlie.

As she slowly turned the doorknob, thoughts raced through her mind: How could Charlie consider moving? It seemed like a betrayal for him to uproot her from home, family, and all she cherished. Evansville lay 150 miles away, and there would be no more popping in next door for Mother's advice or to enjoy a pleasant evening with her and Daddy. They'd leave behind their siblings and close companions, Allen and Catherine. Had Charlie thought about all of this? Of course, Evansville was only a few miles from Charlie's hometown, family farm, and Harold's parish in Morgantown. As they sat together on the parlor sofa, Alice barely listened as Charlie tried explaining the details of his job transfer. Her shoulders drooped as she tried to block out her husband's words.

His voice trailed off as he mentioned a slight salary increase. Otherwise, the Evansville job offered no advancement. He stood up, walked over to the mantel, and stared down at the black-tinged asbestos fireplace backing. Then he turned around. "Are you chilly, Alice? We could use a fire."

Alice sat quietly, still numb. Charlie turned on the gas with a turn of the key; the pilot light took hold. A blue-hot flame glowed and began warming the room. "That's better, isn't it," said Charlie. He returned to Alice and attempted a hug; she remained a stubborn lump. "Come on, it's not the end of the world. We can start our own life. What's wrong with Evansville?"

"Everything!" blurted Alice, barely looking at him. "Everything"

A week before Christmas, Alice was glad to stay home while Charlie escorted Catherine downtown for a day of last-minute gift shopping. Settling down at the kitchen table with a steaming cup of fragrant tea, Alice began writing in her diary. Still unhappy and incredulous over Charlie's announcement of the job transfer, she attempted to form her nebulous thoughts into words. Dappled sunlight filtered through the tall kitchen windowpanes. Alice rubbed her neck to ease some tightness. She took a deep, shuddering breath as she began to write:

> *I guess it's different for a man, anyway for Charlie. He's been away from his roots—at the university, his first job in Detroit, now here. His parents are gone. He's fond of his brothers and sisters but doesn't need them, as I need my family. Maybe it's just me—I couldn't even make it through college away from home. I'm lost without my family, this place, this city. I guess I'm not feeling like the good Biblical wife . . . "Whither thou goest . . ." But I don't want to have my baby in god-forsaken Evansville!*

Alice felt her stomach tighten and cramp. She looked into her Rose Briar china teacup through the last clear sip of chamomile tea. Sometimes tea will do this, Alice thought as she clutched at her lower abdomen. She felt uncomfortable and wondered if she were hungry. "Maybe soda crackers would help," she said aloud. As she rose from her chair, another cramp took her breath away. Alice fled to the bathroom.

⌒⌒⌒⌒

Charlie arrived home an hour later, arms full of paper bags from Stewart's and the Book Nook, a bouquet of red roses for Alice tucked under one elbow. "Alice!" he called, answered by a moan from the back hallway. He tossed bags and roses aside as he rushed to find his wife. Alice, disheveled and speechless, cowered outside the bathroom, holding onto the doorframe as blood streamed down her legs. The sight of more blood splattered on the yellowish linoleum of the bathroom floor and around the toilet terrified him. His heart pounded against his ribs, and he was unable to focus his unblinking eyes. What had she done? What happened here? Not knowing what else to do, Charlie grabbed a towel off the towel rack, wrapped it around Alice's lower body, carried her into the parlor, and laid her on the sofa.

"Did you call your mother?" Alice shook her head. His voice trembled as he phoned Flora, then asked the operator to ring Doc Richards. Alice's wails nearly undid him. As Charlie returned the phone receiver to its cradle, he noticed his hand shaking.

Losing their baby right before Christmas was a blow, an injustice. Charlie knew no way of consoling Alice. He couldn't fathom words large enough to embrace their tragedy. He knew they would endure a quiet holiday season in their borrowed home.

One day as they met briefly in their adjacent front yards, Allen urged Charlie to, at least, buy a Christmas tree. "It will pick up Sis's spirits, your own too. Catherine and I will help you decorate."

Charlie bit his lip. "No thanks. But I really mean it—thanks." Could a man cry? He felt like he might. Allen's kind empathy overwhelmed him. Charlie looked down. Allen's arm draping across his shoulders felt like a hug.

◦◦◦◦◦

Thick snowflakes spattered the windshield of Charlie's Plymouth as he headed home from work two days before Christmas. A serious blizzard heralded official winter as snow piled up on slippery streets, forcing downtown traffic to a crawl. Charlie's feet were numb from standing in the icy slush without overshoes and brushing off his windshield and running board. He appreciated his little car's dual wipers and the heater for thawing his feet. The green Plymouth skidded around a few corners, almost failing to stop for the red light at Oak Street, yet made it home to its usual parking place in front of Uncle Stuart Lea's house. My old faithful, breathed Charlie, patting his car's dashboard. To think, a couple of weeks ago, he'd made plans to trade in his prized coupe for a larger sedan! Now, that deal could be canceled.

As he got out of the car, he glanced toward John Lea's front yard and saw Alice digging in her rock garden. Her red sweater stood out in stark contrast to the snow on the ground and streaks of white whirling around her. "Alice! My god—what in tarnation!" Charlie made his way over to her as quickly as possible without slipping on the sidewalk and steps. The blowing snow frosted his glasses; he took them off and slipped them into his coat pocket. "What in the world are you doing?" He saw her moving rocks around—struggling against a blizzard—and feared she had lost her mind. She had been out of the hospital for only two days!

Alice looked up at him brightly, her eyelashes caked with snow. "I thought we might put a Nativity scene out here."

"Honey, it's snowing and after dark. You're wearing a sweater!" He gathered his wife into his arms, nearly tumbling over in the snow. She clung to the large black boulder. "Let go, Alice! We're going home." She shivered uncontrollably as Charlie pulled her to stand.

Charlie settled Alice on the parlor sofa with a blanket around her, then removed his coat and placed his glasses on the fireplace mantel. He lit the fireplace and watched the flames rise against the fibrous backing. Alice shivered under the blanket in her damp clothes. She stared blankly at the blue-orange blaze in the fireplace as Charlie knelt to remove her shoes, caressing her clammy ankles. "I'll find your slippers," he murmured, then left the room.

On the way to the bedroom, he considered how to bring Alice back to her senses. He thought of a Christmas gift he and Catherine had selected for her. He returned to the parlor with Alice's wooly slippers and a book-sized gift, store-wrapped in red paper, tied with a candy-striped ribbon. Charlie placed it on top of Alice's blanket. For a moment she gazed at the gift before freeing her hands to open it.

"Let me help you," offered Charlie. Together they opened the package—a rare 1920 first edition of Robert Graves's poetry he had found on a back-room shelf at Book Nook.

Alice held the book as if warming her hands on it. "Thank you," she whispered, turning to the first poem entitled *A Frosty Night*.

Charlie watched as her eyes focused on the page and her lips moved slightly as she read.

"My goodness!" She suddenly turned to him. "Listen to this. The poem's a dialog between two people—*Alice* and *Mother*! Can you believe that?"

Charlie smiled. "Must have had you in mind!"

Alice hesitated, breathed deeply, and began to read:

"Mother . . ."

Charlie interrupted her, "You don't need to read it out loud. Just to yourself."

She gave him a hurt look. So he continued, "but you can tell me how it goes. I'd rather hear it from your lips."

Alice nodded and began reading the poem to herself. She quickly read the first stanza, then looked up at Charlie. "*Mother* noticed *Alice* so pale and shaken. She asked *Alice* if she were chilled or frightened."

Charlie gazed as Alice returned to the page and continued, "*Alice* declares she is all right even though the night was frosty. And it appears she is writing a letter."

"Does it say to whom?" Charlie asked.

"No, it doesn't. And the mother keeps questioning *Alice*. It's odd too, that *Mother* seems to notice *Alice's* feet were dancing and stars in her eyes."

Charlie said, "But before, *Mother* thought she might be sick. Are dancing feet and starry eyes a sign of fever?"

Alice chuckled. "Or love? It's like when I was sick and my mother kept questioning me about your proposal; she was so patronizing."

Charlie hadn't known about that conversation but urged Alice, "Go on with the poem."

"Aha—*Mother* is getting nosy and suspects *Alice* has a sweetheart."

"Was she right?"

Charlie waited for Alice to finish reading. Then she looked up with a hint of a smile. "It must be love. *Alice* pleads to her mother to let her go." Alice's eyes misted in the firelight. "I see what this means!"

The book slid off her lap as she reached for Charlie and burrowed her face in his soft wool sweater. Charlie let the book lie on the floor as he held Alice to his chest and smoothed her hair. He felt the weight of her emotions against him but was uncertain what to say, so he kept holding her, hoping Alice would end the spell. What had she meant? What interpretation had she bestowed on this little poem? To Charlie, the words seemed to say that *Alice* should leave *Mother* and follow whoever said he loved her. He hoped Alice saw it that way too.

Daylight dissolved into dusk in John and Flora Lea's parlor, aglow with holiday trimmings to obscure the sadness of Charlie and Alice's recent loss. The family settled around the Christmas tree laden with baubles, garlands, and glitz that Flora had carefully preserved since the pre-Depression years. Emerging out of the attic trunk for the holidays, the clown doll, Flippity Flop, appeared in his jester cap with a tiny bell on the tip, assuming his annual place of honor under the tree with a jumble of gifts. Flippity had been a gift to Allen on his first Christmas. From the kitchen came a wave of tempting aromas—roast turkey, sage, and yeast rolls baking. Sitting on the floor next to Charlie, Alice felt the warmth of Christmas Eve comforting her like a downy quilt. She cuddled closer to her husband.

"Let's see who opens the first present," began John, in his tattered Santa Claus cap of many Christmases, as he reached into the pile of gifts. Everyone waited as he read the tag: *To Alice, all my love Charlie.* The box was wrapped in holly-printed paper from Stewart's Department Store. Charlie had returned the maternity clothes he'd bought the day of his wife's miscarriage and exchanged them for a lacy lavender nightgown. The lid of the box dropped aside, and Alice held up the fancy lingerie. She hugged it to her face, breathing in the lavender-scented sachet in a satin pouch. (The added touch had been Catherine's suggestion.) Charlie glanced briefly at his sister, meeting her smile.

"Thank you, thank you! It's beautiful!" said Alice, letting the nightgown fall into her lap and hugging Charlie.

Alice's brightness signaled a happy start to the round of gift openings as each person around the tree opened gifts, expressing delight and thanks. Alice had a surprise for her husband in a miniature velvet box. She had bought the gift before Thanksgiving and had kept it in her diary drawer. Since Charlie did not have a wedding band, she bought him a ring she spotted in Tafels Jewelers' window. The perfect gift for him, Alice thought. She followed his every move with delight as he unwrapped her gift and saw his face light up with anticipation as he opened the curved lid of the box. She held her breath, hoping he would be surprised and pleased with the ring—a square black onyx set in gold, inscribed with a design resembling the Plymouth ship logo on his coupe. Alice knew how he prized his car, and she appreciated his willingness to give it up for a larger model to accommodate a family.

Charlie tried the ring on his right ring finger. "Hey—it fits!" he laughed. "It's swell, Alice. Thank you. What a surprise!" He planted a kiss on her cheek. Relieved and glowing, she knew her gift was a success.

They moved to the Leas' formal dining room for dinner where the gate-leg table, covered with a perfect white tablecloth, and Flora's family china and crystal goblets awaited them. Elizabeth, the Leas' cook for special occasions, moved like a gray ghost in her uniform, delivering a succulent turkey for John to carve. Alice watched as she kept disappearing into the kitchen, then reappearing with dishes of sweet potatoes, oyster stuffing, cranberries, and freshly-baked Parker House rolls. The scent of coffee wafting from the kitchen forecasted dessert. A sudden enthusiasm for food tickled Alice's gut. Her appetite was rushing back as Elizabeth presented her culinary magic. The family chatted about the food, their Christmas gifts, the economy, and predictions for the coming year. Flora mentioned New Year's resolutions.

"I might eat less," said Allen, his mouth stuffed.

Catherine nudged him. "You said that last year." Everyone laughed.

When the conversation turned to the snowy weather, Alice's thoughts flew to her failed plan for a rock garden Nativity scene, Charlie's admonition, and her worry that he doubted her sanity. She spoke timidly, daring to arouse her family's views on the matter. "I wanted to put a Christmas crèche in my rock garden and had moved some of the rocks around already, but Charlie stopped me."

The room was quiet except for the clanking of Elizabeth's pans in the kitchen. Alice tensed when she saw Charlie grip the edge of the table and shoot a glance at Flora.

Allen's good humor broke the pause. "Great idea, Sis! You should have asked me to help."

"The weather was against you, Peaches," suggested John with an understanding smile.

"Perhaps next year we can plan for it earlier and have a manger scene in place before Christmas," suggested Flora.

"Next year we'll be in Evansville!" said Alice, throwing her napkin on the table. Her face crumpled.

Charlie reached past his water glass to clasp her other hand. "No, we won't, Alice," he said. "After I found you out in the snow the other night, I realized how deeply you feel about home. You—we need to stay here. I am determined to find another, better job right here in this city. Yesterday I made a contact. It'll be okay."

16

*C*HRISTMAS IS OVER. *I went through the motions. It felt good being with my family and dear husband. But something was missing—terribly. I kept thinking about my baby. When I saw Flippity Flop, I felt deeply sad—he comes out of his box once a year to sit under the Christmas tree, but my baby is never to see Christmas or even the light of day. His or her chubby hands will never touch Flippity's limber little body, the silky smoothness of his clown costume, or play with the jingly bell on his cap. I don't even know whether my baby was a boy or girl—how to think of him, her—as I do all the time. I try to keep my tears secret even though ready to burst out at any moment.*

Thankfully, Charlie has given me something else to think about—a new worry. Come February, he will be unemployed—unless he takes an offer, and it's not a sure thing yet—from the whiskey barrel company.

Hard to think of Charlie without a job. Will he be out on the streets, peddling something door to door? I can't imagine it. Without money to buy a home, would we stay on here with Uncle Stuart and Aunt Henny or move in with my parents next door? It would kill Charlie to be so dependent, not his own man.

Now, what about this possible new job? Whiskey barrels is a far cry from Charlie's secure job at the land bank. Ha! Turns out that wasn't so safe. Maybe the business world is a better place, after all, for someone with original ideas. But whiskey?

In her mother's kitchen, above the vertical cream-colored wainscoting, a new calendar with paintings from the Impressionists heralded the New Year 1938. Alice looked at it, sighed, and sipped her first taste of the morning's fresh coffee. Flora busied herself putting away clean dishes. The kitchen noises—glassware clinking, pots clanging, cupboard doors banging—wrapped around Alice like a hug. In contrast, the house next door always felt too quiet after Charlie left for work.

"Mother, I don't know about this whiskey barrel job for Charlie. What do you think?"

Flora paused for a moment, wiping a damp hand on her apron. "What concerns you, dear?"

Alice propped her elbow on the table, rubbed her forehead, and said thoughtfully, "It's a far cry from banking. I hoped Charlie would work his way up—"

"To bank president?" finished Flora. "You are ambitious for him."

"He knows finance and has good ideas," Alice defended.

"Indeed he does," agreed Flora. "And his good business sense will be valuable no matter where he works."

"But the whiskey business!" Alice wrinkled her nose as if sensing something rotten in her coffee.

"What's wrong with that? It's one of our oldest industries. Maybe even safer than banking." Flora chuckled. "It even survived Prohibition!"

"Still—a lot of people think alcohol is wrong. I don't want people to think badly of us on account of Charlie's career." She set her cup into its saucer.

"Alice, you do worry so. There's good and bad to almost anything. It's not as if your husband is becoming an alcoholic. Charlie is Charlie; people respect and like him. No one's going to shun you. If they do, it's their problem—not yours."

"I just wish he would keep his sights on banking. Whiskey barrels seems sort of—" Alice hesitated. "I don't know."

"Lowbrow?" Flora clinked a china teacup against another on a shelf. "Well I, for one, hope he gets the job."

The statement sounded final. Alice kept quiet, sipping her coffee.

She remained at her mother's house after their coffee break while Flora moved on to her morning phone conversations with friends. The comforting morning mood held her as Alice retreated upstairs to her old bedroom, sat on the window seat, and watched the wintry scene on Brook Street. A few cars passed through the gray cityscape. People in dark overcoats pulled tight against the wind walked along the sidewalks. Leftover snow in sooty patches covered the bare roots of street trees. The rock garden lay dormant; the stones lacked sparkle. She smiled at her creation, knowing it awaited the kiss of spring sunshine to revive.

"There you are!" Her mother's voice broke into the silent dream-filled room. "I knew I'd find you here." Flora went across to the bay window where her daughter sat looking out. Alice turned away from her reverie and patted a spot on the seat beside her.

Flora remained standing, bending closer to the window. "Isn't that Mrs. Ritchie's son going in the house over there? He must be home on leave. I heard he got a job—with the Army."

Alice stared across the street, hoping Charlie's job situation wouldn't tempt him to join the Army.

"Anyway," Flora said, her voice brisk, "shouldn't you be a good wife and go home to your chores now?"

Alice frowned. "I haven't much to do at home. If I went, I'd probably just read."

"Suit yourself, then. You're always welcome here. But I need to go out for a while. I'll bring some fresh bread home for lunch—if you're still here."

"Okay, Mother. Keep warm," said Alice, turning back to the window.

During her mother's absence, Alice picked up a tattered copy of *The Little Colonel* from her bookshelf and settled onto her old familiar high bed to read. Running her hand over the front cover, Alice hoped she would someday have a daughter with whom to share these favorite stories about an assertive young girl and her military grandfather. She opened the book to the first finger-smudged page and began reading. The story possessed her until Alice quickened to the telephone's mellow buzz from her parents' bedroom. She rushed to the phone. "Hello. Leas' residence."

She heard Charlie's chuckle. "I tried the Lukas residence first," he said. "You weren't home." Alice knew he wasn't criticizing; his high spirits traveled through the phone line. "I accepted the job, Alice! You're talking with the new chief controller for Limestone Cooperage, a division of Limestone Distillers, Bourbon County, Kentucky."

Alice giggled at his formality despite a panicky thought. "We don't have to move there, do we?"

"No, no," Charlie assured her. "The barrel works is right here in the west end, not too far from the racetrack."

"Good!" Relieved, Alice sat on her parents' bed, nearly sliding off the satiny down-filled comforter, then catching herself.

"Only about ten minutes from here," Charlie added. "I start February first."

"It's wonderful, Charlie," said Alice, catching some of his enthusiasm. "I can't wait to tell Mother." She heard a key click open the front door downstairs. "She's home now. I'll see you tonight. I love you." Alice listened as Charlie echoed her words, then hung up the phone.

Back home, Alice resolved to be *the good wife* as her *Dos and Don'ts for Wives* instructed. She debated inviting her family and Catherine to join them for supper to celebrate Charlie's new job, instead deciding in favor of an intimate meal for two. With the aid of her recipe book, Alice felt able to handle a small feast without the complication of serving guests. She'd let her parents do the family celebration later. Alice braced herself against the cold wind and walked to the corner grocery store to buy ingredients for a special meal in Charlie's honor.

She managed fried chicken and a sweet potato casserole. The chicken skin stuck to the skillet, but Charlie pronounced the meal by candlelight "excellent and elegant!" As a surprise, almost a joke, Charlie had brought home a bottle of Limestone's *Old Dan'l* bourbon. He and Alice raised a toast with their whiskey and sodas. Laughing, they touched their glasses together as Charlie said, "to us—our future—whiskey barrels!" Alice had even purchased a special chocolate cake for dessert with their coffee. More bourbon followed, its sharp sweetness tickling their noses. They relaxed in a jubilant mood.

Pillow talk that night began in sober and uneasy contrast. Alice rearranged her pillows, turned from side to side, and threw off her covers. "What's the matter?" Charlie asked, throwing an arm over his wife. "Is it the bourbon?"

Alice stopped moving. "Well, in a way, it is," she said. "Charlie, I need to know your true thoughts."

He shifted up on an elbow. "About what?"

Alice took a deep breath; she needed to gather courage. "About working for a whiskey company. Whiskey is kind of evil—like tobacco. And I know you wouldn't be caught dead working for a cigarette company." She waited.

Charlie folded his arms under his head. "It's not the same thing. Whiskey is something you can drink on special occasions—in moderation. I don't know anyone who smokes that smokes only a little." Alice lay still, unconvinced, waiting. Charlie went on, "Kentucky bourbon is a special gift—like frosting on the cake. Can you imagine Derby Day without mint juleps!"

Alice turned over, her face close to Charlie's. "But whiskey can cause terrible harm—alcoholics and bad fathers who spend their children's bread money on whiskey."

"Do you know any?" asked Charlie.

Alice thought for a moment. "No, however—"

Charlie continued, "Do you know anyone who drinks bourbon on special occasions? Who mixes it with honey for their children's sore throats?"

"Well, of course—"

"So, you see! It's more a good thing than a bad thing," concluded Charlie. He leaned over to snuggle against Alice's cheek. "I think I forgot to tell you something important."

"What?" She half expected him to say he loved her. She grinned in the shadow of her pillow.

"I was going to tell you on the phone when your mother interrupted. Then tonight, with our special celebration, I forgot I hadn't told you what they're paying me."

Her feelings had been so conflicted about his job that she'd neglected to ask that important detail. "How much?" She held her breath.

Moonlight through the window caught Charlie's bright smile as he leaned on an elbow to look down at Alice. "Twice what I'm making at the land bank!"

"Get out!" said Alice. She sat straight up. "You're joking."

"No, Alice." He was unable to control a broadening grin. "I kid you not!"

After all of the heartache and worry they had gone through, she could hardly believe it. A lump rose in her throat. "Oh Charlie! We can buy our dream house."

Any discussion about demon whiskey came to an end.

◦∽◦∾◦

In mid-February, Charlie had been at his accountant's desk at Limestone Cooperage for a couple of weeks. He wanted to reassure Alice about his job and introduce her to his new employer. He remembered, over a year ago at the Simpson farm, how Alice had romanticized the physical work of tobacco harvesting—he figured she'd be fascinated by the barrel makers' deft handling of staves and iron hoops as they moved barrels through fiery furnaces. The workers' rhythms and the blazing eruptions of the char tunnels should have Alice's heart going pit-pat, thought Charlie.

◦∽◦∾◦

Charlie showed Alice around the rambling brick office building where he worked; it resembled the headquarters of a large ranch operation. Inside the building, Alice caught the scent of leather and the polish of rich woodwork. Charlie introduced her to his new boss, Tom Stevens, the manager of Limestone's barrel division. Stevens smiled graciously, showing perfect teeth, and extended his hand to Alice. "I'm so glad to meet you at last," he said. Alice was impressed with his genuine enthusiasm and gray-haired handsomeness. Had she dressed smartly enough—did her makeup and hair look neat? His manner was easy-going and jovial. Alice relaxed as Stevens pointed to an antique bar sign hung near the main entrance of the office building: *Gentlemen imbibing foreign and alien spirits other than Bourbon whiskey may be requested to pay in cash.* They laughed.

Stevens slapped Charlie on the back. "You two enjoy the tour. Come back to work anytime—no hurry."

Walking Alice across a brick courtyard to the barrel factory, Charlie pointed out the adjacent supply yard where pallets of oak strips were stacked in high columns. "Smells like a lumber yard," said Alice, breathing in the fragrance.

"Yes, white oak smells great." Charlie held onto his wife's arm, like an usher.

Inside, the factory air pulsated with heat. "Feels good," said Alice.

"Wonder how this feels in summer," said Charlie. "Guess I'll find out then—that is, if I ever leave my cool office for this hothouse."

They passed men with sinewy arms aglow with sweat and grime. The workers were standing barrel staves on end inside an iron ring. "Looks like a big basket," commented Alice.

"It does at first." Charlie nodded to a barrel-raiser whose teeth showed white in a smoke-darkened face.

As they moved on through the factory, the temperature increased. Strong-muscled men slammed hoops over the three-foot-high baskets of barrel staves, using machinery to force them into barrel shapes.

"I can almost smell the whiskey!" Alice exclaimed. "They don't put the whiskey in the barrels here, do they?"

Charlie chuckled. "It's the charred oak you're smelling. Charring the inside of the barrel gives bourbon its special flavor," he explained.

Alice saw leaping flames ahead and felt a hot breath charging toward her. Barrels burst with fire from within while the exterior wood remained unscathed. The workers, wearing goggles, were so blackened with smoke that they looked burned too. Asbestos-gloved hands moved the barrels in and out of the char tunnel. The heat of the furnaces bore down on Alice like a smothering blanket she couldn't escape. Suddenly she began to sway and reached out desperately for Charlie's arm. He caught her as she slumped toward the floor.

"Alice!"

Her surroundings dimmed as Alice slipped into a vision of herself at about four years old, falling down the cellar stairs on Brook Street. The coalman with the dirty face and sooty eyelashes grabbed her. Instead of righting her and sending her back upstairs to the yard, the *bogeyman* jammed her face so tightly against his sweat-grimed shirt that she could not scream. Her nose recoiled from his body odor, and she could only breathe acrid dust. The coalman's belt buckle gouged her cheek. She tasted blood on her lips. "Help!"

Alice's vision caught Uncle Stuart crossing the backyard, not glancing toward the cellar, where the coalman held her in terror, pressing his hand across her mouth. Why didn't Uncle Stuart look her way? "I can't breathe."

"Someone let me out!" Alice cried. The coalman loosened his grip after her uncle tromped up the back stairs to the house. To prevent her return to the yard, the coalman threw Alice into the coal bin. She listened for his truck to rumble down the alley, then gathered all her strength to escape from the trough of coal. She floundered and struggled, unable to climb out, as pieces of coal shifted, slipped, and threatened to engulf her like quicksand.

"It's me—Alice. Let me out!"

"Dear God, Alice. Don't create a scene," Charlie pleaded, looking around. He staggered with Alice's weight collapsed in his arms. Workers on the barrel assembly remained absorbed in their work. Clanging and blast-furnace noises from a few yards away reverberated in the air. No one seemed to notice the couple in distress. Charlie clenched his jaw as he half-walked, half-carried Alice toward the door to the courtyard.

"Help me!" Alice wailed.

"Alice, we're outside now. Stop acting loony. What is it?"

The cold air snapped Alice into consciousness; she stared numbly at her husband. "What happened?"

"You tell me," he answered, steadying her to stand on the brick walkway.

The nightmare she had just experienced terrified her. Charlie seemed annoyed and burdened. She feared to explain her strange hallucination. "I'm not sure," she mumbled as they walked unsteadily toward the car. "It must have been the terrific heat—the faces all blackened."

"Faces?" he growled. "How absurd! But I guess the heat—"

"It was so uncanny—nothing like that has happened to me before," she began, her voice trembling.

"You had trouble breathing and said some very odd things. Like 'let me out.' You scared me; I didn't know what was happening to you." Charlie gave her that look again, questioning her sanity. Her heart thudded; she feared he would think her even crazier if she revealed her childhood memory. She clamped her lips tight together, holding in the panic that threatened to emerge. They reached the car, and Alice was thankful to see Charlie's face shifting gears to another thought. "I'll take you home and maybe come back to work if you seem okay," he said, opening the passenger door of the coupe.

⌐⌐

February 21, 1938, Alice logged in her diary:

> *It was a terrible vision going back so long ago. I never told Mother or anyone what happened; she scolded me for playing in the coal bin! Only Allen saw I'd been trapped and pulled me out with a rope. He never told either. And I forgot—until my frightful episode today. Did that time in the cellar really happen? Am I losing my mind?*

17

THE *prosperity* predicted by Herbert Hoover in 1932 finally appeared *just around the corner* for Charlie and Alice in 1938. They purchased their first home and planned to move in May, in time for Aunt Henny and Uncle Stuart to reclaim their home on Brook Street. Alice wanted to start a rock garden for them—a way to say *thank you.* "Shouldn't you be shopping instead?" Charlie asked. "We don't own a stick of furniture."

Overwhelmed by the task of electing a houseful of furniture, Alice resisted. "We can shop on Saturdays—together!"

"You'll need lots of odds and ends—like dishcloths, linens, pots, and pans," her mother reminded her. "It would bore Charlie to tears. I'll go shopping with you."

Alice agreed to shop for basic *necessities* with her mother during the week and furniture with Charlie on Saturdays. She didn't tell her husband and mother about her plan—she was going to move her rock garden, piece by piece, to her uncle's front yard.

On a glimmering April morning, chimney smoke filtering the low sunlight, Alice began to implement her plan. She donned her gardening gloves, old clothes, and a heavy moth-eaten sweater Charlie had discarded. She scurried past the ominous cellar door to borrow a shovel leaning against the sooty brick wall of her parents' home. With the shovel and a shorter-handled trowel, Alice began to dig up a spot in her uncle's front yard. The unyielding clay reminded her of the difficulty of that first groundbreaking in her parents' yard—the day Charlie came along and proposed. She smiled, thinking of how he sometimes brought roses home on Friday nights after work. He planned to start a rose garden in their new backyard on Pleasant Avenue.

The mailman came by, tipped his hat to Alice, then rested his foot on the low concrete wall above the sidewalk. "What's going on here?" he asked.

"I'm moving my garden from over there," said Alice brightly, pointing next door.

The mailman surveyed the obsidian boulder, the multitude of mossy river rocks, and the tender shoots of spring green in the adjacent yard. "That's an awfully big job for a wee lass," he said. "I wish you luck." He tapped his leather mailbag. "I must move on." He pulled out some pieces of mail—bills mostly—for Alice.

"Thanks!" After tucking the mail into the pocket of her husband's gray sweater, she resumed digging, pressing her foot on the shovel, even standing on it and pushing down, to scoop out as much earth as she could dislodge. Frustrated at the slow progress, she knelt on the soil and stabbed the hard clay with her trowel. The thrusting action stirred up buried emotions along with the difficult earth. As she dealt damaging blows to upend patches of dirt, she fantasized violence on someone who had long deserved her wrath. The harder she jabbed, the more release she felt. A planting space began to take shape in Uncle Stuart's yard.

He's the one I'm mad at! An attack of memory rocked her back on her heels. Hanging in the air was a vision of her uncle passing by the cellar door. Why hadn't he turned to notice her plight and rescue her from the coalman? Her chest compressed and she couldn't breathe, reliving the trauma. Her eyes burned, and she wanted to cry out or sob. Uncle Stuart could have made all the difference! Her palm moist on the trowel, she continued slashing the lumps of clay. By midday, Alice had significantly disturbed her uncle's front yard.

Flora Lea flounced out of her front door and down the steps, smartly dressed, pocketbook in hand, ready for a day's outing. At the sight of Alice, she stopped short. "What on earth are you up to? I thought we were going shopping today."

Alice looked blank. "Oh, I forgot." She wiped a drop of sweat off her forehead with the back of one hand.

"What an awful mess! You're tearing up Stuart's yard, for heaven's sake!"

"Just until I move my rock garden over here," said Alice, "It's my going-away gift. After all, the biggest rock belongs to Uncle Stuart."

Flora shook her head. "He gave us that rock. You don't owe it back to him." She looked around at the garden in her yard. "Alice, this is so beautiful—what you've done here. It would take several gardeners to move all of this—and several days too."

Alice rested both hands on the shovel. "Do you really like my rock garden? Do you honestly think it's beautiful?"

"Of course," answered Flora. "Didn't you think we'd look after it when you move away?"

Alice suddenly felt like a naughty child, embarrassed by her foolishness. "I never thought—"

"Well then, you are thoughtless," snapped Flora. "You've given us a lovely garden, and now you want to take it away."

Alice stood still while her mother continued: "I can't imagine Charlie agreeing to this. He'd say you are giving those plants a death sentence."

Alice's heart broke into brittle shards at Flora's reproach. Would Charlie give her that *are you crazy* look again? Her enthusiasm stifled, she dropped the trowel and sank back on her haunches. Tears ringed her eyes and spilled down her cheeks. Here she would stay! She shook her head and refused to go shopping.

"Do whatever you want." Flora waved dismissively. "I'm going downtown anyway." A yellow cab pulled up to the curb; Flora entered, slamming the door shut.

❧❧❧

That evening after work, Charlie parked his Plymouth at the curb. Stepping out, he glanced across the green metal roof of his car and noticed the gouged landscape of the front yard. "Giant gophers!" he said aloud. Walking up the steps into the yard, he saw the shovel. "Alice!" He hurried into the house, not daring to imagine what his wife had been up to.

Charlie found her in the kitchen, calmly stirring a vegetable soup for their supper; pink splotches on her cheeks said she'd been crying. He kissed her quickly. "So, what went on today?"

Alice told him of her attempt to move the rock garden and the mixed messages from her mother. Charlie fought back any judgment of Alice's behavior and put his arms around her. "It's okay, Alice. If it were possible to move your garden with us, I would. But it's best left where it is." He kissed her cheek tenderly.

❧❧❧

A few nights later, Alice wrote in her diary: *I don't know what came over me. It's an exciting new start for Charlie and me but moving to our new house is getting me emotional. I have felt sad, hurt, and angry at Mother and Uncle Stuart. Oh, I hope to leave these feelings behind when we move to Pleasant Avenue.*

Charlie spent half of our furniture-shopping day smoothing out Uncle Stuart's yard and planting new grass.

✧✦✧

They moved into 403 Pleasant Avenue on a Saturday, with Allen, Catherine, and the Leas helping to unload wedding china, linens, and clothes. The heaviest boxes contained Alice's books, introducing a musty addition to the odors of wallpaper paste and fresh varnish. New furniture had not yet arrived. Charlie and Alice knelt on a shiny wood floor, sorting books, preparing to fill just-painted bookcases. "It's not home until my books are arranged," Alice confided. "I'm strange that way."

"Not really," soothed Charlie. "Gotta start somewhere."

"Mother would probably say curtains first," said Alice, her eyes sweeping around to the six windows in their living room. "You watch—she'll probably mention it."

The unfurnished house echoed clattering noises from the kitchen, doors banging, and muffled talking in other rooms. Allen sauntered into the bare living room and bellowed, "Well, Charlie, how does it feel to be king of all you survey?"

Charlie looked smug. "Pretty powerful, and here's my queen right beside me." He drew a beaming Alice tight against him.

Catherine walked up behind Allen and put her arms around his hefty waistline. "Are we next in line?" she coaxed.

Allen grinned, grabbing her pale hands; before he could reply, the sound of a tinkling bell approached through the front hallway between the dining and living rooms.

"Teatime!" Flora's voice accompanied the bell.

Allen and Catherine let go of each other. "What in the world, Mother!" said Allen. Flora carried a silver tray with six demitasse cups. John followed behind with a thermos bottle.

"We have tea!" Flora announced. "Time to celebrate with a toast to Alice and Charlie's new home."

"With tea?" mocked Allen.

Catherine nudged him. "You think of everything, Mrs. Lea," she said, stressing politeness with her little frown at Allen.

Flora motioned them to gather around on the floor as she placed the tray on a cardboard box full of books. Allen groaned, lowering his heft to the floor beside Catherine. Alice and Charlie scooted over. John stood as he removed the thermos cap and began to pour tea.

"Can't you sit?" asked Flora.

"My knees," complained John, whose lanky baseball legs were becoming arthritic. Alice rose to retrieve a stepladder from in front of a bookcase for her father to sit on. "Thank you, Peaches," he said. "Now, if I only had some bourbon," he chuckled.

"I must have some," said Charlie, "in a box somewhere."

"I've got some in my car," offered Allen. Catherine shot him a pained look and covered her mouth with her hand.

"In your car, Allen?" said Flora, "whatever for!"

Allen offered to share the whiskey. He arose, groaning, as Catherine helped by pushing on his lower back. Allen avoided his mother's eyes as he left the room.

Alice wondered why her brother carried whiskey in his car. What else had he and Catherine been doing in his Chevy with the ample back seat? Perhaps the whiskey is a housewarming present, she thought, making allowances.

The bottle Allen presented was half empty. Without comment, John reached toward the bottle. "My knees thank you," he said to his son. He poured a capful into his dainty cup. "I'll pass this around," John suggested, "since Flora forgot the sugar."

Flora bit her lip, then smiled. "Looks like we'll have a proper toast after all."

∽∾∽

To Alice, the house was a miniature Tara—much smaller than Scarlett O'Hara's or even the Simpsons', but this one was her own. The newly-built house boasted fresh paint and clean bricks. Over the front stoop, a balcony supported by two faux columns contributed a southern Colonial effect to this square two-story house. Their perfect home included a screened-in back porch, three bedrooms, two bathrooms, and a tiny middle room upstairs for a sewing room, den, or nursery. The builder lived two doors away in a house with a Dutchy barn-like roof. On either side of Charlie and Alice's house stood two other new brick homes, already occupied.

From their front windows, they looked across to the broad green campus, church, and dormitory buildings of a seminary. When Alice first heard the church bells intone the hourly chime, she couldn't believe her ears. "It sounds exactly like Big Ben—the clock in Mother and Daddy's house!"

"And they say you can't take it with you!" joked Charlie.

Inside her new home, it was easy for Alice to forget the rumblings happening in the world outside. But the newspapers kept intruding on her peace. Daily headlines screamed destruction and violence in Europe—the war in Spain, Hitler's crushing of Austria—and Japan's atrocities in China. It depressed Alice, who suggested quitting the *Courier-Times.* "You can get enough news on the radio or at work," she told Charlie. "It's too scary. I remember President Roosevelt saying an attack on the Western Hemisphere is imaginable! I don't want to know," shuddered Alice.

"With two oceans to protect us, you needn't worry," said Charlie. However, he allowed Alice to cancel the newspaper, saying, "Fewer clouds to rain on our picnic."

On weekends, Charlie busied himself landscaping their backyard. He planted two Elberta peach trees—one on either side of the sidewalk leading from the house to their whitewashed frame garage. He plotted a garden for rosebushes under their living room windows. Next to the windows, he affixed a trellis on the back wall of the house for his new light pink *Dorothy Perkins* to do her climbing and cascading. In summer, the blooms would be visible indoors or out, and the fragrance of the roses could be imbibed through open windows.

To celebrate their new era of homeownership, Charlie bought a can of white paint and a broad brush. As Alice stood next to him inside their garage, he plunged the brush into the creamy liquid and began to paint their name in wide swaths on the wood planks of the garage wall. "Let me help!" said Alice. Charlie loaded the paintbrush to dripping. His hand over hers, together they marked their declaration of ownership:

LUKAS 1938

18

THE PHILCO PLAYED faintly from the Lukases' living room; Louis Armstrong sang an old favorite, *Stardust*. The only other sound was the yipping of the Boston bull terrier next door. Chicken roasted in the oven, awaiting Charlie's arrival from work. Alice sat at one end of the dining room table, composing a letter to Lillian, Charlie's crippled sister with whom she'd felt a bond since the wedding. She wrote:

Sept. 29, 1939—Dear Lillian, We are looking forward to your spending Christmas with us and meeting our new baby. Wish I knew if it's a boy or girl—a John Allen or Judith Alice. By all indications of its kicking, the Kentucky Wildcats might want him (or her?) on their team. How are things in Washington DC? Are you getting around okay? . . . In her puffy maternity dress, Alice pored over her monogrammed stationery, scribbling her racing thoughts to Lillian. She ignored the scent of the chicken skin becoming harsher and was startled as Charlie breezed through the doorway, trailing the fresh air of early Fall.

"How's my girl!" said Charlie, dropping his briefcase on the table. Alice leaned up for his kiss. "Your girls—or maybe girl-carrying-boy—are all fine," she smiled, patting her belly. Then she frowned at the briefcase with its metal trim at the edges. "That will leave marks, Charlie."

"Oh, sorry," he replied, grabbing the offending item.

"Me too." She gave her husband a sympathetic look. "But I know you don't want to scratch our nice new furniture either." The cherry dining room set—chairs and table with claw-foot legs and the glass-front china hutch—were recent purchases and gifts from Alice's parents.

Charlie went to the front hall closet to stash his briefcase, still smelling of new leather. "No matter," he said. "I'm done with it for the weekend." He slammed the closet door shut.

"So, how was your day?" Alice inquired. She set her correspondence aside.

"Good day," he summarized. "Had lunch with Mike Sanders. He had a surprise for me—and a good deal."

"Oh, what was that?"

"Mike offered me his old set of golf clubs at a great price. Apparently, he and Virginia think they need new clubs every other year or so."

"Have to do something with Virginia's money, I guess," said Alice.

Charlie grinned. "I guess so. But Mike's offer was too good to turn down."

"You bought the clubs?"

"Yes, I did. I won't be playing much. Just good to have a set—for when I do."

Alice looked away, picked up then set down her pen.

Charlie pointed out, "Mr. Stevens plays. Might be good for business."

Alice looked up with an approving smile.

Charlie cleared his throat and stripped off his necktie. "I hope you won't mind if I try the clubs out tomorrow—over at Seneca. He waited. "I see you have a letter to finish. I'll be home before you miss me."

Alice noticed a burning scent from the kitchen. "Oh no! The chicken!"

Charlie followed his waddling wife to the stove. She grabbed a potholder and pulled the oven rack with the roaster out of the oven. She looked under the lid to discover juices stuck to the bottom of the pan, scorched black—a familiar result. When Alice's face fell, Charlie laughed it off. "It's the way I like it—well done!"

⌀⌀⌀⌀

The next day, Charlie bounded out of bed earlier than usual, neglecting their Saturday morning cuddle. He had convinced Alice that she didn't need to fix his breakfast. "I know how to make coffee and burn the toast. You get some sleep."

Mourning doves cooed from the telephone wires as Charlie crossed the backyard to the garage, toting his new golf clubs. He was also free as a bird, humming a tune, and looking forward to swinging a golf club again. He hadn't played a round with Mike and Stan since his marriage to Alice.

Few cars traveled the roads early Saturday, except for traffic in and out of the nearby Bowman Field airport. Charlie noted that some of the vehicles were

U.S. military and wondered what was happening. The parking lot at the Seneca Park golf course was already half full. Charlie parked, lugged his new golf bag and clubs out of the trunk, then set off eagerly for the clubhouse. He wondered if he'd see a familiar face, although he knew Mike and Virginia had other plans. Perhaps he'd see Mr. Stevens or someone from the cooperage company or land bank. More likely, the clubhouse personnel would match him with someone he didn't already know. An occasion for possible new friendships or perhaps business opportunities.

As Charlie approached the registration desk, two managers busily checked off tee times for newly arrived patrons. Charlie joined the line. In front of him, a blond woman was explaining something to the fresh-faced youth at the desk. "He was due by now, and I can't wait much longer."

The young man looked up at the large wall clock. "We have an opening in ten minutes. If you can wait—"

"No, I don't want to wait," said the woman.

The woman's pouty voice sounded familiar to Charlie—and that white-blond hair.

The desk man said, "We don't usually allow single players."

"Well, I'm not waiting another minute. Just match me up with—anyone." The impatient woman flung her arm, nearly hitting Charlie as she turned around.

"Bonnie!"

They stared at each other, surprised. Charlie was seeing a vision of loveliness. Had he forgotten how beautiful Bonnie was? He hadn't known she played golf. The young man at the desk spoke. "Sir, do you have a reservation?"

Charlie, flustered, replied. "No, I didn't think—"

"Would you agree to tee off with this woman right about now?" He looked at the clock again and tapped his pencil on the logbook. "All right with you?" the man turned to Bonnie.

"Sure," she drawled, her mouth twisting in an ironic smile. "Charlie and I are old friends. Okay Charlie?"

"Well, okay." Charlie swallowed, uncomfortable. What would Alice think?

Bonnie and Charlie paid their fees and collected pencils and scorecards from the desk. Charlie, dazed, followed his golf partner to the first tee. "It's so good to see you," said Bonnie. "How long has it been?"

Charlie thought a moment. "Well, it's got to be over two years now. What have you been up to since I saw you last?"

"No good," said Bonnie drolly.

"Seriously, though. . . ."

"I'll tell you later. Are you still at the land bank?" she asked, putting her ball on the tee. She looked at her golf partner before taking a stroke.

"No. I've been at Limestone Cooperage for over a year now."

"Oh!" Bonnie swung her driver; with a clean whacking sound, her tiny ball disappeared above the red-tinged oak trees.

Charlie whistled. "Nice hit!" Charlie couldn't help smiling at her graceful form and delivery. She smiled back.

Charlie stepped up for his turn. He set his ball on the tee, studied it, and wiggled his hips as he addressed the ball. "Nice," cooed Bonnie. She cleared her throat. Charlie stopped and turned to look at her. She gave him a wolfish grin. His concentration ruined, he missed the ball as his wooden driver thudded to the ground. Behind him, Bonnie laughed. His face heated. On his next attempt, Charlie regained focus, wiggled his hips despite Bonnie, and drove the ball into the sky.

"Good recovery!" praised Bonnie. "I like your style."

Charlie didn't respond to her comment. Instead, he shouldered his golf bag. "Shall we find our balls," he said.

Bonnie raised her eyebrows, "Have you really lost your balls, Charlie?"

He ignored her wisecrack and inquired again, "What have you been up to—besides no good—since I last saw you?"

"I've been working over there at Bowman Field for the Aero Club." She explained that the club provided aviation services for commercial and private airplanes. "Things are getting busier over there. The government is putting up more hangars. And the rumor is that some barracks for air corpsmen will be built sometime soon."

Charlie didn't like hearing about the military buildup, so he dismissed the rumor. They found their golf balls, Charlie's in the fairway, Bonnie's in the rough. Bonnie drove to the green first. He was aware of her graceful, athletic moves and slim presence. She seemed to attract sunshine, radiating beauty and warmth. And no longer a hint of cigarette smoke as she walked companionably beside him. Uncomfortable, was he enjoying this more than he should?

Walking along the second fairway lined with nodding old trees, Bonnie asked Charlie whom he was courting. He set down his golf bag and laughed to hide his discomfort. "I'm not courting anyone." Well, it was the truth.

"Seriously? Hard to believe that." She paused, giving him a long searching look. "Well, here we are again! We had some good times, didn't we?" Her eyes crinkled in a smile that seemed like an invitation.

Charlie shifted on his feet and shook his head. "Bonnie, I'm married."

Bonnie put down her clubs. "No! Really? You're not wearing a ring."

"Not a wedding ring. But I do have this swell one Alice gave me for Christmas the year we married." He showed her his onyx ring with the quasi-Plymouth logo.

Bonnie touched her fingers to his as she looked at the ring. "You married that Alice?" Her forehead wrinkled as she looked into Charlie's dark eyes.

"Yes, Alice Lea. We're expecting a baby in about six weeks—early November."

"Oh, my! And you're out here playing golf." She stared, looking incredulous.

"Not much for me to do—"

Bonnie snorted. "Yeah, your deed is done, isn't it? I guess Alice doesn't mind you out golfing?"

Charlie reflected that she might mind his playing golf with an old girlfriend. He replied, "Alice is understanding and kind."

"Humpf," said Bonnie, more to herself than Charlie. "What every man needs—a kind wife."

As the golf match continued, the sun on the fall scenery warmed them; they became more at ease with each other. Chatting and laughing as they followed their golf balls and strolled from greens to tees. Charlie learned that Bonnie's current flame was an airfield mechanic who had stood her up for this golf match. "I'll have a serious talk with Joe," said Bonnie. "He'll come around when he hears who I played golf with."

"He wouldn't know me," objected Charlie.

"I have ways of making him jealous." She winked.

Charlie wanted to release the guilt he felt for his renewed attraction to Bonnie. He slammed the ball to the green, closing in on a possible eagle on the eighth hole.

"Have you ever made a hole-in-one, Charlie?" Bonnie asked.

With a self-deprecating chuckle, he said, "No, of course not. I'll be amazed if I make this eagle. Have you ever made a hole-in-one?"

"I don't have the equipment," said Bonnie. "But I'll bet you did—lots of times. Maybe even on your honeymoon." Her voice held a sardonic edge as she gazed pointedly at him.

He ignored her naughty teasing, concentrating on a thirty-foot putt, a near impossibility. Bonnie whistled as he wiggled again. That did it—Charlie's ball flew ten feet to the other side of the hole. He looked at Bonnie and scowled. By protocol, Bonnie's turn was next to drive her ball. Instead, she urged, "Go ahcad, Charlie. Score!"

He made a birdie on the eighth hole and smiled. "Your fault," he said, wishing he'd made the eagle. Charlie retrieved his ball from the hole.

At the ninth green, the clubhouse beckoned. Charlie wiped his brow and glasses with his golf towel; Bonnie's shoulders drooped under her load of clubs. "Had enough?" asked Charlie.

"Nine more?" tempted Bonnie.

Though a touch of exhaustion had set in from golf and battling his feelings about Bonnie, he was enjoying the easy camaraderie and felt encouraged by his birdie on the eighth, followed by a par on the ninth. "Whatever you say. I'm game."

"I'm glad you're game, Charlie. I certainly am." That sexy wink again!

He sliced the ball with his nine-iron from the eleventh tee. On the twelfth hole, he and Bonnie had trouble chipping out of a sand trap. The humidity and temperature were climbing, and Bonnie's vibes were making him feverish. "How about we call it quits?" Charlie wiped his brow again, and his shirt was sticking to his back. Perhaps enough was enough!

"I'll let you buy me a drink in the clubhouse," Bonnie suggested.

Charlie gave her a sideways glance. "Maybe," he said. He wondered if he should be so agreeable as they trudged back to the clubhouse from the twelfth green. By the time they arrived at the building, Charlie decided to put a positive spin on the prospect of a drink with Bonnie. He specified *Old Dan'l* bourbon and water for both of them from the white-coated waiter in the cool upholstered bar. "Good for business!" laughed Charlie, hoisting his drink.

"And for old friendships!" returned Bonnie, clinking her glass to his.

As they said goodbye in the parking lot, Bonnie suggested, "Shall we play again sometime?"

Charlie considered her offer. "Maybe we can," he said, with the mental reservation they might meet again—by accident. Or at her invitation. As a married man, he would never contact Bonnie. Inside his overheated little coupe, Charlie felt limp and drained as he peered through his rearview mirror to see Bonnie maneuver her black Ford convertible out of the lot. Pushing the starter, Charlie breathed a sigh, thankful he had not seen anyone else he knew at the golf course—anyone who'd have noticed him with a woman who was not his wife.

Then the engine died. "Come on!" shouted Charlie, jamming his thumb on the starter. At last, on the road leading home, he considered whether he would meet Bonnie again. A famous quote popped into his head: *When in the course of human events.* He felt a smile forming on his lips.

Then he swallowed. Alice awaited him at home, no doubt eager to hear how the new golf clubs worked. And she was close to delivering their first child. No, he couldn't see Bonnie again. The baby would be his excuse: *Up late last night . . . colicky . . . Alice needs me.* The words of a dead end.

He grabbed the steering wheel as his little coupe swerved left of the centerline. He sweated more than ever, even with the windows rolled down. What's with this car! Is it me? Bonnie? The bourbon? Another thought: how to explain the bourbon on his breath to Alice? She'd wonder with whom he shared a drink. She might not believe his meeting a woman friend—and playing twelve holes of golf with her—a pure accident. Should he lie? Charlie formed a plan. He would rush into the house, drop his clubs, then hurry upstairs to shower. After-shave cologne, his strong Fitch's shampoo, and extra time might cover the scent of whiskey breath.

As he pulled up to the curb in front of his home on Pleasant Avenue, he noticed a car parked smack even with the front sidewalk. The shiny black finish and baroque shark-nosed front end told Charlie it must be the 1938 Graham sedan Harold's parishioners had bought for him. Why had he come—all the way from Morgantown! Had Alice summoned him?

Alice and Harold were standing in the front entry of the house as Charlie approached. She opened the screen door, calling cheerfully, "Look who's here!"

"Harold!" Charlie forced a smile. "What brings you to these parts?" He was eager to know.

"Just dropped by on my way home from a meeting with the archbishop," Harold replied. His neck looked warm and whiskery under his tight clerical collar. The brothers clasped hands.

"Good to see you," said Charlie, relieved that the visit was a casual one. He tried to talk without directing his breath at his wife or brother.

"I got to thinking it's about time I came by to bless your house," said Harold. "You've been here over a year now."

"Haven't noticed any evil spirits about," said Charlie, smiling. "But maybe you can keep them out permanently."

Harold's grayish-blue eyes crinkled under his spectacles as he chuckled at his brother's comment. "That's the general idea—keep the devil out for good."

Charlie motioned to his wrinkled clothing. "I've been golfing. Mind if I take a few minutes to change and freshen up?"

"Swell idea," interjected Alice. "I'll offer Harold a drink while we wait."

"Marvelous," said Charlie, covering his mouth. "Give Harold the best bourbon," he called out while rushing upstairs. With all imbibing, his whiskey breath wouldn't stand out; he hoped they hadn't already sensed it.

Charlie returned downstairs. Alice and Harold were seated on the living room sofa under a still-life painting of hydrangeas in a cream-colored vase. "Maybe we'd better get started on the house blessing," said Harold. They rose, bowing their heads, as Harold intoned a short prayer, "Dear Lord, we thank you for these people and this house. . . ." They went from room to room, Alice leading, as Harold raised his aspergillum and flung droplets of holy water to each corner while mumbling in Latin, "In Nomine Patris. . . ." They walked through every area of the Lukas home, including the back porch, basement, bathrooms, and the tiny expectant nursery at front and center of the second floor. After he had blessed all the rooms, the priest turned to Alice and sprinkled holy rain on her maternal belly. "Lord, bless this good woman and her child. Keep them in good health."

As Harold prepared to leave on his long drive to Morgantown, Charlie ushered his brother to the sedan. "Did you bless your car, Harold? It has a rascally look to it."

"It's a blessed car now, Charlie. I took care of that first thing."

"Well, maybe you'd better do mine. It gave me some trouble today," said Charlie.

Harold obliged, sprinkling holy water on the Plymouth. "Exorciso te, in Nomine Dei Patris . . ." he began. Next, he turned to his brother. "I think you need a blessing too."

"Oh?" Charlie arched an eyebrow.

"This will chase the devil out of you," said the priest, showering holy water on Charlie.

"Gosh, Harold. You overdid it!" His starched shirt dripped.

"You needed a lot," grinned Harold. "Better stay away from whiskey on the golf course from now on!" The priest slid into the driver's seat and reached for his black fedora. Charlie stood still. "Be seeing you, Charlie! Let me know when the baby arrives." The heavy black car roared away.

19

Loew's Theater offered a special pre-release viewing of *Gone With the Wind* in Technicolor—advance tickets, one showing only—on Friday, three days before Charlie and Alice's second anniversary. Close enough for their celebration. Charlie left work early to pick up Alice at her parents' home, where she had spent the afternoon.

In the darkening theater, the couple held hands, anticipating the film version of Alice's favorite book. Excited and content, Alice allowed the romantic ambiance of the old downtown theater to draw her in. The panoramic piazza setting attracted and held her attention during the excruciating wait for the dark surround and bright action to begin on the movie screen. Stars twinkled through cutouts in the illusory sky of a twilit evening; a crescent moon rose on the indigo dome. Stage lights illuminated an Italian village square with balconied buildings and turrets. Windowpanes glowed from within and then began to fade as night fell gradually over the tableau. A meteorite shot across the sky; stars shimmered. It was a magical scene set to transition the audience from reality to illusion.

Alice jumped when the Movietone news logo burst onto the heavy velvet curtain as it rumbled open, revealing the screen. A nasal masculine voice proclaimed the news headlines of the week, accompanied by important military music: The war in Europe.

A beautiful woman with delicate features spoke seductively into the table microphone at a radio broadcast from New York City. Poet Edna St. Vincent Millay said, "If we love democracy, we must love it in England and France. . . ."

Next, a seated President Roosevelt, in his New York accent, spoke about the war declared almost two months ago. He stated that America would remain neutral. Alice gripped Charlie's hand as she focused on the president's message.

The next news piece revealed a setback to U.S. neutrality when on October ninth, a German battleship captured an American cargo ship carrying farm supplies to England. Charlie peeled Alice's fingers off his hand and shook it awake. Alice's eyes sought his for a reassuring smile in the darkness.

The long-awaited feature began, and Alice slipped off into the Deep South to a plantation called Tara, in another time, another foreboding of war. She lost herself in the story of impetuous Scarlett O'Hara and roguish Rhett Butler as the reflection of the flickering screen bounced off Charlie's glasses. Alice assumed the heroine's role; her emotions surged with Scarlett's highs and lows, attraction and revulsion for Rhett. She closed one eye during the grim war scenes. Such violence amid ordinary life shocked her, as did rows of pale, distorted bodies laid out in view of frantic pedestrians on the city commons. After two hours, the film was at midpoint, with the starving heroine swearing revenge on the Yankees who devastated Tara. Alice clung to her chair arms as Scarlett choked on radish root and railed to the sky, "I will never be hungry again!"

The curtain rolled closed as the house lights slowly turned up for intermission. Charlie glanced at his watch, then turned to Alice. "Well, I am hungry! How about you?"

Alice shook her head, refusing. She didn't want food or drink, thus avoiding a trip to the theater's bathroom.

"I'm going for popcorn," said Charlie, springing up from his seat. Other patrons had already filled the aisles, heading for the lobby.

Alice stayed in her seat, consumed by the story unfolding with such intensity on the screen. She noticed a woman seated in front of her sobbing into her handkerchief. The man beside her helped the woman leave her seat, and they walked out.

Alice's thoughts tumbled. She felt she'd never seen so much reality—such beauty, such horror—as revealed in this Civil War epic. She wondered how her mother would view Scarlett O'Hara. Flora might dismiss her as selfish and petty; at worst, ruthless and spiteful. On the other hand, she assumed her mother would praise Scarlett's heroic determination. Alice always felt dominated; Scarlett was her polar opposite. Not a worrier. Instead, Scarlett always said, "I'll think about that tomorrow."

Alice wished she had Scarlett's indomitable spirit but was relieved she didn't have to contend with the surliness of a Rhett Butler. Charlie had his moments, but he was a gentle puppy compared to Rhett.

Charlie returned with a bag of popcorn and offered some to Alice. The smell gagged her; she turned away. "You know," said Charlie, "that hunger scene right at intermission was just a set-up for refreshment sales. You should see the crowd!"

"It had the opposite effect on me," said Alice. She felt her stomach grab under her ribs.

After intermission, the curtain opened to reveal Scarlett on her mission to restore Tara after General Sherman's pillaging March to the Sea. Alone in the mansion, Scarlett's virtue and life were threatened by a wayward soldier on the grand stairway. With her back against the wall, Scarlett shot him in the face in self-defense. Alice's mind rolled back to her childhood summer at the Simpsons' farm when Mattie battered the chicken-yard rat to death. Mattie and Scarlett—such powerful women! Then she remembered her own helplessness against the coalman in the cellar. Scarlett didn't have a brother to defend her. Alice had no weapon.

Back to Civil War Atlanta, Alice watched in fascinated horror as the film continued with ravaging war scenes and the deaths of beloved characters. Lives were forever changed. Yet in the end, a hopeful Scarlett O'Hara rose from the ashes, proclaiming, "Tomorrow is another day."

I wish I could be like her, thought Alice as the epic ended. She clutched Charlie's hand, trying to ignore a gnawing urge in her stomach.

As the house lights went up, the audience stood to applaud the movie. Charlie turned to his wife. "Well!" he exclaimed. "Did you like it?"

"Yes," murmured Alice, not yet possessing words to convey her deeply touched emotions. She knew her impressions would find form later in her diary.

"Where shall we eat?" Charlie asked.

"You decide." Alice didn't think she was hungry despite the cramp in her belly.

As they stumbled up the aisle with others still dazed and dazzled, Alice grabbed her stomach as a stabbing pain surprised her. She clung to a seat back where a man looked up at her, startled. Charlie's embrace surrounded her. "What's wrong?"

A few hours later, in a closeted room on the maternity floor of Jewish Hospital, Alice labored to give birth, as nurses scurried about with charts, thermometers, and needles. She had never been in such a fearful predicament, trapped inside a cocoon of pain, floating in an empty universe. The feral creature within had arrived at a critical juncture—time to find the light. He or she will press on, no matter the pain or damage to me, Alice thought. She vaguely remembered a

Roman myth heard long ago—something about the goddess Juno giving birth to the galaxy. Alice understood how a woman in labor could imagine such an expansive eruption. She would try to remember those feverish thoughts for her diary.

In the hour after the nursing staff whisked Alice away, Charlie finished his pork chops, potatoes, and coffee in the hospital cafeteria. Alice's parents arrived, excited and out of breath with questions for Charlie. Allen, with Catherine, met them at the maternity floor reception desk. A nurse greeted them and pointed toward the waiting room. The expectant group huddled together on two sofas, warming the green acetate cushions with their body heat. Sterile, white walls surrounded them. As the lone family awaiting a birth that evening, they took ownership of the room to shuffle aimlessly, flip magazine pages, wonder, and wait for someone to inform them of Alice's progress.

Near eleven o'clock, Doc Richards entered the room in surgical garb, a mask loose under his chin, a green cap on his head. As they shook hands, Charlie noticed that Doc's naturally ruddy complexion seemed grayer.

Flora rose quickly, demanding, "How is Alice?"

The doctor assumed a level stance, hands on his wide hips, and announced, "I have to operate."

Flora gasped. Catherine rushed toward Charlie as he swayed.

"The baby is having trouble—not coming headfirst. I need to do a cesarean section to get the baby out as soon as possible."

"What does that mean?" croaked Charlie.

"Means I need to cut into the womb surgically to lift out the baby." Charlie grew pale; Doc hesitated. "It must be done, Charlie, so they will both be okay. I'd best get started."

He left the family with their silent questions. Catherine held onto her brother.

Allen spoke first. "The kid intends to walk into the world—or maybe back in."

Charlie grimaced.

"Everything will be okay." Catherine rubbed Charlie's arm, wrinkling his white shirtsleeve.

John, still seated, with his long arms dangling, shook his head. "Why did this happen to Peaches? She already lost one baby."

Flora responded, "No one said she's losing this baby. We can't know God's will, of course, but I have perfect faith in my nephew. He's a skilled doctor. Besides, it's an old operation. Done lots of times."

John removed a white handkerchief from his pocket to wipe his brow.

"I'm going outside," announced Charlie. "I need air."

"Sure, old chap," said Allen. "I'll wear out the linoleum for you."

Charlie walked outside the square brick hospital into the courtyard. The night air felt cool, chilling him in the sweaty shirt he'd been wearing since he left for work that morning. It seemed like several days had passed. He remembered a full moon rising after he and Alice left Loew's, driving to the hospital. Charlie looked up to reconnect with the steady, smiling moon. What had happened to it? He scanned the clear sky and found merely a section of the moon, still bright, as a disc-shaped shadow drew across it. "What in tarnation!" Charlie muttered. This unnatural-seeming occurrence increased Charlie's anxiety about Alice and the baby. He vomited in the courtyard bushes, then wiped his mouth with his handkerchief. "Damn!" When he next looked at the moon, it had transformed into a menacing bloody color, further unnerving him. Charlie returned, shivering, to the family waiting inside the hospital.

Four quiet, worried forms looked up expectantly. Flora's expression said oh, it's you. Charlie felt she probably blamed him for Alice's condition and would prefer seeing Doc Richards walk in.

Catherine jumped up, motioning her brother to sit between her and Allen. "It won't be much longer," Allen assured him, patting Charlie on the back as he slumped to the sofa.

Doc Richards finally returned to the waiting room, shoulders sagging. Facing the worried expressions before him, he relaxed into a smile. Extending his hand again to Charlie, he said, "Congratulations! You have a beautiful baby girl." He added, "Don't worry—Alice is fine. She was magnificent."

An explosion of joy filled Charlie's chest, and he barely heard the others expressing their happy relief. He saw John Lea wipe a tear off his cheek and felt Allen thumping on his shoulders like a bear suddenly freed from its cage.

❧❧❧

Judith Star Lukas entered the world just before midnight on October 27, 1939. Alice's mid-November diary entry would contain memories of that night:

> *I still wonder why I went into labor early. Was it the birthing scene in the film or Scarlett's wild carriage ride through fiery Atlanta? The horseback riding or maybe that awful tumble down the stairs when she reached out to slap Rhett Butler and lost her balance?*
>
> *Giving birth was a long ordeal— I'm just glad I slept through the worst part of the main feature! I'm forever grateful to Doc Richards. What*

blessed relief to have him in charge, not like Scarlett O'Hara with a silly
servant girl to help her give birth! Thank goodness for anesthesia!

When Charlie told me about the moon's eclipse at the time of Judy's
birth, I took it for a sign. The magic in the night sky was no accident. I
decided then and there to change Baby's middle name from Alice, as we
intended, to Star. At first, Charlie said 'no'—that no priest would baptize
her with such a pagan name. But seeing the raw scar on my belly, he
finally agreed to my wish. Our daughter's brightness will eclipse even the
fire of the sun. I am sure of it.

20

A saint's name added to the baptismal certificate of Judith Star Mary Lukas satisfied her uncle Harold and the Catholic Church. At ten months old, she was *The Star*, as grandpa John Lea nicknamed her. On a typical morning, she was the first one awake, rocking her crib. Her parents, who called her Judy, were buried in their pillows, lost in sleep. Charlie, in his sleeveless undershirt, had one arm over Alice. The rhythmic squeaking from Judy's bedroom brought them gradually out of their dreams. Their daughter's room was on the other side of the tiny nursery she had quickly outgrown, with a wardrobe of clothes, stuffed animals, and furniture that included Alice's old rocking chair. If her parents didn't hear her shaking the frame off her crib, Judy would begin chattering and—as a last resort—wailing. For the moment, she happily bounced.

Alice turned her head toward Charlie, groaning. He raised an eyebrow, looking over at his wife to determine her wakefulness. It didn't look good. Charlie moved his arm off Alice and sat up in bed.

He squinted at the clock, unable to make out the numbers without his glasses. The seminary clock began its prelude, then gonged six chimes for the hour. Knowing his alarm would go off at 6:30 anyway, he hauled out on his side of the bed, put on his slippers, tied the string more securely on his striped pajama pants, and trudged into his daughter's bedroom.

"Bottle?" said Judy brightly when her tousled father appeared.

Charlie grinned at his elfin daughter, soft cheeks and dark eyes, ready to begin her day. "Good morning, Sunshine." He picked her up, noticing she seemed especially bottom-heavy and reeked of strong ammonia. "Oh my," said Charlie. "Where is Mommy when we need her? Right!"

Judy squealed. "Dada! Dada!"

"Okay, Kid. Let's do it," he said, laying the baby on her changing table. Luckily for Charlie, it was only a very saturated wet diaper. He changed it quickly despite Judy's wiggling; he remembered to take care which way the pointed ends of the safety pins fastened—away from the chubby abdomen. He slipped fresh rubber pants over the diaper and finished. "Okay, Judy," Charlie said, picking her up. "Now what were you saying?"

"Bottle?" she repeated.

"Oh, that's right," laughed Charlie. "Let's get your bottle warmed up right now."

As they started toward the hallway, Judy suddenly lurched halfway out of her father's arms and leaned toward the crib. "Bunny!" she screamed.

"Oh, of course." Charlie reached into the crib to retrieve Judy's favorite stuffed animal—a long-eared white bunny wearing a flimsy green skirt and a tiny flower corsage at its waist. Judy hugged Bunny to her face and bit one ear as Charlie carried her toward the stairs. Walking past the master bedroom, he called to Alice, still in bed. "I have to work today!"

Downstairs, Charlie busied himself at the kitchen counter, hastily preparing the baby's bottle and pabulum. He turned as Alice straggled in. "Good morning," Alice yawned.

Judy, her hair sticking out in every direction, spooned moist cereal into her mouth and shared it with Bunny's furry chin. "Mama!" Judy reached out, dropping her spoon.

Alice picked it up from the floor. "You didn't cover her legs!" she scolded Charlie. "She'll get cold."

"Sorry. I didn't think about it," he replied. "But I did the safety pins right."

"Swell," said Alice. "You'd better get dressed. Throw down Judy's overalls when you go up."

"Right. I was just starting coffee."

"I'll do it. Go get dressed. I'll clean up this mess too."

Charlie knew Alice's early-morning grumps. Perhaps he'd get a kiss later, maybe a sweet remark as he left for work. I should bring roses tonight, he thought. Hope I remember.

‿๑~๑‿

After her husband left for work, Alice, as usual, had the feeling of a wide plain of time expanding outward to the end of the day. Still a novice in the school of childcare, she had scant experience with babies or toddlers while growing up. Her aunt and uncle, next door on Brook Street, were childless. Another aunt in town had a daughter, but the cousin was near Alice's age, not someone she'd taken care of. The parenting books Alice read emphasized perfection on the mother's part, as did her *Dos and Don'ts for Wives*. So much pressure.

Despite the drag of housework and the uncharted waters of childcare, Alice found her chatty daughter with sunny brown hair irresistible. She and Judy enjoyed storybooks, and Alice found a new talent in making up stories to delight her baby girl.

(She wrote in her diary: *I'm a storyteller and a surprising poet! My childhood adventures with Raggedy Ann and Andy and the Lewis Carroll characters are paying off with Judy Star. We have great fun and she's a swell audience.*)

Even with her enjoyment of Judy, Alice looked forward to breaks. She held her daughter to a regular 12:30 to 3:30 naptime (the book stressed the importance of maintaining a schedule.) The Smith girls next door were always welcome to entertain Judy for an hour or two after school.

Alice also appreciated her parents spending time with them. John Lea's new half-time workweek allowed him and Flora to visit, take Alice and Judy shopping, or go for a drive in the country. One of John's greatest delights was watching his granddaughter eat an ice cream cone at the dairy store. His hearty laugh infected other customers as Judy tried to devour her vanilla ice cream before it ran off the cone, spreading down her clothes. Alice's laugh concealed an inward cringe at the thought of lugging more laundry to the Laundromat.

One evening as Alice and Judy waited for Charlie's return from work, they sat on the living room sofa, enjoying an alphabet book, identifying pictures of apples, cats, dogs, and more. Charlie entered the room and laid his gray hat on the sofa beside Alice. She and Judy looked up at a pale-faced Charlie holding out a bouquet of red roses. Seeing his face, Alice expected the roses to expire any second. What on earth was wrong? Her heart sped up a beat.

"Let's go to the kitchen and get water for these," urged Charlie.

"Look, Judy—Daddy's brought red roses. R is for roses!"

Judy kicked her feet rapidly on the sofa. Alice scooped her up to follow Charlie into the kitchen. She quickly deposited the little girl into the Babee-Tenda with some crackers to crumble and eat. Alice was breathless to learn what troubled Charlie. As she reached up to the cupboard for a crystal vase to contain the roses, her hand shook. Charlie placed his hand over hers and gently guided the vase down to the kitchen counter. Then he spoke quietly.

"Today was a bad day. A man got burned at the char tunnel."

Alice looked at him, horrified. "Will he be okay?"

"They don't know yet."

Charlie had further news. He placed his hand on Alice's back, rubbing gently on her spine. "I read in the newspaper this morning—and talk all over the office—"

Alice turned quickly to face him. "What is it?"

"Roosevelt has just signed a peacetime draft into law."

Alice held her breath. "Meaning?"

"All men between twenty-one and thirty-five must register for it."

"Oh no—meaning you and Allen?"

Charlie nodded. "That's the bad news. The good news is we're not at war. And Allen and I are near the upper end of the age range. In another year, Allen won't even be eligible."

"Would you have to leave us if there's a war?" She looked over at Judy, who was starting to fret.

"I don't know. Nobody knows the particulars. For now, it sounds like anyone drafted would stay in the U.S. or territories around the world."

"Around the world?"

Charlie shrugged. "Not in Europe. Like, you know—Hawaii or the Pacific—"

"Oh my!" Alice's hands pressed her cheeks, eyes burning. "What can we do?"

"Don't worry. I'm not going anywhere—except to the draft office. And that's not even set up yet." He smiled.

Judy cried to be held, arms stretched out, fingers beckoning. Alice picked up her crumb-coated daughter, kissed her head, then planted her face in the baby's warm brown hair. What was about to happen to their family life? Face flushed, eyes reddening, Alice turned to Charlie.

He walked over and embraced his wife and sniffling baby. "Registering doesn't mean getting drafted. There will be a lottery." He kissed Alice's forehead, then bent toward her lips.

She pulled away, worry possessing her. "Oh, like an unlucky number—"

"That's right. I'm usually not too good at having my number drawn."

"Let's hope your—our—luck stays. What would I do without you!"

"Don't look on the dark side. I only wanted you to know the score."

Alice shifted Judy in her arms. "I wonder why this is happening now." She searched Charlie's hazel eyes for a clue to his true thoughts, as fear swirled in her stomach.

***

A sudden thought pierced Charlie's brain like a flaming arrow. Bonnie! What was going on now at Bowman Field, and what about that military buildup? He hadn't seen her since fate brought them together to play golf last fall. It had been a busy year for Charlie as a new dad—just as he'd expected. But he had thought of Bonnie and even hoped to see her beautiful face and shiny blond hair at Seneca the one time he played golf this summer with Mike and Stan. He'd been more disappointed than he should have, not to see her.

Bonnie's sudden appearance in his mind and the possibility of being drafted into war closed Charlie's throat. He began choking and eased away from his family's embrace. He went to the sink and quickly poured a glass of water. After drinking, he set down the glass and stood at the sink staring out the window at nothing in particular, his thoughts jumbled.

21

O N A HAZY October Sunday in 1940, the Leas hosted a midday dinner for John's brother Stuart and his wife Henny, recently home from a Lake Erie cruise. After they finished dessert, Henny held Judy on her lap as the child examined her great aunt's pince-nez on a gold chain. As the adults talked, Judy made expressive pronouncements in gibberish; everyone laughed. Grandpa John reminded them, "She's the Star, you know."

"And sounds smarter than most politicians around here," added Stuart. From a heavy gilded frame on the wall, the portrait of their father, John H. Lea, peered down his banker's nose at them, adding his ubiquitous touch of solemnity.

Allen's *I Hate Wah* button on his shirt pocket caused a stir. "What does that mean?" asked Alice. "Something against my baby crying?"

Charlie chuckled.

"No, Sis. It means 'war' as pronounced by our New-Yawker president," said Allen.

"Well, I wouldn't wear it when we go to sign up," suggested Charlie.

"Sign up?" echoed Catherine.

"You know—register for the draft," Charlie reminded her. "That button would put Allen at the top of the list to go."

"Don't joke, Charlie," said Catherine.

"Well, of course I won't wear it to the draft office," said Allen, rolling his eyes. "But in other places, I want to show my preference for electing Wendell Willkie and keeping us out of war."

Elizabeth bustled around the table with second helpings of fried chicken.

"Are you and Catherine voting for Willkie?" asked Alice.

"The more Roosevelt leans us toward war—wah—the more I lean toward Willkie." He looked at his mother, known as a staunch Democrat. Flora dabbed at her mouth with a napkin, ignoring his look.

"As for myself," Catherine spoke up, "I haven't made up my mind yet. But I'm definitely against war."

Alice thought, if only it were up to us! She glanced at others around the table and alighted on Charlie's gaze. He raised his eyebrows, shook his head, and cracked a half-smile. Is he worried or not? wondered Alice.

"I'm sure we can all agree with Catherine on opposing war," summarized John at the head of the table. Nodding toward the portrait of his father, who had fought for the Confederacy in the Civil War, John added, "However, rare times come along when it is incumbent to serve, to protect what we hold dear. So, are you boys ready? Wednesday's the big day."

"Is the draft office ready for us?" countered Charlie.

"They look open for business," replied John. "On the floor above me at the post office. They've moved into the old passport office."

"The passport office?" inquired Stuart.

"It's been moved to a smaller room," said John. "Stuart, I guess we're lucky at our ages to be more concerned with passports than selective service. As for our sons—"

Stuart nodded, "Sure, definitely. Please pass the biscuits, Flora."

Sometimes Uncle Stuart annoyed Alice. This was one such moment. He's too old for the draft, but shouldn't he care about others—about Charlie and Allen especially?

Flora rang a little bell signaling Elizabeth, in the kitchen, to replenish the hot biscuits. The hum of conversation, punctuated by Judy's happy prattle, continued as the cook marched under the grandfather's portrait with a tray of her baking powder gems. Alice cast a disapproving frown at Uncle Stuart as he grabbed a steaming hot biscuit and dropped it on his plate. Flora nodded her thanks to Elizabeth as the large woman retreated to the kitchen with an empty tray.

❦

Wednesday, October sixteenth, was a virtual business holiday to allow men ages twenty-one to thirty-five to register for the first peacetime draft in American history. Charlie thought it a fine day for golf instead—and maybe a chance meeting with Bonnie. He pressed his lips tight and heaved a sigh as he and Allen joined the queue outside the Selective Service office that snaked down the fourth-floor corridor and stairway of the post office building. It reminded Charlie of breadlines during the Depression. Some men in this line looked jobless and hungry, others prosperous enough. None looked happy. The draft is an equalizer, thought Charlie. There had been no Fireside Chat from the President regarding the draft; Charlie assumed others in line were as informed by rumor as he.

"I see you're not wearing your wah button," Charlie nudged Allen.

"In my pocket," said Allen, patting the pocket of his tweed jacket.

"No lie! I hope it doesn't fall on the floor when someone official is looking."

A stern man with graying sideburns came by, handing out informational papers to those in line. "What's this?" said Charlie.

"For your reading pleasure," sneered the man.

Charlie put on his glasses. He and Allen began reading information concerning selective service, deferment categories, and the lottery procedure, as they shuffled forward up the steps in line.

"I think I'll register as a conscientious objector," said Allen.

"Can you do that?" asked Charlie.

"You know me—I hate wah," he said, slapping his pocket.

"But don't you have to be a Quaker or something? Presbyterians aren't known as war objectors, generally."

"It doesn't say anything about religious affiliation." Allen read further. "Well, there's one guy I know of who won't need to sign up."

"Who's that?" asked Charlie.

"The poor chap who got burned at your factory last month. Good timing."

"Hardly a lucky break," said Charlie, disgusted. "The way it looks on paper, he'll still need to register but will get a deferment for disability."

"Frying pan into the fire," muttered Allen, shifting his weight to another foot.

As they moved forward, the two men didn't talk much. Charlie sensed Allen was lost in thought and wondered if his brother-in-law were rehearsing a conscientious objector strategy in his head. Should he also? As the reality of the draft came closer, he worried how Alice and Judy would cope without him.

More than an hour later, Charlie and Allen reached the office and were handed registration cards by employees of the local draft board. Charlie signed his quickly, scrupulously providing all required information, including his employment, marital, and paternity status. Charlie wished this draft card to miraculously disappear among the millions of similar ones being filled out across the nation. However, he also felt a strong patriotic duty as a citizen to participate if called. Among this throng of men, he felt like a non-entity. He looked around at others near him. Their identities and backgrounds were buried like his, just numbers to be tossed into the lottery bin of war games. Charlie's chest tightened, and his heart felt strangely offbeat as he handed his card to a board member and received his registration receipt. Later, as he turned to leave the room, he noticed Allen in ardent conversation with another draft board representative. Charlie waited in the hall, feeling annoyed with Allen.

"What was all that about?" he asked when Allen, red-faced, joined Charlie in the musty corridor.

"Well, the upshot is I didn't sign for c.o. status after all. I learned it would involve a hearing before the draft board. Let's see if we have a war first. I can change my status later—when I'm more prepared and know what's happening with the war."

"There's the spirit," Charlie slapped Allen on the back. "We'll see what happens. For one thing—the election could change the likelihood of war."

"Leaning toward Willkie too?" asked Allen. "I'll get you a wah button."

"Not now," said Charlie.

On their way downstairs, Charlie passed by two familiar—but grim—faces; he shook hands with Mike and Stan. They wished each other good luck. "God bless America," said Mike. Charlie smiled crookedly as he continued down the steps, his draft card with the official lottery number in his trousers pocket.

Within a week, Charlie and Allen received mail from the draft board explaining the selection process. Charlie guessed he would be classified 3D: *Deferred by reason of extreme hardship and privation to wife, child, or parent.* Allen would probably be classified in category one—*liable for military service*—but lower on the list as 1H: *Age twenty-eight or over.*

⌇⌇⌇

Two days after Judy's first birthday, a blindfolded Secretary of War Henry Stimson drew numbers for the first draftees from a glass fishbowl in the nation's capitol. President Roosevelt announced the first number:

158—The number Allen Lea received from the draft board when he registered.

Despite the unprecedented peacetime draft, Roosevelt beat Willkie by three million votes in a record turnout in the November election, while Secretary Stimson continued drawing the numbers of young men for the selective service.

With nearly half the men chosen disqualified for illiteracy or ill health, the Lea and Lukas families steeled themselves for the day Allen must leave for military duty.

One morning, Charlie and Alice looked out their bedroom window to see a large banner unfurled in front of the seminary chapel across the street. It read *Hail to Union 8* in support of New York theological students who refused to register for the draft. Every morning when he saw the banner, it reminded Charlie how close Allen had come to choosing conscientious objector status.

⌖⌖⌖

Flora and John Lea's Thanksgiving dinner came early as a gala send-off for Allen, who was soon reporting for military duty. Stuart and Henny were present, along with John and Stuart's sister, her husband, their daughter, and some close friends of the Leas. The dining room was crowded, with another table set in the Tiffany lamp-lit parlor. A doorway connected the rooms. Elizabeth's cooking and serving skills were stretched, but she proved herself queen of turkey and trimmings once again. Prefaced with a generous aperitif of *Old Dan'l* bourbon cocktails, the delectable feast and savory aromas put everyone in a relaxed, mellow mood despite the farewell to Allen.

During dessert, while guests enjoyed their pumpkin pie, Allen stood and clinked his water glass with a spoon, commanding attention. Alice returned to the dining room after laying Judy down for a nap in her old bedroom upstairs. She halted in the doorway, watching her brother beneath their grandfather's portrait. Two distinguished soldiers, she reflected. Grandfather Lea had fought for the south in Stonewall Jackson's brigade; Allen would soon go wherever *Uncle Sam* directed.

"I have an announcement," said Allen, reaching for Catherine's hand. "Last night, this lovely raven-haired lady made me the happiest man in the world when we were married by a justice of the peace across the river."

Flora coughed into her linen napkin. Alice grabbed the doorframe as if an earthquake had hit Brook Street. A sudden hush fell, followed by sounds of surprised chatter from both rooms of guests. "And that's not all!" continued Allen, smiling down at Catherine beside him. "We are expecting a baby next June." More sounds of surprise, murmurs. Elizabeth dropped a frying pan in the kitchen; the sound vibrated. Behind her at the table in the parlor, Alice heard a giggle. She turned around to see her aunt and uncle whispering. Cousin Annlea, with an amused smirk, caught Alice's eye.

Alice quickly turned back toward the dining room, holding her breath in anticipation of how her family would react to Allen's news. She knew her mother must wish to vanish from the dining room—even from the house—at this moment. However, Flora's show of composure didn't falter. The perfect hostess, despite everything changing at once, mused Alice. John Lea's frozen smile reminded Alice of the Cheshire Cat's grin.

She didn't feel as surprised as her family obviously did. She had suspected her brother and Catherine were being intimate. She remembered Allen's confession a couple of years ago of having whiskey in his car, and she had wondered what else might be going on between the couple, what other secrets they shared. Now they were married.

To Alice's surprise, Flora rose from her chair and went to the other side of the table to Allen and Catherine and put her arms around their shoulders. "Congratulations, my dears," said Flora. "May all of this end happily." Allen stood to embrace his mother as Catherine looked up, smiling through brimming eyes.

⌇⌇

As they prepared for bed that night, Alice sensed a storm brewing. Charlie, too quiet, had been sitting on his side of the bed, bent over, running his fingers through his hair. In her dressing table mirror, she watched him suddenly plant his feet on the floor and start pacing. He began speaking, spewing his anger toward Catherine and Allen, especially Allen. "Justice of the peace—they're not even married in the eyes of the Church! Lillian and Harold won't accept it. Mama would die again—of shame. I hope Harold gives Catherine what-for and gets her to see the light." Alice turned around, disturbed by Charlie's harangue, her shoulders hunched, limp strands of hair splayed across her pale neck. She watched Charlie's bare feet shuffling back and forth. "And an innocent baby too!"

"But we also—" Alice began, looking up.

"This is different. Don't you see what Allen's done? An instant family is his way of escaping the draft. He's a damned draft resister. Didn't even have the courage to plead a case of conscientious objector. He's cheating!"

Alice cringed at her husband's anger. By her calculations, the baby would have been conceived before Allen had time to consider his draft status. The draft had just been announced in September. Could Allen and Catherine have hatched a plot to conceive a baby so conveniently? Not likely, she thought. She opened her mouth to say so, but her breath left her. Charlie, in his undershirt and pajama bottoms, continued his rant.

"He's been thinking of a way out of the draft since day one. Now he's done it. The draft board will re-classify him as 3D, and he won't see military training after all."

Alice turned away and thought, I'm glad. Shouldn't Charlie be pleased too? His show of temper and self-righteousness made her stomach churn. She watched his reflection in her mirror and barely recognized the husband she loved and believed in.

"Allen's simply an unpatriotic draft resister, using other innocent people to help him. Lowest of the low. He's not welcome in my house again."

Alice gasped. "But it's my house too," she said, facing Charlie. "And he's my brother. Your sister—"

Charlie glared. "I don't care who they are. This is my decision. We'll not harbor draft evaders and unholy marriages in this house." He stomped out of the bedroom and into the bathroom, slamming the door with a force that shook the walls.

Alice stood up, her emotions trailing him. I've never seen Charlie like this, she thought. Is it war nerves that's turning him into a raving autocrat? What more can I say to him, she wondered. I tried to appeal but he's not listening. Surely he'll cool down, and then I will try again.

Judy awoke and began wailing. Alice slipped on her robe with worn satin trim and rushed to comfort her child. Judy stood in her crib, wide-eyed. Had she heard the harsh words? "Dada! Dada!" Her daughter reached up for comfort.

Alice picked her up. "Judy Star, my angel." Swallowing tears of fear and confusion, Alice wrapped her baby's favorite blanket—a snowy white coverlet crocheted by Aunt Henny—around her daughter and carried her to the rocking chair. They moved to the squeaking old rhythm of Alice's childhood. As they clung together, Alice thought about how she loved and trusted her protective big brother, firmly believing he had not used marriage and family to avoid the draft. After all, he would be thirty-five next year, no longer of draft age. He couldn't have known in September that he'd be called up immediately for military service. Besides, wouldn't Catherine have had a say about marriage and a baby?

Her cheeks damp against Judy's sweet head, Alice reflected that Charlie's shunning of Allen (and Catherine) was like tossing him into a coal bin, as dire a spot as the black hole Allen had saved her from in their childhood home on Brook Street. She squeezed her eyes tight and wished for a way to save her brother. She hoped Charlie would soon return to his reasonable nature. For now, Alice resolved to keep her thoughts between herself and her diary. Troubled, she fell asleep in the rocking chair, holding Judy close.

✥✥✥

Charlie came down the hall from the bathroom, observed his wife and child, and withdrew to bed alone.

22

"CHARLIE, CAN YOU watch Judy while I go to Nap's?" Alice called, as she pulled the plug in the kitchen sink, a tinge of whine in her request. Her errands had piled up on Saturday—the first weekend in December 1941. Charlie had driven the Plymouth to work all week, even on Wednesday—her usual day to keep the car. Christmas demands festered. Cards to write and address in her best handwriting. Shopping for presents—for everyone—and when is there time? Charlie was expecting some extra cookie-baking; he'd hinted as much. And a tree to purchase and decorate. It should all be so festive and fun, but it bore down on Alice—even with willing help from her parents and the Smith girls to babysit.

Charlie, already playing with two-year-old Judy in the living room, had clicked on the radio, hoping to catch moments of Saturday's basketball games. Judy squealed for his attention, "Watch, Dada!" as she tumbled headlong over sofa pillows on the floor.

Alice marched into the living room. "Charlie!" Eyeing the displaced pillows, she heaved a sigh, knowing that Charlie wouldn't be the one to put the living room back in order.

"Of course, I'll watch Judy. We're having fun!" He hugged the child as she toddled forward into his arms.

As Alice gathered up her pocketbook, handmade cloth grocery bags, and the stuffed-full wicker laundry basket, a regretful pang of jealousy clouded her mind, seeing her husband and daughter at play while she had chores to occupy most of her day. Charlie worked all week earning their keep. Why then did she feel so left out, put-upon? "Maybe I'll think about that tomorrow," she whispered to herself, borrowing Scarlett O'Hara's words.

Alice tackled her errands with edgy efficiency. At the square-front Laundromat, she tossed and stuffed her family's clothing into the washing machines, careless in separating the colors from whites. In Nap's Market next door, she barely acknowledged the friendly good morning of Mrs. Napolitano; she ignored Mr. Nap, as usual, considering him brusque. Alice went down her list quickly, familiar with what the shelves contained in close-together aisles. She diligently purchased the items budgeted for, nothing extra.

At the checkout, dark-eyed Mrs. Nap spoke in her faint voice. "Where is Miss Judy today? She is always so happy; I miss her singing."

Alice said abruptly, "She's with her daddy this morning."

"Oh, well, here's a stick of peppermint for her. Tell her it's from me."

"Swell. She'll like this," said Alice. Realizing she hadn't been pleasant, she added, "Thank you," and forced a smile. Alice picked up the two bags of groceries and carried them to the Plymouth. She deemed herself fortunate that milk, eggs, and butter were delivered to their front door every other day. It made for easier grocery shopping and lighter loads. She headed home to put the groceries away while the laundry churned in the machines.

When Alice arrived home, she noticed her parents' car parked in front of the house. She hadn't expected them and hoped nothing was wrong.

Her mother greeted Alice at the front door to help carry the shopping bags. Motioning to the living room, Flora said, "The men are busy." Alice saw her father and Charlie seated on the floor next to the radio, rolling a shaggy ball, homemade from a wool sweater, back and forth to Judy. "They're all just kids," added Flora. Alice smiled in agreement, still curious why her parents had arrived.

Flora revealed their mission. "We're on our way over to Allen and Catherine's. I wondered if you and Judy would like to come along. We know how Charlie feels about visiting them, but we thought you might—"

"Yes, it's a wonderful idea." Alice centered a bag of groceries on the kitchen table. The invitation lightened her mood. She didn't see enough of her brother and his family anymore. As predicted, Allen had been deferred from the draft; Charlie was even more adamant in enforcing his year-long boycott now that Allen's so-called plan had been successful. Alice appreciated that Charlie allowed her to visit with the younger Leas, despite his glowering demeanor when she did so. She wished she could see six-month-old Deborah more often. "Judy should get to know her cousin," Alice said to her mother. "Let me put these things away, and next, I have to go back to the Laundromat for the clothes."

"I'll come with you," volunteered Flora.

The prospect of visiting Allen and his family put a spring in Alice's step. With her mother's assistance, she quickly accomplished the bulk of her chores and set the rest aside.

꽁꽁꽁

Alice winced, as always, when John Lea pulled his Chevy onto Allen's paved driveway; if the brakes failed, they would plunge down the steep hillside and crash into the garage below. She saw Allen watching for their arrival at the front door of the brick bungalow. He shot out to the driveway in his shirtsleeves, despite the cold temperature.

"We made it!" said a relieved Alice as she stepped out of the car.

Allen laughed. "Always worried about that hill, aren't you, Sis! Nothing wrong with Dad's brakes. But I'd wonder if you didn't worry. It wouldn't be normal!"

Alice laughed at her characteristic anxiety, as she transferred Judy into Allen's welcoming arms. Flora and John piled out of the car, and Catherine came out of the house, carrying Deborah, hugging her close for warmth. Alice noted that the baby's silky curls had become a crown of reddish-blond ringlets, comparing her niece's coiffure to Judy's stubbornly straight hair, already like a manic halo in the breeze. With her grandmother's too-wide nose, Judy would not be another Shirley Temple, thought Alice, even though she sings like a canary.

Judy reached out toward her cousin's tempting curls. The baby blinked her long eyelashes. "Baby!" cooed Judy.

"She likes you," Catherine said. "Let's go inside so you and Deborah can play." Catherine started toward the house. "I've made a bit of lunch. Hope you're all hungry."

Alice nodded. Suddenly she felt ravenous.

After lunch, the men wandered off toward the master bedroom to listen to the second half of the Kentucky-Miami of Ohio game on the radio. Alice agreed to help Catherine polish her good silver. They sat on opposite sides of the large table that overwhelmed the dining room, an embroidered tablecloth spread with silverware. From her place in Allen's maroon mohair chair in the living room, Flora could eavesdrop on the younger women. The chair, ample for her son, made a cozy nest for Flora and her two granddaughters.

As the girls snuggled on her bosom, Flora sang softly: "There's a wee little man in a wee little house. . . ."

Judy joined in, on perfect pitch: ". . . lives over the way you see. And he sits at his window and sews all day making shoes for you and me."

Flora looked down at Judy with an approving smile; they joined voices for the chorus: "And rappy-tap-tap and rappy-tap-tap the hammers busy go. . . ."

Deborah laughed and kicked. Soon the girls became sleepy in their grand-mother's arms. Flora rocked them and listened to the conversation in the dining room. Alice and Catherine were talking about their mutual shadow of con-cern—Charlie's boycott.

Catherine was saying, ". . . not the fun weekends we used to have."

"I'm so sorry," said Alice.

With a deep sigh, Catherine set aside her cloth and the spoon she'd been polishing. "Why is Charlie such a goody-goody? He's more of a priest than Harold. At least Harold hasn't said anything about our marriage and certainly doesn't judge Allen for getting reclassified by the draft board."

"I know," sighed Alice.

"He's so perfect," continued Catherine, her voice rising. "No smoking. No this, no that. Does he ever wear anything but those starched white shirts? You're probably the only one who sees him in anything less."

Alice's mouth twisted in a wry smile. "The shirts aren't as perfect now that Charlie has quit sending his shirts to Allen's laundry. I'm not much at ironing."

"I'm sorry. I'm being hard on your husband. But he's my brother too, so I guess I have a right to talk—and defend myself and Allen!" Alice looked down at her tarnish-smudged fingers as Catherine continued, "I don't want you to feel bad. It's just that—"

"I know. It's sad—and hard on all of us, even Mother and Daddy." Alice looked over at Flora and the sleeping girls.

"At least Charlie allows you to visit us," said Catherine.

"Yes." Alice thought of her husband's scowl whenever she left the house to visit Allen's family. "I think it's so important for the girls to know each other. Maybe down deep, Charlie does too. And this is his compromise."

From the living room, Flora spoke up softly so as not to disturb the dozing girls. "I have an idea we might try. Maybe Charlie wouldn't object to a meeting on neutral ground." Alice and Catherine turned to listen. "Maybe tomorrow we could all drive up to the Stone Inn at Middlesboro for dinner and see their Christmas decorations. Why not include the Simpsons? Maybe Charlie would agree to join us if we make it a special occasion. Maybe this could be a way back for Charlie. In the Christmas spirit, perhaps?"

Alice glanced over at her sister-in-law and shrugged a shoulder. "Maybe. It's worth a try."

Catherine nodded. "Perhaps. The rest of us could go anyway. It sounds like fun."

Flora said, "Let's try it. Help me lay the girls down in Deborah's room, and we'll phone the Simpsons and the inn."

Alice fretted about how she would sweet-talk Charlie into joining them. Tiptoeing down the hallway with the sleeping girls, the women heard John and Allen cheering from the other bedroom.

"The Wildcats must have won," noted Flora.

Muted December sunbeams slipped through the west-facing windows of the living room on Pleasant Avenue. Slouched in his olive-green armchair, Charlie smiled as the basketball game ended in victory for Kentucky. Looking over at the empty sofa, his smile faded. The room exploded in quiet as he clicked off the radio. He felt disconnected and empty, with no one home to share a toast of *Old Dan'l* to his alma mater. A flash of anger struck. Flora, John, Alice—they all nagged his conscience the way they slid around his boycott of Allen and Catherine. He struck the chair arm with his fist and got up, resolving to displace his bad mood with a diversion.

Pacing the living room, Charlie thought of a precious few Saturday afternoons in the past summer, playing golf with Bonnie, followed by drinks in the clubhouse and a stolen kiss or two. She was beautiful and fun—always good for a laugh. They had established an agreed-upon time on Saturdays for chance golf encounters that, when available, either one or both would show up at the course. The two or three times they both arrived at Seneca, there had been no need to phone her, to break his resolution not to contact her.

But this was wintertime. He missed her. "Just this once," Charlie said aloud as he approached the wobbly telephone table in the hallway. Picking up the black receiver, he shook off an invisible restraining hand. Alice and Judy were not home; he needed someone to talk to, someone fun and flirty. The phone buzzed on the other end; then he heard Bonnie's voice.

Alice tried telephoning Charlie to suggest Flora's idea for tomorrow's gathering at Stone Inn. She chewed her lip, hoping that convincing words might fly out of her mouth. The phone responded with a busy signal. Alice tried to reach

Charlie for nearly an hour, deciding their home phone must be off the hook. Long phone conversations were unusual for Charlie; she would ask him about it later.

She heard Judy waking up, singing in her tiny, high voice. Alice smiled, hearing her daughter's attempt at entertaining Deborah. She cracked open the bedroom door. As she suspected, Judy was sitting up in the double bed, hair sticking out like a scarecrow's, dress wrinkled, bending over her drowsy baby cousin. Deborah's curls lay moist and sweaty, her face red and wrinkled where she'd been lying on a crease of the bedspread. She reached a chubby fist up to Judy, who was gently singing, "Good morning to you. . . ." Alice caught her breath and covered her mouth so as not to interrupt this adorable scene. These two little sweethearts together—a sight to surely melt Charlie's heart too! Alice strengthened her resolve to bring Allen's family back into the fold.

～～～

On Pleasant Avenue, the seminary clock sounded the eight notes of its Big Ben intonation, then struck four bongs for the hour. John Lea pulled his car to the curb, bringing Alice and Judy home. "Oh goodness," said Alice, "I'll have to think about supper soon. Want to stay? It's potluck."

John looked eager, but Flora gently reminded him, "We've got Leather-stocking Club tonight."

John's grin stopped short. "That's right." He adjusted the gearshift, turned off the ignition, and got out of the car to assist Alice and Judy. "Let me take her," he said, reaching for Judy.

"Oh, Daddy—your knees," protested Alice, eyeing the seven steps up the hill of their front yard.

"Never mind. Someday my little Star will be too big for this." Judy clamped her fingers around her grandfather's neck. With a large, gnarly hand on the railing, John made his way to the top step.

At the front door, Alice reclaimed her daughter from John's arms. "Bye, Papa," said Judy, reluctantly letting go of him. Alice, holding Judy, stood on the stoop until John started the car and drove away. She blew kisses to her parents, then turned back into the house to face Charlie.

Judy wanted down and ran into the living room. "Dada!"

As Alice took off her coat, she looked at the hall telephone and saw it resting innocently in its cradle. She picked up the receiver and heard a dial tone. So the upstairs phone was in place too. "Hmm!" Alice stared at the phone, wondering why she'd been unable to reach Charlie. The house was quiet, with no radio playing. Where was he? Did he go out? She wondered.

Judy started up the stairs. "Dada?" They heard the back door open and Charlie's familiar footsteps in the kitchen. Judy hurried down the stairs as fast as her two-feet-on-each-step gait would take her. "Dada!"

"Judy!" Charlie swept her up. "I missed you."

Alice saw he was wearing his black winter coat. Did he have a long phone call and then go somewhere? "Where were you?" she asked.

"Out—like you!" Charlie teased.

"But where?" she demanded.

"Easy, Alice. I was just putting the car in the garage. Did you forget—you left it out front after your errands this morning."

"You're wearing your overcoat!"

"It's chilly out! The car didn't warm up only going around to the alley."

Alice couldn't argue. "Did you catch the end of the game?"

"Yes, of course. Great game—close at the end! Did you know we won?" He lifted a giggling Judy above his head at arm's length, appearing at ease. "Coach Rupp's boys are off to a good start and—"

"I tried phoning you from Allen's for nearly an hour. The line was busy."

Charlie stopped tossing his daughter to stare at Alice. "What for?"

"I wanted to ask you a favor. Were you on the phone?"

Charlie looked down. "Must've been the party line," he mumbled.

"So, it wasn't you?" Alice watched his eyes. They were full of thought. She shifted topics, explaining the plans for the Sunday jaunt to Middlesboro with her parents, the Simpsons, Allen, Catherine, and Deborah. "Can we go?" She held her breath.

Charlie seemed to be twisting his mind around an answer. "Well, I guess so," he replied. "Are we all set then?"

"Of course." Alice was willing to stop puzzling about the hour-long busy telephone as she rejoiced in this moment of Charlie's agreeing to join her family tomorrow. She smiled broadly and repeated, "Of course."

With Judy in his arms, Charlie reached around to enfold Alice in a family hug. She felt their warm hearts beating in harmony. Amused, she moved away and suggested, "Here, let me take Judy so you can finally take off your coat."

Alice walked with Judy toward the kitchen. Turning back, she saw Charlie lift the phone receiver and re-set it in the cradle.

23

"Tonight Judy Star makes her debut at Stone Inn!" Alice said as she lifted her daughter out of the Babee-Tenda feeding table where she'd been drooling toast over Bunny's dress and whiskers. "Ooey gooey!" Alice wiped a smudge of butter from the girl's cheek. "Hope she behaves."

Charlie looked over, chewing his last morsel of sweet roll. "She will. She's a good girl." Getting up from the table, he stretched and said. "Guess I'll see what's on the Philco."

With the Sunday paper tucked under his arm, he sauntered over to the living room easy chair and turned on the radio. Judy, dragging Bunny along the floor, followed him. Charlie spun the radio dial. "Let's see what I can find, Judy," he said.

"Play!" she responded, holding her arms out wide.

Charlie laughed and nodded as he hit a station emitting a cheering-crowd noise. "Pro-football! Giants against Brooklyn!" he smiled. Judy frowned.

In the kitchen, Alice finished her last half-cup of coffee, looking out the window over the sink. So far, she mused, it had been a perfect Sunday. She had done her religious duty for the month by taking Judy to Mass with Charlie. When he added his vibrant tenor to the swelling chorus in the loft, Judy, thumb in mouth, stood spellbound, clinging to Charlie's trouser leg. Churchgoers in their pews turned around with admiring glances. Alice appreciated the choir and organ music for charming her two-year-old, but as Judy grew wigglier, church attendance became more of a chore.

Alice placed her everyday china cup in the sink and began clearing the other dishes from the table, picking up Judy's toast scraps from the checkerboard linoleum floor. With her arms in hot, soapy water and dishes bobbing, Alice gazed out the window, daydreaming about the afternoon ahead. The food at the Stone Inn was wonderful—the world's best fried chicken, gravy and biscuits, plus her favorite—corn pudding. Add in the old-fashioned Christmas décor—poinsettias and festive trees illuminating each room of the old stone house with its wide-planked floors, and she knew it could be a beautiful time. But worry intruded on her bright hope. If only today's gathering at Stone Inn would warm Charlie's heart enough to repair his breach with Allen and Catherine. Sighing, she ran the cold water for rinsing.

Alice left the kitchen, dishes sparkling in the drainer, to join her family in the living room. On the sofa, she grabbed the *Courier-Times*—a once-a-week diversion Charlie picked up on their way home from church. Alice skipped over the grim news on the front page: FDR's troublesome negotiations with Japan, atrocities in Europe. She scanned the funny pages and began reading *Li'l Abner*. Mammy and Pappy made her laugh; Mammy reminded Alice of a hillbilly Flora. Judy climbed onto her mother's lap; Alice began reading the funnies softly to the little girl. Charlie kept his ear to the radio. Judy laughed as her mother read aloud and made faces; after a while, Judy nodded off.

Charlie suddenly clicked off the radio, turning his attention to the pair on the sofa. He and Alice exchanged smiles as she stroked Judy's soft brown hair. "Halftime already!" Charlie announced. "Lots of running; it went fast." He started toward the kitchen to rummage for a snack.

"I'll lay Judy down." Alice gently shifted the sleeping girl and rose from the sofa to carry her upstairs. Judy must be fresh for the evening event. Concern for tonight's positive outcome sloshed in Alice's stomach as she laid Judy in her crib, careful not to awaken her.

Alice closed the door, checking to see that Judy dozed. The seminary clock chimed the half-hour; Alice held still, listening for her daughter to stir. All quiet, she tiptoed across the hall to her bedroom. She took bubble bath from her dressing table, gathered fresh underwear, and headed to the bathroom. A long bath would be a relaxing prelude to the family outing in a few hours.

Alice submerged herself under a mound of lavender-scented bubbles in the bathtub, eyes closed to the tiny black and white tiles and the green and orange fish splashing across the shower curtain. She relaxed, starting a daydream when she heard Charlie taking the stairs, running. He knocked on the door, then barged into the bathroom. He stood over the tub, breathless, hands flailing to express something he searched to speak words for. Had he suffered a stroke, Alice wondered. She sat up, suds dripping off her breasts. "What is it?"

Excited, Charlie blurted out, "They broke in on the football game—Japan has attacked the American fleet at Pearl Harbor!"

"Japan?" Alice wrinkled her forehead. "Pearl Harbor? Where's that?"

Charlie cleared his throat, but his voice strained. "It's in Hawaii—our Navy base in Hawaii." He sat down on the edge of the bathtub, head in hands. "While we were watching the action in Europe, the Japs sneaked up on our blind side." He ran a hand through his hair; the ends stood up crazily. To Alice he looked insane, with eyes bulging behind his glasses.

"What kind of attack, Charlie? How bad?"

"They're just getting the news of an air raid. Lots of bombs dropped on airfields and battleships in the harbor. One ship—the Oklahoma—was set on fire." He paused, then continued in a quivering voice. "American boys—our men—are dying out there. Over 300 killed by one bomb." Charlie shook his head, hands covering his face.

The enormity was difficult for Alice to imagine. She stared at the squares of tiles above the tub. This can't be happening, she thought, as the blacks and whites blurred and converged in her vision. Why today? Why ever? She tried to think of anyone she might know in the service: the Nap's Market family, their oldest in the Navy. Charlie's friend, Stan, recently drafted. Had Charlie also thought of him? Or of boys from the barrel factory who were called up? What if Charlie and Allen had been drafted! She reached out a soapy hand to touch her husband's arm. Charlie looked up, deadpan. His mouth twisted.

Suddenly Alice remembered. "Hawaii! Aren't Henny and Stuart wintering in Hawaii?"

"That's right, I guess." He looked dazed.

"Oh, my goodness. Where would they be? Get me out of here. I must call Mother."

"Calm down, Alice. I'm sure your aunt and uncle aren't at any Navy base."

"But how close could they be? Bombs can miss their targets." She raised herself, creating a tidal surge in the tub.

Charlie reached to grab Alice's towel and help her out, soapsuds and all. His eyes popped at the sight of her glistening body in suds up to her neck. "You should see yourself!" he chuckled, quickly kissing off a couple of well-placed bubbles.

Alice felt agitated. What a time for Charlie to get amorous! "Now I remember—they're at Waikiki Beach. Where's that?"

"Calm down, Shh." He wrapped the towel around his wife and held her close. "I'll go down and find out more," he said against her damp ear. "You get dressed, and try not to worry!"

∽∾∾

Leaving Alice to dress, Charlie heard the phone ring and rushed to answer the bedroom extension. Flora's voice sounded unnaturally loud and shaky: "We've just heard the news about Pearl Harbor. At least three battleships have been sunk. It's horrible." There was a choking pause before she continued. "I wanted you and Alice to know we've canceled our evening at Stone Inn. Under the circumstances—no one can even think!" Flora spoke in staccatos between sobs. Charlie nodded and listened. "We're so deeply worried about Stuart and Henny," she told him.

"Have you heard from them?" Charlie asked.

His mother-in-law took a deep breath. "No. And we don't know whether to expect to or not. It's so uncertain—we all need to pray."

"Yes, of course."

Suddenly, Alice, in her silky white underwear, was at Charlie's ear, grabbing for the phone. "Mother! Mother!" Charlie pulled Alice close so they could listen together to Flora's tumbling words.

"Is Waikiki Beach anywhere near Pearl Harbor?" Charlie butted in.

"Yes, I'm afraid so. John checked the Atlas, and it's on the same island." Alice bit her nails and shifted nervously on her feet. She and Charlie leaned in but heard only a crackling silence. Suddenly Flora seemed to gather herself and asked, "Will you all come to our house for supper this evening? We can face this together. It will help."

Alice snatched the phone from Charlie. "Oh, I hope so," she exclaimed into the mouthpiece. Charlie stepped away and let Alice continue. "Will Allen and Catherine be there too?" she asked. He met her eyes with a grim stare. "Oh, they're already there!" Alice gave a surprised chuckle. Charlie shrugged and turned away. He went downstairs to catch more news on the radio.

∽∾∾

Updates of the Pearl Harbor attack continued breaking through the afternoon's broadcasts. By evening the frightful news streamed across the airwaves: Two surges of attacks from Japanese dive and torpedo bombers sank nineteen vessels, five of them battleships. All aircraft at nearby airfields were damaged or destroyed. Over 2,000 American lives had been lost.

Charlie and Alice listened. One moment teary-eyed, another terrified, she watched her husband, sunk in thought. Was he thinking about his and Allen's deferred military service? What if they had been at Pearl Harbor? Her stomach clenched at the thought. Could she have handled the fearful shock of not knowing their fates? She shuddered. Not wanting to entertain the horrible thought a moment longer, she shook her head to clear her mind. It was bad enough not knowing where Stuart and Henny were at this hour.

Charlie refused Flora's invitation for supper with the Lea families but allowed Alice and Judy to take the car and go without him.

"No. I'm staying with you," Alice said firmly. She longed for Flora and John's comforting wisdom, yet couldn't bear the thought of leaving her sad husband at home alone. She and Charlie sorely needed to see each other through this terrible night. Her parents would have to wait.

A demanding wail from upstairs shook Alice back into Sunday normalcy. Naptime over, she bounded upstairs to welcome Judy into their darkening evening. The radio announcements continued periodically. The child grew bored and fretful with her distracted parents. They had forgotten about mealtime until Judy reminded them with a fit of crying. Charlie clicked off the radio. "Enough for a while," he said. "Let's eat."

They found leftovers in the refrigerator, meager in comparison to the feast at Stone Inn Alice had anticipated. Such innocent pleasures, along with a healthy appetite, seemed part of a past life.

As Charlie and Alice wearily prepared for bed, they were interrupted by the jangling telephone. "Flora?" Charlie, in his striped pajamas, answered the bedroom phone. "Any news?"

Alice raced downstairs, slippers flapping, to pick up the phone receiver in the hall. She heard her mother say, "I'll read the telegram: *In shock, sorrow. Physically okay. Bird watching on Koko Head. Witnessed the bombers. Wish we were home. Return when possible. Love Stuart and Henny.*

"It's such a relief knowing they're safe, at least for now." Flora paused. "Charlie, it's all about family and country, isn't it? When we look at the big picture, can we try to forget our small differences?"

Alice appreciated her mother's words, hoping the admonition would weigh on Charlie. She quietly hung up the receiver on her end so no one knew she'd been listening, afraid to hear his response. Alice guessed she would know soon enough whether he would forgive Allen and Catherine. The world had changed. Could Charlie?

24

CHARLIE ROSE FROM the depths of sleep as if emerging from a bad dream. An attack on U.S. territory felt surreal. Had he and Alice spent most of yesterday feeling victimized, bombarded with the news that war had come to their homeland? Inconceivable—war always happened somewhere else, out of sight, out of mind. With morning light filtering onto the peach-colored bedroom walls, a rush of adrenalin pulsed through him. He wanted to know more, act on the offensive, protect his family and country. Charlie looked over at Alice, still sound asleep. No chatter from Judy's room. He hopped out of bed and tiptoed downstairs, hardly noticing his feet chilling on bare floorboards. He crossed the living room carpet to turn on the radio.

A newscaster talked breathlessly as if hyperventilating. Reports continued about the four-hour attack on Pearl Harbor: battleships sunk, thousands of Americans dead, confused reports of attacks on Guam and the Philippines. Charlie turned off the radio. He would head to work as soon as he dressed and grabbed a bite of toast. In the company of other men at work, he would peruse the newspaper with its heavy black headlines and photographs of warships and airplanes. With the others, he would learn the latest news, discuss the rumors, and face challenges to the peaceful lives they owned the day before yesterday.

Rushing into their upstairs bedroom for Alice's goodbye kiss, he saw her stretching and gazing out the window onto Pleasant Avenue's seminary campus. She turned at his approach. "Why up so early?"

"I need to see how the world's going this morning."

Alice's "Oh—" sounded like a moan.

"I'll be in touch." Charlie kissed Alice's furrowed brow.

She raised a hand. "I don't think I'll stay here today. I don't want to be alone."

Charlie stood gazing intently at her face. "Where will you go?"

"I'll call Daddy to come pick up Judy and me. I'd like to be with my parents today."

"Good plan," agreed Charlie. "Oh—Judy's awake," he added as Judy hollered from her crib for the morning bottle she couldn't yet give up.

He hurried to his daughter's room for a quick hug. "Mommy's coming," he assured her before dashing downstairs, his wingtips clicking on the varnished surfaces. He grabbed his gray fedora off the closet shelf, yanked his overcoat off the hanger, forced the squeaky door shut, and set off to work.

In the wood-paneled fortification of Limestone Cooperage, Charlie listened in with a nationwide radio audience as President Roosevelt addressed a joint session of Congress. Tom Stevens's desk became the gathering spot for Charlie, other accountants, and managers—all men in shirtsleeves, neckties askew, leaning in to catch the president's words over the buzzing radio. The women, mostly secretaries, kept business afloat, answering the few telephone calls that came in. They awaited second-hand news from the men.

⸙

With Judy cuddled in her arms, Alice sat on the floor in front of her parents' Tombstone radio with its inner light and reassuring hum. Her father rested in his Morris chair, staring at fireplace embers dancing on the asbestos; his long legs crossed, feet pushed into leather slippers, arms dangling. Flora bustled about until she heard the president announced. Even Judy, in her blue cotton dress, rumpled by her mother's embrace, listened to Roosevelt's commanding voice:

"Yesterday, December seventh, 1941—a date which will live in infamy—the United States of America was suddenly and deliberately attacked. . . ."

For nearly seven minutes, Alice was frozen to her spot on the floor in front of her father's chair. She peered into the radio, seeking closeness to the president's every word. She paid little attention to John's slippered foot at her backside and Judy's restless little fingers twiddling with her hair. A chill traveled up Alice's spine as Roosevelt declared, "A state of war has existed between the United States and the Japanese Empire. . . ." She exhaled a long-held breath. A war! How vulnerable are we all, she wondered, turning to look at her father.

"Here we go again," sighed John, who had witnessed the First World War as a father with young children. "Doesn't the world ever learn?"

~∽∼◡

Within an hour after Roosevelt's speech, Congress approved the war declaration with only one dissenting vote. The babble of excited conversations quieted as men at the cooperage offices returned to their desks. A few stopped to discuss the news with their secretaries. Charlie heard a cohort say, "I'll be signing up tomorrow." He didn't share the man's eagerness, but it struck a nerve as he realized he and Allen would both be waiting on the sidelines now that war was declared. Their statuses were the same.

~∽∼◡

Alice remained seated on the floor, shock still, staring at the radio oracle with its wooden architecture. Flora came over and switched it off. "I think it's time we ate a little something." Judy, whimpering, hugged her mother's neck. Alice roused herself back into the damaged day. For the second time in two days she'd forgotten mealtime. Groaning, she got up from the floor and took Judy's hand.

"Let's help Grandma in the kitchen."

A short while later, Alice lay Judy down for a nap in her old bed upstairs. The child seemed sleepy, reflecting her mother's exhaustion. Alice resisted the urge to lie down; instead, she curled up in a sunny patch on the window seat. Below her sprawled Brook Street, scarce of traffic. She guessed everyone had been indoors by their radios, listening to the president, too stunned to venture out.

The president's entire speech had been solemn and terrifying to Alice. However, it particularly worried her when Roosevelt said, "American ships have been reported torpedoed on the high seas between San Francisco and Honolulu." She wondered where Stuart and Henny could be. She also worried that war might strike the west coast and continue like wildfire into Kentucky. War scenes from *Gone With the Wind* came to mind. She visualized sudden bursts of black smoke, flames consuming city blocks, the shocking sights of destroyed bodies, and devastation all around.

Alice looked down from the bedroom window upon her beloved rock garden as a glint of quartz caught her eye. Nothing bloomed. The rocks were barren—but not completely. As she gazed, she observed patches of green among the bleak boulders. She remembered how the moss grew, sending up wispy filaments, like threads, bearing tiny beak-like spores aloft to produce future life.

Now is the time for us to imitate the moss, to survive amid desolation, to send up threads of green hope from the dark ground of war. That's good, Alice mused, looking around for a pencil and paper to record these thoughts for her diary.

Tuesday evening, long after their usual bedtime, Alice and Charlie, in pajamas, robes, and slippers, sipped cups of Ovaltine, listening again to President Roosevelt on their radio in the living room. He spoke to calm America's fears, to warn against false rumors, and to explain the necessity of limiting information during wartime.

Charlie had been feeling guilty about seeming unpatriotic while twenty men from the cooperage office and factory had enlisted in the military in the past two days. "Some of us men need to stay at our desks. Mr. Stevens says we might think about hiring women as barrel makers now—can you imagine!" he told Alice. She rolled her eyes.

Charlie took heart when the president said, "Every single man, woman, and child is a partner in the most tremendous undertaking of our American history. We must share together. . . ." The words comforted Charlie, convinced he could play a patriotic role, even if not called for active military service. FDR continued speaking about the sacrifices all must make—without considering it sacrifice—"to give one's best to our nation."

Upstairs, as they got into bed, Charlie began discussing ways they could help the war effort. He said, "The president mentioned conserving food. Can you believe it—back to life in the Depression!"

"I'll be on duty in the kitchen," Alice said, giving a mock salute.

Charlie grinned, then sobered. "He also said metals will be scarce. So I guess no new car."

Alice patted her belly. "We'll be tight in the Plymouth. That is if a new baby is actually on the way."

"We'll manage," Charlie assured her, secretly glad of another excuse to keep his little coupe but realizing four would be a crowd.

Alice assailed her pillow with a forceful whack.

"Don't take it out on a helpless pillow!" He reached over and pulled Alice close against him. She snuggled to his neck as he stared at the ceiling, gathering more thoughts. After a few moments, he spoke again. "I know something I can do right away. And your mother would approve," said Charlie.

"What's that?" She looked up past his chin.

"Pray. We can always pray."

"Good! I'm sure Mother and Daddy will too." She pulled up the covers, turning her back.

A few seconds later, he added, "I'm starting tomorrow. Daily Mass." This affirmation felt like a solid start.

Alice sat up, laughing down into Charlie's solemn face. "What time is that?"

"I guess around six or seven."

"Look at the clock—it's nearly midnight. You'll never make it up that early." Her smile questioned his sincerity.

Not to be taken for a slacker, he replied. "Okay. I'll start Thursday." That was his best shot for helping the war effort—at the moment. He looked forward to a good night's sleep.

～～～

On Thursday, Germany declared war on the U.S., and Congress reciprocated. The world was at war again.

Alice confided in her diary:

Everything is different. We were all innocent babies with wide smiles before Pearl Harbor. Now we are old people with tired, frightened eyes. Charlie and I must shield our precious Judy—and maybe another baby coming—from the horrible realities of this world as long as we possibly can. I'm thinking of the Bible verse that says 'woe to those who are with child or have babies at the breast.' The present time feels like the end of days, but I won't worry for myself. Please, God, let our children grow up secure and happy. Never let them see the hideous face of war.

25

T HE HANDFUL OF people at Monday morning Mass huddled in the front pews, close to the scents of beeswax candles and incense. The daily Mass at Holy Angels felt more serene and intimate than the Sunday version with its full choir and sermon, coughing and fidgeting congregation. The church's open beam ceiling resembled the roof of the Nativity stable on a side altar. Charlie knelt reverently as the priest mumbled in Latin and altar boys, in flowing cassocks, struggled to stay upright on their knees. He focused on the manger scene, with straw bedding, farm animals, and the expectant family (no Baby Jesus in place yet). Pleasant thoughts flitted through Charlie's mind, from his farm boyhood to his present-day life as a family man awaiting his second child. He prayed for Alice, Judy, and their unborn baby. He prayed for his sister Lillian in war-focused Washington D.C.; his brother Harold, likely saying Mass at St. Ann's this morning; and his other scattered siblings. Charlie said a prayer for his friend Stan, who was on war duty in the Pacific. He added a quick *Hail Mary* for Bonnie and asked for God's blessing on Alice's parents.

He stopped, troubled at the thought of Allen and Catherine. Of course, he should pray for his sister and her husband to re-do their marriage vows in the Catholic Church. Charlie had let go of his resentment toward Allen's draft avoidance, as the coincidence of timing with Catherine's pregnancy was unclear. Besides, with the nation at war, Charlie's and Allen's selective service standings were the same. But his sister's marriage by a justice of the peace rankled.

The priest intoned, "Pater Noster . . ." loud enough for the assembly to hear. Charlie didn't need his Missal's translation to say the Lord's Prayer to himself as the priest trailed on in Latin. Charlie came to "forgive us our trespasses as we forgive those. . . ." Alice and Flora wished him to forgive Allen and Catherine. Shouldn't he insist on his younger sister's obedience to the Church? How could he condone what she had done?

At Communion time, the priest came down the steps from the white and gold altar with its cluster of doll-faced angels at the top border. He stood at the altar railing, holding an ornate chalice in one hand, a tiny circle of thin bread in the other, as parishioners rose from their pews to receive the sacrament. With the priest stood a round-faced altar boy wearing an embroidered surplice, holding a flat gold tray. Looks like an angel, thought Charlie, wondering if his next child might be a future altar boy. As he rose from his knees, Charlie heard kneeling benches bang, row after row, like a noisy wave against the backs of pews. Advancing to the aisle, he saw a friend walk past, hands folded—Ted Hawkes from Holy Angels men's club. The short auburn-haired woman in front of him must be Ted's wife. Charlie made a mental note to speak with them after Mass.

The morning ritual ended promptly at 7:45 a.m. for the altar boys to arrive at their desks in the adjacent school building by eight o'clock. Outside in the brisk, cloudy morning, Charlie found Ted and his wife standing on the sidewalk leading to the street. Ted raised his hand in a friendly greeting. Ted Hawkes impressed Charlie as more like an owl than a hawk, with his horn-rimmed glasses and bookish manner. Ted was one of the wiseacres and punsters among the men's club members. He introduced his wife, Theresa. The fluttering of her dark eyelashes made Charlie wonder if she were flirting or had simply applied too much mascara. She spoke softly to him, "So happy to meet you."

In their brief conversation, Charlie divulged his intent to attend Mass three days a week to pray for a quick victory to end the war. "What a lovely idea!" Theresa batted her eyelashes. Turning to Ted, she said, "We could do that too." To Charlie, she explained, "We were only coming during Advent. But continuing daily Mass afterward is a wonderful suggestion. If more people prayed—"

Ted broke in, "Theresa has a direct line to the Man Upstairs. Her prayers count!"

Charlie laughed and said to Theresa, "Glad to make your acquaintance!"

"We're on our way home for breakfast before Ted goes downtown to the newspaper office. Can you join us?"

"Sounds swell," said Charlie. "Could I have a rain check some other time? Alice is expecting me, and then I have to rush off to work too."

In a few more minutes of chatter, Ted and Charlie learned that their offices were only three blocks apart. "Why don't we share rides sometime, save on gas? They say rationing might happen," suggested Ted.

"Good plan," said Charlie as he hurried off to his Plymouth at the curb.

Over toast and coffee, Charlie told Alice about the Hawkes couple and their plans to share rides, even occasional breakfasts after weekday Mass. "Theresa reminds me a bit of my sister Lillian—same color hair, small bones." He didn't mention Theresa's flirty eyes.

"It's awfully kind of them to offer breakfast. But I hope you didn't say I'd return the favor."

"No. I knew you wouldn't be up to it—with Judy and all."

"And morning sickness," Alice reminded him.

The schedule evolved so that Charlie would have breakfast with the Hawkeses on Fridays after Mass. On the Fridays Ted drove them to work, Charlie would take the bus to Holy Angels and meet them there. Alice could have alternate Fridays to use the Plymouth, in addition to her usual Wednesdays when Charlie took the bus to work. One Friday remained for Alice to finish her Christmas shopping.

"Now, don't spend too much," Charlie cautioned. "There's a war on!"

❧❧❧

Alice said to Flora over the phone: "This would be a first for you, Mother—not having the family for Christmas."

"Well, maybe it's time to share. After all, Allen and Catherine's first Christmas in their new home is a special occasion. Deborah's first Christmas too."

Alice felt a pang of rebuke. She and Charlie had not hosted their first Christmas on Pleasant Avenue, nor either of Judy's two Christmases. Alice hadn't possessed the energy to break with family tradition.

Flora continued, "My only regret is that Elizabeth won't have her regular job cooking for us this holiday. Maybe I'll offer her to Catherine. If Catherine doesn't want to use her, I'll give Elizabeth a big Christmas check."

"You always take care of everyone, Mother." She spoke in a gentle tone but reserved the sarcasm to herself. Flora's patronizing of Catherine stung. Alice couldn't help her own lack of confidence in hosting large dinner parties. So all right, if Catherine wants to host this year's Christmas dinner, so be it.

Alice and her mother shared a concern that Charlie might refuse to attend the dinner at Allen and Catherine's. "I'd sure be in a pickle then. Don't exactly know what I'd do."

"Just make him come," Flora clipped.

Alice realized her mother might easily manage her father, but Charlie couldn't be bossed. "Well, maybe I could cry a lot," she replied.

❧❧❧

When Alice told Charlie about the Christmas dinner invitation to her brother's home, he said he would think about it. Later that night, he stretched out on his side of the bed in his undershirt and boxer shorts, waiting for Alice to finish her bath. He bent one arm under his head like a pillow. Atop the green satin quilt, Charlie thought about Catherine and Allen's invitation. Unbidden, his long-dead mother, Josephine, popped into his head, recalling childhood Christmases on the farm. Their whitewashed farmhouse with the rambling front porch became a magical holiday scene each year. The farm prospered; Charlie and his siblings had plenty to eat. On Christmas, bounty rained from heaven: bananas and exotic nuts, stockings by the fireplace filled with oranges and sweets. Strings of cranberries adorned a pine tree Papa had felled. In the kitchen, Mama concocted a pork roast or duckling and cornmeal hushpuppies. Charlie recalled exactly the aroma of Mama's sage dressing. He remembered Catherine, at about age ten, helping their mother make it. His sister's face beamed as she carried the platter of dressing to the table for Papa's approval.

I wonder if she still has that recipe, Charlie mused.

The question remained: should he set foot in this sinful couple's home? What would Mama advise? He almost heard her say, "She's your sister. Love and protect her," as she sent the children off for the day at the country school. He remembered Catherine's cool trusting hand in his.

"It's Allen who has led her astray," Charlie said to the Mama in his head.

She replied, "If Catherine loves him can he be so bad? Is shunning the answer? Does Alice agree with you?"

Just then, the scent of Alice, fresh from her bath, caught Charlie's attention. The *Blue Hour* perfume always excited him. Alice, in her clingy silk nightgown, set down her bottles of bubble bath and perfume on the dressing table. She caught Charlie's eyes in the mirror. "A penny for your thoughts," she said with a coy smile.

"All dull and boring until right now." Charlie propped himself on one elbow.

Alice turned to him over her shoulder. A strand of strawberry blond hair fell over one eye. A blue strap of nightgown glided down her arm.

"You don't look pregnant," said Charlie.

"What do I look like? A wife? Veronica Lake?" With her fingers, she pulled her hair across her right eye.

"You look like that beautiful girl I saw waiting for me at the end of the long driveway at the tobacco barn. Only prettier."

"That was nearly five years ago," said Alice.

"And even younger," added Charlie. He stood up and swept Alice into his arms. They tumbled onto the bed.

"Well, have you thought about it?" Alice asked her husband when she woke up in his arms the next morning, the Saturday before Christmas.

Charlie smiled. "In my dreams." He threw his arm over Alice. "Want to go again?"

She pulled away, laughing. "I meant—have you thought about Christmas?"

Charlie squinted, trying to refocus. He figured out what Alice meant but teased, "We can do it on Christmas too."

"Oh Charlie!" Alice pushed him away. He chuckled at her pretend exasperation, enjoying the playful moment.

Later in the day, Charlie phoned his brother Harold at the parish in Morgantown to seek counsel on Catherine's *situation*.

"My advice?" said Harold. "Let it go. Allen and Catherine have done nothing to hurt anyone. Yes, they did wrong marrying as they did, but you're not correcting that by how you're treating them."

"I can't approve. How can you?"

"Forgiving doesn't mean approving. Put it in God's hands, and you'll be happier. You'll make everyone happier. Guaranteed! It can be your Christmas gift to the family."

Charlie didn't reply. Then Harold said, "I hope to see you at Catherine's on Christmas."

"You're going to be there?"

"I wouldn't miss it. And I want to see you, Alice, and Judy too."

Charlie couldn't argue with his older brother—and a priest to boot. He imagined the sunshine of his mother's smile as he placed the phone in its cradle. He went to find Alice and tell her of his decision to attend the family's Christmas dinner.

⌇⌇⌇

Christmas came to the Lea and Lukas families at Allen and Catherine's bungalow, perched over its snowy backyard resembling a ski slope. Inside, the living room was crowded, the temperature rising. Catherine had disguised the usual cigarette scent with cinnamon candles assisted by the aromas of roasting and baking. The women chatted in the cramped kitchen, then shifted to the hallway to allow Catherine room to prepare the meal, including Mama Josephine's sage dressing. Flora and Alice stood ready to assist with preparations and serving. The men—Charlie, Allen, John, and Harold—entertained the younger generation by exploring the Christmas tree, rattling the festively wrapped presents, and playing with Allen's childhood clown doll, Flippity Flop, freed again from the Leas' attic trunk. As Allen talked for Flippity in falsetto, Judy and Deborah squealed with laughter.

Catherine announced, "Soup's on!" The family quickly filed into the pristine dining room, a table set with gleaming silver and china, tapered Christmas candles, and ruby red water glasses. Seven chairs plus two high chairs were placed close together, but no one seemed to mind jostling elbows.

"Isn't it grand being together! It's lovely, Catherine," said Flora. "Thanks to you and Allen for doing all this."

Missing from the scene were Henny and Stuart; they had made it back from Hawaii by passenger ship as far as Los Angeles, deciding to rest there awhile. Lillian Lukas was also absent; she had been afraid to venture away from home, with her disability, when she knew the trains would be packed with the military.

The family stood behind their chairs, heads bowed, waiting for Harold's invocation. Alice lifted her eyes as far as she could without lifting her head to disrupt the circle of downward chins. Allen looked so proud and fatherly holding baby Deborah, curly locks crowning her head. Alice felt like a queen mother, watching princess Judy enthroned in her high chair, a bib tucked over her royal red velvet dress. The child waved her curved-handle baby spoon as if to hurry up the proceedings.

Harold's eyes were shut tight. "Let us hold hands." Alice took hold of Deborah's soft fingers as she perched on her father's right arm. At the table's head, Allen reached over to Charlie on his left. The others joined hands.

༺ঞঞ

Charlie couldn't believe he and Allen were touching, as he glanced at his brother-in-law, whose big head bowed reverently.

Harold prayed: "God, through your son Jesus, who was born this day, we ask you to bless all the family here and those not able to join us. Enfold us in your love, keep us safe from harm. Bless our nation in the cause of righteousness we defend. Bring the light of peace to the world. Let us give thanks for each other and the bounty we are about to receive. Amen."

"Amen." echoed Charlie. He released Allen's hand, conceding to himself that forgiveness would take place—in time.

Christmas afternoon flashed into evening, with the family returning to the kitchen at intervals to glean leftovers. They listened to Christmas music on the radio and opened gifts, as the Christmas tree shed its pine needles and prickly scent. Deborah clutched a new teddy bear as she nursed her nighttime bottle in Catherine's arms. Judy kept herself awake, playing with Flippity Flop amid the opened gifts and tissue paper under the Christmas tree. The grownups' talk turned to the subject of the war.

Charlie's heart fluttered as he announced that he had signed up to be a captain for the civil defense office and would be in charge of neighborhood air raid drills. He would soon receive training and a shipment of helmets and supplies to distribute to the block wardens. He smirked as he felt all eyes on him. They should now plainly see he would do his part for the war effort.

John's announcement knocked him for a loop. His father-in-law said he would have to register for the draft. "That's right! Men eighteen to sixty-five are now required to register. I barely made it under the wire." He took the shine off Charlie and now looked like the patriot in the room.

"That's hard to believe," Charlie mumbled, not knowing what else to say.

"Yep. It's an old man's war now," said Allen.

"I can't imagine they would allow you into any battle—with your knees!" said Flora.

"Well, I can't either, my dear," John agreed. "However, I can do a mean job holding down a desk—if they actually get around to drafting me."

Allen broke in with a further announcement: "I'm leaving my job at the Pauling Laundry and will go to work at the munitions plant opening up in about a week."

Charlie felt a shock wave sweep around the room; it rattled his confounded nerves. He sought Catherine's eyes as she avoided the family's incredulous gazes. She shifted Deborah to her other shoulder. As the questions began tumbling at once, Catherine excused herself to put her daughter to bed.

∽◗◖∼

Alice, silent during the men's announcements, scooped up Judy from her playthings on the floor and followed Catherine and Deborah into the hallway.

"Ready for bed too?" Catherine whispered to Judy. The girl nodded.

"We really need to go home," Alice told her sister-in-law. "But I can't leave yet—I think I might faint. Daddy registering for the draft—and Allen!" Her voice quivered. "He's just started managing at the new branch laundry. Why in heaven's name!"

A half-smile flickered on Catherine's face. "He's decided. It's what he wants. Mr. Pauling has been very good about it too." They listened to the men and Flora's jumbled conversation in the living room.

Allen's voice rose above the din. "The laundry business may slow down with a war on. The future is uncertain at this point."

Alice walked back into the living room, as Catherine escorted the little girls to the bedroom. Electricity surged through the group; everyone's face looked pale. Or was she projecting her bereft feelings onto everyone else?

Allen was saying, "I'll have a supervisory position at the factory. I'll be serving my country. The plant makes and tests gunpowder for ammunition in military rifles."

"I don't like that one bit. Isn't it awfully dangerous?" asked his mother.

"It can be," acknowledged Allen. "So happens that safety is part of my job—to make sure the factory is kept spotless. Cleanliness is important because of the dangerous materials. I guess they liked my laundry background. Figured I was the guy to keep things clean!" He chuckled; the family stared. Alice swallowed a sob. How could Allen make so light of this?

⁓⁓⁓

On the ride home, the Plymouth hummed and bounced Judy to sleep, as Alice held her tight. Biting his lip, Charlie kept his eyes on the road, alert for snowy patches. He could feel the gravity of Alice's mood. Reading her thoughts, Charlie took one hand off the steering wheel to reach across the hump of their sleeping daughter. "The pay is good, you know."

"It had better be," said Alice. "Allen is giving up a lot. And despite his cute remarks about keeping things clean, it sounds like a dangerous job to me."

Her mouth a taut line, she moved her hand away from Charlie's. He watched her turn and stare out the window into frosted darkness.

26

A WINTRY NIGHT in January 1942. Moonlight streamed through the windshield of the Plymouth. Between her parents in the front seat, Judy smiled back at the friendly pale face she knew from *Old Mother Goose*. Happy with Grandma's coconut cake and RC Cola in her tummy, Judy nestled against her mother for the ride home. The scent of Alice's *Blue Hour* perfume and rabbit fur boa tickled Judy's elfin nose as she laid her head on the bump of her mother's belly. The car's heater was on high; Judy, with her eyes shuttered, toes cozy, waited for her father to begin singing.

The Plymouth's percussion section started as the tires slapped a steady beat on the pavement. The hum of the motor, accented by rising tones of the shifting gears, provided the overture for Charlie's clear voice: "Oh, give me a home where the buffalo roam, where the deer and the antelope play. . . ." When he reached the chorus of "Home, home on the range . . . ," tears seeped from under Judy's eyelids.

She tried not to sniffle as she heard her mother say, "She's doing it again."

A passing car's horn beeped two notes, and Charlie suggested, "How about this one!" He began with an upbeat tempo, "Yippee Ti Yi Yo, get along little dogies. It's your misfortune and none of my own." More tears trickled down Judy's cheeks.

"She's getting me damp," complained Alice. "It's the 'doggies,' I guess. Please, no more cowboy songs."

Judy heard a deep chuckle as her dad said, "I sure have the gift. . . ."

The girl's head popped up. "Gift?" she repeated, wiping her face with her hand.

Charlie laughed and patted the top of Judy's head. "Not that type of gift—a talent! Singing is my gift to you. Sorry to make you sad."

Judy felt puzzled about a gift not wrapped and tied with a bow. Her head too heavy for thinking, she lay back down against Alice's warmth. "No gifts, Daddy." She rubbed her moist nose against her mother's coat before settling to sleep as the car rocked and hummed.

∽⌒∾

After a while, Charlie said, "By the way, Theresa Hawkes invited me to join the Holy Angels choir."

"So, somebody else thinks you can sing," responded Alice in a teasing tone. She considered herself the biggest fan of Charlie's vocal talent.

"Why yes! Somebody who knows music."

"A musician then?" Alice said dismissively, spurred by a pinch of jealousy.

"She has a beautiful soprano voice—outstanding!"

"I guess I've heard her belting it out in the choir," said Alice. Theresa's effusive singing annoyed Alice.

"She's not showing off, you know," defended Charlie. "Her voice carries naturally. She's a leader."

Alice didn't answer, not wanting to sound negative and invite further praise of Theresa. The quiet roar of the heater and sloshing of tires on the wintry street filled a lull in their sharpening dialogue.

"You'd like Theresa and Ted if you got acquainted," Charlie commented.

"Well, I appreciate them feeding you breakfast and sharing the drive to work." Although the fellowship that excluded her festered.

"But you don't know them. We could be good friends. They play Bridge. We could—"

"And we don't, not that much—with Mother and Daddy sometimes. Mother loses her patience."

"I know. Theresa wouldn't though. She's very considerate."

"So, you think I need that? A friend to overlook my mistakes!" Alice's irritation spilled over.

"Just at Bridge." Charlie cleared his throat and looked at Alice cautiously. "I'll take that as a maybe," he concluded.

∽⌒∾

In late February, they accepted Theresa and Ted's invitation for an evening of Bridge. However, the announcement of an air raid drill postponed their get-together. The afternoon before the drill, Charlie prepared the block wardens and checked instructions and supplies for the east-end neighborhoods' blackout practice. He confirmed the readiness of the first-aid post at Zachary Taylor School, in the block adjacent to Nap's Market and the Laundromat. Neighborhood residents had received instructions: lower window shades, extinguish lights at night, and cover any necessary illumination with red plastic to hide from virtual enemy bombers.

When the siren blew that night, Charlie set out to patrol the neighborhood in his helmet, with a flashlight covered in red plastic. Despite his efforts, the first air raid drill did not go well. Charlie saw lights at the seminary's campus store and from many dormitory windows. The Smiths left a basement light glowing. A gas station on Lexington Road blatantly ignored the siren, leaving its Neon sign lit. A car fire blazed near Bowman Field, exposing the airfield to eyes in the sky. A Buick with headlights refused Charlie's stop order at the corner of Pleasant Avenue and the seminary driveway. Sightseers in parked cars and on porches lit cigarettes, reminding Charlie of fireflies.

Charlie read the next day's headlines in the *Courier-Times* decrying the first air raid practice as a failure in most areas of the city. Editorials urged the populace to perform better on the next drill in May. What's wrong with people, Charlie wondered. Don't they care that there's a war on, or are they just stupid and careless? He had followed all his training protocols for the air raid practice. Why couldn't everyone else just follow the rules? The neighbors! He tossed his Sunday newspaper in disgust and went to join his family, finishing breakfast in the kitchen.

On a Saturday in March, Theresa and Ted Hawkes issued another invitation for Bridge. Alice enlisted the Smith girls next door to care for Judy, with their parents as backups. Arriving at the Hawkes's cottage, Charlie parked the coupe in the driveway.

Theresa intercepted them at the back door. "No one ever comes to our front door but salesmen," she said as they approached.

The woman's pleasant humor encouraged Alice, but she stiffened when Theresa reached out to embrace her. Too much warmth, too soon. In the tidy French Provincial kitchen, Alice noticed fresh-baked brownies and coffee bubbling in the percolator. She sensed the aura of a proficient homemaker and hoped Charlie wasn't taking notes to compare her kitchen skills with Theresa's.

Ted moved beyond into the living room, placing chairs at the card table in front of a broad window covered by maroon drapes. "Hey Charlie!" Ted said, turning toward them. "And the beautiful Alice, I presume." He extended his hand, and she accepted with an embarrassed giggle.

"So, who else would I be with, Ted?" Charlie laughed. Ted helped Alice off with her coat and reached for Charlie's overcoat to hang in the closet behind the kitchen. They made their way to the living room, where the Bridge table awaited them.

At one point, between Bridge hands, Theresa exclaimed, "So, you two are expecting another baby!" Theresa reached over and vigorously patted Alice's arm.

Alice saw burgundy fingernails against her pale green sweater. "Yes," said Alice, hoping the conversation wouldn't become too personal.

"You two seem like the ideal parents," said Theresa. "And how lovely for you to give your darling Judy a baby brother or sister."

Alice gave a quick smile and glanced nervously at Charlie.

"So, which do you want?" Theresa continued and winked at Charlie. Alice didn't know what the wink meant. Did Theresa assume Charlie was angling for a son? Alice intended to hold her cards close and not indulge this woman's nosy questions and gushing manner.

Charlie replied. "We don't care whether boy or girl as long as it's healthy."

"And when are you due, may I ask?" probed Theresa.

"About the first week of August," answered Alice.

"We think," Charlie added. Alice hoped this line of questioning would end. This woman who seemed so chummy with Charlie made her squirm in her chair.

"Oh, you are so lucky—blessed by God, really," cooed Theresa. "Ted and I have not been blessed in that way." She smiled at her husband across the table.

"We have each other, our good health. Friends, family, and our Faith. We're happy," supplied Ted.

Alice remembered Charlie quoting Ted about his wife's direct prayer line to God. Had she prayed for children? Alice wondered, not that praying caused it.

"Whose deal?" boomed Ted.

"The cards are here," said Alice. "So mine, I guess." She began dealing, her hands shaking as everyone watched.

When the evening ended, Charlie and Alice rushed to the Plymouth in a sudden downpour. Charlie hustled his wife into the car and ran around to enter the driver's side. As he shut the door against the slanting rain, Alice said, "I shouldn't go out with you anywhere." She saw a happy grin on his face slide away. "You really don't need to embarrass me in front of people we hardly know."

Charlie opened his hands. "What did I do?"

"You know perfectly well. You did it so many times you can't remember," she replied. Lightning tore through the sky. Alice jumped at the thunderclap.

A drop of rain fell from the curly lock on Charlie's forehead onto his nose. "Well, tell me just one incident." He reached to press the starter.

Alice began. "How about when I played a heart on that spade trick and you moaned."

"No one heard but you," Charlie said between tight lips.

"Oh, that's not true. They both exchanged looks."

"Looks, hah!" He turned on the headlights and shifted gears. The windshield wipers began beating against the rain; Charlie swung the car out of the driveway.

"And then—the time you practically swore at me when I went down a trick when we were really in the wrong suit because of your bidding."

"My bidding?" Charlie challenged. "No, ma'am. Three spades was the right bid, and I simply told you how you might have made it."

"Do you always think you've got it right, and I don't know anything?"

"Do you think you can't learn from your mistakes?" Charlie countered.

"My mistakes? What about yours?"

"Okay, Lady. What mistakes did I make that you're only now telling me about?"

"You could have played some cards differently. At least I was considerate enough not to say anything in front of your friends."

"Oh, I see. You're the model of politeness—I'm a brute," said Charlie.

"You said it. Not me."

They drove on without talking, listening to pounding rain, crashing thunder, and splashing tires. Headlights tunneled through the rain as lightning flashes turned night into split seconds of daylight. Two blocks from home, Charlie turned a corner. "Did you notice how Ted cheats?"

"You mean when he kept looking at the bottom card and un-cut the deck so he could deal it to himself?"

"Exactly," said Charlie. "If he saw a high card, that is. Now that's what I call rude."

Alice laughed. "And annoying."

"Otherwise, how do you like Ted and Theresa?"

"Nobody's perfect," said Alice. "But I guess they're okay. At least Theresa didn't break out singing, and she never got her arms around me."

She was glad to hear Charlie laugh. The coupe stopped in front of the garage. Charlie stepped out to open the door. Reaching skyward to check for raindrops, he announced, "It stopped raining. Storm's over!"

"For now, anyway," said Alice, as lightning flickered on the horizon.

27

CHARLIE SLEPT THROUGH the seminary clock's morning chimes but not the raggedy ring of the wind-up alarm clock. "Dad-burn clock!"

Saturday, August fifteenth—the Feast of the Assumption of Mary into Heaven—a date requiring Mass attendance for Catholics. Charlie looked up at the ceiling and sighed. August fifteenth—the baby should have arrived by now, but Doc Richards had revised Alice's due date. The cesarean operation was scheduled for Monday. In two days Charlie would be a father again. What luck if it's a boy this time, he thought.

Charlie looked over at Alice, who managed to stay asleep during the alarm clock's jangle. Poor dear, he thought. She looked like a huge animal—a bear, maybe, hibernating under a summer blanket. She slept on her side; Charlie sympathized with her difficulty finding a comfortable position. "Monday it will be over," Charlie whispered, then realized a new baby in the house would also make sleeping difficult.

So he focused on today's agenda: a quick early Mass—no singing. Afterward, home for breakfast on the run and a quick check-in with wife and daughter before heading off to the Seneca golf course. Alice promised Charlie she'd bear up okay; she said she wanted him to enjoy this last golf outing before the baby arrived.

Charlie hurried to dress and tiptoed downstairs, hoping not to awaken Judy. As he left the house, Charlie smiled to himself. He pictured Bonnie waiting for him later at the golf course, slim and golden, smiling her audacious smile, in the shade of the spreading chestnut tree outside the clubhouse.

Back home after Mass, eating breakfast, Charlie listened to Alice's groans whenever she rose from her chair. Her footsteps dragged as she padded about the kitchen in her slippers. She recently complained of her legs feeling weak. Charlie wondered if polio could recur; Alice assured him the baby was pressing on nerves. Doc Richards had said so.

"Go lie down," Charlie suggested.

"No—no, there's no way to get comfortable. I might as well be up and doing."

They heard Judy singing from her crib upstairs. "Good morning to you, good morning to you. . . ."

Charlie had to laugh. "She's our little bird."

"And this one's almost out of the nest." Alice patted her belly.

The thought of having twice as many children gave Charlie pause. "Yep. On Monday," he said, taking a sip of coffee. "I'll get Judy. You sit down for a bit."

Dressing Judy hadn't been on Charlie's original agenda, but seeing his big-eyed urchin peeking at him through the slats of her crib tickled his heart. "How are you and Bunny this morning?"

Once he situated Judy in the Babee-Tenda at center stage in the kitchen, he let Alice take over. He gave his wife a peck on the cheek. "Well, I'm off! That is if you're sure you're okay?" He paused, brow furrowed.

Alice waved her hand toward the door—a green light signal to Charlie. On his way across the floor of the screened porch, he took out his pocket watch. Good! Still in time for tee-off!

In the garage, Charlie placed his golf bag in the car's trunk. As he shut the lid, he reflected on how he missed his trusty steed—the Plymouth coupe. Two weeks earlier, he had traded the coupe for John Lea's Chevy sedan, as Charlie and Alice needed a larger car for their expanding family. With the war on, new autos were unavailable. They were happy to employ the Leas' roomier car, and Charlie chuckled at how driving the sportier Plymouth gave his father-in-law a youthful glow.

Charlie was still adjusting to the feel of the Chevy and the different knobs in strange places. As he drove to the golf course near Seneca Park, he remembered how Judy threw a tantrum and stiffened her body against being put into the sedan the day they traded cars. *Soon you can ride in the Plymouth with Grandpa* didn't stop her bawling as she watched through the back window as John Lea drove away. Charlie understood; he missed the old car too.

The dewy morning felt cool to Charlie as he approached the clubhouse; he visualized the air turning to steam before he and Bonnie completed the eighteenth hole. He would loosen his collar and roll up the sleeves of his pristine white shirt, soaked with perspiration. He looked forward to a cool drink at the bar after the last hole—all part of the summertime golf scene—with delightful Bonnie.

Entering the clubhouse, he saw a familiar figure ahead at the registration desk. Ted Hawkes in his Scotch plaid golfer's cap! Immediately Ted turned toward him. "Charlie—come on up here! We need a fourth."

Uh-oh. Charlie's luck at remaining incognito at the golf course had hit a snag. He tried to smile as Ted's two friends turned toward him. Charlie recognized one as an usher at Holy Angels. "Thanks Ted, but I'm waiting for my foursome—some guys from work," he lied. He hoped Bonnie wouldn't show up at that moment.

"Too bad. Then, another time." Ted tipped his hat. "Say—how's Alice?"

"Swell, thanks! The baby comes on Monday." Charlie slunk back out the door of the clubhouse to intercept Bonnie, should she suddenly appear. He needed to carefully time their approach to the first tee to avoid Ted Hawkes. He imagined the gossip if Ted found out about Bonnie, especially after he lied about meeting three other men. Charlie was already sweating.

Bonnie arrived ten minutes later, her bright hair bouncing in the sunlight. "You're as blinding as ever," Charlie greeted her. He loved to make her laugh; she sparkled.

"I've got a new driver," said Bonnie. "Can't wait to try it! Have you signed us in?"

"No. You weren't here yet."

"You could have signed us up for the usual time. You knew I'd be here—on your last day of golf before fatherhood!"

Charlie looked around and ushered two couples ahead of him and Bonnie into the clubhouse, lengthening the distance between them and Ted Hawkes.

"Are you feeling okay, Charlie?" asked Bonnie. "You look sort of pale."

"Sure." His underarms felt soaked already. "It's the humidity, you know."

Finally out on the first tee, Charlie kept glancing over his shoulder, on the lookout for a certain red plaid golfer's cap amidst the course's greenery. On the fifth tee, Bonnie had endured enough of her companion's inattention. "Watch me!" she called, reminding Charlie of his daughter's frequent demand.

As Bonnie and Charlie walked the fairway, he kept an eye out for the Hawkes foursome, knowing that fairways for other holes sometimes passed within proximate viewing range. "Charlie, what's the matter today?" questioned Bonnie. "You're so jumpy."

"Just keeping an eye out for gossipers. You know."

"It doesn't usually bother you. Today you act like a fugitive from justice."

"Well, maybe I am," said Charlie, his conscience assailing him again at an inopportune moment.

"It's not like we smooch all over the golf course," teased Bonnie.

Charlie remembered well the first time they'd kissed on the golf course, hidden by trees in the rough. It happened last summer when Bonnie's ball flew into a copse of pine trees, and they took advantage of the moment. Looking around for her tiny white ball, Bonnie had said, "It must have snuggled under these vines."

The word *snuggled* split his heart and triggered an irresistible urge in Charlie's thighs. He squatted down beside Bonnie, rummaging through the ground cover. Their shoulders touching, Charlie reached one arm around Bonnie, nearly tumbling her. As she faced him in surprise, he planted a firm kiss on her bright lips. She pulled away for a moment, then succumbed to an even deeper kiss. They rolled onto the cool spreading vines. Excited, Charlie's hands began to search for Bonnie's breasts. Then they heard voices coming from the adjacent fairway. Charlie snapped back into reality. "Sorry Bonnie," he said. "That was wrong." He stood up and brushed leaves and dirt off his trousers. She looked up, smiling. "Yes. But very nice." Charlie extended his hand to help Bonnie stand up. As she reached down to steady herself, she felt something hard on the ground. "And here's my lost ball!"

Since then, they commemorated that kissing site whenever they met to play golf. Here they were again at the trysting spot by the pine trees. But Charlie didn't like being reminded—not today. "There'll be no kisses for you, my girl," he muttered under his breath, smacking his ball emphatically. Much too dangerous, even though desirable.

"Whoo-hoo!" cheered Bonnie. "You're on the green—I think!"

They raced ahead to see; Charlie forgot about forbidden kisses and the threat of Ted Hawkes's eyes. His mind returned to golf for the moment.

Bonnie scored a birdie on the ninth hole, and Charlie hugged her. He pulled back, remembering Ted Hawkes again, especially when he knew the ninth hole could be seen clearly from the eighteenth. He hoped Ted's group wasn't finishing quite yet. Charlie looked across and didn't see the plaid cap.

As they walked along the fairway toward the twelfth green, Bonnie told Charlie of her new career plans. "I'm taking a course at Bowman Field. The Air Force started something called the flight evacuation school."

Just then, a bi-wing plane flew over on its way to the landing field, skimming low enough for Charlie to read the number forty-four on its fuselage. "What will you do after you finish the class?" He didn't understand a woman's interest in flight evacuation, whatever the heck that meant.

"I'll study to be a medical tech." She tossed her head proudly. "Eventually I hope to help out with the wounded soldiers in battle."

Those were difficult words to hear. Charlie stopped walking and set down his golf bag. "You?"

"Yes, little ole me," laughed Bonnie. "I've got guts, after all."

Charlie didn't doubt it. "But where will they send you?"

"Well, Dummy. Naturally, I'll wind up in a war zone. Europe or the Pacific, I suppose."

Charlie shook his head, disliking what he heard.

Bonnie continued, "Joe joined the Air Force. They might start glider combat training here. He's real interested in that."

Charlie considered that Bonnie's enthusiasm might be sparked by wanting to be with Joe. A twinge of jealousy seared him.

"Just doing our part to win the war," said Bonnie

Charlie remained dumbfounded, thinking. While he kept to his job and played golf on Saturdays, people he knew were jumping in for the war effort—the barrel makers at the cooperage, his friend Stan, Allen at the munitions factory, and now Bonnie. He gulped; something stuck in his throat. "No more golf then."

Bonnie giggled, hugging his arm. "Silly! You're about to be a daddy again anyway. You'll be busy!"

As they approached the fifteenth tee, a clubhouse employee on a bicycle hollered at them. "Charlie Lukas?" the young man called out.

"That's right," Charlie answered.

The boy leaped from his bike almost before stopping it; the frame crashed to the ground. Running to Charlie, he called, "Message for you!" and waved a piece of paper.

"What in tarnation!" Charlie exclaimed.

Before handing Charlie the note, the breathless boy announced, "It's your wife—having a baby!"

"Oh my gosh," said Charlie.

"Steady, there," said Bonnie, grabbing him as he swayed.

"I been all over this course." The boy took a breath. "Checking all the groups of men." He wiped a hot hand across his brow and looked at Bonnie. "I thought—I didn't know you'd be with—"

"That's all right," said Charlie, tempted to identify Bonnie as his sister. The note said John Lea had taken Alice to the hospital while Flora stayed with Judy. Hurry home.

"Thanks for your trouble." Charlie reached into his pocket for change. "Buy yourself a lemonade. You've earned it."

The young man grinned. "Congratulations to you—and your wife." He cast another curious look at Bonnie as he headed off to mount his bicycle.

Charlie and Bonnie walked back to the clubhouse as fast as possible, shouldering their golf bags. As they entered the clubhouse, Charlie noticed Ted Hawkes at the registration counter, laughing and joking with his pals. They had just finished the eighteenth hole. Charlie tried to duck out the door, too late. Ted saw him. "Hey there!"

As Ted turned away to respond to a friend's nudge, Bonnie whispered to Charlie that she was going to the powder room. "Go!" replied Charlie, urging her forward. He saw Ted coming over and hoped that golfers milling around the desk and display area had blocked Ted's view of a certain blond companion. To shrug off Ted, Charlie sputtered, "Alice is having the baby! She's already at the hospital, had to shorten my game."

"I wondered," said Ted. "We saw the boy on the bike looking for you."

"He found me all right. Gotta go now. We'll call you with the news. So long!"

Charlie made straight for his father-in-law's Chevy and didn't wait or even look around for Bonnie. He said one of his most fervent prayers ever: "Don't let Ted have seen me with Bonnie." He couldn't know but placed his blind faith in God.

As he settled his golf bag in the trunk, he saw Bonnie from the corner of his eye. Her shiny black convertible sat on the opposite side of the lot. He snapped shut the trunk and waved in her direction.

Bonnie blew him a kiss. "Godspeed, Charlie!"

By the time Charlie arrived at Jewish Hospital, Alice was in surgery; Doc Richards had been called from a social gathering at his home to deliver Alice's baby. Charlie joined John Lea and Allen in the waiting room to receive news of the baby's birth. "Didn't expect this today, did we!" chuckled Allen, indicating Charlie's unkempt appearance.

"Nope! I'm straight off the golf course. Alice wanted me to play one last time." Charlie grabbed John's shoulder. "Thanks for taking care of her. Guess I should've stayed home after all."

"It's all right. Babies have their own schedules," John said.

Soon Doc Richards entered the room, surgical mask dangling around his neck. Charlie became the center of congratulations over his new baby son—all seven pounds, nine ounces of him. Doc's words were an added blessing: "Alice came through with flying colors once again."

That evening, after a brief visit with a groggy, happy Alice and their cherubic son, whom Charlie referred to as *a duckling with white down*, the new father returned home for a shower and a hot meal prepared by Flora.

She had taken over the kitchen and told him she planned to stay the night and next morning to look after Judy, "So you can go back to the hospital to be with Alice and your son."

Flora reported that Judy was fussy after the day's turmoil. As Charlie scraped the bottom of a dish of chocolate pudding, he heard his daughter wailing from her crib, "Mommy! Dada!"

"Poor thing," said Flora. "Her world's turned upside down today."

"I'll go to her," said Charlie, rising from the kitchen chair and wiping his mouth with a fresh napkin. "Does she know about her baby brother yet?"

"Yes, I told her, but she wants to know his name." Untying her apron strings and lifting the garment over her head, she added, "So do I."

Charlie smiled at his mother-law. She was the first to hear: "It's Benjamin Charles Lukas."

While Charlie soothed Judy and described baby Benny with white fuzz for hair, he dismissed the ringing telephone and Flora's barely audible conversation with the caller. After Judy settled again into sleep, with Bunny tucked between her chin and shoulder, Charlie finished the nighttime routine by singing, "Goodnight sweetheart, sleep until tomorrow . . ." as he slowly stepped down the stairway.

When he reached the floor below, Flora came through the dining room to face him in the hallway. "Who is Bonnie?"

Charlie grabbed for the smooth curve of the newel post. Her question caught him off guard.

"Someone named Bonnie called to ask about Alice and the baby. She said she saw you at the golf course today when you got the notice about Alice having the baby." Did Flora's eyes flash with suspicion? Charlie hoped not.

He recovered his composure. "Yes. Bonnie is a secretary at the cooperage company," he lied. Then, shading the truth: "We spoke in the clubhouse when I took off for the hospital."

Flora seemed satisfied. "I told her the news—you have a son named Benjamin Charles, and Alice is fine. And I said you're okay too."

"Thanks for giving her the news, Flora." Charlie took a deep breath and smiled.

Relieved of returning Bonnie's call, he hoped Flora wouldn't mention it to Alice. He wanted Alice to remain disinterested in his golfing arrangements. So far, she seemed convinced that he liked picking up foursomes at the course and making new friends.

Now, Charlie supposed, he'd be on Ted Hawkes's list of golfing companions, but it didn't matter. He shrugged. New-father duties would exclude golf for a while, and Bonnie planned to join the war effort—a turn of events still hard to comprehend. The sad, inevitable ending had arrived, Charlie realized. In his role as a family man, he needed to focus entirely on his wife, daughter, and—a son! He wouldn't meet Bonnie again. In his heart, he blew her a final kiss and returned her godspeed.

28

As Charlie pruned the lilac bush with a quick snap of his shears, the blue-purple blossoms rewarded him with an explosion of fragrance. "Ah—smell that, Judy!" He beckoned to the barefoot child trailing behind him, one of her chubby arms dragging Bunny through the grass. Judy looked up from thumb-sucking and smiled. Charlie plucked a bloom and tangled it into a strand of hair behind his daughter's ear. "Here's one for your sunny hair." She reached up to touch the blossom, knocking it to the ground. "Okay—for Bunny then!" Charlie stuck the purple bloom into the faded ribbon around the toy rabbit's waist. Judy giggled. A speck of yellow whimsy floated in the pure blue sky, and Judy chased after the butterfly until it ascended over the garage roof next door.

Charlie continued his tasks, up and down on his knees in the backyard flowerbeds, tending and weeding his roses and other lush plants that prospered under his care. He wished Alice enjoyed the outdoors more. He looked over to the rose bed in front of their garage. I'll find a rosebud for Alice, he thought.

Charlie eased back from weeding the roses and sat on his heels, the knees of his khaki pants stained with mud and grass. His heart stirred at the sight of his three-year-old daughter wandering aimlessly, clutching her stuffed rabbit, and humming softly. She was lonely, having lost her mother's undivided attention with the birth of her baby brother last summer. Charlie tried to help by reading stories to Judy as soon as he came home from work each evening. But she was usually in a grumpy mood by suppertime and complained he didn't say the words right. Alice's story-reading talents were a hard act to follow. "Come over here, Judy. Let's sing something!" The girl dropped Bunny on the grass as she ran to her daddy's arms. Charlie re-tied the dangling sash of Judy's favorite red and white gingham dress, then twirled her around to face him. "What shall we do?"

Judy paused, put her finger to her mouth, and rolled her eyes upward, dramatizing her thinking process. "How about—This is the way we wash our clothes," she shouted.

"With the motions?" asked Charlie.

"Yes." Judy nodded her head up and down as hard as she could. They began to sing and scrub on an imaginary washboard.

᠃᠁᠃

From the living room, Alice heard Charlie and Judy singing and longed to join them outdoors. She patted Benny on his back to dislodge a bubble in his tummy. The baby squirmed and wrinkled his lower lip, about to cry. Alice lifted him at arm's length to look her son in the eye. His blue eyes, the color of a summer sky, looked away. "You are so beautiful," said Alice, "like a pretty doll with your curly blond hair. Why don't you like your mama? Why can't I reach you?"

Benny started to cry. "I could cry too, my Benjamin," whispered Alice at the window. Judy had been such an easy, responsive, happy baby. Why was Benny like a little sack of flour? No chubby arms reaching up to be held, no eager feet kicking, no giggles. And he lost interest in being held or cuddled after he was full of breast milk. His little body would arch stiffly as he cried to be laid down. He cried a lot—for reasons she and Charlie couldn't always identify.

Alice blinked back a tear, seeing the rest of her family in the flower-ringed yard. "Let's go," she said to Benny. Alice carried him to the back porch and grabbed a heavy cotton blanket covering a lounge chair. Juggling blanket and baby, she opened the screen door and picked her way down the steps.

In the middle of "this is the way we sweep our house," Charlie and Judy stopped when they saw Alice and Benny. Judy ran to her mother, who responded with a wide smile. Charlie took the blanket, spreading it on the grass. Alice knelt and placed the boy face down on the woven surface.

Judy, on all fours, faced her brother and grinned as he raised his head. "Hi Benny!" She plucked a lone dandelion from the lawn to tickle the boy's chin. He didn't respond until she laid the bloom in front of him on the blanket. His eyes focused on the yellow head as he began to reach for it. Judy quickly snatched the bloom and placed it farther from him, forcing Benny to move toward it as his parents watched. Alice caught her breath and clapped her hands to her mouth. This was the first time she'd seen her son wiggle forward with his arms.

Charlie said, "You're teaching Benny to crawl. Good girl!"

Judy continued the game. She led Benny off the blanket onto the grass, where he jerked back with a sharp, alarmed cry when he touched the cool, prickly texture. When his cherubic face started to implode, Judy acted quickly.

"Look at that, Alice," whispered Charlie. "He doesn't like it, and Judy's helping him back to the blanket. Isn't she something!" Alice nodded and smiled.

Charlie went back to his gardening. As Alice watched Judy attempting to play with Benny, relief washed over her that the boy was not crying. Then the thought of chores pending seized her attention. But on such a glorious Saturday afternoon, she couldn't keep from stretching out on the blanket. Her worries slipped away as sunshine colored her world orange inside her sleepy eyelids. She felt the weight of her body on the earth and inhaled the fresh scents of grass and blossoms perfuming the air. The neighbors' bulldog gruffed near the fence. A cardinal whistled and repeated its five-note song. Alice sank deeper as a happy moment held the children. For now, all was harmonious in her world on Pleasant Avenue.

As she heard the chip, chip, chip of Charlie's hoe in a flower bed, she remembered his new vegetable garden would soon come to fruition, and her kitchen would become a small-scale canning factory. *I'll think about that tomorrow.* She was pleased that Scarlett O'Hara's dauntless words came to mind, strengthening her.

Alice was awakened from her reverie by a rich fragrance like a delicious berry and a tickling sensation on her cheek. She opened her eyes to see Charlie's tanned, whiskery face close to hers. He held a rosebud in his teeth. She laughed and quickly sat up. "You look ridiculous!" she said, taking the crimson bud from his mouth. Charlie laughed too, tumbling onto her lap. Nestled on their blanket island in a sea of sweet grass, close to their children, Alice felt the warmth and joy of a June afternoon flooding her body and filling her heart. Worries and disappointments fluttered away like gossamer butterflies. No thought was given to their return.

29

I N HIS TALL hat and suit of American colors, *Uncle Sam* commanded the nation to pull together, work harder, and sacrifice for the war effort. A government poster campaign, *Plant More in '44,* aimed to increase the production of vegetables. Another poster read *Our Food is Fighting.* Charlie had rented a large plot of land for a Victory Garden at the corner of Lexington Road and Aubrey, the street east of Pleasant Avenue. He reclaimed his boyhood role of farmer, planting rows of corn, beans, tomatoes, and potatoes to provide for his family and reduce the cost of vegetables to the War Department.

Charlie continued his volunteer air raid warden duties as well as his efforts for peace on another front—daily Mass as often as possible and a faithful commitment to the Sunday choir. A side benefit of Friday Mass was the weekly breakfast with Theresa and Ted Hawkes; choir practices offered further opportunities to grow their friendship.

War posters abounded. One in crayon colors urged *Can All You Can.* As Charlie's Victory Garden burgeoned, Alice fretted that her housedresses were even more dowdy, covered by aprons. She spent most of her time in the kitchen, canning vegetables and making jelly (using the least possible amount of sugar—a precious commodity requiring ration stamps). Her great slog of effort tired and depressed her, and worries about Benny's development added to her feverish exhaustion. Another burden was the awareness that Judy needed her share of attention without distraction.

Providing healthy foods acceptable to the children's finicky tastes was a daily chore. Benny disliked certain textures and colors and wouldn't eat anything yellow, including cheese and butter (which were rationed anyway). Judy refused to eat peanut butter sandwiches on the thin white bread sliced lengthwise to stretch one slice into two.

As weariness bore down on her, Alice noticed her legs occasionally weakened, causing her to stumble under the daily strains. She had trouble sleeping at night because her legs and feet ached. Relief came from a liniment that burned her nose with its licorice odor. She wished Charlie would offer to rub her achy limbs, but he turned away from the smell of the Iodex.

Alice felt isolated. She missed seeing Allen, Catherine, and Deborah as much as she wanted. Allen worked long hours at the munitions factory, and Alice worried for his safety, as did the entire family. Perhaps that was why Catherine smoked more, even though her favorite brand of cigarettes was being shipped to soldiers overseas. Catherine involved herself with the war effort as a block volunteer. She organized neighborhood groups to recycle tin cans, clothing, and bacon grease for the war effort. Pushing Deborah in her Taylor Tot, she visited her neighbors to circulate information regarding volunteer services, Victory Gardens, war savings bonds, and blood donor programs.

❧⸎❧

One Saturday afternoon, Charlie stomped into the kitchen from his vegetable garden with a basketful of the season's new potatoes, clods of mud stuck to both shoes. Alice sat in the kitchen, staring at a stained cheesecloth bag full of purple grapes dripping into a dented metal bucket on the floor—the first step in preparing grape jelly. "Where are the kiddos?" asked Charlie.

Alice looked up. "Napping."

"Looks like you're the one who needs sleep, with those shadows under your eyes. Is Judy napping too?"

"Yes. She and Benny wore themselves out banging themselves back and forth on the Davenport." She sighed, feeling she also had taken a beating.

"Then the Davenport should be worn out too."

Alice ignored Charlie's pun. "I can't make Benny stop doing it. And Judy joins in!" After a moment's hesitation, her words rushed onward. "Oh, Charlie! What's wrong with our son? He will be two next week, and he doesn't talk. He doesn't like me to hold him. Is it me? Is it him? I'm almost at my wit's end." She drew a deep breath, suppressing a sob that tried to emerge.

Charlie frowned. "I know. Benny seems different from Judy at that age. But, you know, she might be the exception. Are all kids supposed to have words by age one? At least he's walking, finally. He's just slower."

The grape juice dripped steadily, pinging and splashing into the bucket. Alice sighed. "It's not only that he's slow. He's different. Not happy. Except when he's doing something like banging the springs out of the couch. And he won't pay attention to us!" She shook her head, watching the spreading purple of the grapes through the cheesecloth.

A pause, then Charlie said gently, "I know."

Straightening her back and attempting a determined note, Alice said, "I'm going to see Doc Richards about Benny. I've almost decided."

"Okay, then." Charlie picked up a new potato from the basket, rolling it between his soiled fingers.

Alice glanced at the basket and envisioned more work ahead. "Thanks," she said. A forced smile stretched her lips while she felt she would suffocate.

❧❧❧

The day after Benny's second birthday, Alice took him to see her cousin Doc Richards in his paneled offices in the Francis Building downtown. Flora Lea accompanied her daughter and the children. Benny squirmed and fussed in his mother's arms as the elevator rose nine floors. Judy tried tickling behind his chubby knees, but the boy screamed. Alice frowned and clicked her tongue. Flora remained calm, smiling at the woman operating the elevator, as numbers flashed by on the door. When the elevator stopped moving, the operator rose from her stool to open the door for the family. "I hope he ain't sick," she said.

Judy hopped out of the elevator, waving goodbye to the attendant.

"Sick might be easier," Alice murmured to her mother as they walked down a narrow corridor.

"He will be fine," Flora assured her. "I think it might be a case of Mommy needing more rest."

Alice opened her mouth, but her frustration wouldn't form into words. Her face flushed. Flora laughed gently, "See what Doc Richards says. Mark my words."

"How could I rest more?" Alice fumed, as Benny whimpered and squirmed.

"For a start, you don't really need to carry the child everywhere. He does walk now."

"And likes to run away too," Alice reminded her. "Can't you just see him running into the traffic on Fourth Street?"

"Maybe find a nanny to help," suggested Flora. "Or your daddy and I can take the children more. We've been way too busy with the war bonds. We'll do better."

Alice took a deep breath and forced her shoulders to relax. "Thanks, Mother. We'll see."

Alice knew her parents were throwing themselves into the war effort. Since John retired from the post office, he'd experienced a respite from his arthritis and showed renewed energy. He and Flora were full-time volunteers, knocking on doors in their neighborhood and other downtown residential areas, urging the purchase of war bonds that promised a generous return in ten years, while helping to finance this terrible *Second World War*. Besides the door-knocking, Flora and John grew a Victory Garden consisting only of yellow squash in their gritty backyard, and Flora still tended Alice's rock garden.

Alice, Flora, and Benny turned down another corridor lined with war posters imploring *Sock Your Money in War Bonds* and warning *Loose Lips Sink Ships*. They approached the pebbled glass door with Doc Richards's name in black letters. Judy had skipped ahead in her patent leather shoes.

"Judy, come back, Darling," called her grandmother, motioning to the girl.

As Flora opened the door to the dark, empty waiting room, a lone shaft of sunlight shot through the panes of a high window onto Judy's face. "Sunshine meeting sunbeam," Flora noted to Alice as they walked into the chair-lined room.

Judy dashed to the bookcase wall where storybooks beckoned from the bottom shelf. The women, with Benny, were about to settle onto a wrinkled leather couch when a gray-haired nurse opened the inner door, motioning Alice and her son into the suite of examining rooms. Flora gave Alice's arm an encouraging squeeze as she left, carrying Benny.

In the examining room, Benny looked around at the sterile hard surfaces and white walls. He bellowed, clinging to Alice, smearing tears and mucous on the bodice of her navy chambray dress. "Shh, shh," she repeated in her distraught toddler's ear, rocking him.

Suddenly the door opened wide; a jovial white-coated Doc Richards entered. "What have we here?" his voice boomed. Benny stopped to listen for a moment and then continued his wail. The doctor approached the child, released the stethoscope from his ears, and handed it to Benny.

The boy stopped in the middle of a raspy inhale to grasp the strange object with long tubes. "What do you say to that?" asked Doc Richards. Benny refused to look at the man, instead concentrating on the chest piece of the stethoscope.

"Finally quiet. Thank you." Alice smiled.

As Doc Richards examined the child without alarming him, Alice unleashed her list of worries regarding her son as she stood by the table. The doctor listened while registering the child's heartbeat, appearance, and other vital signs. Alice noted her cousin's gentleness and his talent for focusing on multiple tasks at once. She trusted him and awaited his wisdom regarding Benny.

"Does he talk at all?" asked Doc Richards.

"No," replied Alice. "Not words—nonsense syllables. He makes sounds, gestures, throws tantrums."

"Does it get him what he wants?"

"Usually." Alice added proudly, "Our Judy is wonderful at interpreting what he wants. She's almost able to read his mind."

The doctor continued. "Your son looks normal, bright enough," he concluded. "He may just be slow in developing speech. But his remoteness is disturbing. There's a term we've heard recently—childhood schizophrenia. I've not seen it myself, and it's too soon to diagnose Benny. Keep trying to make contact with him. Judy might be your best ally."

He lifted the boy from the table, handing him to his mother. "Alice, may I ask you something?" Her pulse quickened as she stood up to take Benny in her arms. "As your cousin and doctor, may I ask—are you and Charlie happy?"

Alice felt her legs falter; she grabbed the cold examining table with one hand. "Why—yes! I hadn't thought. We're always so busy."

The doctor smiled. "Make time for yourselves—and this young man."

Shocked, Alice said nothing more, even though she had wanted to probe further about the newly discovered medical condition. She and Benny were being pushed out of the examining room. "I want to speak to that bright young daughter of yours," said Doc Richards, with his arm around Alice's shoulders, "and say hello to Aunt Flora."

That evening as Alice prepared supper, Charlie walked into the kitchen, arriving home from work at the cooperage company. He kissed her, then asked, "How did the doctor visit go?"

Alice had much to confide, so this time she didn't mind the children tossing themselves back and forth on the living room couch. "I heard a new word today—schizophrenia," she began. "I don't know what it means—if it's a disease or what. Doc said it's too soon to diagnose Benny. But one of the worst moments of the visit was Judy's behavior."

"Judy?"

"Yes. She acted like a perfect dummy after I bragged about her smartness. When Doc tried to talk to her, she started babbling like Benny. Even Mother's frowns couldn't make her stop doing it. I was so embarrassed. I'm sure Doc Richards thinks we have two disturbed children on our hands." She flinched, remembering those awful moments in the doctor's office.

Charlie laughed. "You should know by now our Judy is not a performer. She doesn't like it when people try to show her off. She's no Shirley Temple, as you've often said yourself. Her talents lie elsewhere."

"Doc was impressed when I mentioned she might be a big help with Benny," said Alice. "But that was before he tried to talk sense with her."

Still smiling, Charlie said, "There's no worry about Judy. We both know that."

"And he told me to keep trying to make contact with Benny. Those were his exact words!" Alice went on. "I've done nothing else but try to reach that child. What more can I do?" Feeling overwhelmed and inept, she dissolved into tears, turning her face toward the white-painted cupboards. A lid began chattering on a pot of savory vegetable stew on the stove.

After Charlie reached over to reduce the heat, he embraced Alice and turned her around to face him. "Look," he said, "we're in this together. It will all come out right somehow."

Alice pulled away. "And—oh, Charlie! Doc asked about our marriage."

Charlie raised his eyebrows above his glasses.

"Are we happy, Charlie?" Her cousin's question had hit a nerve that was still vibrating.

Charlie held her at arm's length, his hazel-flecked eyes penetrating hers. "Well, don't you think so, Alice? I do."

She nodded, stifling a sob. Charlie's quick answer seemed patronizing, dismissive.

He wiped a tear off her reddened cheek with one finger. "Okay then—no tears, please."

Alice sniffled and tried to smile while worry simmered in her brain. She had no appetite; her stomach felt hollow. Was her husband truly happy with her? Was she the best mother she could be? Dinnertime beckoned. She turned toward the pot on the stove and said over her shoulder, "Okay. Get the kids. Time to eat our vegetables."

"That's my girl," said Charlie as he turned away to gather their bouncing children.

30

THE CORN STOOD high in Charlie's Victory Garden, but Alice wilted in the late August heat. Eyes shut tight, she reclined on the frazzled cushions of the living room Davenport as Charlie hovered. "Don't worry about the kitchen," he said, placing a cold washcloth on her forehead. "I'll clean up the mess when we come back." Her eyelids fluttered. "Just rest," he added, applying two cool cloths to her legs. "I'm taking the kids over to the garden."

The morning started quietly, with a gentle breeze to stir the pressure-cooked air. Through the alley they marched, Charlie in the lead, pushing his wooden wheelbarrow loaded with tools. He glanced over his shoulder at his son and daughter. "Judy, this is important," he began. "You simply must hold Benny's hand tight until we are across Aubrey."

"Okay Daddy," she replied, squeezing her brother's right hand. Benny dragged a stick with his left. Charlie had them halt at the curb. "We always look left and right, then left again," he reminded his children, even though few cars passed by on Aubrey Avenue. "When we get to the garden, you two stay up by the tomatoes and potatoes. Don't go in the corn!" Charlie warned. The corn plot covered the farthest reach of Charlie's garden, separated by a strip of grass from Lexington Road—Route 60—where traffic streamed by in a hurry.

"Okay Daddy," said Judy.

Charlie and the children reached the garden, where he began unloading tools from his wheelbarrow at the near margin of the field. Benny ran to a spot of plowed ground shaded by an elm tree. He sat down among the dry earth clods and began picking them up, one by one. Judy wiped her sweaty hand on her dress, made sure Benny was settled, and then walked over to her father to watch him begin work.

As they pulled weeds and checked for ripe tomatoes, Charlie and Judy also kept watch on Benny, his blond curly head preoccupied with his own garden project. Judy ran to where he had organized a pattern with lumps of soil. "Good work, Benny!" The boy paid no attention. Judy ran back to her father, who sent her to the wheelbarrow to fetch a basket for collecting tomatoes. She kept busy running back and forth between Charlie and Benny.

In less than an hour, the sunshine made its mark on the hatless trio. Judy's face flushed; Charlie sweated through his gray work shirt; the tops of Benny's legs reddened as the shade retreated from where he sat on the ground. "Time for a break!" Charlie called, holding out a bright red jewel of a tomato. Judy ran over to accept it; Benny stayed put. "Benny—want a tomato?" Charlie called to him.

The child didn't look up, continuing to sift and sort lumps of garden soil. Judy rushed over to show her brother the tomato, but he demonstrated no interest. The girl shrugged and returned to the tomato rows.

"Here, Judy—let me wipe off some dirt." Charlie took the tomato from her hand, examined it, and then wiped off some sulfur spray and soil on his salty shirt. He smiled, knowing Judy liked her tomato seasoned that way. She bit into the fruit, and the juice spilled down her chin. Charlie laughed and bit into a tomato; this one squirted juice and seeds. Judy's giggle lightened his heart, drawing away his concerns about Alice's gloom. As Charlie took another bite of tomato, a military glider flew overhead, holding their attention, as it silently winged its approach to Bowman Field. When they turned back toward Benny under the elm tree, he was gone.

At the far edge of the plot, high corn tassels moved without wind. A crow flew out, squawking its alarm. Judy pointed. "There, Daddy!" They raced toward the south end of the garden through rows of potatoes and beans. Too soon, they heard the heart-rending sounds of car horns and screeching brakes from Lexington Road.

"Oh my God!" Charlie cried out. His heart pounded in his throat, and he could scarcely breathe. Charlie broke into a full-speed run toward the highway, leaving his frightened daughter behind, panting, to follow him. His legs ran on their own steam, fear blinding Charlie as he reached the sight he couldn't bear to view:

Cars had stopped on Lexington Road, blocking traffic. In the far lane, he saw a tow-headed figure in blue shorts curled in front of the shiny chrome bumper of a Ford that looked vaguely familiar. Crazed with terror, daring to hope, Charlie's eyes darted to the driver in the near lane—a lanky young soldier in an olive-drab uniform—dismounting from a dusty black pickup as if dazed on a battlefield. The young man started toward the crumpled child, then snatched off his peaked cap and folded it against his chest. Charlie approached, wheezing and unable to speak. "Your child?" the soldier hailed.

The answer came from Charlie's trailing cry of "Oh—no, no . . ." as he fell on his knees beside the boy lying motionless in the street.

A man and woman scrambled from the blue Ford—Theresa and Ted Hawkes. Theresa screamed, "It's Benny Lukas!" Charlie looked up, paralyzed and dazed. She reached out to embrace her friend, tears streaming down his face. Ted gently lifted the small body from the street and carried him to the grassy shoulder of the road. Onlookers gathered.

The soldier followed and told them, "He ran right in front of my truck."

As Charlie stared into his son's face, Benny opened his eyes. He looked at Ted, then reached out for his father. "Oh Benny—you're alive!" Charlie cried, hugging the trembling child.

Ted offered, "We didn't hit him!"

Theresa added breathlessly, "We were driving east, going home, and saw this child run out in front of that pickup."

"Luckily, my reflexes are good," said the soldier, smiling tentatively. "I didn't see the boy until he was right in front of me!" He made a colliding motion with his hand. "I just missed him!"

Theresa continued. "We stopped instantly. He fell in front of our car, but we didn't think we hit him. It happened so fast! He must have been panic-stricken. When I saw you coming, I knew it was Benny. Look how he's shaking. Oh, Charlie! Is he in shock? God have mercy!"

Charlie examined his son, seeing scrapes and bruises, nothing obviously broken, and took a breath—his first complete one, it seemed, since Benny had run off. "He's had a bad scare. We all have. Thank you, everyone," he said thickly. Acid rose in his throat. He was trembling and sweating, as he enfolded Benny to calm his tremors and ragged crying. Charlie gently carried his son across the highway to where Judy waited, staring. He had forgotten her as the terrifying scene took place. He was stung by the realization that he'd forgotten Benny too, focusing on his garden work. How would he justify to Alice his careless inattention? And Judy? She looked up at her father, fear and sadness crumpling her sweet face, anguish hollowing her eyes. It took all the energy Charlie could muster to respond calmly to his daughter. "He's okay, Judy. Let's go home."

Charlie felt as limp as a scarecrow, moving by sheer willpower as he carried Benny along the edge of the field back to where the wheelbarrow rested. He felt like his mind and body had separated, as thoughts of the past moments ran through his brain like a sped-up newsreel. His body moved sluggishly as in a dream. Judy trudged alongside. To Charlie, it seemed like another lifetime since he had parked the wheelbarrow to begin the morning's work. He told Judy, "I think Benny needs to ride home in the wheelbarrow," although his arms didn't feel strong enough to push it home.

"What about me?" said the girl.

Charlie knew it had been an exhausting and frightening episode for her too; he couldn't resist. "Okay, Judy. You hop in too."

He piled his tools and the basket of tomatoes into the wheelbarrow with the children. As Charlie wrestled his load down a slight incline to the street, the Hawkes's car pulled up to the curb. Charlie set down his load as Theresa opened the passenger door and stepped out. "Is everyone okay, Charlie? You've had a terrible shock."

Charlie nodded. "I think we're okay now."

Ted got out of the car too.

"Thank you for stopping in time," said Charlie. "Benny could've been killed. I don't know how to repay you." His shoulders shook, and he choked on his words.

Theresa hugged him. "Saving your little angel is reward enough."

Ted nodded in agreement. "What a close call! Thanks to God."

Charlie took control of his emotions and reached into the wheelbarrow for the basket of tomatoes. Judy reached to stop him, but Charlie gave her a warning look. She made a mewing sound. Charlie handed the basket to Theresa. "Here, at least take these. Alice and I are forever indebted to you." He looked at his children, huddled securely, and added, "Judy and Benny are too."

Theresa accepted the basket. "Thank you, Charlie. Now, can we get you home?"

Ted grabbed the wheelbarrow handles from Charlie's quivering hands. Theresa asked Judy if she'd like a ride home in the car or the bumpy ride in the wheelbarrow. Judy chose "the bumpy way," holding her brother around his waist. Ted pushed the wheelbarrow as Charlie dragged himself along beside them. He still felt dazed and not sure how he'd find words to describe the morning's near-tragedy to Alice. He imagined her still lying on the sofa in the darkened living room under her damp compresses.

In a dozing fog, Alice heard the rumble of the wheelbarrow as it rolled along the backyard sidewalk and Charlie's voice talking to another man. Who? She raised herself with one arm painfully off the living room sofa and stumbled to the back window to look out. What was Ted Hawkes doing here? Groveling for free vegetables?

Then she heard a car door slam on Pleasant Avenue. Moving to the front window, she saw Theresa walking toward the house. Surrounded! What a time for the Hawkeses to visit! Couldn't Charlie tell them how bad I'm feeling today? Alice primped her hair and smoothed her wrinkled housedress as the doorbell rang. Then she heard Judy open the back door and run through the kitchen. "Mommy, Mommy! Benny is hurt!"

"What?" shrieked Alice, just as she was opening the front door to Theresa. Judy threw her arms around her mother. Alice was struck by Judy's announcement and couldn't manage *hello* to Theresa. But the look on Theresa's face warned of bad news.

Ted and Charlie, with Benny in his arms, were soon behind Alice in the front hallway. She turned to see her sniveling boy with scratches and bruises on his face and skinny arms, blood matting his blond curls. Alice let out a wail and reached for him. Charlie put his other arm around her and urged, "Come on. Let's all sit down."

They gathered in the living room, the Lukases on the sofa, embracing Benny, as Ted and Theresa stood anxiously, their backs to the small brick fireplace. "What happened?" Alice demanded, her voice clogged with tears. Judy cuddled up to her mother, as Charlie began to reveal the morning's near-tragic event. Theresa and Ted, in soft voices, added details from their perspectives. They all spoke of the soldier who had barely avoided hitting Benny as he ran into the street.

It was even worse than she had anticipated at first sight of Benny. Alice realized her world had almost ended that morning, but for the quick action of an alert soldier. Why had Charlie been so careless? She'd never let him take Benny to the garden again. Alice refused to look at any of the adults, wishing they would all go away. She held on to Benny and buried her face in Judy's soft hair. Tears stung her eyes.

Alice could barely cope with family duties the rest of the day. Her legs hurt more than ever, and her back was stiff. Charlie seemed more than willing to take on all the chores, including heating leftovers for their dinner. Serves him right! Alice believed he was trying to make up for his guilty behavior.

She wanted to punish him further. The Victory Garden was a harvest of fatigue and grief. Never mind that they had plenty to eat. But all the canning and preserving was driving her to madness and weariness unrelieved by sleep. And now—the garden project had almost caused her son's death or permanent injury. She wished to destroy Charlie's precious garden. But exactly how could she do that? Impossible, probably, without setting fire or dynamite to it. A large truck mowing it down? Nice to ruminate on vengeful thoughts rather than grieve over what could have happened to Benny.

☙✑❧

In the early coolness of the next morning, his family still asleep in their beds, Charlie took his place in the choir loft for Sunday Mass. His pure tenor voice rang out in grateful praise and thanksgiving. He stood between Ted and Theresa and felt like hugging them. On the spot, he decided to share half of his entire vegetable garden harvest with them for their part in saving Benny's life.

Charlie wished he had thought to ask the name of the young soldier who had stopped his pickup on a dime, avoiding Benny as he dashed into the street. At least I told them all thank you, Charlie consoled himself. He wished he knew more about the young man with good reflexes. Was he home on furlough or stationed nearby at Fort Knox? In the few words spoken, Charlie recalled a slight Tennessee drawl. Probably a tomato squeezer like me, he mused. He beseeched God to reward the soldier. Now that the war in Europe had turned a corner after Normandy, it didn't seem like too much to ask God to let the young man return home, safe from battle.

"Praise God from whom all blessings flow . . ." the choir began to sing. Charlie's glasses fogged over.

31

CHARLIE FELT CONTENT. His Victory Garden had produced a bountiful harvest. Alice rose to the challenge, lining their basement shelves with rows of home-canned vegetables and peaches. Judy proved an able apprentice, applying labels to the jars. Benny spoke a few words. Flora Lea quoted a saying that summarized their situation in the fall of 1944: "God's in his heaven, all's right with the world."

Even the war was going better. Charlie felt his near-daily Mass marathon had paid off. General DeGaulle had returned to Paris, and the Allies needed only to finish off Germany for victory in Europe. So far, none of the horrific war casualties had been friends or family—nor anyone they knew—except for two men Alice remembered from grade school who lost their lives in the D-Day invasion.

Charlie's friend Stan had returned home from the Pacific in August, recovering from burns and a broken leg. Charlie visited him in the hospital and heard stories of the victory in Guam. "The thing about Guam," Stan told Charlie, "We called it the Japanese liquor cabinet. Those nips were drunk as hell when they tried a counterattack. They screamed like mad and gave away their positions. Like ducks in a shooting gallery!"

Charlie threw back his head, laughing at how human failings could alter history. "Were they drinking bourbon?"

"Straight from Kentucky, I'm sure."

⌒☜⊙☞⌒

The breakfast ritual began as usual on a Saturday morning in October—the day after Judy's fifth birthday and two days before the Lukases' wedding anniversary. Charlie opened his newspaper to see Bonnie's photograph facing him under the front-page headline, *Local Woman Killed in Pacific*. Charlie slammed his cup, toppling its saucer, as coffee spewed from his mouth. He wanted to scream, "Bonnie—No!" The cry reverberated in his aching head.

Alice turned from where she waited for the flopper toaster to stop ticking and ring its bell, signaling the toast was done. "Charlie! What's the matter?"

"I knew her!" Charlie pointed to Bonnie's picture and stood up from his chair.

Alice squinted to see the likeness better. "Do I?" Alice asked.

"No. I knew her from work."

"Oh, my goodness!"

Charlie began reading aloud: "Bonnie Fines, of the Women's Army Corps, was killed in a bomb attack on Leyte Island, October twenty-second." He stopped reading and almost stopped breathing. Charlie felt his brain erupting into a rolling boil like a kettle of peach preserves on the stove. He slammed the newspaper on the table and walked away so that Alice wouldn't see the turbulent emotions that must be playing on his face.

⌒☜⊙☞⌒

Alice watched as the dining room door swung behind him, revealing flashes of the decorated table set for their daughter's birthday party. She picked up the newspaper, reading further:

> *Army Lt. Bonnie Fines valiantly kept communications open at Leyte after the Sixth Army landed on October twentieth. She worked among the WACs on night duty, taking messages from the communications center and sending alerts to front-line units when fatally injured by shell frag-ments. By the end of the day, the invasion gained a successful foothold as General MacArthur announced his return to the Philippines. Forty-nine heroic lives were lost.*

More details followed, recounting Bonnie Fines's service history, but no mention of her surviving family or her association with the land bank or Lime-stone Cooperage. Alice wondered how Charlie could have known her. Who was Bonnie Fines? Judy's hollering and Benny's screams from the living room drew Alice's attention; she dropped the newspaper. "Not again!" she sputtered, rushing to quell the riot in the living room.

⌒⌒⌒

Judy had behaved spitefully to Benny the last few days since he lost Bunny on a walk to Nap's Market. Alice remembered Judy had allowed her brother to play with her favorite stuffed toy that day. As they were leaving the store with lollipops from Mrs. Nap, Judy turned to request a treat "for Bunny too!" When she reached for her rabbit, Benny didn't have it. The stuffed bunny with its green organdy skirt and flowers tied to its waistband had vanished. Benny probably dropped it from his Taylor Tot as they walked to the store; neither Alice nor Judy had seen it fall. They searched for Judy's *best friend* on the way home without finding it. By the time they reached home, Judy was bawling. Since then, she had acted teary and cross with her mother and brother. She sobbed into her father's starched collar as he read from a book that had been one of her favorites, *The Runaway Bunny* by Margaret Wise Brown. "Stop!" wailed Judy. "Don't ever read me this story again!" As Alice entered the living room, she found that Judy had knocked down the wooden alphabet blocks Benny had carefully arranged on the carpet in front of the fireplace screen. "Judith Star Lukas, I am tired of your behavior," Alice fumed. "Do you want your birthday party this afternoon or not? I can cancel it very easily with a few phone calls!" She wanted to shake Judy but controlled herself with clenched teeth. She knew her daughter was angry with Benny and grieving for her lost toy rabbit.

Judy stood up, stared at her mother, and ran from the living room, sobbing loudly.

Alice heard her daughter clattering up the stairs. "You and your father!" Alice muttered, hands on hips. "You two deserve each other." She knelt to help Benny gather his scattered blocks.

⌒⌒⌒

The awful weekend ended with an outpouring of troubling emotions for Alice. She had not written in her diary since Pearl Harbor—nearly three years ago. On the last Sunday night in October 1944, she wrote again:

> *Where to begin! I'm bombarded with woes. At first, Charlie couldn't wait to give Judy those shiny roller skates. He hoped it would take her mind off losing Bunny. On Saturday morning everything changed. Instead, Charlie barely made an appearance at the party. He was off in the yard—gardening, for heavens sakes!*
>
> *Luckily, Mother and Daddy helped serve the cake and ice cream. They both entertained the girls, especially Daddy, with his funny squirrel imitations. Everything else fell flat. The roller skates ended up in a pile with*

other presents. When Charlie did make an appearance at the party, his eyes looked red—like Judy's. They were both a 'sight for sore eyes'—their own! Directing those party games frustrated me. Judy didn't seem to like the other little girls I'd invited. She only wanted to play with Deborah. After all my efforts with her party, will I ever try that again?!

And Benny! I couldn't give him much attention with all I had going with the party. Thank goodness for Allen—in a way. He totally took over with Benny. Benny truly wanted to be with Allen. He was all over him! Even said his name 'Unca Allen.' Benny has never shown such great interest in another person, except sometimes Judy. Not even Charlie and me, after we've tried so hard with that child!

When the party finally ended—thank goodness—Benny screamed and cried when Allen said goodbye. I tried to hold him back; he showed super strength, wailing and reaching for Allen. I asked Allen and Catherine if they'd like to take him home, only half joking. My heart breaks for my son. I pray he will grow out of his strangeness. He's still only two. I must keep hoping.

Now Charlie! I know it caused a shock wave when a woman he knew was killed in the war. The same for me a few months ago, when I learned that two of my favorite buddies from grade school were killed in Normandy. With the great number of casualties you hear about, it's no surprise there's someone you know. It hit Charlie extra hard for some reason, though he didn't want to talk about it. I'm disappointed he didn't get more involved with Judy's party. I'm sure it added to her funk over losing Bunny. I've never seen a child enjoy her party less. When I scolded Charlie later, he said he felt 'in the way' and pointed out he did give Judy her skates, after all. What could I say?

Then today, after church, Charlie was gone the whole afternoon at the Hawkes'. He took a load of potatoes and carrots over—I can understand his gratitude to them. But why did he stay away so long? I was beside myself, trying to help Judy with her new skates and making sure Benny didn't run out of the yard. Also, my legs ached terribly. I was in tears when I finally called Mother. She invited us for supper whenever Charlie came home—no matter how late. God bless Mother and Daddy! If anyone saved this miserable weekend, they did! I began wondering if Charlie left me. He finally came home about six. Didn't say much, and he didn't look like I'd better ask.

Tomorrow is our seventh wedding anniversary. The way Charlie's been acting, I hope he hasn't forgotten.

⌒✑⌒

At the Leas' on Sunday night—the night after Judy's party, Flora had turned to Alice as they washed the supper dishes. "You were right keeping Judy home from kindergarten this year."

Alice heard her father's laughter and Judy's high-pitched giggles drifting into the kitchen from the parlor where John, Charlie, and the children were listening to radio comedies. "I'm sorry—what did you say about Judy?" said Alice, returning to the conversation.

Her mother repeated her remark.

"Why do you think my decision was right?"

"The way she acted at her own party," Flora continued. "She doesn't play well with other children."

"So, you think I have two problem children?" Here she goes again judging me, thought Alice. Resentment swirled in her stomach as she braced herself for her mother's words.

A smile flickered on Flora's lips. "No, I didn't mean that at all. I just think Judy needs more time and some practice socializing with playmates. Her shyness could detract from learning." Flora had taught kindergarten a few years before she married John; she spoke with authority.

"I'm sure you know what you're talking about, Mother, but we don't have many neighbors with children, and those seminary children seem so—"

"Unkempt?"

"Yes, sort of waifish. Besides, I don't let Judy cross the street."

"But they're certainly nice enough children, I'm sure. Judy needs friends."

"I'll try calling other mothers to find some girls her age." Alice sighed.

"Why not show her how to cross the street safely?" Flora raised an eyebrow. Alice offered no response and bit her tongue to hold back bitter words on the tip. She carried dishes to the kitchen sink and, feeling picked on, deposited plates and cups without her usual care.

Flora opened another subject as she picked up clean dishes from the drainer and headed to the pantry. "Charlie certainly wandered off into his own world this weekend. And tomorrow is your anniversary."

A china dish crashed into the sink. "Oh, it broke!" said Alice. Her mouth crumpled, and tears started down her cheeks.

Flora hurried to her daughter's side. "It's all right, honey. I'm sorry I said those things. I just thought we should have a good talk."

Alice nodded, swallowing. "Yes. Another time. It's been a hard weekend. I need to think about it."

"And write in your diary?"

Alice looked down at her chapped hands in the porcelain sink. Maybe penning her thoughts would lift troubling burdens. Yes, it was a splendid idea. She had resolved to return to her diary that night.

32

Earlier that Sunday afternoon—the day after Judy's party—Charlie knew that Alice was still upset about how the party had flopped, and he decided to disappear from her wifely frowns for a while. He would deliver a promised supply of potatoes and carrots to Theresa and Ted. Charlie had only intended a short stay, but the Hawkes's rolling backyard and easy conversation were such a relief to the shock and sadness he felt over Bonnie's death, he lingered to follow Theresa on a tour of her garden. As she bemoaned her chrysanthemums' dead heads, Ted remarked, "better on plants than people."

As they moved around the yard, Charlie took turns laughing at Ted's droll comments and siding with Theresa's points of view. Theresa expressed delight with her new St. Francis statue; Ted remarked how the birds used it for a target. Charlie laughed and suggested moving the statue away from the mulberry bushes.

Theresa, with freckles scattered across her nose, auburn hair tied back under a bandana, reminded Charlie of Maureen O'Hara in one of last year's picture shows—a good one about the French Resistance.

"What should I do about these asters, Charlie?" Theresa asked.

He surveyed the plants, suggesting where she might trim them back. As they circled the large grassy yard, Charlie had a mental image of leading Theresa by the hand, and he noticed Ted fading out of the picture, losing interest in the tour.

"I'm going back to my book!" Ted called as he turned toward the house.

Theresa and Charlie waved to him. "He's quite a reader." Theresa giggled. She turned back to her green spaces. "I'm thinking a rock garden might look attractive over there." She pointed.

A flood of déjà vu swept over Charlie. The moment brought him back to the summer of 1937 when he was smitten by a lovely woman planting a rock garden on barren soil. And—oh—where Alice's garden path had led him!

"I'm sorry, Charlie. I'm asking too much," said Theresa. "You look like you could use some lemonade. Let's go in."

Did she grab him by the arm momentarily? Charlie followed Theresa into her yellow and blue kitchen. He watched as she removed her bandana, letting her shiny hair tumble to her neck.

Theresa took a pitcher of lemonade from the pudgy Kelvinator and a tray of ice cubes from the freezer compartment. Charlie helped her pry open the metal divider, releasing the hard-frozen cubes in a crashing spill. As Theresa picked up stray ice cubes from the table, she called out to Ted, offering lemonade.

"No thanks! I've got a beer!" came his reply from somewhere in the house's interior.

"Now then," said Theresa as she and Charlie seated themselves at the kitchen table. "Let's hear about your family. How is that darling boy of yours?"

"Well, he seems just fine. His scrape with Lexington Road traffic didn't faze him much. He still tries to run away."

Theresa's eyes crinkled as she sipped her drink. "What do you and Alice do about that?"

"Watch him like a hawk."

"It must keep you busy."

"Yes, I don't take him to the Victory Garden anymore. It's a shame." Charlie swirled the ice in his glass and stared at it. "I'm thinking of building a sandbox in the backyard to occupy him. Thank goodness for Judy—she's five now and helps us watch Benny."

"Good for her! But she's only a child." Theresa paused. "If you'd like me to watch him sometime, please let me know."

A smile flickered on Charlie's moist lips. "Thanks, Theresa."

"I mean it." Her hand found Charlie's arm and gripped it firmly through his gray mohair sweater.

At Theresa's touch, a tingling sensation traveled up his arm and tickled his heart.

She continued, "Benny is a precious child. I'd enjoy taking care of him. He gives me a boost—watching him zig-zag around and walking on his tippy-toes like he does."

Charlie chuckled and reluctantly moved his arm from Theresa's grasp. "Yes, he's got energy, all right. But sometimes he just sits and stares. He's day and night."

"I don't care. He's precious, and I'd love to help you out. You've been so generous." Theresa motioned to the baskets of root vegetables on the counter.

Charlie knew Theresa wished she had children of her own. "Okay. Thanks. Maybe sometime—when we take Judy to a picture show. That would be helpful."

"I'd welcome Judy too, of course," added Theresa.

"She'd be a help to you rather than a bother," said Charlie. "Usually," he added, chuckling.

Theresa refilled Charlie's lemonade glass.

Charlie turned solemn. "Judy didn't have a very nice weekend. Neither did I." He relayed the story of Judy's lost rabbit, followed by her subdued birthday party. Then he revealed the shocking news about Bonnie's death that assailed him Saturday morning.

As he talked, Charlie surprised himself at the depth of his feeling of loss. Theresa listened with such a sympathetic ear, he began telling her how he had met Bonnie on his lunch hour one day and how they remained friends through the years. He even mentioned they had played golf together "a few times." Charlie added, "Of course, Alice wouldn't understand. She's the jealous type."

Theresa nodded, then leaned forward, intense. "Somehow, you must resolve your troubled feelings about Bonnie. You owe that to your family."

Charlie was impressed. "You talk like my mother!"

"Sure sounds like a compliment." Theresa smiled and flashed her brown eyes.

"The thing about Bonnie," Charlie continued, "I wish I knew more about her. I'd send my sympathy to her family—if I only knew who they were. There was her boyfriend, Joe. I never knew his last name. It's hard to resolve . . . ," Charlie faltered.

"It's okay, Charlie." Theresa patted his arm again. "I will try to find out all this for you. It will be my special project—aside from my garden, of course. I'll start with the newspaper article and go from there."

Charlie's mouth went slack. Surprise muted his voice; he shook his head.

"Really," Theresa emphasized. "I would love to do it." She added, "And I'll not say anything in front of Alice."

Suddenly, the air felt awkward between them. Charlie realized he'd revealed way too much. He wished he could stop Theresa's probing into Bonnie's background. But *the cat was out of the bag*, as his mother-in-law Flora would say. No *stitch in time* now.

Ted sauntered into the kitchen. "Just checking on you two. Gotta keep an eye on Charlie," he winked at his friend.

Charlie recalled a certain day two years ago—the day of his son's birth—when he worried that Ted had seen him with Bonnie at the golf course. Ted's teasing remark made him wonder again. Charlie squirmed in his chair, thinking maybe he should head home. Late afternoon already!

As Theresa walked Charlie to the door, she reminded him. "See you Wednesday night for our extra choir practice."

"Right you are," Ted chimed in. "We can't let that *Te Deum* get us down! Even though it's tedium."

Charlie forced a laugh and said goodbye. As he turned his father-in-law's Chevy around in the driveway, he didn't feel like going straight home. He didn't think about the time or Alice missing him. The car practically drove itself to the Seneca Golf Course. The parking lot was empty except for a scattering of vehicles. Anyone playing golf this late in the season had likely finished several hours earlier, thought Charlie. Perhaps those cars belonged to clubhouse employees.

He got out of the car and walked to the first tee, hands in his pockets, the breeze riffing through his wavy hair. He stood still, weight shifted to one leg, remembering the first time he'd played golf with Bonnie and how she liked making those smutty little remarks. He smiled, then shook his head. How was it possible that he'd never see her again? He walked over to the eighteenth green, remembering how he and Bonnie enjoyed drinks in the clubhouse bar after finishing their rounds of golf. And those delicious kisses under the pine trees! Despite the many times he'd tried to tell Bonnie *we can't meet again*, there had always been another tee time.

Now all was over, completely over, finished forever.

Charlie noticed a youngish man with a receding hairline rushing toward him from the clubhouse. "Can I help you, sir? I'm afraid we're closed for the day."

Charlie regarded the man, whom he'd probably seen many times before, and adjusted his glasses with a push of one finger. "No. Never mind. I lost something here. But I didn't find it."

Head down, he returned to the parking lot.

He hesitated going home and, instead, drove to Bowman Field, where Bonnie had worked and trained. He parked outside the fence. Through the chain links, Charlie commanded a good view of the landing field with runway lights aglow. Around the perimeter, he saw mechanics in coveralls and some of the Negro Air Force personnel. Everyone moved briskly and efficiently. He watched a man with headphones direct a mammoth B-17 to its parking space near the hangars. A glider landed. Charlie admired the slow, graceful landing and the pilot's ability to fly an engineless aircraft so precisely across currents of air. Like a spirit floating unencumbered. Like Bonnie. She haunted the panorama of the airfield before Charlie's eyes; the canvas turned gray and surreal as daylight fled. Those workers out there—had any of them known the brave woman who died at Leyte Island? Was her name mentioned? Did anyone else cry in his soul over her passing?

Charlie took a deep breath and pushed back into the Chevy's well-worn upholstery. He relaxed his grip on the steering wheel. As his right hand stretched across to the passenger's seat, the Plymouth ring caught his eye—the ring Alice gave him the first Christmas of their marriage.

Suddenly, he realized the day was over, darkness closing in, and Alice would be worried about him. Charlie hoped she hadn't phoned Ted and Theresa, as his index finger pressed the starter. Driving through the twilit park underneath towering old oaks, he suddenly remembered his and Alice's wedding anniversary. Today—tomorrow? He swiped a hand over his face. Good Lord, he thought. What am I turning into? Guess I'd better pick up some roses for Alice tomorrow. Charlie bit his lip and pressed his foot to the gas pedal.

33

I N THE HOLY Angels choir loft, Theresa whispered an invitation: "Come over for coffee after practice. I have some news."

Charlie knew she'd been searching for Bonnie's family. He nodded. Guilt and curiosity vied for his emotions as a fever rolled up his neck. He whispered back, "Okay. I'll phone Alice from your house."

The choir director glared and cleared his throat for attention. "Let's begin now—*Adeste Fidelis*." Charlie and Theresa re-focused on the music. Behind them, Ted smirked.

Later, outside the church, snow began crystallizing in the night air. Large snowflakes played with Theresa's long eyelashes; Charlie thought she looked beautiful—like a snow queen. Ted hustled her toward their car and waved to Charlie. "See you at the house!"

In the Hawkes's warm kitchen, Theresa scurried to brew coffee and set out her best dessert plates for Dutch apple pie; the aroma of baking filled the room. Charlie's mouth watered as he tried to remain focused on Ted's conversation: "One thing the war has done for this country—we're now giants of production. Amazing the thousands of airplanes we've produced, and that's not even half the story."

The mention of airplanes brought Bonnie to mind, but Charlie replied. "I'm just waiting for the day we can buy a new car!"

Theresa said, "Well—it's nearly Christmas. Why not ask Santa?"

They laughed.

Ted concluded, "Let's ask Santa to end this war; the sooner, the better."

"We'd better go to Santa's boss instead," corrected Theresa. "We must pray until the finish line."

Charlie nodded in agreement, his eyes on the pie Theresa was bringing to the table. She began slicing it with an enamel-handled pie cutter. Ted assisted by holding a glass plate toward his wife. "A big piece for Charlie!"

"Of course," laughed Theresa. "He looks hungry."

Charlie commented, "Choir practice takes a lot out of a person!"

Theresa poured coffee; the three friends dug into their pie and conversation. After the plates were scraped clean and the last crumb dabbed from satisfied mouths, Theresa poured another round of coffee. "You make the best pie and coffee," said Charlie. "Ted's a lucky man."

Theresa blushed, hurrying across the kitchen to place the glass pot in the sink. Ted winked at her as she returned to the table.

"Now then." She gave Ted a serious look and sat down. "I'm sure Charlie wants to hear the news I promised him."

Ted looked as if he'd suddenly tasted a bitter apple seed. "I'll let you two go at it. I'm off to my book."

Theresa paused, addressing Ted as he rose from his chair. "Oh, okay then. I guess you already know the news I have," she said. Ted left the room.

Theresa turned to Charlie, explaining, "One of his greatest joys is reading. He always has a book handy." She changed the subject. "Guess what—I found Bonnie Fines's family!"

Charlie had expected as much, but he silently panicked at the burden of hearing the news. And now, he was apprehensive that Ted likely knew the whole story. Charlie didn't like having Ted as a witness.

Theresa continued, "It turns out Bonnie's parents are both deceased. However, I tracked down a sister in Columbus."

"How did you find her?" His heart beat faster.

"Some help from a *Courier-Times* editor. And a lucky break. It seems the sister was making inquiries at about the same time."

Charlie cleared his throat. "Then, what?"

"I wrote to the sister. Her name is Jane."

He frowned. "What did you say about me?"

Theresa giggled. "Don't worry. I was very discreet. I said that friends who knew Bonnie before the war wanted to know—"

"Did the sister write back?"

"I just heard last week. I'm sure it was hard for her—I'll get the letter."

Theresa quickly retrieved the letter from a kitchen drawer. Charlie put on his glasses and took the folded document from its lavender-scented envelope. He opened it slowly, observing black penmanship scrawled across two pages, boldly handwritten—as Bonnie would have done, Charlie reflected.

The letter revealed that Bonnie and her sister Jane had been estranged, causing Jane enormous guilt as well as grief over Bonnie's tragic death. Charlie sighed, remembering his shunning of Allen. He looked up at Theresa and commented, "Sad that the sisters didn't reconcile." He continued reading.

Jane wrote that she felt proud of her heroic sister and wished to honor Bonnie's memory and atone for her own failings in a public way. She revealed more: Bonnie was newly, perhaps secretly, married before being sent to the Pacific. The husband, Joe Green, had informed Jane of Bonnie's death.

Charlie put down the letter and stared straight ahead at Theresa's bright yellow kitchen wall. Joe! The guy from Bowman Field who stood her up at the golf course.

"Are you okay, Charlie?" Theresa shook his arm.

"Sure." Charlie smiled. "Thank you—you did an amazing job finding out all this. I'm grateful." He carefully re-folded the letter.

Theresa fluttered her eyelashes. "My pleasure."

"But now," Charlie began. "I'm not sure what to do. Bonnie mentioned Joe, and I knew he had joined the military. But I never met him. And the sister Jane—"

"Do you wish to contact them?" Theresa intercepted.

Charlie looked down at his hands on the folded white paper and played with his ring. "That's about right. Although Joe, wherever he is now, probably wouldn't want to hear from me. Don't know what I'd say to Jane."

"Well, maybe it's enough, knowing Bonnie had a husband who loved her and a sister who is proud of her. Could that satisfy you?" He heard the concern in her voice. As she waited, Charlie felt his eyes smarting.

Theresa touched his arm again. "I'm so sorry."

Charlie tried to shake off his feelings. "Don't be. I'm grateful to you for finding out. Yes. I think it's enough for now. I feel sort of—relieved."

"Good!" said Theresa. "I hope you, Alice, and the children can enjoy a wonderful Christmas."

Impulsively, Charlie leaned over and kissed Theresa's flushed cheek. His lips lingered another moment. "Merry Christmas, Theresa!" She laughed, her fingers touching the spot where his lips had been. The kitchen suddenly felt ten degrees warmer.

34

As springtime 1945 rolled around, Charlie began turning the backyard into a playground for his children. Under a shady peach tree, he placed an outdoor dollhouse for Judy and built a sandbox for Benny's sifting, digging, and musing. Charlie constructed a two-seat swing set where the boy liked to sway, tummy down on the seat, watching the ground move forward and back beneath his feet.

Judy enjoyed sweeping high in her swing above the flower-lined backyard to look across at the neighbors on both sides of the backyard while she sang at the top of her voice. The Smith girls often waved and applauded from next door while Topsy the dog barked through the opposite fence. Judy also appreciated a smooth sidewalk from front yard to the back, which was handy for practicing her roller-skating glides and quick turns.

Alice regarded her five-year-old daughter as happy, busy, and content. She didn't appear to need friends. Finding companions for Judy could wait a while longer. Besides, Alice depended on Judy's everyday assistance—entertaining and interpreting for Benny.

The boy began showing interest in books but did not follow stories as Judy did. One book might interest him for an hour while he flipped through and randomly fixated on pages, babbling to himself. Benny wore out pop-up books in a week. Two tougher books were hardbound copies of *The Hole Book*, with a circular hole perforating through every page, and *The Slant Book*, shaped like a rhombus, in which a baby goes for a wild ride in a buggy. Benny often sat on the couch with his books, enjoying rocking back and forth, wearing down the cushions. Sometimes he stopped to listen as his mother and sister, cuddled in the easy chair, read stories aloud—*Raggedy Ann, The Wizard of Oz*—or poems from *A Child's Garden of Verses*. "Up in the air and down!" he parroted over and over as he rocked, repeating the last line of a poem about swinging.

Judy sensed her brother's needs and wishes. One day, as Benny began tuning up for a lunchtime tantrum, she warned their mother, "He only wants the peanut butter—not the mayonnaise. He doesn't like touching it."

Alice paused with her hand on the vertical slicer, ready to divide a piece of white bread in two. "Thank you, my dear." She sighed. "Does he want a sandwich or not?"

Judy scrutinized her brother's babbles and gestures. "No. Just an apple."

Alice laughed despite her frustration. She picked up an apple from a bowl on the counter and began slicing it.

"Peeled!" commanded Judy.

Alice slammed the knife down and turned to her daughter, one hand on her hip. Alice knew there was nothing wrong with Benny's vocal mechanisms. He could repeat and repeat any phrase that fascinated him. Such a quirky, stubborn child! "Judy—now that he's quieter, do you suppose you could teach Benny some real words?"

The girl's hazel eyes sparkled. "Benny, can you say *apple*?" He shook his head wildly. "But I'll bet you *can*!" she insisted.

From then on, Judy accepted her mother's challenge. During playtimes, bath times, mealtimes, and walks to the market, she prompted her brother to pronounce words. In tantrum-prone situations, she encouraged, "Benny, use your words." He paid attention when she pointed out simple words on the pages of alphabet books. Printed words and letters of the alphabet—on signs, billboards, cans, and box labels—became his new fascination. For the first time, he began listening to his family as they spoke.

Benny learned some words but limited his expressions to wants and needs or parroting phrases he'd heard. "At least we have fewer tantrums these days," Alice noted to Charlie one evening after a peaceful meal in their dining room.

"Yeah," replied Charlie. "I wonder when he'll tell us what he's thinking. Wouldn't you love to know?"

"Yes. If he has thoughts."

Charlie frowned. "Of course he does! In his own way."

❧❧❧

Three weeks after Benny's third birthday in 1945, he surprised the family by engaging in their celebration over the end of World War II. He announced: "Now we can go!" He shouted the phrase repeatedly, propelling himself off the couch cushions.

Alice confided in her diary:

We had no idea Benny understood our rationing, scraping, saving during the war, and how the war held everything back. No new cars, gas rationed for our old cars, so we couldn't go on any extra sightseeing trips, no adventures by car. Little no-talk Benny exploded with his "now we can go!" Daddy nearly fell out of the living room chair, laughing. Charlie smiled ear to ear with pride. For once, our boy seemed in tune with the rest of us—what joy! But Judy seemed annoyed with him.

A few days later, it was sunny with a hint of autumn in the air; tips of yellow painted the Sweet Gum leaves. Alice's painful legs needed exercise, so she and the children walked to Nap's Market. Benny rode in the Taylor Tot, which would double as a grocery cart on the return trip. Inside the store, Alice responded cheerfully to the Napolitanos, who greeted her like a welcoming committee. The end of the war had put them in a rejoicing mood.

"And your son did his part. You must be so proud," said Alice. "Thank heaven he made it home safe!"

The store proprietors beamed and chattered together about their family's blessed relief over the war's ending. Mrs. Nap's hands accentuated her words.

The couple laughed when Alice told them Benny's remark about the end of the war allowing for more car trips.

"He's right!" agreed Mr. Nap. "Smart boy!"

More fuss over Benny triggered Judy into action. She took her brother by the hand and hid midway in the aisle where canned foods met the bread display. She whispered a prompt to Benny, who began pulling his T-shirt off his head. He whimpered for help. "Shh!" said Judy as she tugged the shirt over his head.

Alice continued chatting with the storekeepers about the victory in the Pacific, how sad and unfair that President Roosevelt hadn't lived to see the final curtain.

Judy giggled quietly as she helped Benny untie his brown oxford shoes and remove his ribbed socks. Her merriment increased as she unzipped his shorts. Benny pulled down his white training pants in a flash.

"Where are the children?" Alice asked, looking around.

"I saw them go that way," said Mr. Nap, pointing toward the canned goods.

By then, Judy's giggles had turned into shrieks. Too late, Alice encountered the children as naked Benny ran out the other end of the aisle toward the meat counter at the back of the store. He ran into a very startled Mr. Nap. "Whoa, there!"

Benny turned and ran down another aisle, where he collided with Mrs. Nap. She held a package of cupcakes, slapping it toward Benny's tiny penis aimed directly at her. "No, no!" she warned.

Judy, right behind her brother, laughed giddily over the uproar. Alice, red-faced and breathless, was gaining on the children. "Judy! Benny! What are you doing!" She brushed past her daughter and caught up with Benny who had been corralled by Mrs. Nap in the cereal aisle. The two women looked at each other.

"I'm so sorry," said Alice. "I can't believe they did this."

"You mean Benny!" Judy piped up.

Alice turned angrily. "Young lady, I know he had help. You will both be punished when we get home."

Judy's laughing mouth turned downward.

"Go—get his clothes—right now!" Alice ordered Judy, then followed her to the canned foods aisle, carrying Benny in his nakedness. She dressed her son quickly as Judy stood staring at the dark linoleum floor. Benny began wailing as Alice dressed him roughly. "Here—you carry his shoes and socks home." She shoved the items at her daughter. "And you, mister, are riding home in the Taylor Tot." The boy screamed louder as Alice slammed him into the seat. They left the store without groceries.

Embarrassed, Alice didn't even say goodbye to the storekeepers. "Come back soon!" called Mr. Nap from behind the meat counter. Was there a note of laughter in his voice?

On the walk home, Alice didn't speak to her *naughty children*, who were both crying. She paid no attention to neighbors who waved, walking in the opposite direction with a black Labrador on a leash. I need help, she thought. Child-rearing was an increasingly complex endeavor. Who could shed some light? Flora, though an experienced mother and teacher, had a critical edge and always insinuated that Alice needed to change. Maybe she ought to consult Doc Richards again. He had always been wise and kind. In a few days, Judy would start kindergarten. Alice hoped they would all turn a new page.

35

THE WAR HAD been over nearly a year in the summer of 1946—a time to breathe easier and step into the waiting line for peace and prosperity. Charlie and Alice had ordered a four-door Ford, and John Lea awaited a new Chevy. When their new cars came rolling off the assembly lines, they hoped to sell their old vehicles to young men just home from the service—if anyone preferred buying a used, rather than new, car.

The Victory Garden on Aubrey Avenue thrived because Charlie enjoyed the escape of physical work. He became an expert rose grower too. In the backyard, he had dug a deep pit for drainage near the garage and filled it with layers of sand and peat to plant roses. He and Alice awaited the arrival of a unique hybrid they had ordered from a catalog. The Peace Rose, which began its cultivated life in France and escaped to the U.S. as a *war refugee*, becoming a symbol of hope and survival. The waiting list was long; every gardener wanted a Peace Rose.

The Lukas children spent hours in the backyard, playing, swinging, and singing as Charlie worked. Alice occasionally brought out a picnic lunch and spread it on a blanket under a peach tree, where they all took a break. When the sun blazed, Judy played indoors with paper dolls cut out from women's magazines. Benny pitched himself back and forth on the sofa or pored over his books. He was starting to copy entire pages by hand with his special fat crayons. Running out of paper caused tantrums. Charlie solved the problem with weekly supplies of used scratch paper from the cooperage company.

The Lea and Lukas families felt extraordinarily blessed when Allen returned to his manager's position at the Pauling Laundry after three years as overseer in the munitions factory. Alice thanked God that the factory hadn't blown up while producing weapons of war. She admired Allen for letting his patriotism outshine his anti-war feelings. After the atomic bombings in Japan, he had said, "Was annihilation necessary?" At least the war was over, and Allen could resume his ordinary life.

⌇⌇⌇

One night in late June, well past the children's usual bedtime, Alice hurried through the last pages of a storybook with them. Benny, nestled beside his mother and sister in his new double bed, tried to slow the pace by grabbing each page as Alice reached to turn it.

Judy snapped, "Stop it, Benny!"

Alice sensed the two would be wide-awake and fighting before the end of the story. She was about to abruptly close the book and try a different tactic (a song and back rubs) when she heard the telephone ring.

The hour was late for a phone call. Alice listened for Charlie to answer the downstairs phone. She heard a surprised exclamation, and then his voice quieted. Alice tiptoed from Benny's room to the top of the stairs. She didn't hear Charlie say anything. When he replaced the phone receiver, Alice called down softly, "What is it?"

She watched him, hunched over the table in the hallway below, his hand gripping the black telephone receiver. He didn't respond, as he slowly replaced the phone in its cradle and began to straighten his back like a much older man suffering unspeakable agony.

"Charlie?" She whispered, stepping down the stairs.

He turned and approached her. Alice had never seen his eyes so dark and sad. "There was an accident at the laundry," said Charlie. "A bad one—an explosion. Allen is missing."

The words exploded in her head, and Alice felt ripped out of her own life. She collapsed, sinking to a stair step. Her arms reached out to Charlie, for breath, for a desperate hope that he hadn't spoken of such devastation. She inhaled from a hollow place deep inside. A moan escaped her mouth like an ugly spirit. Then came the tears—a rising tide she couldn't staunch. An infinity of tears would never be enough to ease her loss. Charlie embraced his wife and helped her walk upstairs.

Judy came padding out of Benny's room. "What is it, Mommy? Daddy?"

⌇⌇⌇

Before the funeral on a bright Thursday morning, the Lea and Lukas families gathered at Catherine and Allen's home. As she arrived with Charlie and the children, Alice envisioned the house dead, too, without Allen. Such a precious summer day, with cobalt sky and birds flitting through the maples and sycamores, was out of harmony with her family's tragedy. Later she would write in her diary:

> *Life so abundant surrounded us. I noticed every living and beautiful thing because my brother was so opposite, now so dead, so suddenly absent—forever. How he'd revel in a perfect day like this for driving around the countryside. I know I'll never again see such a day and not think of Allen.*

～❀❀～

Charlie stepped out of the Chevy onto the driveway, noting that Flora and John's Plymouth, formerly his own, had already arrived and parked ahead of them on the downward slope. Walking across the overgrown dewy grass, he thought of Allen's big hand on his shoulder, always ready with welcome. Charlie felt the warm spot where Allen's firm pat would have landed. He straightened his shoulders and ushered Alice and the children into the house. As they entered, he noticed the reek of cigarette smoke in his sister's house, worse than ever.

Catherine staggered toward them, eyes swollen and red, face ashen, and hair hanging. She reached out to her brother and fell limp into his embrace. Flora and John stood close behind Catherine. John had aged ten years overnight, and Flora's complexion looked gray, her eyes sunken. Alice rushed to the comfort of her parents' arms; all three were crying. Charlie felt apart, yet responsible for keeping this family grounded. He held his sister.

Judy, neat with her braids and fresh cotton dress, looked around the living room as if on another planet. Benny held her hand tight. The Reverend Harold Lukas sat on the sofa by an open window. A breeze stirred the yellowing curtains. "Come here, Judy, Benny." His gentle smile beckoned the disoriented children.

Judy asked her uncle about the whereabouts of her cousin Deborah, whose fifth birthday party she'd enjoyed only ten days ago.

"She's with the cook, I think," answered Harold. "You know Deborah is very sad."

Judy's eyelashes fanned out on her cheeks, as she looked down at her patent leather shoes. "We're sad too. We miss our uncle."

Benny jerked Judy's arm and began screaming, "No, no!" Harold reached forward to calm the boy, but Benny's wail strengthened.

Nearly at once, Elizabeth, the cook, came through the dining room, with Deborah clinging to her apron. "Come along," said the woman, her velvety tone comforting yet commanding. Deborah, russet curls tumbling over her somber face, reached for Judy's hand, and the three children followed Elizabeth into the kitchen.

⁓⁓⁓

Alice swept a damp lock of hair from her cheek. Over Flora's shoulder, she noticed the maid herding the children, including Benny, whom she feared would have a difficult day. His bawling had stopped under Elizabeth's influence. "She is so good with them," Alice said to her mother as she wiped her eyes.

Flora dabbed a crumpled tissue at her own tears. "Yes. We think it's best she keep the children here this morning. A funeral is no place for them."

Looking at her grieving father, Alice replied. "No place for any of us."

John nodded, unable to speak.

Alice wondered how it must be for her parents to lose their only son. She couldn't imagine the well of sadness if Judy or Benny passed away. She absolutely couldn't face it. And, what of the moppet Deborah, with no father to love and guide her from the tender age of five—would his image, the sound and feel of him eventually fade from her mind? We shall all have to help Deborah grow up, Alice mused. Her eyes stung, and her chin trembled as she pressed hard to control her emotions.

Later that evening, she would write about Catherine in her diary:

This is Day One of her new life without her husband. So many roles are wrapped up in the word 'husband,' and she will face life from now on without Allen's love, comfort, and support. We shall find out whether Catherine is a strong enough woman to endure. With God's help, she will.

At the burial site in Cave Hill Cemetery, the wide circle—immediate family and cousins, a multitude of friends including the Simpsons and their maid Mattie, Alice's former boss Mr. McNulty, the Paulings, postal workers, church members both Catholic and Presbyterian—extended out to the horizon in Alice's misty view. The men in suits were reverent, holding their homburgs and fedoras; the women wore proper gloves and Sunday hats with veils covering red eyes. Alice hoped the words of the minister's eulogy carried to the far edges of the crowd. Near Allen's casket overlooking the burial hole, soon to swallow his broken body, she huddled close to Charlie and her mother. Harold Lukas delivered a prayer for his brother-in-law's eternal sleep in peace. Catherine sobbed uncontrollably; Charlie held her tight as if she might jump into the burial pit. It should be pouring rain today, thought Alice. The sunshine seemed a mockery.

The dark hole in the ground reminded Alice of the coal bin where she'd been trapped long ago. Allen had come to her rescue. As he reached into the bin to grab her arms, he'd laughed and said, "How'd you get so buried?"

Alice bit her lips. Allen was her *resurrection and life*, the words she'd heard in a prayer today. Since the re-surfacing of her memory of the coalman's abuse and Allen's rescue, Alice had meant to ask her brother to recall his version of the experience. But it had been so many years ago and seemed so other-worldly, so out of the context of their adult lives, that she had never found the right time to bring it up. Now, she'd never be able to ask, would never receive Allen's confirmation that the incident really happened, was not a dream nor a storybook fantasy. Staring at his casket, soon to disappear below ground, Alice whispered to her brother, "I wish I could have saved you this time. If you could come back to me, I'd never let you go!" Tears rolled down her cheeks, and she couldn't stop them.

After the funeral, Elizabeth served lunch at Catherine's house. The children had already eaten and were playing quietly outdoors. Flora and Elizabeth took turns watching them from the kitchen and dining room windows. Catherine ate nothing and hid in the master bedroom, sprawling on the bed she had shared with Allen, her face buried in the pillows. In the dining room, conversation came hard to the others. Even Harold, in his practiced role as an empathetic clergyman, seemed pressed to say something appropriate. Elizabeth, silent and respectful, served the meal.

Flora broke through with a suggestion: "Catherine and Deborah must come home with us and stay at our house tonight—and for as long as they want to stay."

Alice agreed. "They shouldn't be alone."

Her father cleared his throat and said, "Catherine is our daughter now, too, more than ever."

Alice watched his thin neck swallow hard; he said nothing more. She picked up her fork and began nibbling a polite share of the meal without pleasure and felt apologetic for the supreme effort Elizabeth had spent preparing the food. The afternoon continued gray within the walls of her brother's house, and then Alice and Charlie gathered their children and returned home.

Flora had invited them to share the evening meal and help Catherine and Deborah get settled in the house on Brook Street. Toward evening, Charlie packed a bushel basket of garden vegetables into the trunk of the Chevy. He, Alice, and the children set off for Flora and John's.

As Alice followed the children and Charlie, with his basket, up the steps from Brook Street, she looked over at her rock garden. It's alive and Allen's gone, she thought. A memory glided to consciousness—Allen and Catherine bringing fall flowers to the garden for her wedding nearly nine years ago. Now, the purple sedum flourished vividly among the stones, and the mosses and pastel blossoms produced their richest colors. But frost will come, thought Alice. The flowers eclipsed at their prime—like Allen, taken too soon. Was this all real? How could today be happening? It was a nightmare, with Alice desolate in the middle of it, yearning to wake up.

Uncle Stuart and Aunt Henny arrived from next door to offer their support to Catherine and Deborah, whom they described as "at sea in a lifeboat, adrift."

To Alice, Allen's widow and daughter indeed seemed lost among the grieving family. They have lost their anchor, she reflected. Will their lives ever be righted? And would she herself ever be the same, with her brother snatched away so suddenly? She watched the children as they ate in Flora's kitchen. Alice looked at her curly-haired niece and thought, she truly is *Orphan Annie* now. Deborah sat quietly while her cousins giggled and stuffed their mouths with cream cheese and cucumber sandwiches.

"Do you have any fudge, Grandma?" Judy asked. "Fudge would make Deborah feel better." Alice shook her head and frowned at her daughter.

Flora bustled to the pantry door. "I did make fudge just for you children," she said. She placed a glass candy dish of sugary dark candy on the table and watched the children's eyes bulge. Flora whispered to Alice, "I had to keep busy, and I couldn't think of anything but making fudge—Allen's favorite."

The adults made sandwiches from the offerings Flora set out on the dining table. Alice was glad to see Catherine, red-eyed and weary, at least picking at the buffet. But her father was not at the table. He sat in his Morris chair in the parlor, staring at the cold fireplace. Alice went to him. "Can I bring you a plate of something, Daddy?"

He shook his bald head. "No thanks, Peaches." He paused. "I buried my son today." His voice seemed to come from far away.

Alice knelt by his chair. "I know," she said and patted his long, limp fingers.

"Where's Benny?" Judy burst into the parlor, followed by Deborah.

"I thought Benny was with you girls," replied Alice. A slight worry nudged her mind. Benny had opened his secretive little heart to Allen. How might her son be reacting to this great loss? She rose to follow the girls.

Approaching the front door, they heard a heart-piercing wail break loose outdoors. "Unca Allen! My Unca Allen!" Benny's blond hair seemed electrified in the glowing sunset as he howled to the sky. "I want you! Come back!"

He was sobbing hysterically between pleas for Allen to reappear. And Alice noticed something else—he had done a pretty thorough job trampling her rock garden.

36

Sadness expanded to the walls of Charlie's brain. He couldn't shake the shadows that clouded his thoughts. When Alice commented on his mood, he blamed it on grief over Allen's death, which, while true enough, served as a convenient cover for mourning Bonnie. He realized Alice needed empathy and support after losing her brother but found his resources lacking.

The recovery of his Plymouth coupe provided a diversion for Charlie. John Lea's new Chevy had arrived; he agreed to trade back the Plymouth to Charlie for the older-model Chevy and sell it. The Lukases became the first two-car family on the block. Their garage accommodated one car, so the coupe and a new maroon Ford sedan took turns competing for parking space with seminary students' vehicles on Pleasant Avenue.

The week they regained the Plymouth, Judy waited each evening on the front sidewalk to greet her father as he arrived home from work. Charlie felt flattered by his daughter's focused attention but curious about her motive. Did she need reassurance after the sudden loss of Deborah's father a few months ago? As he pulled up to the curb, Judy hopped down the front steps, pigtails with bright ribbons bouncing off her shoulders. He turned off the motor, opened the door, and leaped around the front of the car to hug his daughter on the sidewalk. He needed her explanation.

"Honey, all week you've been meeting me after work. It's swell you're so glad to see me. . . ."

"Of course, I'm always glad to see you, Daddy," said Judy. "Specially seeing you in the little green car!"

Charlie laughed, swept his daughter off the ground, and spun her around. "That's my girl! We love our old car, don't we!"

༄༅༅

Having a second car freed Alice from the tight scheduling of household errands. Shopping, laundry, and other duties required less time; she drove the new sedan to Catherine's nearly every day for a visit over morning coffee while the children played. Once school started, Judy entered first grade at Holy Angels, and Deborah was a fledgling in public school kindergarten. On the second morning of the school year, Alice arrived at Catherine's house, unencumbered by children.

Catherine, in her cotton robe, cigarette in hand, strolled out the front door, as Alice alighted from her car. "Where's Benny?" asked Catherine.

"He's with that church friend of Charlie's, Theresa Hawkes." The women walked into Catherine's house; Alice took her usual place at the dining table.

"Benny's with a friend of Charlie's?" Catherine inquired, sidestepping into the kitchen as she looked back at her sister-in-law.

Alice nodded.

"She's not your friend too?" Catherine called out while gathering the coffee pot and cups on a tray.

Alice pondered a moment, waiting for Catherine to reappear. "I just don't know her very well."

"And you let her keep Benny?" Catherine poured coffee into a delicate china cup.

"She's watched both children before. Judy likes her. Plus, Theresa claims she enjoys Benny. She's offered to watch him any mornings I choose."

"But what about Benny? Did he mind you dropping him off without Judy?" Catherine reached for her pack of cigarettes.

Alice smiled wistfully and shook her head. "Oddly enough, no." She watched Catherine flick her lighter and inflame the cigarette tip. "Theresa used to be a teacher; I think she's sad not having children. Benny gets every ounce of her attention."

"I'm sure he likes that." Catherine exhaled a puff of smoke.

Alice sipped her coffee and dodged the cloud.

"Sorry!" said Catherine. "I'll blow this way." She turned her head.

"It's a relief for me," continued Alice. "Sometimes I simply can't cope with that child's tantrums and strange needs—either for constant attention or to be left alone."

"He's usually all right with the girls," Catherine pointed out.

"But at home with me—I can never figure him out. He'll be doing something like lining up his books around the living room. I'll sit down beside him. Right away, he's agitated and starts fussing. It's like I ruined something for him. Then he'll be cranky, demanding one thing or another for hours."

"What ever happened with the rock garden?" Catherine asked. "Such a loss!"

"Mother and Daddy are working on it, re-planting saxifrages, sedum, everything. It breaks my heart to see the ruins and watch them try so hard. But my precious garden gives the poor dears something to think about. . . ." She hesitated, "besides Allen."

Both women fell silent. Catherine blew a smoke ring toward the ceiling. Then Alice said, "I've enjoyed these mornings."

"Me too." Catherine smiled faintly, offering a cigarette.

"No thanks." Alice took a deep breath and resumed a previous topic: "Charlie pays Theresa to sit with Benny."

Catherine looked surprised. "It doesn't sound like my frugal brother. I can't believe that arrangement will continue much longer."

"Charlie understands I need a few hours off, I guess. With Judy in school . . ."

"Judy is your trustworthy helper with Benny." Catherine stubbed her cigarette in the ashtray. Immediately her long fingers reached for the Lucky Strikes. She held the pack out to Alice; one cigarette dangled from the open end.

Alice smiled. "No. I can't."

"Sure you can," tempted Catherine. "Try one. It will help you relax."

"Charlie would be so angry."

"He wouldn't have to know."

"He'd smell it right away."

"He'll smell it from me smoking in your face. Just tell him it's me. Have one!" She shook the pack, and a cigarette slipped out.

Picking it up, Alice said, "Okay—only one! I'm curious. What's the attraction?"

Catherine reached across the table with her lighter to start Alice's cigarette, the sleeve of her wrapper brushing the coffee cups. "Now, inhale it!"

Alice did as instructed, choking wildly, her face turning red. Catherine laughed. "This is relaxing?" said Alice between spasms of coughing.

"You'll catch on," Catherine encouraged.

"I don't think I want to," gasped Alice, thumping her chest.

However, the next day she tried smoking again, and the next. . . .

"I can't believe smoking's so easy now," Alice remarked two weeks later.

"It's relaxing, isn't it? It helps perk me up," said Catherine. "And before bed-time, I smoke and think of Allen. With a nip of bourbon—it helps me sleep too."

Alice nodded. Her brother's loss had left a hole in the fabric of the family; she couldn't imagine it ever mending. She ground one cigarette into the ashtray and reached for another. I need to start buying these. We're always smoking yours."

"You'd better be careful. If Charlie found out, he might cancel the sitting business with Theresa," said Catherine.

"You're right," agreed Alice. "So far, he believes it's the smell of your smoke on me. And the coffee covers my breath. Chewing gum helps." She rapped her knuckles on the table. "Knock on wood."

The visits with Catherine continued on weekdays whenever Theresa Hawkes had time to watch Benny.

"He brightens my day," Theresa, sun-tanned under her straw garden hat, told Alice one afternoon when she arrived to pick up Benny. Theresa had been helping him collect Sweet Gum leaves in her spacious yard. The colors—deep crimson to bright yellow—varied in patterns and intensity on each leaf. Benny had placed them in separate piles on the back doorsteps. "I'm not sure what he's thinking," said Theresa, "but I enjoy watching how serious he is. He's fascinating."

"I never know what's going on in his mind," Alice replied. Then she called to her son, rummaging for leaves in the yard. "Come on, Benny! Time to get Judy at school!"

Instantly, he let the women know he wasn't ready to stop. With high-pitched wails and high stomping feet, he ran in circles through the leaves. When he began punching his head with his fists, Alice stood helplessly while Theresa hurried over to the boy. She embraced his thrashing arms tight against his body and spoke softly, "Ten more minutes, then you and Mommy can take the leaves home to show Judy."

He stood there, tear-streaked. Theresa returned to Alice. "I think we have time for coffee," she offered, motioning toward the house. "Be careful of the leaves stacked on the steps!" Her teeth sparkled as she smiled, ushering Al-ice into her bright kitchen. Alice felt upstaged by Theresa's easy competence. Over coffee, the women kept their eyes on Benny through the back door. Alice wished she had a cigarette.

37

Benny endured a taste of kindergarten in September 1947. At the classroom door, he wailed and raged, gripping Alice's right leg. Her skin, beneath shredded nylons, suffered the imprints of his fingernails. Sister Helena, in her heavy black wool skirt, black Rosary beads dangling, attempted to embrace the disturbed child and coax him into the room. Benny's eyes widened at the stiff white headgear hiding all except Sister's face below her eyebrows, and he screamed, diving onto the concrete floor. Over the ruckus, Sister Helena shook her head at Alice, signaling *it's no use.*

Alice took her son home and tried again the next morning. Benny's tantrum erupted as she wrestled his unwilling arms and legs into the back seat of the sedan. Judy sank into the front seat beside her mother. Benny tossed and kicked, bellowing, "No, no! Help, help!" Alice made sure the windows were rolled up as she drove through neighborhoods.

When they arrived at the school, Alice let Judy out of the car and kissed her. "Have a good day, Sweetie." The girl hung back, clutching her school satchel and lunch box, awaiting the outcome for her brother. Alice shoved her toward the school. "Go on, now. You'll be late." Benny wailed, kicking the front-seat upholstery and banging his head on the back seat. Alice drove him home and gave up on kindergarten that year.

Alice made another appointment with Doc Richards. Before the visit, she wrote down specific observations about her son's behavior so that she wouldn't become flustered or forgetful during the discussion:

Benny spent one hour this morning rocking himself back and forth against the back of the Davenport. He made a humming sound with his voice most of the time, except for when he started coughing. He usually walks on his tiptoes. A bit later he spent over an hour on his tummy, swinging in the backyard, making those same humming noises. He had temper outbursts at lunch—the wrong kind of crackers. In the afternoon he took off his shoes and socks in the yard. Refused to put them back on. Threw a fit. Finally, calm while swinging. At afternoon snack (when the right crackers were served) he got interested in spinning a milk bottle top and didn't finish eating.

After Judy came home, he settled down (sort of) to his writing. This time, he's copying the book about a bunny saying goodnight to the moon. Even though he's absorbed, I can't be too far away. He demands that I tell a word, or peel his crayon, or bring more paper. Always something! If I don't—another conniption fit.

Alice invited her mother to accompany her and Benny during the doctor's appointment. Perhaps she would offer supporting observations of Benny's behavior. For the consultation, a nurse ushered them into Doc Richards's paneled office, furnished with medical books, framed diplomas, and certificates. A family photo of Doc with his wife and teenage daughter was framed on his polished desk. The nurse pointed toward two business-like chairs opposite the desk before she left the room.

Doc Richards entered, hands clean and chafed, jolly as always. He hugged his aunt Flora. Alice remained seated with Benny on her lap, as he drove one of his miniature metal cars around the edges of the mahogany desk. The boy didn't acknowledge the cheerful giant even when Doc sauntered over to ruffle his blond hair. "Some pretty curls there!" Followed by, "Where'd you get those, little man?"

Benny paid no attention. Alice chuckled inwardly, imagining her son parroting the doctor's remarks later.

Doc's large frame settled into his groaning swivel chair as he faced the women with calm authority. "Well, we're here to talk about this handsome young man. . . ." He looked over at the boy who paid no notice.

"I've written sort of a diary here about Benny," offered Alice, rummaging in her stiff new handbag. She passed the papers to the doctor, who put on his glasses. After he finished reading, he followed up with a few questions. Her mother confirmed what she'd written about Benny. Alice breathed a thankful sigh.

The boy continued tracking a car around and under the desk, even running it over one of Doc's shiny black shoes as he began a route along the border of the Oriental carpet. Doc chuckled. "That's a footbridge, sonny!" Benny remained focused on his occupation. Then the doctor leaned back in his chair, thumbs under his belt, and concluded, "It's beginning to look like a classic case—of autism, sometimes called infantile schizophrenia." He cleared his throat. Alice leaned forward as he continued, "Some say it's caused by a catastrophe, but I don't think so in this case unless there's a trauma I haven't heard about."

Alice shook her head. "Of course, there was Allen's death. But this sort of behavior started long before that."

Doc continued, "There's a theory it's caused by parents pressuring the child to be perfect. I've observed some of that with your handling of Judy. . . ." His steady look held Alice. She flinched, realizing she did indeed have high standards and expectations for Judith Star Lukas, but Judy behaved normally.

Flora took up Alice's defense. "Often such is the case with the oldest child, especially a girl. Of course, we believe Judy is next to perfect." She cleared her throat. "With Benny, we have hopes and prayers—and try to maintain order."

Doc nodded. "Some say the condition is caused by parental doting or over-involvement, others by neglectful parenting. It appears parents can't win." A wry smile drew his mouth sideways as Alice straightened in her chair. He went on: "What I'm saying is—none of us are perfect. We do our best as parents; the children usually turn out fine."

Alice eased.

Doc advised, "Wait a year, then try him in school again." He paused, then added a statement that shocked Alice, "Down the road, if all else fails, institutionalizing is a possibility." He ended the session by placing a copy of *Today's Psychology* into her shaky hands, pointing out an article on troubled marriages and autism.

The women and Benny made it out of the doctor's office onto the busy downtown sidewalk, noisy with traffic. Alice blinked in the sunlight. "Did I hear right—an institution?"

Flora grabbed her daughter's arm. "Never you mind. We won't let that happen to Benny. Over his grandparents' dead bodies!" She looked down at her grandson and stroked his sunny curls. Alice's lips were tense as they walked toward the parked car. She tossed the magazine in the first trash container they passed.

∽∼∾

Alice couldn't say *no* to her mother's piling mismatched furniture into the Lukases' home on Pleasant Avenue. Her parents were remodeling their house on Brook Street in preparation for moving to the first floor and discarding unneeded furnishings. Living on the main floor without stairs would accommodate John Lea's arthritic knees. They hoped to rent out the second floor for extra income. Despite the rising tide of furniture creeping into their home, Alice held onto items she couldn't throw away—outgrown toys, newspapers and magazines she might read someday, clothes that no longer fit. But the grain of sand irritating her oyster shell was Charlie's habit of parking his golf bag and cart in the dining room between an antique washstand and a side chair. His grass-stained golf shoes often sat on the other side of the crowded furniture. Every time Charlie came home from golfing, Alice's anger increased because she knew he realized her displeasure and ignored it. "You did it again!" she railed.

"There's no better spot for them," he countered.

"What's wrong with the back porch?"

Charlie never complied, and Alice didn't move the clubs herself. Only when they expected company were the golf clubs removed from the dining room—a compromise in an ongoing skirmish.

❧❧❧

In the past year or so, Charlie puzzled over the faint staleness of cigarette smoke building up in the house, but he could never pin down the source. Alice surely didn't smoke. She'd better not! Does she? Alice claimed the scent came into the house with other people and on her clothes after visiting Catherine. For sure, his sister was a smoker. His not-so-gentle suggestions that she quit the habit went unheeded. Okay, as long as she doesn't do it in my house, he thought. But why was the stink building up here?

A typical face-off with Alice had Charlie wrinkling his nose and fingering the dining room curtains, slightly greasy with dust. "Can't you take these to the cleaners?"

"If you help me take them down and put them back up."

"Well, sure."

"But now isn't a good time."

It never seemed like the right moment for this chore. Charlie knew Alice disliked entering Pauling's Laundry now that Allen was gone. In a way he understood, but the ashy redolence in the house annoyed him. He determined not to budge on buying that washing machine she wanted or one of those newfangled dishwashers until the house smelled normal again. *Expensive luxuries anyhow!*

Summertime 1948 brought some sunlight into the shadows. Friends and family often migrated to the Lukases' backyard, especially during berry and peach seasons. Charlie loved showing off his prize roses, too—the Peace rose and his yellow and crimson varieties. Theresa and Ted Hawkes were admirers. Theresa swooned over the fragrances of Charlie's roses; she called him a *master*. Charlie always took pride in selecting a perfect blossom for Theresa. Ted's prize was a basket of fruit.

One Saturday in August, a family with seven children breezed in like a cloud of starlings. They had driven from Morgantown and claimed a cousin relationship. Armed with ladders, they virtually stripped one of Charlie's peach trees.

"Now, who were they again?" Alice asked after the family had left, their car visibly lower to the ground as it lumbered off.

"I thought they were your cousins," answered Charlie. "I never saw them before!"

Alice and Charlie could only laugh and agree that in the future only *certified cousins* would be allowed to pick their peaches.

In the fall, Judy attended third grade, loving geography and reading books from the library. She had a few girlfriends in her classroom, although she sometimes complained about being teased or not being *chosen* for games. Alice reasoned that Judy wasn't popular because of her brain and talent. Besides, Alice couldn't spare time or energy for concern with Judy's school experiences when the major dilemmas involved Benny, soon to attempt first grade at Holy Angels School.

Charlie took a morning off work and accompanied Alice to ensure the boy made it into the classroom and sat down as instructed. Judy helped by reading to her brother from her third-grade reader as they rode to school in the back seat of the Ford sedan. As he walked with his parents down the tunnel-like corridor to the first-grade room, Benny tuned up his whine and quickly approached full throttle. Charlie yanked the boy to attention, looking him in the eye, "Remember—ice cream with Grandma and Grandpa after school—if you don't fuss."

Benny stopped, bit his lip, and allowed the black-robed nun to lead him into the classroom. She ushered him into a child-sized chair at a low table for eight students; each had a drawer at his place. Benny looked back at his parents, who waved and smiled from the doorway.

Charlie mouthed, "Ice cream!"

At the end of the school day, when Alice and Judy stopped by the first-grade classroom to pick up Benny, the teacher told them he was no longer there. "I couldn't control him, and the principal sent him back to kindergarten." Alice imagined her son running away, the involvement of school personnel, and the chaos caused by Benny's misbehavior. The nun continued, ". . . refusing to sit down, tiptoeing all over the classroom and throwing books and chalk. Talking out of turn, yelling nonsense words, making odd sounds. Some of the children laughed. Others seemed frightened."

In a white-hot-pounding panic, Alice grabbed Judy's cool hand and raced downstairs to the basement kindergarten room, her legs shaking. Judy cried out as her mother clawed into her hand. Sister Helena greeted them with a beatific smile. Benny stood quietly beside her, waiting at the classroom door. "I think he'll be fine now. I can work with him," said the nun. Alice realized she had a young, pretty face under the penguin garb. "He likes books," said Sister Helena. "That's a very good start."

In the car, all the way home, Benny chattered in his flat-toned voice about "Little Her."

"Who is Little Her, Benny?" Alice asked and kept repeating, as he did not acknowledge her question. She thought Little Her must be a book character or a classmate. Benny kept prattling on.

Finally, Judy figured it out. "Little Her is his teacher, Sister Helena."

Alice smiled at Judy's cleverness. "Let's hope Little Her can give Benny a big year in kindergarten at last."

38

"I KNOW WHAT happened to Bunny," Judy began, fresh and dripping, just out of the bathtub.

Alice, on her knees, enveloped her daughter in a threadbare towel and hugged her close. "Really? After all this time?" Alice was surprised to hear about the rabbit toy, lost years before. Yet she had learned not to underestimate eight-year-old Judy's memory and insights.

The girl snuggled inside the familiar softness and began whispering: "Bunny was a runaway—like the bunny in that story we read." Her volume increased with excitement. "Remember how his mommy said she would go find him no matter what he turned into? A rock, a flower, a fish . . ."

Alice joined in, remembering, "A sailboat, a bird, a circus performer."

Judy's eyes were bright. "Even a little boy!"

Alice squinted, trying to fathom Judy's thoughts.

"I looked and looked for Bunny everywhere," Judy said. "I actually thought he'd turn up as a flower or rock in your garden at Grandma's. But I finally realized he ran away and became a real boy!"

"Interesting," Alice mused as she dried Judy's damp hair with the towel.

"It happened that day in the Taylor Tot," said the girl, her head bobbing as Alice rubbed. "We didn't see it because it was magic—Bunny turned into Benny!"

Alice stopped toweling Judy and rested on her heels. "Amazing! Why do you think Benny is your toy rabbit?"

"I always knew Bunny wanted to be alive and be my friend who could talk to me! I finally figured out he did it when we weren't looking." She gestured, holding out both arms like a magician under the towel. "Bunny was gone—there was Benny!"

"But your brother didn't change," Alice countered.

"But he did, bit by bit—afterward." Judy numbered the ways: "How he walks—on his tippy-toes. The way he talks—not like a regular person. How he doesn't understand some things. . . ."

"And he loves carrots," Alice surrendered.

"Yes!" Judy bounced up and down off the tile floor. "You see! And the names—Bunny and Benny—it all fits!" She threw her arms around Alice's neck, kissing her cheek.

Alice could only smile at her daughter's certainty and delight. That night she wrote in her diary:

> *I hadn't realized the depth of Judy's sadness over losing her bunny. It's been four years—half her life. In her childish way, she's kept her hopes alive of someday finding it. Without any help from us, Judy has thought about it and found a solution. A child's imagination is a glorious thing, like a garden where beautiful ideas come alive. Santa Claus, fairies, now Bunny, transformed into her brother! It makes me sad in a way too. If Judy had more friends, would she have tried so hard to bring her rabbit back to life? At least for now, her dreams are happy.*

On the weekend, Charlie and Alice wanted to see a picture show at The Vogue. *Sorry Wrong Number*, a thriller with Barbara Stanwyck and Burt Lancaster, seemed the perfect escape to Charlie. For a couple of hours in the darkened theater, he and Alice could munch popcorn and hold hands like in the old days, forgetting the doldrums of everyday life. "I'll ask Theresa to look after the kiddos," he told Alice.

"No—I'd rather you didn't," said Alice. Charlie raised his eyebrows at her determined tone. "She sees enough of Benny after kindergarten during the week. And Mother has complained we don't bring the children to them more often."

Charlie nodded. "Okay. Ask Flora, then."

"It makes perfect sense. Mother and Daddy can come here and put the children to bed. Or—better yet—the kids could spend the night with my parents and watch that new television. It would give us all night."

Charlie caught her eyes sparkling. He figured there might be love scenes in the movie to ignite Alice's sexual desires, as they often did. Hoping for delights under the bedsheets later, he smiled.

Alice continued. "Besides, I haven't quite understood for a long time why you pay Theresa so much for sitting with Benny. It's a lot more money than we pay the girls next door."

Charlie needed a logical explanation. Clearing his throat, then speaking calmly, he said, "Money stretches further with young girls. What do they need money for, anyway?"

Alice shrugged. The telephone rang, ending the discussion.

❧❧❧

Waiting for Mass to begin Sunday morning, Charlie cracked his knuckles and anticipated Theresa's arrival at Holy Angels's choir loft. He saw Alice downstairs in a pew with the children, already hushing Benny. Then he glanced toward the stairway and saw Theresa entering the loft without Ted.

"Nothing serious, I hope," said Charlie offhandedly when he learned Ted was nursing a cold. His gaze swept Theresa from head to toe. She looked striking with her burnished hair tamed under a blue velvet beret. She stood up straighter in her plaid dress and smiled brightly.

Charlie pulled her aside from choir members just arriving. "I think our scheme may be coming to an end," he whispered.

"Oh! What's the matter?"

"Alice wants to cut back on your sitting time with the kids." Theresa frowned. "Her parents want more time with the grandchildren. John Lea is pretty much housebound. . . ."

Theresa patted Charlie's arm. "I understand. The children are an entertaining diversion for him."

"And Alice is grumbling about paying you," Charlie continued. "How much more do we need?"

The choir director motioned for the members to take their places and open their hymnals.

Theresa whispered, "Don't worry, Charlie. We've saved nearly enough. In fact, it's all we need. It's virtually paid for."

"Are you sure?"

The director tapped his baton on the podium; muffled conversations and shuffling motions stopped.

Theresa smiled at Charlie as she turned to pick up her book. "Yes, positive."

The organist attacked the keys and drowned out further conversation. Exultant chords of the processional thundered through the aisles up to the church altar.

⌦⌫

Downstairs, Alice rummaged in her purse for a blue Tootsietoy car Benny was on the verge of screaming for. Trying to keep calm, she wondered if she had remembered to pack it in the flushed hurry to prepare for church. Her fingers hit the tiny metal object. Lucky! She handed the little sedan to Benny. Relieved, she collapsed against the pew back. Through the solid oak wood, the bass vibrations of the pipe organ tickled her throat and throbbed in her chest. Happily retracing a moment from last night's lovemaking, Alice turned to spot Charlie in the choir loft above. Her expectant smile froze as she observed her husband cheek-to-cheek with Theresa Hawkes.

39

S NOW FALLING SOFTLY on a November morning gave notice of the holiday season approaching. Catherine phoned Alice to request a favor. "Can you please help me take down the curtains so I can wash them before Thanksgiving?"

Alice hesitated because she was exhausted and her legs ached, but she knew she shouldn't refuse her widowed sister-in-law. "Which ones—just in the dining room?"

"Pretty much the whole house. Drapes too. I'll send those to Pauling's. But I need help taking them down. I'd ask Charlie, but—"

Alice laughed despite feeling put-upon. "I know. He'd choke and cough and complain the whole time."

Catherine jumped ahead. "I take it you'll help, then. It's my only hope of getting Harold here for Thanksgiving dinner. Last time he was here—too long ago—he complained about the cigarette smell. He didn't stay long. My sainted brother doesn't complain about much. When he does, you know it's bad."

"Okay." Alice let Catherine hear her long sigh, then realized, ashamed, that she was acting like an old woman. She straightened her backbone and agreed to help Catherine a week before Thanksgiving.

The agreed-upon workday arrived soon enough. The hours stretched ahead, with Benny and Judy in school all day. Catherine had sent Deborah to school despite a cough. Alice drove through wet streets, powdered with snow, and arrived at her sister-in-law's house, stoically prepared for housework that also needed doing at home.

Catherine opened the door, mixing cold fresh air with smoke from the stub she held in her hand. "Come in, come in!" Glenn Miller's upbeat jazz issued from the record player; the scent of percolating coffee upstaged the usual stale tobacco smell. "We've got all day. I thought we'd start slow," said Catherine, swinging her hips as she ushered Alice through the living room into the adjacent dining room.

Alice noticed one of the pale green drapes already down and folded on the floor. Good start, she thought, readily accepting a *Lucky Strike* from the package Catherine tossed onto the tablecloth.

"I really should wash all the tablecloths, too," Catherine mused.

"Thanksgiving is a lot of work," Alice commented.

"Especially for smokers." Catherine snickered. "But never mind that for now. I have something to show you." She drew a folded envelope from her apron pocket. "Something of concern—from Lillian."

As Alice drew on her cigarette, she read the letter from Catherine and Charlie's sister in Washington DC. One word stood out as if electrified—polio! She hastened to read on:

> For several months now, I've felt tired and weak. It's an effort to take a step off a curb. Twice I fell when walking two blocks from the bus stop to Capitol Hill. Such a bustling place—and lately I've felt I don't belong here.

Alice looked up at Catherine. "How dreadful! Lillian has always been on the go despite her crippled leg."

Catherine shook her head. "It's sure hard to understand."

Alice continued reading to herself: *I thought whatever is wrong might eventually pass. But two weeks ago, I was really scared when I had trouble swallowing. I went to the doctor, and he kept talking about my having polio as a child. The swallowing difficulty has occurred several times. The doctor said there's a possibility I could choke, and I ought not live alone anymore.*

Lillian's letter continued with more details about her symptoms and difficulties, along with her doctor's assertion: *contagion unlikely.* He gave no reason for Lillian's weakening condition, only strong advice to change her living and work arrangements. The letter ended with a simple request to Catherine: *May I move in with you and Deborah?*

Alice slammed the letter down. "No! Possible polio and she wants to live here and expose Deborah—and you!" Her voice shook. "And my children too!"

"Don't get excited," Catherine soothed. "It's a big decision and lots to discuss. Nothing's happening yet. Of course, we'll consult Doc Richards too."

"I just don't want to see polio in my life again." Remembering the miasma of her own sickness, the thought of revisiting the trauma on her family made her struggle for a breath.

"Of course not. None of us do. But I'm worried about Lil living by herself—and choking."

"I know," said Alice, sighing. "Maybe she could find someone to share her apartment and stay in Washington." Away from us, she thought.

⁓⁓⁓

Before Christmas, Lillian had quit her secretarial position and hired a practical nurse to stay with her at night. The expense took a bite from Lillian's savings. Her letters to Catherine became more plaintive.

She wrote: *I need to work in a quieter place where I can find transportation to a job. I need to be with family. Catherine, I think we could help each other. I can pay you for my lodging; I can watch Deborah sometimes, and I can cook. Remember what a good cook Mama turned me into—and you too, of course.*

When Alice heard of Lillian's suggestion, she bristled, especially at the mention of caring for Deborah and cooking.

"With polio! How can she dare?" Alice raised her concerns—and her voice—to Charlie as he listened to the radio after the children's bedtime. Charlie tuned out John Cameron Swayze's commentary on Communist traitors and gave ear to his wife.

His hazel eyes flashed amber. "For Chrissake Alice! The doctor practically certified Lillian's not sick and not contagious. They don't know what's wrong with her, but she certainly needs our help."

"I understand. She's your sister, and you want to help. But. . . ." She bit her lip, recalling Charlie's shunning of her brother during the war years.

Charlie's hostile stare ended the discussion.

While her husband prepared for bed, Alice turned to her diary:

Am I wrong to protect my children? I just know Lillian has polio again. I'm afraid of what's happening to me too. The aches and weakness in my legs that come and go. I hope I won't become as desperate a case as Lillian. I know how much she needs family. I just don't want my children's lives put in danger.

Flora and John Lea jumped into the fray over Lillian's plans, even offering to open their home to her, as it sat on a convenient trolley route to downtown. Alice raised objections. Flora countered, "Judy and Benny are probably more in danger of polio exposure at school and playgrounds than they'd be with Lillian."

Alice wondered why life presented such adversity. *Why don't people understand my viewpoint? If only I had the spirit of Scarlett O'Hara, I'd put off my worries and enable life to flow happily.*

Harold, in Morgantown, offered to share his parish residence with Lillian. But she declined, preferring to live in the larger city where she might transfer to another federal job. Christmas was bearing down fast. As nothing had been decided, Lillian would remain in Washington, sharing the holiday with her practical nurse.

Alice realized she was the main obstacle to her sister-in-law's resettlement plans, and she knew Charlie and Catherine were right to welcome their sister. But Alice's fear of polio and her instinct to protect her children were strong and sharp. The conflict in her soul added headaches to her bodily woes. At Christmas, she added a note to Lillian's card: *Surely hope you will be feeling better soon and back to your busy, happy life as usual in 1950. Happy New Year! We send our love.*

40

ALICE DIDN'T KNOW what to expect from the meeting with Benny's second-grade teacher. Sister Mary Magdalene had been brisk on the telephone. Of course, reasoned Alice, her son was an unusual and sometimes difficult child, but he had adapted to school, as far as she could tell. He seemed happy enough, if tired, each day when she collected the children after school.

She dressed in a new tweed skirt and jacket with a frilly blouse pinned at the neck by a cameo that reminded her of Martha Washington. Her sensible oxford pumps with arch supports never varied. But she should wear gloves and a hat—her gray felt one would do—for the meeting with Benny's teacher, an Ursuline nun, who wore black serge to her ankles and a starched white head contrivance topped with a black veil. Interesting, thought Alice, the contrast in our prescribed *uniforms*.

The steely February sky hung low as she walked from house to garage. Driving to Holy Angels School, she predicted Benny might be restless after school, with both recesses probably canceled due to wintry weather. The principal's commanding the class during her meeting with Sister Mary Magdalene would be a stressful change of routine for Benny. After such a day, Alice knew he might explode physically and emotionally when he hit home, resulting in a headache for her.

But on a positive note, Benny's appetite for reading and writing had taken great strides this year. Santa Claus had brought a set of encyclopedias down the chimney at Christmas, and Benny was already wearing out the pages of M, D, and S. Limestone Cooperage hardly produced enough scrap paper for Benny's ongoing lists of minerals, dinosaurs, and facts about the forty-eight states. His rosters of invented names and places were amazingly creative leaps; how did he think these up?

Benny loved reading to Judy and listening to her read. Alice alternated between feeling left out and enjoying free moments to herself. Benny sometimes criticized his sister's reading style, demanding, "Say it out!" Judy then appeased him with more drama in her voice.

But she often teased Benny as he read: "They can hear you in the next town!" Their mother, in the kitchen, would chuckle to herself as she listened to them reading and chattering on the living room couch.

Alice hoped for a good report at her conference with Sister Mary Magdalene—at the very worst, a solution to any problems. She parked the sedan at the curb in front of Holy Angels Church and walked past the heavy wooden doors inlaid with stained-glass crosses, around to the two-story brick school where earthbound angels sat at their desks. Sister Mary Magdalene reminded her of Eleanor Roosevelt in a habit, wearing glasses. She anticipated the nun would be as wise and humane as the former first lady. They met in a tiny room off the principal's office, barely big enough for a sofa and straight chair. Sister offered Alice the sofa, then checked her gold watch dangling on a chain down her heavy black skirt. Alice hesitated, wondering if she had mistaken the appointment time.

The nun closed the door and then sat down in the chair, her high-laced black shoes planted firmly on the floor. "An hour isn't much time," she began, leveling a polite smile at Alice. "So I'll get right into it. I'm sorry I must tell you this, but Benjamin is practically unteachable in my classroom."

Alice felt a bubble bursting around her, and she was treading water under an engulfing wave. She struggled to say something, but nothing—not even an exclamation—came out of her open mouth.

Sister Mary Magdalene continued. "Oh, he's probably smart enough—who can tell!" She shrugged. "But he's off in his own world—his own curriculum, it seems like. He can't be disciplined or even made to listen. He disturbs the class."

Alice collapsed onto the plush velvet upholstery, seeking support; she couldn't believe what she had heard. Yet, as the nun proceeded, she could picture Benny's behaviors.

"I sometimes wonder if it's a hearing problem," said Sister. "He'll be up and wandering around the room during a lesson. Looking out the windows or rummaging in the bookshelves. All the students know the shelves are restricted for silent reading time on Fridays. Benny doesn't follow the rules and seems deaf when I tell him to sit down. If a normal child did that. . . ."

Alice clutched her arms tight around her at the word *normal.*

The nun coughed softly into her fist and continued. "At other times, when it's noisy in the room, Benny will be sitting on the floor with his fingers in his ears."

Alice spoke as firmly as she could muster. "He is not deaf."

"Oversensitive, perhaps?"

"He can be." Alice recalled times when the blaring radio or sudden sharp noises startled her son into a crying fit.

"Does he get enough sleep?"

Alice bristled. "Why do you ask?"

"He seems tired a lot and will sometimes put his head down on his desk. Sometimes he hums to himself, and I have to shake him."

Alice looked down at the tweed skirt stretched across her lap. She realized Benny often appeared anxious and comforted himself by humming or flapping with his hands. She knew stress could wear him out. Her throat tightened with an inability to summarize Benny's condition and the family's coping attempts. "I don't know—we do see a doctor," Alice murmured.

"What does the doctor say about his imaginary friends and lack of real friends among other children?"

"Imaginary friends? I didn't—"

"Yes. He talks about someone he calls Little Her. Babbles about her, especially during recess."

A hint of a smile curved Alice's lips. Judy had reported that Benny often sought out his former kindergarten teacher on the playground during morning recess. "He just loves Sister Helena," Judy had said. "I've seen him hugging and hugging her. Sister doesn't push him away. She is always kind."

Alice eyed the forbidding woman in front of her and could understand her son's seeking refuge with Sister Helena. "We know about Little Her," she responded.

"What concerns me most is that Benjamin is completely off track. Hardly seems to know the other children exist unless they are noisy or bothering him."

Alice shuddered at the word *bothering.* Surely, the nuns could protect him from bullying!

"And he pays no attention to what I'm teaching." The nun stopped abruptly. "Except the other day. I was teaching about homophones—words sounding the same but spelled differently, having different meanings."

Alice nodded; of course, she knew about homophones.

Sister huffed, "Well then," as she began recounting: "Benjamin lit off on homophones. He was writing and scribbling almost faster than I could write on the blackboard. The students shouted out words to me as they caught onto the idea. As far as I can remember, your son never participated. But he kept writing and running his finger down pages of a book on his desk.

"When I questioned him about his activity, he just looked around with a blank stare. 'Benny, are you doing homophones?' I asked. He wouldn't answer, so I marched over to his desk. And, indeed, he'd been writing down all the words from the blackboard plus more from his storybook. His head was down on his desk by then, so I dropped the matter."

She continued, "But just before dismissal when the children were taking turns reviewing the day, Benny began shouting out, virtually interrupting each child whenever they spoke a word that was a homophone. 'W-o-n and o-n-e' he would spell out, or 'no and know, see and sea'—whatever the children would say prompted him to spell the words out loud. It bothered the girls, but the boys got into it with Benny, copying him or making fun of him, jumping out of their seats. It became a near riot before I threatened them all with *after school*."

"Well," said Alice. "They certainly learned their homophones."

"Indeed," snapped Sister, "but it was disruptive."

Alice had planned to share some pleasant examples of Benny's at-home learning and the imaginative lists of names and book titles he created, such as *Goodbye Yellow Wind* or *The Cat Who Sat on Kentucky*. She had hoped to brag to her son's teacher that perhaps he'd write one of those books someday. But now, her pride in Benny's brilliance would appear foolish.

Sister Mary Magdalene adjusted the starched white bib attached to her head covering and said, "I will consult with our principal, Sister Jude, after her experience with Benjamin in my classroom this afternoon." She waved toward the hall lined with classrooms.

The nun's conclusion hit Alice like a thunderbolt: "It might be well to find another placement for Benjamin."

Alice's mouth dropped. She couldn't speak, as dizziness prevented words from forming in her brain.

"You're not Catholic, are you?"

Alice lowered her gaze and shook her head. Frustration caught in her chest. Hadn't she promised to raise Charlie's children Catholic? And hadn't she done her best under complicating and exhausting circumstances? Why was her religious faith now a mark against her? And Benny too?

Sister went on, "I'm not suggesting the public school, of course. That would be even more chaotic. But maybe another private school. Or a boarding school for—"

Alice didn't hear the woman say *institution*, but she knew what was implied. She didn't remember getting up from the sofa and grabbing her purse, but she saw herself flee from the parlor, felt rage and humiliation heating her face, and heard the glass rattle in the door as it slammed behind her. She ran to the car. Shaking and sobbing, she sat in the driver's seat, anticipating the sharp ring of the school's dismissal bell and the buzzing swarm of children spilling out onto the sidewalks around the church.

Soon Judy, followed by Benny, bounced onto the side of the car and jostled the door handles. Alice looked over at Judy, noticing her daughter was quick-ly outgrowing her favorite windowpane-checked dress. She was growing like a bean sprout and becoming almost pretty despite her fine, straight hair and freckles—on the cusp of adolescence. Judy opened the door and slid into the front seat. "Hi Mommy!" she said brightly, tossing her book satchel onto the floorboard.

Alice reached over the back seat to help Benny open the back door. Lately, he demanded to ride home stretched out on the back seat—something to do with the car's vibrations. "Good day, Benny?" Of course, he didn't answer and immediately sprawled face down on the back seat, ready to go. My beautiful son, thought Alice, and the emotions of the past hour strangled her breath and misted her vision. Judy's chatter about her average school day enabled Alice to focus on the drive home.

That evening when Charlie tromped into the kitchen with a load of leftover paper for Benny, Alice could hardly wait to confide in him. However, she was patient, allowing him to warm his hands over the stove, shake off the mood of his workday, and greet the children in the living room. Finally, he wandered back into the steamy kitchen with its suppertime smells, came up behind Alice at the countertop and squeezed her around the waist. "What are the sniffles for?"

"Onions," she said, showing him the half-sliced bulb.

"Sure?" he said. "You're shaking."

Alice's shoulders slumped as she related the events of the afternoon's meet-ing. Occasionally, she paused to turn to the stove and lift the lid on last summer's green beans, smelling harshly overcooked. The nun's words still crackled in her ears like static as she recalled every detail of Sister Mary Magdalene's tirade.

"They can't expel Benny just like that." Charlie snapped his fingers. "They might want to expel you, though. You just walked out on that nun?"

"Maybe you'd have done better," she retorted, her heart filling with rage. You're the Catholic here, she thought, and you have such respect for nuns and priests, no matter how they behave. You should have sat in with that nun today, but on the other hand, you might have betrayed our son. In a barely controlled voice, she said, "Can't you understand how angry and upset I was?"

"Well, I wish I'd been there. I suppose someone from Holy Angels will be telephoning. Either the principal or the pastor."

"I'm sorry. It's really serious, isn't it?"

"Don't worry. We'll see. I'm sure they can't expel Benny without going through some procedures. If necessary, we'll get Harold involved."

Alice sighed. The mention of her well-respected, clerical brother-in-law held promise. "Would he help?"

"Harold might take it to the bishop!" Charlie's laugh made Alice smile.

The children came clamoring into the kitchen. "We're hungry!" announced Judy. "When is supper?"

"Right now!" Charlie beamed, picking up a bowl of wiggling cherry gelatin. He signaled Judy to hold the swinging door and led the way into the dining room.

41

B Y April 1951, Lillian Lukas had been living with Catherine and Deborah for over a month. Catherine, needing more income than Allen's insurance and pensions, began working as a cafeteria hostess in the 620 Building downtown, where Charlie used to work. Lillian was able to find a federal secretarial position in the same building.

Deborah, nearly ten, was adjusting to her new lifestyle, before and after school at a sitter's home, but also happily spending more time with her grandparents and cousins. Flora had learned to drive after John's disabilities prevented him from doing so. She enjoyed wheeling about, picking up Deborah, Judy, and Benny for various outings and visits.

One Friday evening after supper at the house on Brook Street, the three children were enjoying Sid Caesar's television variety show with their grandfather and Uncle Stuart from next door while Flora made fudge. The Leas had turned their parlor into a bedsitter with John's Morris chair facing the fireplace and mantel that displayed sepia-toned graduation photographs of Alice and Allen. Next to the fireplace sat the television where John could watch it by the hour, sometimes even staring at the test pattern. Across the room stood his hospital bed, and at the foot, a daybed for Flora.

Often, Benny sprawled on Flora's narrow bed to watch television or lounge with his books and writing tablets. But this night, he perched on the arm of his grandpa's chair. John observed him closely. "Stuart, come here," John whispered, beckoning to his brother seated near the windows. Stuart gave a nod and drew closer. "Look at Benny," said John.

"I see."

What they observed was reported to Alice when John phoned her soon after. "Benny was sitting on the arm of my chair. He was very stiff, so I reached my arm around so he wouldn't fall."

"Stiff?" said Alice.

"Yes, a bit paralyzed. And his eyes were sort of flickering. We were watching the television. I guess Stuart thought it would help if he turned off the set."

"Paralyzed?" A heavy cramp filled Alice's stomach as thoughts of polio raced through her mind.

"Yes, but it was all over in a minute or two. Benny began joining the girls in protest at Stuart's turning off the Sid Caesar show." He chuckled.

"Thank goodness," said Alice, but worry clung to her voice. "Is he all right now?"

"Yes, just fine. The kiddos are getting ready for their overnight with fudge and storytime. Don't worry."

But Alice knew she would worry. "Call me any time there's a problem."

"Of course, honey. I just thought I should mention this, as it seemed out of the ordinary. And if this had happened before—"

"No. I don't think it has. I never saw that happen, and if Charlie or the teachers ever did, they never told me." But would they? She rubbed her forehead as a headache threatened.

"So, probably nothing important. Good night. Sleep tight."

The following Sunday evening, Alice, Charlie, and the children gathered at the Leas' home on Brook Street for a casual meal and the evening's television programs, starting with the Ed Sullivan show. Lillian, Catherine, and Deborah had joined them. Alice still felt uncomfortable having Lillian in their midst, but Doc Richards had assured the family: "Late effects of polio, not now contagious."

Dining space was tight, so the children ate at a separate table in the high-ceilinged kitchen adjacent to the dining room where the adults were seated.

"Moon pies for dessert!" Flora announced to the grandchildren, who clapped their hands in unison.

In the next room, Alice smiled at the commotion. She kept one ear to the children as the adults talked quietly around her. She heard Judy announce, "Oh, he's a real good bunny!"

Deborah giggled. Benny's high-pitched laugh bounced off the kitchen wall.

It amused Alice how well Benny had taken to the idea of being Judy's reincarnated stuffed rabbit-turned-boy.

"Look at his bunny nose," shrieked Deborah. "Look how it twitches!"

"Good boy, Bunny!" Judy praised. "Bunny? Benny?"

After an abrupt end to their chatter, Alice heard a crash of dishes and the girls screaming. She dashed into the kitchen, where her son lay convulsing on the linoleum floor. Broken glass, chipped dishes, and a moon pie with one bite missing, surrounded him. Charlie was quickly beside her, scooping up his son from the debris.

"What happened?" Flora asked the two girls standing back, speechless and pale.

"His eyes went funny, then he fell over," said Judy.

"Like he was trying to look inside his own head," suggested Deborah.

Alice ran to the telephone in the hallway to call Doc Richards.

"Tell him I'm taking Benny to the hospital," ordered Charlie.

Alice had reached Doc's wife on the phone as she looked at her boy in Charlie's arms, unconscious and a grayish-blue color. "Hurry!" whimpered Alice into the receiver.

Charlie, in a sweat, was immediately out the front door. Alice looked across the hall and saw her father with Lillian, still seated at the dining table, unable to help, talking in concerned tones. Catherine had gone to the kitchen to clean up. Flora took the girls into the bedsitter and sat down with them. Alice heard John telling Lillian about Benny's *flickering* episode on Friday night. When Doc came on the phone, Alice talked as fast as she could, relieved at last that her cousin, the doctor, would be rushing to the hospital.

"I need to be there too," said Alice as she returned to the dining room.

Catherine spoke from the hall. "I'll take you. Let's go."

As the two women raced down the front steps to the sidewalk, Alice turned to her sister-in-law. "It might be polio!"

Catherine said nothing as they hurried to the car. Once inside, Catherine reached over to the glove compartment to grab a package of *Lucky Strikes*. From the passenger-side window, Alice looked out onto the shadowy forms of her rock garden, fearing for her son's life. The Chevy pulled away from the curb.

The two women smoked in silence as they sped through dark streets toward the hospital. Alice prayed silently that each stoplight would let them pass. She sighed with relief on seeing the red neon hospital sign ahead.

Doc Richards, in his knee-length white coat over corduroy trousers, put his arms around Alice and Charlie in the hospital corridor outside the tiny white room where their son lay. "Benny had an epileptic seizure, but he's coming around," said the doctor.

A dart shot through Alice's heart. "What could've caused that?"

"Injury or trauma. Sometimes we don't know what makes the brain go haywire," answered Doc. "He will need to be watched closely in case this happens again." He nodded to a nurse clicking her heels as she walked past in the hallway.

Suddenly Alice thought of how Sister Mary Magdalene might react if her son had such an attack during the school day. "Should Benny go to school?" she asked.

Doc shook his head. "He won't go anywhere for a while. We'll keep him here and see how he does for at least a week."

Alice gasped and tried to loosen Doc's grip on her shoulder. "I must go to him."

She insisted on staying the night in her son's room. Hospital orderlies wheeled in a cot for her. Charlie looked at it with a clenched jaw. "I'll go to pick up Judy. She has school tomorrow."

Alice kissed her husband distractedly and turned toward Benny's bedside. The matter of sleeping all night in her clothes seemed irrelevant.

◦⌒◦⌒◦

After Benny suffered another seizure the following week in the hospital, his release date was moved back again. Doc Richards called Charlie and Alice into his office. "With the frequent seizures he's having now, I called in a specialist who deals with epileptic patients. This doctor will take another look at Benny next week and do some tests."

Alice's heart sank to the pit of her stomach. "We miss him at home." Alice had spent two weeks driving to and from the hospital. Charlie, who checked on his son each night after work, voiced concern about his progress in school.

"Yes, well . . ." Doc Richards adjusted his tight shirt collar. "We can send him home soon, but I think your boy needs constant attention. The epilepsy expert and I agree that spending some time under supervision in a specialized hospital would be the wiser choice for your son." He paused, eyes darting between Alice and Charlie, then continued, "At St. Thomas Colony in Middlesboro, he could receive schooling as well as excellent medical care."

Alice felt pale, a tightening in her chest. "You mean he'd have to stay there? All the time?" She saw it again—the dreaded shadow of an institution for Benny.

Charlie cleared his throat. "Is it necessary, do you think?"

Doc nodded. "It would be best until we get this condition under control. I would do it if it were my daughter. St. Thomas Colony is the best place. It's designed specifically for children with epilepsy and other mental conditions."

Alice shuddered at *other mental conditions*. A catchall, somewhere to conveniently put her son out of the way. Her fingers tightened around her purse handle. She wanted to escape the suffocating room and shake off this nightmare. Her voice trembled. "How long would he have to stay?"

"Time will tell," said Doc. He stared briefly at the floor, then squared his shoulders and spoke softly to the couple, "That's the most honest answer I can give."

Two weeks later, on a tear-stained page in her diary, Alice wrote: *Tomorrow we send Benny away. My worst nightmare is real. Charlie keeps telling me it's a temporary thing, but I wonder. You hear of people spending their lives in such a place, never able to get out once they're in. I want so much to refuse sending Benny there. But then, if he had another seizure sometime, the worst could happen. And it would be my fault! This is the blackest time of my life, what a horrible decision.*

The next day, Charlie and Alice prepared to pick up Benny from the hospital and drive him to the Middlesboro facility, not far from the Simpson farm. The Ford sedan was packed with Benny's clothes, the encyclopedias, a box of paper and pencils, a few toys and books, and a new copy of *The Runaway Bunny*. Judy had selected the book for him when Flora took her shopping downtown.

Judy cried loudly in the back seat of the car, pleading with her parents to let her see Benny and say goodbye. Instead, they intended to deliver her to her grandparents' home on their way to the hospital. They had decided an emotional goodbye would not be good for Judy and probably worse for Benny. "You'll see him again soon," Alice promised bravely.

Charlie had to carry Judy into the Leas' house; she cried, kicked, and fought him as he struggled up the steps and sidewalk past the rock garden. Flora, her face like a mask of tragedy, met them at the front door and gathered Judy into her arms. Alice remained in the car, watching with horror as her grief-stricken daughter disappeared behind Flora's closing door. The trauma was sure to continue inside. Alice held down a lump in her throat that tasted like guilt. She could only pray that Flora and John, in their kind wisdom, would know how to comfort and contain Judy.

Alice sat in the back seat with Benny as they drove away from the hospital. Benny knelt on the seat to stare back at the red neon *Hospital* sign. "Judy! Where's Judy?" he cried out.

"She's with Grandma and Grandpa." Alice tried to sound calm although she was shaking.

"I want them—now!" Benny ordered. Then he plunged onto his mother's lap and buried his face in the folds of her light spring coat. Alice fondled his blond curls and listened to his sobs.

"You'll be back home soon," she said, hoping to heaven this was true. She saw Charlie's eyes watching her in the rearview mirror, hazel-brown eyes full of worry. She continued rubbing her son's back and head as he lay crying, face down on her lap; she could feel a damp patch where her coat didn't cover her dress. "You'll be back home before you know it," she said continually.

With a sudden jerk, Benny raised his head and looked down on a shopping bag packed with his toys and books. *The Runaway Bunny* was on top. He picked up the book and sat up next to Alice. He began turning the pages gently as if reading and pondering the brightly imaginative illustrations. "From Judy," Alice commented, smiling. Benny nodded and kept paging through.

I'm the opposite of that mother bunny, thought Alice. Instead of challenging each obstacle to reach my little bunny, I am sending him away—miles from home. She choked on the thought.

"You okay, Alice?" said Charlie.

She swallowed and squeezed out a weak "Yes."

The long drive to Middlesboro seemed like passing through a tunnel, as Alice paid no mind to views outside the car. Her eyes and thoughts were on Benny. As they neared the destination—*the final destination*—Alice worried about how she could be strong enough to encourage Benny to go forward into the foreign environment where his health required him to be. How would she let go of him and allow strangers to take him under their wings? She hoped they would be safe, protective, and nurturing wings. Alice knew she should trust Doc Richards's judgment, but it would be the most challenging moment she'd ever faced.

There was no light at the end of that tunnel, only bleakness and apprehension, as the Ford arrived at the entrance to St. Thomas Colony. Yet Alice knew she must radiate positiveness and hope for Benny's sake. She and Charlie must try to be strong, even cheerful—could they do it? For Benny, they must.

Somehow, she and Charlie played their parts and went through the motions. Alice managed to be untypically perky, and Charlie was the strong, pleasant dad. A friendly and efficient cadre of staff helped ease the dreaded transition moments. Alice held Benny's hand as they registered at the main desk in the lobby. Charlie and some young male assistants brought Benny's luggage and toys from the car.

As they finished paperwork with a grandmotherly receptionist, a red-haired male intern walked over and squatted beside Benny, fixing an open, friendly gaze on the boy's face. Benny stared back. "Would you like to see our ocean fish?" asked the young man, whose name badge read Bruce.

Alice held her breath for Benny's response. Evidently, he was tempted and allowed Bruce to lead him by the hand across the large lobby to a bubbling aquamarine tank flashing with bright-colored and iridescent fish. Alice exhaled and smiled at the woman at the desk.

When it was time for Bruce to show Benny to his room, Alice and Charlie followed but had been given instructions not to prolong the goodbyes. They were shown to a small bedroom with windows looking out to a park-perfect lawn bordered with spring flowers. A red and blue striped quilt covered the single bed, and on the wall hung a framed print of *The Guardian*—two children protected by an angel as they cross a rickety bridge over turbulent water. Alice tried to take it all in, so she could picture where her *little bunny* would lie down each night and wake up every morning.

She knelt and took Benny in her arms to say goodbye. She didn't want to let go and didn't until Charlie tapped her shoulder and said in a joking way, "My turn now." When they both let go of their son, Alice saw his face was flushed and his eyes wide and reddening. She realized, at that moment, that Benny had been playing a role too—that of a strong soldier boy doing his duty. They had both been holding back tears.

"I love you, Benny," said Alice. Giving him one more quick hug, she said, "You are my little bunny." The boy turned away toward the windows as his parents fled the room.

42

The house on Pleasant Avenue had been a tomb after Benny was sent away. Judy wasn't home either. Inconsolable after her parents left her with the Leas on the day of Benny's trip to Middlesboro, Judy had chosen to stay with her grandparents awhile. Even though she was missing her second week near the end of the school year, Charlie and Alice lacked the will to force their daughter's return.

Their home, empty and silent without the children, Charlie watched Alice fade and withdraw emotionally. Quiet and gaunt, her complete dissolution seemed possible; she was like a ghost in her grave.

Daily phone calls from Brook Street provided reports on Judy's status. "She feels threatened," Flora told Charlie on the telephone early one morning, "as well as missing her brother."

"Threatened?" Charlie clipped, raising one eyebrow.

"Well, yes. Think about it. She's angry you've abandoned Benny. Judy's probably wondering if it could happen to her too."

"Oh, that's nonsense. Judy saw Benny's attack. She knows he was sick." The black Bakelite receiver felt damp on his ear.

"True," agreed Flora, "but a hospital is one thing. Being whisked away for who-knows-how-long is quite another."

"Flora, just please—reason with her. I've got problems here too. Alice won't get out of bed."

233

"I'm sure it's devastating for Alice," replied Flora. "It is for all of us. You and I must hold up for everybody."

This burden was already annoyingly obvious to Charlie. "Okay." Chilly in his undershirt and sweating profusely, he scratched his chest. With a heavy sigh, he added, "I guess I'll be late for work today—until she comes around."

"Call me if I can help," Flora offered.

"Well, you've got Judy," Charlie reminded her. "That's a big help."

Charlie replaced the receiver on the bedroom phone and looked toward the sheet-covered lump on Alice's twin bed. He shook his head, baffled. "Alice!" She didn't respond. He tromped to the bathroom to shave. Returning to the bedroom, he tried again, this time shaking his wife to awaken her. She groaned, turning over, not opening her eyes. "Alice—for crying out loud!" How to make her respond and come back to being herself? He stomped over to his side of the bedroom and finished getting dressed. Mumbling under his breath, he opened and shut dresser drawers and rattled his keys. Alice remained motionless, snoring softly. Charlie stood by the bed watching her, feeling helpless. He marched out of the room and down the stairs.

He slammed cupboard doors and clanked dishes, preparing his breakfast. He dumped cereal into an amber cut-glass bowl Alice had acquired in a box of laundry soap flakes. A moment of satisfaction, as well as the refrigerator bulb, lit up his mood when he spotted a bowl of strawberries, fresh-picked last evening after work. Yes, I do keep up my end of things, reflected Charlie, retrieving the cache of sweet berries.

He sat down at the kitchen table to enjoy his breakfast. Then he thought of the newspaper and went to the front stoop to pick it up. "Ah," breathed Charlie, settling down to read about the nation's problems. But his own rivaled the headlines. "Damn it," he said, slapping down his cloth napkin, stained with several days' use. He checked the kitchen clock on the wall. "I'll be late," he muttered, rising from the chair, determined to shake Alice from her torpor.

He tried another tactic. "Alice!" he boomed. "I'm leaving!" He hoped his announcement might imply more than just *leaving for work* in this gloom-filled house. He tried again, "I'm leaving you!" This time he heard a thumping noise upstairs. Charlie smiled. He listened for her slippered footsteps in the upstairs hall. He waited at the bottom of the stairs. Suddenly, Alice whooshed by him on her backside down the stairs, a look of pain on her astonished face. Charlie rushed over as she lay motionless on the hardwood floor, her head resting on the first step.

"My legs," she groaned. "I can't walk."

He tried to hoist her up, but she was dead weight. "Alice, try," he urged.

"No. I mean it. I had to crawl down the hall. My legs were numb." She began to sob.

Charlie stood up, hands on hips, gazing down at his wife in her disarray, hair unkempt, her face blotched and tear-streaked. "I'll get Doc Richards."

As he stepped to the phone, he hoped to catch the doctor before he left for his office downtown.

"Charlie, get me a pillow," Alice pleaded in a hoarse voice.

He walked around to the living room, took a throw pillow from the couch, tucked it behind Alice on the bottom step, and then made the phone call. As the doctor lived close by on Lexington Road, he was soon at the Lukases' front door, ringing the doorbell. Doc rushed in, no time wasted on formalities, and the men helped Alice to the couch. Her legs offered no assistance. As she lay on her back, she looked up at her cousin, "Please, help me!"

Charlie, exasperated and puzzled, left Doc with Alice in the living room. After briefly examining his patient, Doc sought Charlie to convey his findings. He wandered into the kitchen.

"Have a seat," beckoned Charlie. "Instant coffee?"

"No thanks," Doc raised his palm to block the offer. He sat down, his belly filling the space between table and chair. "Alice told me you are leaving her. Is that true?"

Charlie snorted. "Only to work, Doc. I was leaving to go to work. Look at me—" His hand quickly fanned from necktie to polished shoes.

"I had hoped so. I told her she must have had a bad dream, falling. . . ."

"So, what's wrong with her?" asked Charlie, hoping to get past the subject of his treatment of Alice. He pulled out the other chair and sat down.

"Nothing broken. It could be late effects of polio—like your sister has."

Charlie nodded; he had lived with Alice's complaints of leg cramps and weakness for years.

"However, the suddenness of complete paralysis makes me think of another possibility."

"What's that, Doc?" Charlie leaned in.

"Hysteria. Psychological."

"What?" Charlie jerked back in his chair.

"Caused by her tender emotions. I don't know if she really thought you were leaving or if your marriage is on shaky ground, but I do know that sending your son away was quite a trauma for Alice. And with Judy gone too, it must seem like her family has broken up. Her outlook is quite dark right now."

Charlie worked his jaw as if chewing on the doctor's explanation. "She has me, Doc."

"She needs you. Don't even think of leaving her—not now." He searched into the depths of Charlie's hazel eyes. "My cousin is one of those sensitive girls whose emotions can make her physically ill. I hate to think she might harm herself. . . ."

"You mean it's all in her mind?"

The doctor shook his head. "Not so easy," he warned. "It's physical now too. But the road back is through her heart and soul. She needs your love. She needs rest and happiness, a change of scene—away from Benny's empty bedroom."

"It's just like when she had polio," Charlie mused.

A series of family discussions began, and arrangements were made with the Simpsons for Alice's recuperation at the Middlesboro estate once again. An additional benefit was the location—within a few miles of St. Thomas Colony, where she could visit Benny.

Flora and John suggested that both their granddaughters join Alice at the Simpson plantation. A summer of new adventures on the farm promised a happy solution for lonely Judy and a deliverance from sitter-care for Deborah. The girls enthusiastically endorsed their grandparents' plan. Charlie said "Yes" easily, as he looked forward to a quiet summer of work, gardening, golf, and, he hoped, many pleasant evenings with Theresa. And Ted, of course.

⌒⌒⌒

By the first of July at the Simpsons' farm, Alice was nearly recovered from her paralysis and depression, and she looked forward to finally visiting Benny. A hired man at the farm gave Alice a ride and helped her into the main entrance of St. Thomas Colony. Mattie looked after Judy and Deborah at the Simpson house.

Alice nervously waited to see her son in the living-room-like lobby of the Colony's children's home. They'd been apart nearly three months—long, dark months for Alice. Benny would be nine years old next month! Where had the days, months, years gone?

The boy arrived in the lobby, attended by a pretty, young nurse. In the doorway, he stopped and stared at Alice. "Mommy!" He ran to his mother in a flash and flung himself on her before she could arise, stumbling from the stuffed chair.

"Benny!" she cried, tears stinging her eyes. She threw her arms around him, and the two held on for long moments. The nurse moved away. Alice and

Benny looked at each other, crying and laughing simultaneously. This was the first time she had experienced a depth of loving emotion from her son. Her heart nearly burst with joy.

"Let's go outside. It's a beautiful day," Alice said when speech was possible.

As they walked around the carefully tended green-grass campus of St. Thomas Colony, Benny clung to his mother, and Alice hugged him close. Roses bloomed in the flower beds along the pathways, reminding Alice of Charlie and his roses. A whiff of sadness floated up with the fragrance of the blossoms, as she realized how much had changed since the early days when she and Charlie fell in love.

A tug from Benny distracted her thoughts. After all, she was here with her precious son. When he smiled at her, it was like sunshine. She returned his smile and squeezed his hand as they walked.

That night Alice wrote in her diary:

July 2, 1951

> *Tara again! My life with Charlie has come full circle in fourteen years. My legs failed me once more, and here I am recovering at the Simpsons' farm. Enjoying short walks to the chicken coops and tobacco barn to gain my strength. But how different to be here with my daughter this time! And Deborah. How wonderful that they will have childhood memories of this place, as I do. Those girls make the halls ring with laughter and bring smiles to Mattie's wrinkled old face. Bless her heart—she will be here until they carry her out in a pine box.*
>
> *How glorious to be with Benny today! He was glad to see me and wouldn't let go. Being within a few short miles of him makes me feel lighter. I don't walk, I float. My legs can carry me again. And Doc was right. St. Thomas Colony is a caring place and doing well by Benny. He looks healthy, his cheeks are rosy, and thanks to the medicine, his seizures have stopped. And now I know he does love me!*
>
> *We hope to see Charlie Saturday. He didn't come this past weekend, and I don't think he's seen Benny in over a month. Social engagements, golf meets, choir, church. Seems he's a social butterfly when we're not around. I wonder if he remembers my birthday is Thursday. Surely, Mother will remind him. She is amazing—at her age. Driving out here to see us and visit Benny. And how lovingly she takes care of Daddy. How splendid to see a marriage so vital and everlasting!*

43

LUNCH WAS OVER, the dishes cleared, and Charlie had returned to the back-yard until time for the football game. Alice sat at the kitchen table again and rubbed the center of her forehead with her index finger. She stared at the pink rose in its vase beside the radio. "Enjoy your beauty while you can," she told it. Sighing, she reached on top of the radio for the *Courier-Times* dated September 7, 1991, folded to display the day's *Scramble*. Stiffly she turned to find a pencil in the string drawer. Her neck hurt from twisting so sharply. But the jumbled letters of the first word in the puzzle grabbed her attention.

The word was *misfit*. The second word fell into place quickly: *banish*. Alice often wondered if her dear Benny, the *Scramble* author, sent messages through the puzzle. Some days—like today—the words shot straight to her heart. The next word was *pardon*, the fourth *orbit*. She rarely saw her son, tucked away in his reclusive lifestyle in Chicago. She felt thankful for his job and his assisted living apartment near Judy's neighborhood. Alice felt Benny's presence daily in the word game.

It had been a long road back after Benny's two years at St. Thomas Colony. He spent his third and fourth-grade years there but was well enough to return to Holy Angels for the remainder of his grade-school education. Those years were now a blur, at the time a whirlwind, as Benny plowed his way through to high school graduation. She remembered that his uncle Harold Lukas's advocacy had helped Benny over the bumps.

She remembered something else—a deep hurt upon her son's return from the institution: He never forgave her for the death of his grandfather John Lea. Alice's father had passed away on a Sunday in October during his nap. Miserable with arthritic pain and no longer the funny grandpa with a ready laugh, he had leaned forward painfully in his bed to receive Judy's tender kiss that afternoon. Near suppertime, Flora called her family to tell them John was gone. Alice hadn't told Benny for nearly two years. She didn't want to upset him away from home. When he returned, the boy was shocked by his grandfather's death and found it hard to accept his absence. It didn't help that the rest of the family had begun to move on from the loss. He held his mother responsible for this extreme upset in his life. Now Alice wondered if the word pardon in today's puzzle signified a good omen for their relationship.

A short while later, Charlie marched in from the backyard. Alice was in the living room, sorting through old mail accumulated on her corner desk. One of Judy's watercolors hung on one wall above the desk—a fuzzy blend of autumn reds and gold splashes. Alice listened to see if her gardener husband would stop to remove his shoes. No, he continued walking through the hallway, his footfalls clunked as heavy as before.

He headed upstairs, shouting, "The Wildcats are on in half an hour!"

She recognized the signal for her to get the snacks ready before the kickoff of the season opener between Kentucky and Miami of Ohio. Alice resigned herself to spending the rest of the afternoon watching the football game on television.

⌒⌒⌒

Upstairs, Charlie rummaged in his top dresser drawer for his new pill prescription. Where had he put the bottle? His fingertips touched a packet of letters bound with a rubber band. What is this, Charlie wondered, drawing them out. The rubber band broke when he removed it. These have been here awhile, he thought. Oh yes, he recognized the general character of his niece Deborah's handwriting on the envelopes, although the individual words swam before his afflicted eyes. Their niece's letters had annoyed Alice, so she tossed many of them away. "Always asking for money," she had said.

Charlie would correct her, "Not really asking, just hinting."

For years he held onto this batch of letters, always intending to send Catherine's daughter *a little something*. When Deborah divorced her husband, Charlie changed his mind. "A sin against God and the church," he had declared. Yet he'd kept these letters.

Now, what's this? His fingers landed on something like apple seeds on a chain. My old rosary from back in the fifties, he discovered. Charlie felt a smile coming on and a lightness in his heart as if seeing an old friend. He held the black beads up to the light and to the periphery of his vision to view them better. The rosary looked dull and worn, but then how many times had his fingers moved along the chain of beads? "Maybe I prayed too hard," he chuckled. He wondered where the cross was. Sending his fingertips back into the drawer to search, he felt the hard, blocky shape of the silver crucifix. "Always falling off," he muttered.

His mind drifted back to the days of the Family Rosary Crusade, strongly encouraged at Holy Angels parish in the 1950s. Benny had been gone for the start of the campaign. Judy, then starting sixth grade, easily complied with her father's pledge to recite the prayers of the Rosary every day—for an end to wars and the conversion of Communist Russia. When Benny returned from St. Thomas, he didn't seem to mind the daily Rosary routine. Mumbling the prayers by rote seemed to launch Benny into his own thoughts anyhow. Except for that one time.

They'd been driving home one evening from Flora's house—or a ballgame or some other occasion; he couldn't recall that detail. Charlie told the children they'd be late for bedtime, so they needed to recite the Rosary on the trip home. The night air held warmth, so the car windows were rolled down. Like typical boys, Benny sometimes needed to annoy his sister. He stuck his head out the window and began crowing, "Our Father who art in heaven. . . ." As other cars drove by, windows open, Benny continued yelling at the top of his voice, "Hallowed be thy name!"

Charlie remembered Judy diving to the floor of the car in embarrassment, and Alice saying, "Let's stop this nonsense."

Such experiences might have led to Judy's renouncing her Catholic faith as an adult, thought Charlie. A shame. He shook his head. As for his son—maybe he goes to church, maybe not. I'll keep on praying for them, he thought. Maybe I should start saying my Rosary again. He placed the beads on top of the dresser with his change, car keys he no longer used, and the Plymouth ring he always removed when gardening. Alice barely noticed his cluttered dresser top and no longer nagged him about it, thank goodness. She hadn't washed the embroidered linen runner in at least a year.

Now, what was he looking for? Oh yes, the nitro tablets. Continuing to search in the drawer, his fingers came across a hard lump wrapped in tissue paper. Charlie sucked in a breath as he tore open the package. The pearl cluster pendant Alice wore on their wedding day—the necklace Harold said had belonged to their mother as a bride. Charlie didn't remember why Alice had given it back to him rather than placing it with her own jewelry, nor when she'd done so. Now here it lay for him to ponder—a pity no one gave it to Judy to wear at her wedding. Maybe someday, granddaughter Amy. . . .

His thoughts swirled away to his mother, Josephine. How would she view the string of marriages that began the day she wore the pearl cluster more than 100 years ago? He held the brooch closer to the light, where the edges of his vision caught the sparkles. It's still fresh and new, he marveled; it will still exist when we've vanished from the earth. His parents and all his siblings were gone. Their marriages dissolved by death; one of these days, he and Alice would become dust of the earth too.

How would Josephine view his fifty-four years of marriage to Alice? Surely, she would be proud they had raised a family and stayed together. Would his mother confirm he had chosen the right woman for his wife—the right choice to wear her wedding pearls? If he'd married Bonnie instead, all those years ago, she'd possibly be alive today instead of lying cold underground in a veterans' cemetery. Charlie stopped himself. "No, don't go there," he admonished himself, eyes starting to burn. That path would lead only into shadows with no Judy, no Benny. And what would have become of Alice? She had been so desirable with her sapphire blue eyes and pouty lips. With her fragile health and childlike dreams, she had needed him; he'd given her his best years.

Charlie shook his head, fighting back emotions and reflecting on the many ways life can change and how even solid rocks wear out over time. But like his mother's shining pearls, some things endure—his bountiful garden, financial security, children and grandchildren finding their places in the world. Being this old has certain advantages, he reasoned, like seeing how so much of the past has finally turned out.

He shoved the letters back into the drawer, re-wrapped the pearl pendant, and replaced it. Now, where was that nitroglycerin Doc Richards' successor recently prescribed? Young Doc said Charlie might need it if he became too excited watching the Wildcats' games this season. The doctor said the blood pressure pills would help, but too much agitation could cause his heart to do flip-flops. Nitroglycerin under the tongue could be his salvation.

Charlie shut the drawer with a bang. Next drawer down. Ah—the package of nitro tablets! He placed them on top of the dresser. After he cleaned up and shampooed his hair (for Alice's benefit), he went downstairs and placed the nitro tablets in a lamp table drawer beside the living room sofa, handy in case of emergency.

❧❧❧

The Lukases settled on the sofa for the kickoff of the Kentucky-Miami game. From the start, Alice watched how her husband breathed deeply with excitement. The blood practically rose in his face as he inched forward to the edge of his seat. She was fascinated at how a football game—even the first one of the season—inspired such intensity in men. Her brother Allen had been the same way—a regular cheerleader for the Kentucky Wildcats; God rest his soul.

That afternoon's football game would later be referred to as a *squeaker*. As the clock ticked the final minutes of the game, Charlie held his breath. Coach Curry's prized fullback ran ninety yards for a touchdown. Charlie exhaled. Kentucky's win was assured! He let out a yelp and jumped a few inches off his seat. Alice couldn't help laughing. Then she saw how red his face had turned as he stood clutching his chest. "Are you okay?" she asked in alarm.

"Think I will be," he whispered, reaching toward the drawer for his nitroglycerin. He popped a tablet into his mouth, then flopped back onto the cushions beside Alice.

"Any better?" she asked nervously.

He reached over for her hand and relaxed with a smile. "Yes, much."

44

O N THE LAST Saturday in March, Charlie looked forward to watching the NCAA basketball regional finals between his beloved Kentucky Wildcats and the Blue Devils of Duke University. When he awoke that morning, his eighty-four-year-old body felt like jumping out of bed. He felt proud of the Kentucky team this season, how they had broken scoring records, won tournaments, and persevered through disciplinary actions of the basketball conference. He could hardly wait until evening to see his alma mater beat heavily-favored Duke and proceed to the Final Four. Charlie knew they could do it.

But first, spring yard work had to be done. Raking up old leaves, checking for new growth on the roses, and maybe spraying the peach trees again. After lunch, he looked forward to a visit from Theresa Hawkes to practice songs for the Holy Angels choir. Alice would extend a grudging welcome to Theresa, but Charlie was eager to see her. That is if he could see very well. He couldn't see anything straight on, needing to focus at the sides of his eyes. *Macular degeneration*, Young Doc called it.

With Charlie unable to read the pages of his worn-out church hymnal, Theresa had been stopping by every Saturday to tutor him in memorizing and practicing the music for Sunday's Mass. Alice would sink into her chair in the living room, burying her nose in a newspaper or book. Sulking like a dispirited old cat, thought Charlie. On the other hand, Theresa was such a joy—a delightful combination of his mother, Bonnie, and Alice the way she used to be.

He sometimes wondered if Ted were pouting too, the way he'd wait in his car at the curb in front of 403 Pleasant Avenue during Theresa's visits. She always assured Charlie, "No. Ted is perfectly fine. He reads his books while he waits. Then we do errands. He's happiest driving and reading, so grateful he can still do both."

Charlie would heap more thanks on Theresa for helping him stay in tune with the church choir and on Ted for driving him to church on Sundays and often to the Hawkeses's for breakfast.

"Always our pleasure," Theresa insisted. Nearing eighty, her auburn hair turned white, she still batted her eyelashes at Charlie.

After Charlie finished the yard work, he and Alice had lunch at the gray table in their gray kitchen, brightened by a handful of pink hyacinths fresh from the backyard. The radio sat silent as the clock on the wall produced a scratchy sound. Alice didn't speak, her lips pinched with annoyance. "The game will be really exciting," he said to spark a conversation.

"I know," she said, rising from the table to carry her dishes to the sink.

The doorbell sounded its brash buzz. "You can get it," Alice said. "You know who it is."

Charlie pushed himself up from the table and thudded through the hallway to the front door. "Theresa!" he greeted her. "Ted! What in the . . . ?"

Theresa attempted a laugh. "I sprained my foot really bad. Ted had to help me up the steps." She showed off the cast on her foot.

"Well, come on in—both of you," Charlie urged. "Here, Theresa, let me help you." He led her to a chair at the dining table where his dusty tape recorder and oversized magnifying glass lay. He took her light raincoat to hang in the front hall closet.

Ted remained standing just inside the front door. "Darndest thing about Theresa's foot," he began. Charlie motioned for his jacket. "Oh no—I'll go back to the car," Ted responded.

"No need to. Alice is here. You two can visit. Alice!" he called toward the kitchen and took Ted's jacket.

⌒⌒⌒

Alice tried to make the best of this visit forced upon her. With a smile pasted on her face, she came out of the kitchen, wiping her hands on her white apron. She hoped Ted would take the hint that she had business in the kitchen.

"Good to see you, Alice," Ted said, sounding apologetic.

He looked so uncomfortable standing in the hall that Alice took pity. "Come in and sit awhile." She led him into the living room.

Alice claimed her stuffed chair by the front window, motioning to Ted to sit on the slipcovered Davenport. "Not often I get to hear those two practice," said Ted, inclining his good ear toward the dining room. He sat down.

"They sing together nice," Alice commented. "Charlie couldn't stay in the choir without Theresa's help. He can't read the songbooks anymore."

Ted nodded. "We all get to the age of needing help." He was thoughtful for a few moments. "Theresa and I don't see much of you, Alice. I often regret the four of us don't play Bridge anymore."

"Well, Charlie's eyes, you know. . . ."

"True enough. But even when we played Bridge, I think us men didn't let you ladies visit much." He chuckled.

"Yes," agreed Alice. "Charlie played serious Bridge." She tensed, recalling how he focused on her trifling mistakes.

"Maybe one of these days we'll have more time to know each other better," said Ted.

Alice thought the remark odd after the long years they'd been acquainted. "Why? What do you mean?" she blurted.

"I'm just thinking ahead to when we all move into the new Holy Angels assisted living. . . ."

"What?" Alice had heard about the parish's new construction plans but hadn't considered it of interest.

"They're taking applications for apartments already, and Charlie, Theresa, and I have been talking." Alice looked stunned. "Didn't he say anything to you?" Ted asked.

"No. Nothing at all," said Alice. "I have no plans to ever leave this house. Ever! Never!" She crossed her arms and turned her back on Ted, hoping to send the message *conversation closed, visit over*.

"Now you must feel like a fifth wheel—like I often have."

Ted's remark spun Alice around. She clutched the chair arm to steady herself. "Why do you say that?"

Ted cracked a wry smile and nodded toward the dining room. "Didn't you ever feel left out with those two?"

Alice felt her face reddening as she looked at Ted. Of course, she'd been jealous of their friendship for years. But Ted had always been part of the relationship, a chaperone of sorts. Hadn't he?

Ted turned sideways on the sofa to face Alice. "Of course, I knew what was happening. I just let it pass. I had my books, other friends."

What is he saying, thought Alice—this man I didn't even invite into my home. Now he is greatly upsetting me. She was suddenly on a Ferris wheel, dropping dizzily. "What was going on?" she asked breathlessly.

"Mostly the Bonnie thing," Ted began. "Did you know about that?" He cocked his head, looking glad to finally have this conversation.

Alice clawed into the soft upholstery of her chair. "What bonnie thing?"

"Well," he drawled. "I'm glad you're sitting down, Alice. This might take a while." He paused to gather his thoughts, preparing a confession, perhaps. Ted began: "I've always been uncomfortable about the affair with Bonnie."

Alice collapsed into the back of her chair. "Whose affair? Who is Bonnie?" Alice spoke in a hoarse whisper.

Ted shook his head. "Guess I'll have to back up a ways." He shifted his sitting position, clasped and unclasped his hands. "I assumed Bonnie was a friend of Charlie's you knew from his workplace."

"How long ago?"

"Before the war."

Alice's eyes focused somewhere in the distance, outside the living room, trying to remember. She couldn't think of anyone named Bonnie.

She and Ted heard Theresa and Charlie from the dining room, their voices blending in *O Sacred Head Surrounded*. Charlie's tenor sounded as beautiful as when Alice first heard him sing in the Catholic church in Middlesboro. A time before the war. Her eyes reddened. "I don't remember any Bonnie," she told Ted. "What is it I don't know?"

Ted related his knowledge of a woman named Bonnie Fines, who often played golf with Charlie and joined the WACs to serve in the Pacific during the war.

Alice's chest tightened at Ted's words. Did Charlie play golf with a woman? Panic was growing in her heart. "I never knew," said Alice faintly. She kept repeating, "I never knew . . . I never knew."

Ted squirmed and pushed on with the story. "After Bonnie was killed in the war, Charlie had Theresa find out more details about her death, her life, even her family."

Alice's heart lurched as a memory soared like a meteor: the newspaper headlines streaming news of a local woman killed in the War in the Pacific. She remembered how Charlie had become upset and walked out on Judy's fifth birthday party—in October 1944. "I remember now. The news that shocked

Charlie so bad, but I didn't know. . . ." She had difficulty finding words and waited for Ted to say more.

The harmonious singing continued to float into the living room.

Ted hesitated. "I'm sorry. I've hurt you."

"Is there more?" Alice could hardly breathe. She held one hand to her chest, hoping not to start coughing.

"Guess I might as well finish this; I've gone so far. I'm sorry, Alice. I truly am. I shouldn't have started." Was he expecting absolution?

"Please. I want the truth," said Alice, her voice raw. "More than anything." She stared, challenging him with her blue eyes.

Ted met her gaze, then looked down at his shoes. He shook his head. "All right. I might as well finish."

Ted ran a finger under his shirt collar as if giving himself room to breathe. He began: "Theresa could write a book about Bonnie—all the stuff she found out from letters she got from Bonnie's sister Jane."

Alice puckered her forehead, trying to sort it out. Had Theresa known this Bonnie? She lacked the strength to ask as Ted continued with the story.

"It seems Bonnie Fines left a lot of people feeling remorse after she died— her sister, her husband—and Charlie." Ted's eyes found Alice's again.

"What happened next brought all of those people—and Theresa—into a conspiracy of sorts. I tried to stay out of it but felt like a spare part." He jerked his head suddenly. "Of course, you couldn't have known. The plan wouldn't have worked if you'd known."

"What plan?" Alice hoped she wouldn't choke and interrupt Ted's flow of words.

"Jane had the idea to start a fund for a memorial sculpture with a plaque to commemorate Bonnie's ultimate sacrifice in the war. Bonnie's husband, Joe, favored the idea; so did Charlie. Theresa was like a giddy schoolgirl, she wanted so much to help."

Alice couldn't imagine why. Had Bonnie been Theresa's friend too?

Ted went on. "Remember when Theresa took care of your son Benny several days a week while you went out—errands and visits, I suppose." He waved his hand as if the detail didn't matter.

"Yes. Charlie suggested the idea. It gave me a lift."

"Exactly! And for a few years, Charlie purposely overpaid Theresa for her sitter services. The total of that money went to Jane for Bonnie's memorial fund."

Alice realized in despair that those were the years she spent so much time with Catherine and began her smoking habit. A tight fist enclosed her heart.

No wonder Charlie let me run around so freely in those days, she reflected. Back when Theresa took care of Benny so much, Charlie must have realized I'd started smoking with Catherine. He needed to channel the money through Theresa, so he didn't complain about the smoking. Now, I can't sleep nights for coughing. And Charlie—he's in there singing with Theresa!

Alice unclamped her jaw. "Our money spent for the memorial! Was it ever built?" A tear started down her cheek.

"Yes, paid for and built. Please know that Theresa truly loved caring for your little boy. She felt a bit responsible for him after the time our car nearly ran over him."

Alice swallowed hard. The memory touched a tender spot.

"Theresa wanted no money for her sitting services, and every penny went to Bonnie's sister. By 1948 they'd finished raising the money. The sculpture was completed a year or so later and placed in the vets' cemetery in Columbus.

"Maybe I shouldn't tell you this, but in 1951—if memory serves—when you and your children were away for the summer, I drove Theresa and Charlie to see the memorial, and we met Jane."

Alice's stomach turned inside out as a memory rushed over her. 1951 was the summer she spent in Middlesboro at the Simpsons', recovering from paralysis and a breakdown, while Benny resided at nearby St. Thomas Colony for epileptic patients. She had been brokenhearted when Charlie didn't show up for her birthday and hadn't even sent a card or a rose. Alice hung her head, struck with a blow that Charlie had fled to Bonnie's family in Columbus when his own family needed him most.

She sensed Ted staring hard at her, probably wondering about her thoughts. Holding back tears, Alice had one more question for him. With a ragged breath, she asked, "Why did Theresa get involved?"

Ted shook his head. "It mystified me for a while." He paused. "We didn't have kids of our own to dote on, and Theresa is the motherly type. After Benny's near accident and Charlie's generosity with his garden, she took Charlie under her wing. She had a soft spot in her heart for him, always has. I guess she felt compassion for his grief. . . ."

"For another woman," finished Alice.

"I know, I know. And I blame myself too, for the cover-up. I knew about it, but I couldn't tell you, couldn't stop Charlie or Theresa." He hesitated. "Guess I didn't try hard enough. That woman certainly deserved the memorial, and as long as you didn't know. . . ."

"So why did you tell me now?" Alice whispered.

"I had to shake it off my shoulders sometime—it just happened to be today. It's been eating on me. I knew you'd been left out of things, of knowing the whole truth, if any. You know, I couldn't carry this burden to the grave. I'm nearly ninety."

Alice stared out the window as the March wind began to stir dead leaves on the lawn.

"I'm sorry, Alice," said Ted. "Selfish of me, in the end." His voice sounded weary, leaden. "Maybe I should have kept quiet after all." He sniffled, rising stiffly from the sofa.

Alice continued gazing out the window at the blank sky. She was unaware when Ted left the living room or when he and Theresa bade their goodbyes to Charlie and exited the house. With a sigh, she noticed their black sedan pull away from the curb. When she turned from the window, she saw Charlie standing silently, watching her from the hallway.

45

"How was your visit with Ted?" Charlie asked.

Alice realized she was clenching both fists. She let them drop by her side and replied coolly, "He is an honest man."

Charlie looked puzzled, as if he wanted to ask what she implied, but said only, "Well good. I'm glad you got along." He then turned sideways as if being pulled back to the dining room.

"Go on!" Alice waved him away.

Charlie returned to the recorder player on the table to listen to Theresa's voice on a tape she had left for him to practice with. The sounds drifting into the living room jolted Alice, as the machine continually stopped to replay sections of the tape. Theresa's voice irritated her, repeating the musical phrases over and over, starting and stopping. Charlie sang along, sometimes missing a note, beginning again.

Charlie and Theresa, the interruptions and repetitions exacerbated her anger and deepened old wounds. She hadn't felt this hurt since Charlie failed to show up for her birthday at the Simpsons' in 1951—now she knew where he'd been! Alice's fingers tightened as painful memories erupted like a sleeping volcano awakened to explosive fury. She re-experienced the heart-numbing pain of Charlie's *are you crazy* looks whenever she mentioned her most terrifying childhood memory, slamming an emotional doorway between them. Never had she felt such fury since Charlie shunned Allen during the war—Allen, her brother and childhood ally. Those months of estrangement had been an unspeakable shame, casting a forever shadow.

Ted's revelations today seemed worse, disclosing Charlie's betrayal over many years, secrets he'd shared outside their marriage, and his obsession with another woman. She wondered if he still thought about that woman, Bonnie. Even if the flame had died, the memory of the relationship was maintained by his friendship with Theresa, who claimed so much of his time. Also, what about Charlie's discussion about moving into assisted living with the Hawkeses? Had she been included in this scheme, or did her husband have other plans for her? Resentment and grief cut a swath through Alice's heart.

Ted's long story had been a heavy load, but knowing a long-hidden truth gave her solid footing to take action. She had been a victim of deceit for too long. "No more," She whispered. "No more." Blood rushed to her face, and her hands trembled. She drew a deep breath, pulled herself up by the arms of her stuffed chair, and steadied herself. Anger took over like an animal dragging her off to uncharted territory. Rage empowered her; she felt clear-headed, ready to grapple.

How to get even? Charlie needs to be punished for the way he deceived me, she thought. It might be satisfying to get him confused, befuddled, to doubt his senses. Maybe even to think he was going crazy, not just blind. Alice walked over to the windows facing the backyard, pondering. She turned around, pacing, and stopped at the lamp table beside the couch. Charlie's glasses lay on the table; they weren't much help to his vision these days. Perfect, thought Alice, I'll stash these somewhere, and he'll wonder what on earth he did with them.

Thinking better of that idea, she considered he might not look for the glasses, as nearly useless as they were. The drawer of the table was slightly open, giving her a better alternative. She pulled out the drawer where Charlie had stashed his nitro pills; she took out the box and slipped it into her apron pocket. This will throw him a punch, she thought, knowing he might need the tablets if this afternoon's basketball game proved overexciting. Predictably, it would—at such a crucial point in the NCAA tournament. She pictured Charlie's panic when his heart started racing and he couldn't find his pills. At the last moment, she'd locate the pills, restore balance, and become the darling heroine. She felt cunning and strong, like a young Scarlett O'Hara. Imagine me plotting revenge! Alice smiled.

Charlie, practicing hymns at the dining table, faced away from Alice as she started up the stairs. On her way to the bedroom, she glanced out the upstairs hall window at the budding peach trees in the backyard. She went to Charlie's dresser and placed the nitro pills in the top drawer. He'll just think he's losing his mind when I find the pills for him, Alice told herself.

Then she noticed the packet of Deborah's letters Charlie had recently uncovered. "What? He kept these?" More secrets! She grabbed the letters and threw them into the wastebasket. Would strong women like Flora and Mattie put up with a man who kept so many secrets? She stuffed the letters further down into the trash and brushed off her hands.

The dresser drawer remained open; when Alice returned to close it, she saw a rumpled tissue paper package inside. She opened it and gasped at seeing the pearl wedding pendant she'd worn as a bride. Tears came to her eyes. I wore his mother's pearls, yet he betrayed me, she thought. She grabbed the package, carried it to the wastebasket, and dropped it in. The pearls sparkled at her as the necklace lay on the crest of trash. Alice's eyes blurred, gazing at it. Then, thinking of Charlie's mother, she retrieved the pendant with its wrapping and replaced it in the drawer. She saw the black rosary. All that praying and church, she reflected, what a hypocrite! She snatched the beads, slammed the drawer closed, and threw the rosary into the trash.

☙❧

Charlie took a break in the afternoon to ramble around the yard, re-checking his earlier work and making new observations of spring growth. He returned to the tape recorder in the dining room, to the sound of Theresa's voice—like the sweet lingering scent of her *Chantilly* perfume. Heavenly, he thought, smiling. He continued listening to her singing *Panis Angelicus* awhile, even after he had mastered the Latin hymn well enough for tomorrow's Mass. During a pause between hymns, Charlie heard another voice: "It is six-thirty," a small electronic speaker told him. He looked at his wristwatch but couldn't read the numbers. The voice was *my Chinese Lady* from a special watch Judy and Benny had given him when his eyesight dimmed. He chuckled at the mechanical voice and remembered his children's thoughtfulness. The seminary clock chimed once, confirming the Chinese Lady's statement of the time.

He realized less than a half-hour remained until tip-off for the Kentucky-Duke basketball game in Philadelphia. Time enough for Alice to prepare a snack for their supper. "Alice!" he called out. "Where is she now?" he muttered.

Charlie prepared the coffee table by removing old newspapers, then settled on the couch with the television volume turned up. He didn't want to miss a second of the game. Alice puttered around, serving a tray of cheese, cold meat, and crackers; she set out glasses and RC Cola on the coffee table. The game was in its second minute when she sat down heavily next to Charlie. He was already leaning forward at the edge of the sofa, absorbed in the televised action.

The teams were well matched; the lead went predictably back and forth as first, the Kentucky Wildcats dribbled down to their end of the court; next, the Duke Blue Devils took the ball, heading to their basket. At the first commercial break, Charlie let out a long sigh and leaned back onto the cushions. He smiled, reaching over for Alice's hand—a cold fist. He laid his palm on top of her curled fingers. "They're good—the Wildcats have got what it takes this year," he said.

Alice said nothing as a cough rattled in her chest.

"Could be like 1948 and 1949 all over again," he went on.

"Why?" she asked.

"Remember—they won the NCAA championship both years!"

"I don't remember that."

"Well, I sure do," he said spiritedly, eager to watch the continuing action as the break ended. As he leaned forward, he felt a rip spread in the back of his plaid shirt, where his shoulders pulled it tight. He'd have Alice mend it later.

As both teams scored, the game progressed with raucous cheering from the televised arena. Charlie munched on the cheese and crackers. Absently, he sent crumbs flying onto the sculptured light green carpet. Alice nudged his arm and handed him a napkin. "Watch your crumbs!" He nearly knocked over his cola and ice cubes while flinging his arms, but Alice moved his glass away just in time.

As the second half of the game drew to a close, Charlie could hardly stay seated. As Kentucky pulled ahead by one point, he was on his feet. He paced as a commercial came on during a time-out. He felt Alice watching him. After the commercial, a Kentucky forward, John Pelphrey, made a free throw. Another timeout, and Charlie had to dash to the lavatory during the commercial. Just as it ended, Charlie returned to his seat. "Made it!" he panted.

A Duke player missed a shot. The final buzzer sounded as time ran out; the score tied 93 to 93. The crowd in Philadelphia erupted in a roar. Charlie flopped back, clutching his chest. "Oh no—overtime! How much more can we take?"

Alice smiled.

He reached over to the lamp table drawer and began rummaging. He felt with his fingers, shuffling papers and items in the drawer.

"What are you looking for?" Alice asked.

"My nitro tablets!" He jumped to his feet and pulled the drawer completely out of the table, spilling the contents on the carpet.

"You'll never find them now," she chided.

"They must be here someplace!" he cried out in desperation, all the while his heart pounded on his rib cage.

"You probably took them back upstairs," suggested Alice. "You just forgot."

"No. I don't think so." Charlie, on his knees, sweaty and confused, searched the whorls of the carpeting. "Where could they be!"

"They must be upstairs. I'll go look in a minute," she said. "Wait—it's starting!"

Charlie crawled back to the sofa but stayed seated on the floor to watch the overtime play, his energy running low. His heart was racing and turning flip-flops. Why hadn't the Wildcats sealed a victory in regulation time? Now he was beside himself with anxiety both for the game and his misplaced nitro tablets, now that his heart was pounding at a dangerous level.

♾

The extra five minutes proceeded much as the rest of the game, with baskets made back and forth like a conversation among skilled players. Alice watched the scoring and Charlie's reactions; she bit her lip and wadded a napkin in her hand. As the game clock ticked away the final seconds, Charlie's mouth hung open, and his eyes glistened with hope. Kentucky's Sean Woods shot a basket off the backboard with two seconds left. The Wildcats of Kentucky were about to win—by one point! Duke called a timeout. Charlie squirmed and gasped for breath as the last seconds of the game were held in suspension. Alice watched him try to relax and slow his palpitating heart. How would the game end? Despite her focus on Charlie, she too tasted the excitement of the moment. And she still had the upper hand over her husband, knowing where the nitro tablets were hiding. She would retrieve them in the nick of time.

Watching Charlie's torment, Alice's emotions began to waver. Could his heart give out over a basketball game? Unbelievable, in a way. With the game clock stopped again, she watched him writhing and breathing painfully. Troubling images came to mind: Scarlett O'Hara shooting a Union soldier at close range, and Mattie at the Simpson farm smashing a rat's head with a piece of wood. The visions frightened her. What have I done? thought Alice. What would Mother say? Mother, who so tenderly nursed her husband through his last suffering years! Could Charlie die here? She had only meant to scare him, shake him as he deserved, not kill him. Panic rushed through her like a hot wind, then icy cold. She wanted the game to end so Charlie could revive. And she would find those nitro pills soon enough.

Back into play, Duke's Christian Laettner caught an eighty-foot inbound pass. He turned and fired off a shot near the foul line, making the basket at the final buzzer. Duke won the game 104-103!

Charlie keeled over on the floor; his head struck one leg of the coffee table. Alice called out and reached toward him. This had been her little game of revenge. Had she overplayed it? The suspense of the basketball game and watching Charlie had held her to the sofa. Had she waited too long? She had intended to hurry upstairs to retrieve the packet of nitro tablets, but now he lay on the floor at her feet. In a blinding, roaring panic, she willed herself to fly up the stairs to their bedroom and grab those pills from the dresser drawer. She tried to rise from the sofa, but a weight held her down, and her legs failed. Once again, her paralysis returned and left her unable to move. With Charlie unconscious, she was alone, with no one to help her rise from the sofa or retrieve the lifesaving tablets.

⌘

That Kentucky-Duke basketball game, an NCAA regional final, was later cited as the *greatest college game ever played*. Afterward, Duke went on to win the 1992 tournament championship. Charlie Lukas would never know.

46

A WEEK AFTER Charlie's funeral, Alice and Judy held each other in a farewell embrace. They stood in the front hall of the house on Pleasant Avenue, Judy's childhood home. From the corner of her eye, Alice saw a sporty vehicle pull up to the curb, as afternoon traffic from the seminary flowed by. "Ron's here," she said, sniffling, her eyes red. "I'll walk out with you."

"No, Mom. You stay right here. It's cold and windy." Her fingers nestled into her mother's gnarled hand. "I hate to leave, but we've got to head back to Chicago. Time to check on Benny, you know."

"Thank you for staying as long as you could. I'll be okay." Alice knew her neighbors had promised to check on her, and her refrigerator and pantry were stocked.

"Do you know how to work this?" asked Judy, fingering an alarm device around her mother's neck. When she pressed the correct button, a signal for help would register at an emergency call center.

"Yes, yes," Alice replied. "I'll be fine."

"Promise?" Judy gave her mother another quick hug and kissed her. She touched a tear on Alice's cheek. "Don't cry." Tears streamed down her own face. "I'll call as soon as we get home."

"When will I see you again?" Alice clung to her daughter.

"We'll be back for Easter—less than two weeks."

"Good. I'll hold my breath until then."

Judy laughed through her tears. "Me too."

The seminary clock chimed four. In the next instant, Alice waved goodbye to Judy and her husband, Ron O'Leary, as their silver metallic Subaru moved slowly away from the curb. She stepped onto the front stoop and kept watching her daughter's hand waving out the car's window as they turned onto the side street.

Easter, thought Alice, shuffling back into the house. Charlie would be singing the joyful hymns at Holy Angels if she hadn't tricked him by hiding his nitro pills at the crucial time when he desperately needed them. She wasn't to blame that Kentucky had lost the game by one point at the last second. And she couldn't help the paralysis that immobilized her in that moment of panic. She had meant to save Charlie after taking her momentary revenge. If only she could have foreseen. . . . As her mother Flora had often said in her lifetime, "Hindsight is twenty-twenty. . . ."

Alice remembered how their young next-door neighbor Brad had come over that afternoon to commiserate about the basketball game and had found Charlie unconscious and her in a daze, stumbling on crippled legs. The telephone rang, jarring her from her tragic memories. Alice took a few steps to the phone table in the hall. "Brad! I was just thinking about you . . . Yes, I'm fine just now . . . I'll let you know . . . Thanks for calling."

She ate supper alone late at the wobbly table in the kitchen, with little desire for food since Charlie had been carried from the house on a stretcher that terrible afternoon. Remarkably, neighbors had been there for her—even Theresa and Ted. Judy, Ron, and Benny had arrived so quickly after they heard of Charlie's emergency. My life is alone now, what's left of it. I must be a brave Scarlett O'Hara, with Tara in ruins.

Scarlett's appearance in her mind led to another thought—her diary—a companion she'd shared many of life's crises and heartaches with. When had she last written? Why had she stopped? Yet she remembered exactly where those soul-filled books were tucked away. Alice pushed her half-finished dinner aside as a thought more enticing than food tempted her. She would uncover those diaries at bedtime tonight.

Anticipating a grand reunion with the pages written by her much younger self at various stages of her life, she went upstairs to her bedroom much earlier than usual. Yes! She might even share some new words with her diary. The thought gave her a warm feeling.

Settled for the night in her flannel nightgown, her face creamed, hair net in place, Alice climbed into her twin bed and reached for the stack of diaries she'd retrieved from the closet and placed on the bedside table. Somehow, she couldn't bear to turn the pages back to her earliest entries—not yet. Instead, she picked up the most recent volume. The date of the last entry surprised her—1951. She had written it while at the Simpson farm that summer with Judy and Deborah. "Over forty years ago!" she breathed, incredulous at the passage of time. She felt the urge to pick up her pen and continue writing, to recapture time, to say *I'm still here*!

Alice found a pen in the table drawer and began to write. The words flowed. She wanted to bring Charlie back to the present, too, with his bed opposite hers so glaringly empty. She wrote of the last day of her husband's life—March 30, 1992—when he lay still in the hospital, a machine breathing for him. As her thoughts poured onto the pages, midnight approached.

The jangling telephone interrupted her. She had to lay aside her writing, throw off the covers, and get out of bed. Whoever was calling kept ringing. When Alice answered, she heard Judy's voice: "Sorry to phone so late, but I knew you'd be waiting."

"Yes indeed. So you're home safe! Thank you, Judy Star. . . ." Speaking aloud after hours of silence made her cough suddenly.

"Mom? Are you okay?"

"I'm fine. Really." Alice wiggled her bare toes and looked over at the diaries on the bed.

After she hung up the phone, Alice returned to bed, relaxing on her propped-up wedge pillow, content. Then she began reading what she'd just written in her diary:

> I felt like a helpless child, watching Charlie lie there so still. He wouldn't even be breathing if he weren't hooked up to a machine. I couldn't help him anymore. I saw his pale shoulders and the top of his chest bare above the thin hospital covers. My fingers kept reaching to pull up the blanket around his cold skin, but it was tucked so tight and wouldn't budge.
>
> In the sterile quiet, a door suddenly flew open. I almost expected Doc Richards, but he's long ago passed on. Instead, Theresa Hawkes trounced in, followed by a very hesitant Ted. He nodded and smiled at me. Did he guess what I'd done to Charlie? Theresa was right away hugging me, then pushing in next to Charlie at his head, replacing me where I stood. I felt so angry watching her, but my main feeling was sadness that Charlie would not recover and was slipping away from me.
>
> Theresa began singing softly in his ear. "The Lord is my Shepherd." It made me cry. Then she repeated his name over and over. "Blink your eyes

if you can hear me," she whispered to my Charlie. He did not respond.
She sang more church tunes, then she reached for where his hand lay
tucked under the blanket and uncovered it. "It's Theresa; Alice is here too.
Squeeze my hand if you can hear me," she told him. He gave no response.
She kept this up awhile longer, then looked at me and shook her head. She
then went to sit down on a straight chair beside Ted.

I took Charlie's limp hand and just kept holding on. Ever so often I'd
whisper, "Charlie, it's me, Alice." And once, when I said it, he blinked
his eyelids. Then I felt him lightly press my hand. I wasn't imagining
it. His eyes fluttered, and he squeezed my hand again, a little harder. I
didn't tell Theresa. The moment passed just between Charlie and me. In
that one precious moment, I knew he forgave me, and I forgave him. All
past troubles and unhappiness were washed away as he lightly gripped
my hand. What I would have given for him to open those hazel brown
eyes again and come back into my life. We could start again. Instead, he
slipped away to sing with the choir of heaven.

Before turning off her bedside lamp, Alice added the following:

Now I'm heading into my darkest hours, surely the loneliest years of my
life. I have only one thing to look forward to—being with Charlie again
in our eternal home. I'll think about that tomorrow, as Scarlett would
say. Now, to sleep, to dream. . . .

One early June night, as Alice lay dreaming in her twin bed, she heard a
knocking at the front door. Stunned, she sat up. A caller during the dark of
night should frighten her; instead, excitement mixed with curiosity. Who could
it be? She tossed aside her light coverlet and looked out the window. A car
waited at the curb, headlights beaming.

Alice rolled out of bed, turned on the bedside lamp, and shuffled into her
slippers. The knocking at the door continued. "Okay, I'm coming," she whispered. She saw herself reach for the blue cotton robe she'd laid across Charlie's
empty bed. "I'm coming. I'm coming." She tied the robe securely around her
nightgown and hurried to the stairs.

It was unnecessary to steady herself on the banister, as her legs felt strangely
fluid and graceful as she descended. It was like floating down the stairs to the
front hallway—a delightful sensation. She reached the front door and opened
it, expecting who?

Charlie stood before her, a smile on his handsome young face. He was dressed to kill, complete with a white shirt, tie, and buttoned-up vest. The one he wore on their wedding day? He carried red roses, dewy fresh. "Are you ready, Alice?"

She felt tears starting though she couldn't help smiling. "Charlie—you've come back!" She reached out to him, trembling.

He tenderly took her hand. "Come on. I've brought the Plymouth. Are you ready to go?"

"Yes," Alice replied. "I've been waiting."

Epilogue

Letter from Judy Lukas O'Leary to her daughter Amy:

October 10, 1992

Dearest Amy,

I have much to write, so I hope you're sitting down. So many things on my mind, in my heart. Buckets of tears—happy and sad.

As you know, your dad and I are down here clearing, cleaning, and sorting in your grandma's house. Trying to decide what to keep, who to give things to, what should go to auction, what to toss. Mom left a few instructions—notes on cabinets, backs of picture frames, etc. We've saved some furniture, dishes, and mementos for you and Benny. Someday we must decide how to deliver it all to each of you. Would you like my painting from over your grandma's living room desk?

This is the first of many trips, I'm sure. The Subaru is already nearly packed full. Ron is so patient as I look through all of Mom and Dad's old things.

Amazing discoveries:

I noticed Mom's diaries stacked up on her bedside table when we were all here for her funeral in June. I didn't have the heart to look then, but this time I did. It seemed as if Mom had written these entries for someone to read. Her language was careful and precise. But I found some of her thoughts too personal to read comfortably—especially the writings about her romance with Dad and heartbreaks as a young mother.

I looked for the marriage date, hoping for a happy few pages. Nothing was written on that date, but some weeks later, she did write about their wedding. What a shock to find she'd been pregnant! Not with me—instead, a baby she lost. I felt her sadness.

Now here's a happy part, and it concerns you, Amy. Mom wrote about a lovely pearl cluster pendant she'd worn on their wedding day, October 30, 1937. My uncle Harold, a priest, had given it to her just that morning. The pendant was previously worn by my dad's mother when she married in 1896!

While looking through dresser drawers, I found that very pendant wrapped carefully in tissue paper. At least I thought so. I later confirmed it when I saw my parents' wedding photo. Yes, the same pendant! It's tucked safely in my purse to bring back to Chicago, to give you the next time we're together. I hope you'll wear it when you and Dan get married. It's a gorgeous family treasure.

(As for your wedding, be sure to give us plenty of notice about the date and location. You know, Uncle Benny, with his disorder, has to plan things so carefully and so far ahead.)

Another surprise from our trip:

Somehow, word got around that your dad and I were in town. We received a phone call from the young couple who recently moved into my grandparents' house on Brook Street. The Millers had found an interesting old trunk in the attic. They assumed it belonged to my grandma and grandpa, as they were the first owners of the house, and the trunk looked Victorian. So we drove down to take a look.

I held my breath, returning to the old house downtown. Would it be anything like I remembered? When had I last been there? I recall the last time I kissed Grandpa goodbye—the day he died. I was around twelve or so, in the early 1950s. I visited Grandma Flora there until she died in 1964. Twenty-eight years later, what a shock to be in that house again, to see what was different and remained as I remembered. My latest memories occurred when my grandparents lived only on the first floor, so it was a revelation to go back in time to the second floor of the house. I remembered the exact spot where the grandfather clock, Big Ben, stood at the top of the stairs. A vertical painting on the wall—a Mondrian with lots of *lines and colors—has replaced the clock. I suddenly missed Big Ben's awe-some presence. (You know, it's the clock in your uncle Benny's apartment.) It's perfect that my brother inherited the clock. He had a fascination for it, staring at it for long periods. When I was a child, I thought my parents named Benny for the clock!*

I enjoyed meeting the Millers—Mark, a young dentist, and his wife Liz, taller than Mark and very gracious. At one point in our visit, she took me outdoors to view the rock garden in the front yard. The one Mom started before she married! I'd missed it on the way in—covered with fallen red oak leaves and bright green moss. Happily, the rocks are still in place—even my forever favorite, a large obsidian boulder. Liz said that restoring the rock garden would be her first project. Hearing of her plan surely made my day! How I wished Mom and Grandma could know.

A further surprise: Liz showed me the trunk in the attic. It contained mostly old clothes—some I remembered from playing 'dress up' with Benny and Deborah. But the real gem was my mother's baby book from 1908, where my grandma had fondly recorded her baby girl Alice's earliest years. When I opened the first page, a pair of pressed baby booties fell onto my lap. They were light blue leather with dainty moccasin stitches at the toes, and a ribbon (now colorless, once pink?) to draw the booties around tiny ankles.

The book includes only one photo of my mother as a baby, and it's so precious. She is about a year old, standing tentatively, holding onto a kitchen stool. She has short blond hair, a fringe of bangs across her forehead, and wears a long white dress covering all but her toes. She is looking away from the camera—for help? A hopeful half-smile is on her sweet face. Wow—it's Mom, all right—that same dreamy look! She was always Alice from the first days of her life. I wish I had a picture of my dad at the same age. I wonder who he was back then!

Well, Amy, that's all for this trip. I'll call you when we return home. Take care! We send our love—

Acknowledgments

For the time period of my fictional story, I tried to adhere to historical facts. But in one instance, I took liberties: in Chapter 19, a premiere showing of the movie *Gone with the Wind* takes place in October 1939. The movie actually premiered in Atlanta on December 15, 1939. However, an unannounced preview was shown on September 9, 1939, in Riverside, California, after which David O. Selznick received a thunderous audience response for his masterpiece. For the sake of my novel, I allowed *Gone with the Wind* a further preview showing for the enjoyment of my characters, Alice and Charlie Lukas.

I paraphrased lines from "A Frosty Night" by Robert Graves, 1919. The first poem in collection, *Country Sentiment*, 1920. Also in *Collected Poems: 1941-1947* by Robert Graves.

Song lyrics assumed to be in the public domain: "Home on the Range" (1873) by Dr. Brewster M. Higley VI, "Git Along Little Dogies" (1893), "The Little Shoemaker" (American, U.S. Traditional), and "All Through the Night" (Welsh lullaby).

For background music I thank songwriters and musicians Duke Ellington, Hoagy Carmichael, Koehler and Arlen, Fats Waller, Glenn Miller, Benny Goodman, Frank Sinatra, Phil Collins, and Louis Armstrong.

Inspiration flowed from *Gone With the Wind* my Margaret Mitchell; from Margaret Wise Brown's children's book, *The Runaway Bunny*, and another of her books, *Goodnight Moon*; from Peter Newell's books *The Hole Book* and *The Slant Book*; as well as from books by Johnny Gruelle, L. Frank Baum, Annie Fellows Johnston, Lewis Carroll, W. Somerset Maugham, and Robert Louis Stevenson. I reviewed the facts contained in *The Last Great Game: Duke vs. Kentucky and 2.1 Seconds that Changed Basketball* by Gene Wojciechowski (2012). In

Chapter 7, I referred to Wendell Berry's essay and James Baker Hall's photographs in *Tobacco Harvest: An Elegy* (2004). I am grateful to all for the wonderful words and images.

A huge shout out of *thanks* to my editor, Abigail Henson, at Sunbury Press for her diligence, patience, and gracious assistance. Also, I am forever grateful to my developmental editor, Teri Brown, who encouraged me during a major revision and had faith in my novel, chapter by chapter. She enabled me to go deeper into my story through techniques that allow the reader to experience the feelings, thoughts, and motivations inside a character's head. And thanks to Teri, I have a better handle on using point-of-view consistently without making those little slips that are so easy to slide into. I am now more conscious that prose, as well as poetry, requires rhythmic beats of language. Both Abigail and Teri provided knowledgeable guidance and thoughtful reading that made editing and revising my novel a joyful pursuit.

I also want to thank my readers and those who encouraged me as I wrote and revised my novel. I am grateful to my daughter Nancy Pilotte and my brother Charles Luckett for their encouragement, thorough reading, title suggestions, and thoughtful editorial advice. I am indebted to my late husband, John Harkin, for his support, enthusiasm, patience, helpful comments, and answering many questions about cars, golf, and gardening. Special thanks to Sheila Deeth, who read and commented on every chapter and allowed me to use her poem as a stepping-stone into my story. And additional thanks to Sheila for formatting my 2019 revision of the novel.

Thanks to editor Kristin Thiel for taking a first look at my story and giving me some editing advice. I am grateful to members of the Writers' Mill group in Beaverton, Oregon, for critiques and helpful assistance in my writing. Thanks to James R. Dubbs for reading my book and commenting. Thanks to Rosemary Luckett and Louise Young for additional brainstorming on titles. Thanks to Pat Smiley for reviewing Chapter 7.

About the Author

JEAN HARKIN is the author of *Night in Alcatraz and Other Uncanny Tales*, an eclectic collection of short stories published in 2016. She lives in Portland, Oregon and has had a varied writing background.

She graduated from Creighton University and pursued a career in journalism, beginning as a direct mail advertising copywriter for "Better Homes and Gardens" magazine in Des Moines, Iowa. After she married and was raising her family, she wrote news and features, along with photography, for a community newspaper.

She later wrote interviews and took photographs to create newsletters for the Iowa State University Foundation in Ames, Iowa. During that time, Jean took a course in creative non-fiction and discovered a different style of writing. After a move with her husband to Portland, Oregon, she completed the switch from journalism to writing fiction, when she joined the Writers' Mill writing group.

Her short stories, poems, and some essays have appeared in various anthologies, mainly *The Writers' Mill Journal* series from 2008 to 2022, also *Itty Bitty Writing Space* (2019); and *Strongly Worded Women* (Not a Pipe Publishing, 2018.)

Jean began writing her debut novel, *Promise Full of Thorns*, in November, 2007. As an unpublished novel, it was selected as a finalist in the Maple Lane Books publishing contest, 2016. Since then, the book has gone through numerous revisions and edits.

Jean's blog appears at www.goodreads.com/jeanatwritersmill.

Made in the USA
Middletown, DE
13 February 2023

24035440R00163